AT THE STROKE OF
MIDNIGHT

JENNI KEER

Boldwood

First published in Great Britain in 2024 by Boldwood Books Ltd.

Copyright © Jenni Keer, 2024

Cover Design by Alice Moore Design

Cover Illustration: Shutterstock and iStock

Every effort has been made to obtain the necessary permissions with reference to copyright material, both illustrative and quoted. We apologise for any omissions in this respect and will be pleased to make the appropriate acknowledgements in any future edition.

A CIP catalogue record for this book is available from the British Library.

Paperback ISBN 978-1-78513-969-7

Large Print ISBN 978-1-78513-970-3

Hardback ISBN 978-1-78513-968-0

Ebook ISBN 978-1-78513-971-0

Kindle ISBN 978-1-78513-972-7

Audio CD ISBN 978-1-78513-963-5

MP3 CD ISBN 978-1-78513-965-9

Digital audio download ISBN 978-1-78513-967-3

Boldwood Books Ltd
23 Bowerdean Street
London SW6 3TN
www.boldwoodbooks.com

Monica Allan
Born February 1923
Still hanging on in there August 2023

1

SUMMER 1923

Before time completely stopped for Pearl Glenham, she was more concerned with stealing it.

And yet, paradoxically, the very reason for stealing it was an attempt to hold on to a moment that had long since passed. By commemorating a specific instant in her life – her birth – she was desperately clinging to that fraction of a second when both she and her mother had been alive. She was a level-headed girl and knew that nothing would change with her sentimental action, because time marched forward relentlessly. It was unstoppable. But one delightfully sunny afternoon in July 1923, the universe decided to toy with her. It let her live and relive a few short hours in order to prevent a death.

Not her mother's, however, but her own.

* * *

Pearl was, in many ways, an unremarkable young lady. Her hair, although white-blonde as a child, was now a nondescript shade of mousy brown. She had blue eyes, but not the sort of blue to attract any attention or be remarked upon – a cloudy sky, just before the rain, almost grey. She had been academically advanced as a young child, but her potential had dwindled away, with little encouragement and no opportunities open to her. Her build was slight, she kept her head bowed low, and her voice was barely above a whisper.

But people who appear unremarkable can hide remarkable secrets.

Wearing the neatly pressed uniform of a housemaid, Pearl stood outside Boxley Hall, in a village six miles from where she lived, and watched a scurrying mass of staff prepare for the annual Midsummer Ball. Gardeners were clipping and sweeping, as delivery carts, or in the case of the butcher – a smart, black, liveried Model T van – pulled into the yard to deposit their wares. She witnessed the occasional hustle and overwhelming bustle of people getting in each other's way, and could hear the frantic instructions of the housekeeper desperately trying to oversee it all.

Her heartbeat was already racing as she began to walk towards the servants' entrance clutching a pile of folded linens. But she did not work at the hall, and the linens were from her closet back home. She was an imposter and was terrified her presence would be questioned.

Avoiding eye contact with anyone, she slipped through the door, down a narrow corridor, and up the back stairs, hoping that one girl in a black cotton dress and freshly ironed white pinny was much like another. No one cared who she was, only that she was busy. She passed a footman holding a tray of silverware. Her heart jolted as she recognised him from church, but he saw through her without really looking and hurried on his way, presumably to work his magic with a tin of Silvo liquid polish.

She slipped quietly into a small morning room. Glancing about with inquisitive eyes, she noticed an impressive black chinoiserie clock on the mantel, far too large and valuable for her tastes. Then she spotted a smaller Bakelite desk clock on the writing bureau near the window. With swift and silent feet, she swept across the room and pocketed the clock, before returning downstairs.

After stepping out into the bright June sunshine, she returned to the back of a small shed, where she had earlier deposited her bicycle. Placing the linens in the wicker basket, she finally let out a relieved breath and allowed her shaking hands to steady. It took moments to untie the apron and bundle it on top of the tablecloths, before mounting the saddle and pedalling up the road.

Twenty minutes later she was heading towards a modest cottage at the bottom of an isolated lane, as the tick, tick from her basket reminded her that, however much she wished it was otherwise, the onward march of time was inevitable.

'Where have you been?' Pearl's father asked as she stepped into the hallway, her cheeks rosy from her exertions, and her hair starting to come loose from the low bun fastened at the nape of her neck. She wished she was daring enough to get it cut in a more fashionable bob, but instead had compromised by shaping it around her face and tucking the length of it out of sight.

'Into the village, to purchase some more fabric for my undergarments.' She clutched the linens and their concealed treasure to her chest, knowing he would not enquire further if the answer to his question was in any way intimate, and that he did not have the necessary understanding to ascertain whether she was holding two yards of voile for the creation of a chemise, or three folded tablecloths borrowed from the linen cupboard. 'I wasn't expecting you back so early, Father.'

It was unusual for him to be home at this hour as he always caught the five-fifteen bus from the nearby market town where he had his offices. It dropped him at the top of Parsonage Way at twenty minutes to six without fail, giving him ten minutes to walk the length of the lane, and a further ten minutes to deposit his hat on the coat stand and freshen up before dinner. He was a man of alarmingly regular habits who lived an ordered life, and only events beyond his control disrupted this routine.

Despite the balmy nature of the day, her father looked unusually clammy and uncomfortable as he wiped the back of his hand across his forehead. He was unsettled and that, in turn, unsettled Pearl. She noticed he was clutching a small cream envelope, and wondered if the arrival of this correspondence might be the cause of such a radical deviation from his schedule. It was addressed to his place of work, yet had *Personal* scrawled across the top in deep blue ink. Her eyes quickly flicked back to her father. She didn't want him to think she was prying.

'Troubling matters have arisen and I have come home to attend to them.' He glanced at his inexpensive pocket watch and then returned it to his waistcoat. The gold half-hunter that he'd inherited from his own father sat forlornly in a glass dish on his dressing table. It was only handled by Pearl when she dusted, and only ever displayed the correct time, four minutes past ten, twice a day, by default.

'We have been invited to a place called Highcliffe House a week next Saturday, down in the west country, for a luncheon and evening dinner party. I will make the necessary travel arrangements, but I need you to oversee the packing. My plan is to leave on the Friday for London, where we can catch a train from Waterloo to Weymouth. I shall book accommodation there overnight so that we arrive fresh, sometime late morning, to meet our host the following day. The house is not straightforward to access.'

Pearl was confused by such out-of-character spontaneity. Social functions were to be avoided at all costs, and they rarely stayed away from home.

'That's an awfully long way to go for a dinner party,' she pointed out.

To her knowledge they had no connections in Dorset, and the whole trip would incur great expense at a time when they did not have money for such extravagances. She was often frustrated by their ever-fluctuating financial situation, never understanding why sometimes they had a surplus, and on other occasions he was asking her to make economies. Surely his salary from the accountancy firm was a steady wage?

'I agree,' he said. 'But we are going, and that's an end to it.' His eyes scanned the invitation again. 'You must organise suitable clothes for two days' travelling and formal wear for dinner. How I detest long journeys, stuck on trains with... people,' he added, almost as an afterthought.

'May I at least know the purpose of the visit?' she enquired. 'Is it to see friends? Or a matter of business?'

'Purely business. I do not know the people nor the house, but this trip may lead to a change in our fortunes, so you are not to challenge my decision.'

He looked over to his daughter and then briefly wrinkled his nose, as if considering his attitude might be lacking. Her father had a plain way of speaking, but occasionally caught himself and tried to accommodate what he considered were the frivolous feelings of others, for the sake of good manners, if nothing else.

'Highcliffe House is situated on top of the limestone cliffs of the Jurassic coast, which should please you. There is a small private cove beyond the gardens that you can visit, as you are forever harping on about the sea. Pack appropriate footwear.'

Pearl felt an unbidden flutter of excitement because, alongside her obsession with time, she had an equally enduring fascination with water. However, she was confused by her father's blatant contradiction that he did not know the house, when he was obviously familiar with it. She was also wrestling with her own conflicting desires. She had no wish to attend a dinner party (a social occasion she had no personal experience of) with people she did not know, nor to travel halfway across the country in order to do so. And yet, at the mention of the sea, her heart skipped. If she packed her bathing costume, there would surely be an opportunity to visit the cove he'd mentioned and swim in the ocean. It was nearly enough to offset her unease about meeting new people and leaving the sanctuary of their home.

Ultimately, however, her opinion would not be taken into consideration, so she would have to do her best to alleviate her worries. They were going because her father decreed it, and it was not open to discussion.

'I assume, despite your gadding about the village, that there will be a suitable meal on the table for six o'clock?'

With money often tight, they had not employed a cook for seven years, ever since he'd decided his twelve-year-old daughter was perfectly capable of running the household. Knowing she would be absent for some of the day, she'd already boiled a small ham that morning, so only needed to mash some potatoes and open a jar of pickled beetroot.

'Of course, Father,' she confirmed, as she mounted the narrow stairs and excused herself.

The landing was dark and gloomy, and the deteriorating thatch that overhung the tiny bedroom windows excluded the light even further. Ducking under the low oak lintel, she entered her bedroom and slid the small clock out from between the tablecloths. It was not particularly valuable and neither was she short of a timepiece – quite the opposite, in fact. She pulled out the bottom drawer of her tall chest and lifted the corner of a thick knitted blanket, under which eleven small clocks and wristwatches nestled amongst the spare bedding. As she slipped her latest acquisition next to the others, she tried not to contemplate which unfortunate member of staff might be blamed for the missing item.

She would return upstairs when the clock had wound down, and move the hands to the same hour as her other concealed time-pieces. Because, as she caressed each glass face before closing the drawer, every single one was set to exactly four minutes past ten – the moment her mother had breathed her last and the time her father had also set his gold pocket watch to.

Mindful her father would be cross if the meal was served even one minute later than he'd requested, she scurried down to the kitchen to peel the potatoes.

2

During the week, from the serving of breakfast until the preparation of the evening meal, Pearl's time was largely her own. As long as the household chores were completed and there was food on the table *exactly* when required, her father was largely content. He had high standards (the cutlery must be laid out just so, and he struggled if she dared to rearrange the ornaments) but she was generally a compliant daughter, who tried to avoid giving him reasons to complain.

They had been at the former parsonage for ten years now, which was quite a relief to Pearl because they had moved about so much during her early childhood. The house was in an isolated location, and so it was natural for Raymond Glenham to assume his daughter spent her free hours housekeeping, reading and gardening. To be fair, much of her time was spent this way, but since finishing her education at fourteen, she'd found other activities to fill her time, most of which revolved around her love for the water.

Even in her sleep, the sea came to her, edging endless rolling sands and disappearing into the thick blue line across the distant horizon. She would dream of the beautiful white horses of spume running along the crest and, as the waves folded in on themselves and into the shoreline, that beautiful whooshing sound as they broke. Sometimes, she envisaged her legs stretching down the beach, as the tide brought each wave a little closer to her toes, before receding, and coming at her again. And the repetitiveness of such a thing, much like the repetitiveness of her days, was inexplicably soothing.

Always a child who conformed, largely because that was the only way she received her father's approval, Pearl often wondered how she might have turned out had her mother still been alive. Her father positively loathed the sea, so they had never lived anywhere coastal, and when she talked of it, he visibly shuddered. She occasionally engineered day trips with friends to Lowestoft or Felixstowe but, living in the heart of Suffolk, it was far too arduous a journey to undertake often, so instead she gravitated to inland bodies of water.

She spent a lot of her free time walking along riverbanks in the winter, and playing in Lackley Lake during the summer. Just before the war, as a small girl, her interest in swimming as an activity had been piqued when women were finally allowed to compete in the sport at the Olympic Games. Self-taught, she became a surprisingly competent swimmer, and perhaps even imagined herself winning medals for a while. A veritable mermaid, her friends said. And, although her life was not terrible, it was suffocating, so she relished in the freedom that came to her when she swam in the lake, cutting through the water like a fish, and diving beneath the surface to escape everything above.

The day after her escapades at Boxley Hall, she spent the afternoon with her friend Harriet Crawley. It was particularly humid for late June and so they headed for the lake on their bicycles. Harriet had learned that if she wanted to spend time with Pearl, it would invariably involve water and, on such a sultry day, she had readily agreed, even though Pearl knew her former school friend would spend more time lying on the banks, regaling her with gossip, than actually swimming.

They set a blanket down at the water's edge and within minutes Pearl was splashing about in the middle of the lake. Her body was hot, making the contrast of the icy water even greater but, as always, this sudden shock to her system was a welcome one. It made her feel alive. As her slender arms swept out in synchronised semi-circles, and her legs kicked furiously beneath the surface, she became increasingly frustrated by the weight of her costume.

How she longed for her childhood, when she'd taken to the lake in nothing but her drawers. Unfortunately, an elderly rambler had come across her when she was thirteen, which put paid to such liberty. Instead, she had rather daringly purchased a one-piece cotton knit bathing suit in navy blue from a department store in Ipswich – preferable to the high necks, long sleeves and woollen stockings of costumes from before the war, but still somewhat restrictive. Many parents would be scandalised by such a purchase, but as with most matters regarding his daughter, her father was generally uninterested in anything that fell outside her domestic remit. Besides, the only person who saw her in it was her best friend Harriet, who owned a similar article, but whose parents had little say in their headstrong daughter's choice of swimwear – in fact, they had little say in anything she undertook.

'This will all come to an end once you're married.' Harriet wriggled into her bathing suit but remained on the bank, watching her friend flip over onto her back, tip her head up to the blue cloud-dotted sky, and bob both feet to the surface. 'Your days will be filled with the company of tedious society ladies, flower arranging and organising church bazaars.'

'I shan't marry him,' Pearl said, with more conviction than she felt.

'You will because you always do what you're told. I've never once heard you say no to your father and, as he has determined that you will marry Simon Trowbridge, it will happen. But we both know you'll be desperately unhappy. The man has no interest in you – that much is plain to see.'

Pearl swished her hands through the water to paddle herself closer to Harriet. It was the very point she, herself, had failed to comprehend. Why had Simon Trowbridge singled her out for special attention? She had no fortune, in fact the opposite was true; the match would bring her and her father the much-sought-after financial security they craved, as well as a certain admiration for being wed to a highly decorated and respected war hero. Simon professed to find her charming and attractive, but his eyes were insincere and she could not warm to him. It bothered her that he clearly disliked his potential father-in-law, and she couldn't help but wonder if he was beholden to him in some way, especially since the potential arrangement included her father living nearby. It seemed she would never escape her familial duties.

Harriet stretched out her long legs and wiggled her toes, far happier bathing in golden sunlight than icy waters.

'I love you dearly but it worries me that you've not lived a life, and if you don't do so before you marry, you can be certain there will be little opportunity when you have a family and endless domestic responsibilities.'

'I already have endless domestic responsibilities.' Pearl kicked her feet, twisting her body to one side, and began to swim in small circles, revelling in the gentle caresses of the water and the glorious sense of weightlessness that accompanied it.

'Exactly. So, I will ask you again to accompany my family on our transatlantic trip next month. Father will happily pay your ticket because Mother says I need a companion to keep me in check, and she likes you for all the reasons that you frustrate me; you are suitably sedate and well behaved. Perhaps a little of each of us will rub off on the other. Now, wouldn't that be a splendid outcome? And there's sure to be adventures to be had in such a modern country. The prohibition of alcohol may be inconvenient – you know how much I love a tipple – but there will be other distractions. New York City truly is the capital of the world; we can dance to jazz in Harlem, watch baseball in the new Yankee Stadium, and admire the skyscrapers of Manhattan.'

Pearl shook her head. Her friend was so much braver than her. The thought of engaging in salacious dance moves in public spaces, or watching a ball game she didn't understand, surrounded by excitable young men, frightened her. Harriet embraced new opportunities and revelled in mischief. Pearl was like her father; she felt safe with the familiar. And yet there was a part of her that was curious about the unknown, and even the utterly reckless. From browsing the books in her father's modest library, she wondered what it would be like to see the mighty lions of Africa, gaze upon the ceiling of the Sistine Chapel, or walk through the street markets of India. It would be thrilling to behold the vibrant colours a photograph could not convey and to breathe in the exotic spices that she had never tasted.

But her father's voice echoing in her ears always held her back: 'We aren't that sort of people, Pearl. These are dangerous places – anything could happen.' And a small part of her always wondered if that wasn't rather the point.

So, whilst she was exhilarated by her stealing, the terrifying part was over in moments. For a trip of the magnitude her friend was proposing, the fear would last for weeks.

Harriet stood up and dipped her toes into the icy lake. She shivered.

'You're a water personality, Pearl. Your father surely must have sensed it even as you were born, for you couldn't have been given a more appropriate name. It's like you came from the sea, as the pearl comes from the oyster. Look at how you come alive when you are swimming. If only you would embrace other areas of your life so eagerly.'

They'd had this conversation many times before. Her eager friend pushing her to be bolder and braver, but if Harriet's faith in the centuries-old belief of the mystical nature of the four elements and her passion for astrology were justified (not that Pearl believed in such nonsense) then it rather explained her fear and lack of trust. She was calm and competent, sensitive and reflective. Which was, apparently, all down to the positioning of various celestial objects on the day she was born.

'I wish you had more fire in you. What I wouldn't give to see you punch a door, scream in frustration, or weep openly at something that has moved you. It's not healthy to keep your emotions buttoned up.'

True to form, Pearl remained emotionless, reflecting that it was an unfortunate display of such behaviour from Harriet's father, Mr Crawley, that had led to the family's decision to embark on their imminent trip. The punch on the nose he'd delivered to a well-respected gentleman in a public arena, when he'd overheard a scandalous rumour relating to his wife, only served to grab the attention of an unscrupulous journalist, who decided this made the rumour true. Escaping abroad for a while seemed sensible. Pearl had determined that wheresoever she decided to further her knowledge of the world and the adventures undertaken across it, it would certainly never be from the newspapers, whose salacious and headline-seeking falsehoods destroyed lives.

Harriet finally ducked her body under the water and let out a tiny squeal. Pearl smiled and swam over to persuade her into deeper waters. She took her friend's hands so that her body could float on the surface, finally letting go and allowing Harriet to kick her legs for a few yards, before she lost confidence and found the soft, silty bottom of the lake with her feet.

It wasn't long before Harriet's limbs became weary from her exertions, and she clambered from the water, hanging her heavy soaking wet costume over the branches of a low bush to dry in the sun. Pearl swam back out to the middle of the lake. Her fingers were wrinkled prunes and her body was tired, but she was reluctant to leave her happy place. She took a deep breath, and ducked below the surface, closing her eyes. The sound of her heartbeat amplified, and everything around her became muffled – cushioning her from the challenging world above. If only she could stay down here, away from all the pressures and demands of those around her, because she had an uneasy feeling about the proposed trip to Dorset.

Here, in the water, she was safe. Here, she felt her mother was nearby. Here, she was truly at home.

* * *

It was only later that evening, when Pearl was drawing the curtains in her father's immaculately organised study, that she stumbled across a genuine reason to be anxious.

With a view to being better informed about the trip, she reached for the envelope he'd been waving about the day before and slid the single sheet of paper out. She cast guilty eyes towards the door, worried that her father might enter and catch her prying, but the house was silent. The invitation began in a formal manner, covering the details she already knew: they were cordially invited to attend Highcliffe House for the Saturday and over into the Sunday, where they would attend an intimate dinner party. It would be in the best interests of Raymond Glenham to attend as financial matters relating to the Brockhursts had now been settled, the implication being that he was in line for a sizeable payout.

Pearl had never heard of the Brockhursts, but assumed they were distant relations, perhaps on her mother's side. The invitation went on to say that he and his daughter would be made most welcome, and staff would be on hand to ensure they had a pleasant stay. But it was the last lines of the correspondence that made Pearl freeze. She reread the final paragraph, just to make sure she had correctly interpreted the dark nature of what was a very thinly disguised threat.

...I strongly suggest you accept this invitation, as the consequences of any refusal to attend will prove catastrophic – forcing me to reveal dark secrets that I am certain you would rather remain hidden. You must have known that your past would catch up with you eventually...

Yours faithfully

Mr Badgerwood

3

The bus dropped Pearl and her father in the centre of Morton Peverell, a picturesque south Dorset village twelve miles from Weymouth. It was a hot day and she was glad of her straw hat to protect her from the fierce sun. Their journey had taken most of the Friday, and she was pleased that her father had suggested an overnight stop. Arriving irritable and dishevelled at a guest house was one thing. Turning up to a private residence in such a state was quite another.

Pearl could smell the sea as the bus pulled away, even though she could not yet see it. Walking down to the esplanade in Weymouth the previous day had, naturally, been the first thing she'd done after depositing her suitcase in the tiny attic guest room. The lateness of the hour, however, had prevented her from spending longer than a few minutes walking along the glorious, flat sandy beach. Today, at Highcliffe House, she hoped there would be an opportunity for her to bathe, and the sticky air surrounding them made this an even more appealing prospect.

A painted village sign, depicting a small fishing boat sailing in front of high cliffs, stood in the middle of the open square, mounted on a tall, whitewashed post. A smattering of shops surrounded them, including a bustling fishmongers, which added to the salty coastal smells, and a quaint tea room with a large bay window.

'We need to find someone prepared to take us to the house,' he said.

'Can we not walk there?'

'It would not be practical with our cases and in this heat.'

'Perhaps we could ask in here,' and she pointed to the Morton Peverell general stores. The signage announced the proprietor was a G. W. Lane, and that it also served as the village post office. If they dealt with the post, they would surely know the location of all properties in the area.

Her father hesitated a fraction before striding ahead of her, through the open door, and into the murkiness of the shop – which was made worse by the contrast of the blindingly bright day outside. As her eyes adjusted to the low light, Pearl noticed a figure standing behind the counter. There was an array of shelves running around the walls, stacked with tins and packets of every description, and sacks of flour and rice on the floor. Along the wooden counter stood a mechanical cash register, a set of brass scales, and a neat display of Fry's chocolate.

'Mr Hardinger?' The voice was female, and the woman leaned forward and frowned at her father.

'Mr Glenham,' her father corrected. 'You must have confused me with someone else. I'm not local.'

'So sorry, I do apologise. The mind plays tricks... especially when you've been around as long as I have.' She shrugged. 'Must've seen thousands of people pass through these doors over the years.'

'Not at all. I believe I have one of those faces.' He smiled briefly to indicate that he'd not taken offence. 'My daughter and I need transportation to Highcliffe House, if at all possible. Would you know anyone prepared to help us in this regard?'

'You're in luck. Gerry is making a delivery there shortly – there are some items that got left off the order yesterday. That house has been shut up for so many years, whilst the Brockhursts gallivanted around the world. The vicar's wife received the occasional postcard to say all was well, but now it would appear they have finally returned and opened up the place, as we understand they have guests.' She paused. 'I can only assume that you are some of the guests?'

'It is a large gathering, then?' her father asked, looking faintly surprised. The invitation had described the dinner as intimate.

'Not especially, but my husband is delivering supplies for seven or eight. We had an order placed in writing a week ago from a Mr Badgerwood, with more than sufficient payment enclosed. Strange way of going about it, if you ask me, but money is money.'

Pearl recognised the name from the invitation, and so did her father.

'What do you know of this Mr Badgerwood?' he enquired. 'Is he perhaps a solicitor, or agent of some description?'

'Never heard of him before. He's certainly not local, so I'm assuming he's related to Virgil. Pretty sure the Warren line ended with Lenora.' Remembering the man before her was a stranger, she elaborated. 'The Warrens owned Highcliffe House for decades, and not long after they died, their only daughter married some fancy American called Virgil Brockhurst. The young couple then spent several years travelling the world. About twenty years ago, they indicated they were planning to settle back here, only to dash off again almost immediately in the middle of the night, and they haven't been back since.' She leaned forward to emphasise her point. 'Who does that with a tiny baby in tow? You can be sure that something scared them away, or someone forced them to leave. It never sat right with me.'

Pearl's father shrugged. Gossip wasn't his thing. Nor were

people. But she was unnerved. Meeting new people was bad enough, but nothing about this visit sat easily with her. The house clearly had a peculiar history and her father was being blackmailed into attending the dinner party.

Because she was absolutely certain that the invitation was exactly that – blackmail.

4

___

Highcliffe House, apart from its size, was in no other way magnificent. It was a typical Georgian-style box, with very little ornament or intrigue, and built from the creamy-white local stone that Pearl understood was used in such prestigious buildings as St Paul's Cathedral and Buckingham Palace. A Greek portico marked the main entrance, which gave it a mildly interesting focal point, but she preferred houses with more character – the higgledy-piggledy rooftops and overhanging first floors of a Tudor town house, the steep-pitched roofs and glorious red-brick chimneys of the Victorians, or the pink-washed low thatched cottages of her home county.

The surrounding landscape *was* magnificent, however, and she caught her breath as the G. W. Lane liveried van spluttered to a halt after travelling up the long drive. A cerulean blue sky, with the merest smudge of cloud, supplied a splendid backdrop to the vibrant green lawns and lofty, ancient trees that had surely graced the landscape from a time long before she'd been born. Flower beds danced along the drive, haphazard and overcrowded but recently tended to, nonetheless. And then a glimpse of the dark blue streak of ocean between the horizon and the top of the dramatic coastal cliffs that must have been the inspiration for the house name. She could smell the sea, carried on the air that was rushing in through the open window of the van – a salty freshness overlaid with the tang of fish.

Mr Lane deposited them at the front of the property and she stepped out onto the gravel. A smart red Austin motor car was abandoned near a fading mauve rhododendron bush. Pearl didn't know anyone wealthy enough to own such a vehicle and was both intrigued and anxious about meeting someone with that kind of money. As the grocer's van started up again and disappeared round the back with a crunch of tyres on the loose stones, a young man, dressed in the black suit and crisp white shirt of staff, appeared at the front door.

'Mr and Miss Glenham?' he enquired, immediately following up with a wide smile. 'My name is Ellery Brown and I will endeavour to make your stay at Highcliffe House as comfortable as possible. I trust that you both had a pleasant journey?'

Her father didn't reply but merely nodded to indicate the cases on the ground by their feet before walking up the stone steps and through the open door. Pearl followed meekly behind, used to her father's lack of social skills.

The young man raised an eyebrow, and it was only then that she noticed his extraordinary eyes. They were a startling amber, with flecks of gold that reflected the ascending summer sun, with a darker ring of brown around each iris. His thick hair was parted at the side and had a glossy sheen to it, doubtless from the liberal application of Brilliantine, which only made those orange eyes stand out even more.

'Someone needs a lesson in manners,' he muttered under his

breath, and Pearl considered that he might need a lesson in manners, too. However dismissive her father had been, this young man was employed to assist and defer to the guests of the house, and he should know it was not his place to openly criticise, least of all to the gentleman's daughter.

He picked up their cases, one in each hand, and nodded for Pearl to enter the house, following behind as she stepped over the threshold. Shuffling past them, he then deposited the cases at the foot of the main staircase.

Pearl gazed in wonder at the great number of strange objects and colourful artworks that confronted them as they entered the spacious hallway. She felt as though she'd stepped into a museum gallery. The square open space was crammed with glass display cabinets and mounted exhibits, displaying everything from stuffed mammals to brass instruments, and a whole host of things in between.

'Overwhelming, isn't it?' he said. 'And all down to Lenora and Virgil Brockhurst.' Ellery drew their attention to a huge oil painting above the staircase that dominated the hall, positioned so that the couple could look down on all who entered their house. Virgil was seated on a lush green velvet chair – a self-satisfied smile across his wide, whiskered face. Lenora stood beside him, one delicate hand resting on his shoulder, wearing a late Victorian gown of pale pink satin. Her dark hair was piled high on her head, with tiny curls framing her face. You could tell she was a force to be reckoned with, if only by the confident way she stood: her shoulders back and her chin held high.

Pearl felt uneasy under their intense scrutiny and returned her gaze to the objects dotted about the hallway.

'Is that a shrunken head?' she asked, incredulously, and rather hoping that it wasn't. A wooden carving of one, perhaps?

'I'm rather afraid it is. It's Ecuadorian – look at the label. The indigenous Shuar boil down the heads of their enemies to keep their souls contained and prevent them seeking revenge – or some such.' The young manservant was surprisingly well educated and articulate for someone working in service. 'Brockhurst really liked his macabre curios. Rumour had it that he once briefly owned the finger of some medieval Catholic saint but the Vatican got involved, and I suspect he and the finger were quickly parted. He also had a large jar containing the pickled bodies of conjoined puppies. My mother informed me this particular item was taken off display after the mayor's wife came for afternoon tea and fainted. Such tales travel fast in this part of the world, and you know how the local rags are always desperate for a good story.'

Pearl did indeed know – her dearest friend had suffered as a consequence – but wished she hadn't asked and chose not to investigate anything else, instead returning her attention to the walls, casting her eye across the paintings of exotic landscapes, classical ruins and city skylines.

'They travelled an awful lot,' the young man explained, following her gaze.

Her father began to tap his foot – a sure sign he was agitated and bored by this meaningless interchange.

'I'll take your luggage up to your rooms,' Ellery said, 'whilst Mrs Dawson, the lady engaged to cook for the party, serves you welcome refreshments on the terrace. We are the only two members of staff employed for this occasion, so our roles are numerous. Please be understanding if things take longer than anticipated.' He gestured to the door on their left. 'Mr Standfield arrived not half an hour before you, and is currently enjoying Mr Badgerwood's... *hospitality* outside.' The twinkle in his mesmerising eyes was unmistakable. This was a man who was brimming with mischief and opinions, and struggling to contain them.

'And our host?' her father asked. 'Is he with this Mr Standfield?'

'Ah, no, but there you probably know more than me, as Mr Badgerwood and I have never met—'

'You've not met your employer?' Her father was incredulous.

'Neither myself nor Mrs Dawson have had that pleasure. We were engaged through a third party and our instructions for this gathering have all been via letter. I understand the gentleman will be arriving at some point this afternoon, and will be attending the dinner this evening, but there is no sign of him as yet, sir.'

'This is simply unacceptable,' Mr Glenham continued. 'We've been dragged halfway across the country and he isn't even here to greet us. I was hoping for some enlightenment as to the precise nature of our visit, as I have not met the fellow either,' he admitted. 'Never even heard of him.'

'How odd. Mr Standfield said something similar. Rather curious to my mind, as you are both invited guests.'

'Curious, indeed.' Her father rubbed at his chin. 'Is Badgerwood the current owner? Or some sort of legal chap, overseeing the intricacies of the Brockhursts' affairs?'

The young man shrugged. 'I can only reiterate that I have been employed from the Friday through to the Monday – the temporary nature of the position suited me – but it would appear that you know even less than I.'

Pearl was confused. Her father didn't know Mr Badgerwood? That meant he was effectively being blackmailed by a stranger. She would not dare to question him over the matter, as she didn't want him to know she'd been snooping, but if it wasn't the sender of the invitation he had the connection with, then it must be the place. He'd been to Highcliffe House before but was not prepared to admit it, of that she was certain.

Voices tumbled out into the hallway, so Pearl and her father followed the chatter and found themselves in a spacious drawing room. The walls were papered in a pleasing flocked print of pale blue, both above and below the dado rail, and the furniture was a curious mix of solid English country pieces and alarmingly ostentatious oriental items – such as the gaudy black and gold chinoiserie sideboard along the back wall.

Pearl noticed a slender older woman holding a tray of drinks, silhouetted in the sunlight as she stood at the open French doors. Behind her on the terrace, was a portly gentleman sprawled across an overly fancy wicker chair that looked far too fragile for his bulky form. His hair was thinning, betraying his age, but he had a vibrancy about him that was refreshing, with a booming voice that was certainly more melodic than her father's monotone speech. Pearl was used to his sedate inactivity and gentle stillness, yet the other guest was waving his hands about and pulling the most expressive faces. His casual clothes (tennis sweater and tweed jacket) spoke of serious money, and it was quickly apparent that he had the arrogant demeanour to match.

'Enough with the elderflower cordial and repeated offers of tea. A fellow needs something stiffer if he's to endure this ridiculous pantomime. It's not too early for a White Lady, you know. You have crème de menthe, I assume? Really, one's drinks cabinet is hardly complete without it.'

'I'm sorry, sir,' the lady replied, dipping her head, and taking a step back. 'Please do bear in mind, this house has not been occupied for nearly twenty years, and Mr Badgerwood has only had delivered what he considered necessary for this gathering.'

'Crème de menthe *is* a necessity. As is an ashtray. What's a chap to do with his ash?'

'I'll see what I can find, sir.' She turned back to the room and the pair spotted the new arrivals simultaneously.

'Good God!' The abdominous man stood up as the Glenhams

approached, but before he could say anything further, her father interjected.

'Raymond Glenham. Delighted to make your acquaintance. And this is my daughter, Pearl.'

The pair locked eyes momentarily and then shook hands.

'Harlow Standfield. The pleasure is all mine.'

Mr Standfield nodded at Pearl and gestured for her to take a seat, before hitching up his cream flannel trousers and returning to the wicker chair. She noticed that he sat slightly more upright than previously. Clearly something had piqued his interest and she suspected they were the something.

'Mrs Dawson, at your service,' the woman half-curtsied as she introduced herself. 'Do help yourselves to a glass of the elderflower. I will return presently.'

'Well, this is quite the to-do,' Standfield said, reaching for a packet of cigarettes on the small circular table between them all. He held it out to both in turn but they declined. 'Gathering people for a dinner party, and not even here to greet your guests. That cook woman informs me that a Signor and Signora Ravello are also on their way, and then I understand our little party is complete. Do you know the Ravellos?'

Her father shook his head.

Pearl poured her father and herself a small glass of the cordial, and promptly drank hers in one go. Travelling in the heat was exhausting, and even though she was thankful fashions were increasingly for simpler clothes, she still had on more layers than she would have liked. If only she could sneak away from this unnerving gentleman, retrieve her bathing suit from her case, and escape down to the sea. Out on the terrace, she could hear it calling to her. The screams of the gulls and the hush and hiss of breaking waves were carried on the slight breeze that came from the sea not three hundred yards beyond where they sat.

She realised with a start that the bumptious gentleman had been speaking to her, but her mind had been elsewhere.

'Oh, pay her no heed, Mr Standfield—'

'Harlow, please.'

'And you must call me Raymond. She's not one for conversation. Doesn't much like people and has very little of value to contribute.'

Her father's leg began to bob up and down almost unnoticeably, but it was a sign that something was bothering him. It was one of his little tics. She followed his eyes and saw the dusting of cigarette ash that had fallen onto the table. He did not cope well with mess, or things not being in their proper place. If they were at home she would have jumped up to find a brush, but it was not her place to do so, and she luxuriated in this knowledge.

As she sat back in her chair and allowed herself a moment to enjoy being still after so much travelling, the most glamorous woman Pearl had ever encountered sashayed out through the French doors. She was wearing an exquisitely tailored bright blue suit, with cream silk details. A voluminous orange scarf was casually slung about her neck, its tasselled edges nearly reaching the floor – and across her eyebrows sat a tight-fitting toque hat in a blue that matched the suit. Her heavily mascaraed eyelashes curled upwards to meet the thin brim. She was followed by a handsome, slender gentleman, who was inadvertently slapped across the face by the gloves she was holding, as she waved her arms about. Mr Standfield and her father both got to their feet and exchanged a glance that Pearl didn't understand.

'Céline Ravello and this is my husband Aldo,' she announced, stretching out her elegant hand and graciously allowing both men to kiss it. The woman had a strong Gallic accent, even though Ravello was surely an Italian name. '*C'est un plaisir* to meet you all.' She met the gaze of the gentlemen with incredible self-assurance.

The necessary introductions were made, but everyone was

unusually reticent to expand much beyond their name, and then Aldo said several sentences in Italian, where the only word Pearl thought she recognised was *mangiare*. This, she assumed, was to eat, like the French *manger*, as he put his fingers to his lips to suggest exactly this.

'Well, I say, an international union. How charming. At least you married an ally,' Standfield said to Signora Ravello, shaking the proffered appendage.

'*Oui*, and a most fortuitous union at that. Lucky for me, he has wealth, if not intelligence.'

'I say, how much does the fellow understand?' Standfield asked, frowning at the husband, whose face betrayed nothing.

'Very little. It suits him that way. He has made no attempt to learn any language other than his own, and to be honest, he uses little of that unless he is angry with me. Quite frankly, I do not understand why he bothers to speak at all.' She gave her husband a disdainful look, and he raised an eyebrow in return, so she said a few words in his native tongue that seemed to satisfy him.

'You should have married an Englishman. We're jolly bright.' Standfield gestured for her to take a seat.

'Perhaps,' she purred, 'but you are not, I think, as accomplished loverrrs.'

The way she emphasised that last word, stretching it out and allowing that guttural R to roll around the back of her throat, made Pearl nearly spit out her freshly poured cordial. She made a gurgling sound as she swallowed her drink, and hastily retrieved a handkerchief from her sleeve to pat her mouth.

After seating his wife, Aldo took a chair that was slightly away from the group and proceeded to slip a small brown leather volume from his inside jacket pocket. *Ars Amatoria* was down the spine in gold and he quickly became absorbed in his book, only looking up when Mrs Dawson reappeared with a saucer-sized engraved brass bowl that she placed on the table.

'I couldn't find an ashtray, sir, so I'm afraid this pot will have to do.'

'*Non!*' Céline jumped up from the table and stuck out an imperious hand. Mrs Dawson, wide-eyed, handed it over and the Frenchwoman turned it around in her elegant hands. 'This is seventeenth century. Persian. These are talismanic cartouches, and here, about the rim, is an Arabic invocation. To use such an item will be summoning the malevolent spirits, and things are certainly strange enough without such recklessness. Something more taken from the people it belonged to,' Céline said, with a forlorn look across her face. '*C'est dangereaux* to treat the sacred objects of others as mere trinkets.'

Mrs Dawson looked slightly embarrassed as Céline returned the bowl to her.

'Well, I'm very sorry, madam, to be sure. I'll see if there isn't a saucer or something in the cupboards that will suffice.'

Pearl was fascinated by the description of the little bowl. She loved learning about anything beyond the staid and silent four walls of home. Her life might be dull, but her interests weren't, and books allowed her to escape into a life their finances and her timidity didn't permit. Once, when she was younger, she'd determined to read through the entirety of the eight volumes of her father's old encyclopaedias. She only got to page 94 of volume one because its alphabetised nature did not lend itself to chronological (or, indeed, engaging) reading, but she now knew an awful lot about the Danish port of Aalborg, who Abdul-Hamid II was (the sultan of the Ottoman Empire), and had a basic understanding of aeronautics.

'Dinner will be served at seven o'clock, prompt.' Mrs Dawson eyed the assembled company to stress the necessary punctuality of the meal, and Pearl noticed her father's discomfort at the news his meal would be an hour later than he was used to. 'Pre-dinner drinks will be held in the drawing room at half past six. As all guests are now present, would you like an early luncheon? It can be served on the terrace or in the dining room, if midday suits?'

The general consensus was that everyone was indeed peckish; in fact, Aldo looked decidedly animated when his wife translated the question. All had risen early to travel, and the clement nature of the day lent itself to outside dining, so the older lady rang the bell next to the fireplace, summoned the young manservant and ordered that the larger wooden garden table be set accordingly.

There was an hour to spare, and Pearl had hoped to visit the cove to satisfy her increasingly desperate desire to swim in the sea, but her father had other ideas.

'The luggage needs seeing to. I would like my suits hung up or I'll be no better than a tramp this evening, dining in a crumpled rag.' He didn't need to explicitly make the request. She was being told to attend to this matter, and promptly.

'Of course, Father.'

'Would you show my daughter our rooms?' her father asked Ellery, who had now appeared, and the young man nodded his assent.

'You're brave, old chap,' commented Standfield. 'Letting the pair of them head up to the *boudoirs* unchaperoned.' He gave Pearl an unpleasant wink. 'I'd offer myself, if I knew which room she'd been put in. We could test the firmness of the mattress.'

His comment was wholly inappropriate and Ellery's amber eyes flashed wide. For a moment, she thought he was about to put the older man in his place but, possibly remembering his position, he thought better of it. Pearl, on the other hand, wanted to curl up and die right there on the terrace, preferably before slithering between the gaps in the paving slabs.

They had been at Highcliffe House less than an hour and she was already desperate to return to the sanctuary of the parsonage. This trip was proving far, far worse than she ever could have imagined.

5

Ellery extended his arm to direct an embarrassed Pearl back inside the house.

'Why did your father not say something when Mr Standfield made that inexcusable comment?' Ellery asked in a hushed voice, as he led her out into the hallway.

She shrugged. 'He doesn't think like that. Besides, I'm certain it was just a joke, and Father doesn't really understand jokes.'

As they began to mount the main stairs, Pearl paused. 'Do you know the purpose of this dinner party?' she asked. 'It seems strange to gather people together who have no prior acquaintance.'

'We know very little,' Ellery said, looking across at the cook, who had just that moment appeared in the hallway carrying a refilled jug of cordial.

She'd obviously caught the end of their conversation.

'It is bewildering to me that *everyone* who has been invited to Highcliffe House knows very little, including the staff,' Mrs Dawson almost whispered.

'I did some research into the history of the house when I knew I'd got the job, if it helps,' the young man said. 'It was built by the

Warren family – that was Lenora Brockhurst's maiden name – and, when I asked my mother, she assumed the Brockhursts still owned it. She lives just outside Weymouth, so near enough to hear the local gossip. Apparently, Lenora and Virgil were great travellers and often away from home for months at a time, but the fact that they haven't been seen for so many years is curious, don't you think?'

'I'm not local. Don't look at me,' the older lady said.

Pearl knew some of this information already from Mrs Lane but kept quiet.

'Mother said the marriage was quite the scandal because she was engaged to someone else,' Ellery continued. 'And Virgil was rather the playboy, with more money than he knew what to do with. He spent his twenties travelling around the world, splashing his fortune about and buying up artworks and antiquities left, right and centre – including some pretty controversial artefacts, like those you see about you. Signora Ravello probably has a point when she says they shouldn't have been plundered from their people.' He seemed unusually keen to enlighten her. 'The Brockhursts travelled extensively after their marriage and only returned to England when they had a child. Back for a few days in the spring of 1903 and then disappeared off again. There was the occasional postcard to friends mentioning their latest destination, but nothing in recent years. Makes me wonder if something dreadful happened to them in some foreign clime. And if so, was it an accident or something darker?'

'Not everything in life has to be a great drama,' Mrs Dawson said. 'Perhaps they are simply back from twenty years of travelling and want to surprise everyone.' She shrugged, clearly not as enthralled by the mystery as Ellery.

'Perhaps,' Ellery concurred. 'Perhaps not.'

'Either way, we don't have time to stand about chatting,' she reminded him. 'And Miss Glenham is probably keen to unpack before luncheon.'

'If there is no specific agenda for the afternoon, I was hoping to go down to the cove. Is that allowed?' She felt unusually bold to ask such a thing, but as the alternative was to spend time with the disconcerting company on the terrace, she decided it was the lesser of two evils.

'As far as I'm aware, the guests are free to wander anywhere within the grounds,' Mrs Dawson said. 'The cove has a private beach that belongs to Highcliffe House, so you are unlikely to be disturbed. It's rather a steep climb down, I'm afraid, but apparently worth it. I'll serve lunch on the terrace at twelve, but you are free to amuse yourself after that.'

Ellery took her upstairs and directed her along a wide corridor to a pleasant enough room, decorated in shades of green, where her case was waiting for her at the foot of the bed on a dark mahogany luggage rack.

'Your father is next door, should you wish to unpack for him also.'

She nodded her thanks and began to find drawers for her limited wardrobe. The only dress she owned that was suitable for such a formal occasion was placed on a wooden hanger – a simple dropped-waist gown in pale pink, with magenta details. She'd made it herself, frustrated that fashions were changing but her clothing was not. The one benefit of the current simple styles and straight silhouette was even those with limited home dressmaking skills could run themselves up a passable wardrobe.

She placed her hairbrushes and a small bottle of violet water on the dressing table. There was little to her beauty regime, despite Harriet's best efforts; just the application of Pond's cold cream at night, and a pinch of the cheeks and some face powder to take off the shine during the day. Harriet, on the other hand, had started to wear mascara and lipstick, which horrified Pearl, who disliked drawing attention to herself at the best of times.

When her suitcase was empty, she set about unpacking her father's clothes: hanging up the shirts she'd pressed and folded the day before, arranging his shoes in pairs, and placing a set of cotton pyjamas on his pillow. She put his collars, cuffs and undergarments in the chest of drawers, and his grooming supplies on the more masculine dressing table that stood in front of the long sash window. Both rooms had a view across the front drive and she could see Standfield's motor car abandoned in front of the rhododendron, as she arranged her father's shaving paraphernalia on the marble-topped washstand.

As she headed downstairs, she turned the quarter landing and met Céline Ravello on her way up – one hand, she noticed, was behind her back. Perhaps it held a cigarette and she was embarrassed to be seen smoking in the house, although the confident Signora did not strike her as the sort to bow to the expectations of others.

'So terribly tiresome to have to do the unpacking ourselves, *non*? I am most put out to attend such a gathering without adequate staff, and find it irritating in the extreme that the assumption is the women will deal with such matters. Do you not agree, *ma chérie*?'

Pearl shrugged. She was unaccustomed to staff and was responsible for her father's wardrobe, whether they were at home or away. It would not have occurred to either of them that he would unpack his own belongings.

'Oh, I don't mind,' she replied, trying to sound cheery, and continuing down the stairs, not wanting to get drawn into a conversation with the older woman. Having fulfilled her father's request, there was now not enough time for her to visit the cove, as luncheon would be served in a quarter of an hour. She could hear Mr Standfield and her father skirting around their differing politics

on the terrace and was not inclined to join them, so she opted for
the library, which she stumbled across by opening various doors on
the ground floor.

It was a dark, but welcoming room, which smelled musty but
was not as dust-covered as she'd expected for a house uninhabited
for so long. It had the typical floor-to-ceiling bookcases lining the
walls, and an overspill of books heaped in unstable piles, like small
towers of cairn stones dotted about the floor. She scanned the horizontal rows of gold-embossed titles on the leather-bound volumes
in various shades of red, green and brown, and then turned her
attention to the large elm desk in the window, with piles of folded
maps at the back, and a gigantic and colourful atlas open at the
front. The Ottoman Empire covered both pages, but a large section
of the page had been bleached by the sun where it had fallen
between the half-drawn curtains, suggesting the atlas had been in
its current position for many years.

Was this where the intrepid Mr Brockhurst had headed off to so
suddenly in 1903 with his young family? And, if so, what had subse-
quently befallen them in those foreign lands, ensuring they would
not be heard of for many years?

Because Aldo's choice of reading material had been puzzling
her (she'd noted the title, *Ars Amatoria*, by Ovid) she selected the
appropriate encyclopaedia volume and took the opportunity to
look the fellow up. A Latin poet, born in 43BC, Ovid wrote poetry
about how to find love and, more importantly, keep it. Perhaps
Aldo's wife's flirtatious behaviour was causing him some concern...

There was a low writing bureau to the left of the desk, with a
row of china figurines dancing along the top, and she turned the
brass key in the fall, letting it drop forward. Inside, the neatly fitted
interior of pigeonholes and drawers was cluttered with papers and
writing accoutrements, but it was the silver ladies' pocket watch
that caught her eye. Plain and functional, rather than decorative,

Pearl picked it up to examine it closer. It had long since stopped ticking and her heartbeat began to accelerate as she considered moving the hands to the exact time that held such a personal significance for her – four minutes past ten.

At three minutes past ten on the 6th of June, 1904, her mother had been breathing – her heart pumping blood around her soft, warm body. And then, as the big hands of a hundred thousand clocks jerked forward to the number four, she had taken her last breath, and that warm body had begun to grow cold.

The familiar conflict erupted inside Pearl. It was wrong to steal – to take an object that didn't belong to her – but she had to have it. She could easily slip the watch upstairs now, and tuck it safely in her luggage as she went about Highcliffe House for the duration of her stay, knowing she was unlikely to be suspected of the theft, should it be discovered missing. The thrill was palpable. Or would it be preferable to wait until the following day to carry out her crime, perhaps as they were leaving? This would eliminate the possibility of the theft being noticed beforehand. It could be awkward if Mr Badgerwood arrived and started questioning the staff about its disappearance. As she contemplated slipping it into her pocket, she was startled by a voice from behind.

'Does the young lady have a specific interest in pocket watches? Or is she considering stealing it? Should I warn my employer that a thief is casing the joint – as the gangsters might say?'

It was Ellery's voice, and her face flushed as she hastily returned the timepiece to the bureau, unable to face him.

'Um... No, of course I wasn't about to—'

He gave a cheery laugh. 'I was having you on, miss. You hardly strike me as master criminal material.'

'I was just... it's not the item itself that I was drawn to,' she tried to further explain. 'Rather the concept of time. The onward march of our existence and the inevitability of death, perhaps.'

She turned back into the room, relieved to find his face was not accusatory, but amused.

'I say, that's rather maudlin for a sunny Saturday lunchtime,' he said. 'And it's far too glorious a day to be thinking about such things. I feel certain you have a long and happy life ahead of you. These are thoughts to have when you are eighty-three and rocking by the fire, nursing weary bones and struggling with laboured breaths.'

'My mother died giving birth to me. Death is a very real part of my life.'

'Ah, I did wonder why it was just you and your father attending. I'm sorry.'

He strode towards her and she froze, afraid of what he might be about to do. He noticed her reaction.

'Goodness me, are you one of those young women frightened of her own shadow? I'm merely putting the furniture back in order.' He leaned past her and closed the drop of the bureau. 'We don't want people thinking you've been snooping, do we?'

'Of course not. I wasn't though... I was just—'

'No need to keep apologising. I'm quite tempted to have a good rummage about, myself – not that I would, of course. But Highcliffe House has been untouched for so long, with many of their domestic items simply abandoned, as though the Brockhursts could return at any moment. It's a veritable treasure trove of curiosities, many of questionable origins, but it all reinforces their reputation as great travellers and collectors. It's quite a wonder no one has ransacked the place over the years. However, as intrigued as we both are, may I suggest that rifling through a bureau that does not belong to you might be seen by some as a violation? I'd advise you to stay out of trouble during your stay – there's a good girl.' He raised a warning eyebrow and she felt her stomach collapse. He thought her a naughty child.

She blushed but said nothing further. Being alone in the company of this forthright man made her feel awkward, and not just because he was suspicious of her and her motives. She was of an age where every encounter with the opposite sex did peculiar things to her body. Harriet relished such company. Pearl actively avoided it.

'Excuse me, miss, but Mrs Dawson will be wondering what is keeping me.' He gave a slight nod of the head and departed, failing to close the door behind him, as he probably expected her to follow shortly.

Pearl returned to the window and stared out across the lawns. Two dots of white cloud hovered either side of the bright sun, and the dark blue strip of the ocean created a definite underline to the pale blue sky. The sea was calling to her. She felt the pull like the magnetic force that drags the compass needle to the north – invisible and powerful. Embarrassed at being caught snooping by Ellery, hot from travelling, and anxious at the thought of two days of social interaction with the other guests at the house, she felt like striding into the sea and swimming to France. How liberating to step from the water onto foreign shores and be whomsoever she wanted to be. A stranger with no history, someone not judged by their past actions. If only she had the courage to be a woman like Céline – glamorous and unafraid. Was she to spend her life being overlooked and underestimated?

A brass gong sounded in the hallway, announcing luncheon. Oh, to get this meal over with and escape to the cove. She turned to the bureau and unlocked it once more, slipping the silver watch into her pocket, even if only to spite that patronising manservant for calling her a good girl.

6

Céline had all eyes on her from the moment she stepped back onto the terrace to join them for lunch. A waft of expensive scent both preceded and followed her, and her movements were graceful and considered. She had changed into another stunning ensemble – a yellow and turquoise jewelled turban was about her head, and she was swathed in yards of matching oriental-style silk. It was all terribly modern, and far too extravagant for daywear. The blue suit was obviously just her travelling ensemble, and Pearl wondered how many changes of clothing the woman usually wore during the course of a day.

A pleasant, if simple, meal was served, where Pearl contributed little, but observed a very great deal. Her father immediately rearranged the cutlery and glassware set before him so that everything was perfectly aligned, looking across at his daughter as he did so as if to imply this was something she should have seen to. But it was Céline who held most of her attention. The older woman casually brushed the arms of the men and frequently ran her tongue across her painted red lips. (She only ever wore red lipstick, she confided, as it was the most sensual. Poor Pearl didn't know how to respond.) There was a considered pause before the Signora spoke and, was it Pearl's cynical imagination, or was the woman deliberately stretching out those Gallic vowels in her honey-coated voice, just to trap the buzzing insects of men seated around the table?

Mr Standfield, on the other hand, was all bluster and impetuous pronouncements.

'Dammit, it's so hot, a fellow could strip to his undergarments and throw himself in the sea.'

Everyone looked up from their food, even Aldo, who Pearl noticed was finally looking engaged, if only by his plate of cold chicken pie and salad.

'I have no desire to go to the cove,' Céline said, pulling a face that demonstrated exactly how objectionable the thought was to her.

'No, well, quite,' Standfield said. 'Perhaps a cold bath is preferable. The sea is for paddling children and impoverished fishermen.'

Pearl said nothing but thought he was being rather snobbish, considering Queen Victoria herself had been an exponent of the health benefits of an ocean dip.

Despite their protestations otherwise, it quickly became apparent to her that, with the possible exception of the silent Aldo, the other three guests had met before. There was something about the way they sat, bodies tilted away from each other, and the awkward pauses in the conversation. Everyone was still avoiding the usual civil enquiries about family, occupation and background, which convinced her this was a trio of people who had a shared history but, for some unfathomable reason, were not prepared to admit it.

Ellery came to the table with a bottle of white wine in a pewter cooler. He poured for Céline first, as the most senior female present.

'Darling, do something about the nasty insects,' she purred, reaching for his hand. 'Make them go away.'

'Go bother the English guests,' the young man said, waving his hand ineffectually in front of her face. It seemed to pacify Céline, but Pearl thought he must surely be mocking the Frenchwoman.

'Pearl doesn't drink,' her father announced, as Ellery hovered the bottle near her glass.

The manservant gave her a questioning look, a chance to disagree and overrule her father, but she shook her head and he proceeded to Standfield.

The talk over the meal moved from polite chit-chat to the more scandalous admissions of Signora Ravello. Perhaps she'd decided to liven the whole affair up with her salacious tales, or at least distract everyone from the awkwardness while they awaited the arrival of their elusive host. But, as soon as it was polite to do so, Pearl requested that she be excused. The sea was calling her, and she was worried she would get sucked into a whole afternoon of excruciating conversation if she hung about for too long.

She scurried upstairs and changed into her bathing suit, concealing the pocket watch under a chemise in her drawer, and grabbed a cotton print robe to cover herself. Once downstairs again, she slipped silently through a back door near the kitchens. A winding flagstone path led from the rear of the house down towards the sea. It met a small wooden gate near the top of the cliffs, presumably to stop children or dogs from straying without proper supervision. She unlatched it and walked through, as the flagstones came to an abrupt end and met a run of deep stone steps cut into the hillside.

When she reached the bottom, and was finally able to appreciate her surroundings, she let out a contented sigh. Highcliffe Cove was as beautiful and as dramatic as she'd hoped. Enormous limestone boulders had tumbled down the cliffs and half into the ocean – probably many hundreds of years ago judging by their smooth, sea-eroded edges. The beach was a fine shingle, with sandy patches, and the cliffs cupped covetously around the tiny bay, as a scattering of those huge rocks, with their bizarrely angled strata, protruded from the water. She watched, hypnotised, as the waves slapped repeatedly against them and sent a white foamy spray up into the air.

There was no one in sight, as Mrs Dawson had predicted, so she let her robe slide from her shoulders and puddle at her feet, before slipping from her striped canvas shoes. The sun felt hot against her skin and she knew she would burn if she was exposed to it for too long, so she hastened towards the water, thrilled by the first icy wave that reached her toes. She stood for a few moments, watching the sea ebb and flow around her ankles, dragging larger pebbles with it as it retreated, before shunting them back up the slope of the beach again. The hiss and hush of the water was whispering secrets, of that she was certain, but what exactly was it trying to tell her?

She walked further in, aware that she was not familiar with this coastline, and perhaps should have enquired if the beach fell away sharply, or whether there were rip currents or undertows she should be wary of, but decided that the bay was probably safe, so long as she remained within its protective arms. One minute the water was swirling around her feet, the next she'd waded out to waist-height. Not allowing herself too long to think about the temperature, she dropped her body to submerge her shoulders and began to swim back and forth parallel to the shoreline, tasting the delicious saltiness as the occasional wave brushed across her lips.

The tension that had been building in her shoulders began to seep away and dissolve into the surrounding water. It always had this calming effect on her, as though the weightlessness she experienced lifted the weight of her troubles. There was something comforting about the unceasing nature of the waves, raising and dropping her slender body as they rippled towards the shore.

After a while, she noticed a figure cross from the bottom of the steps to the far side of the cove, where a smaller cluster of rocks had tumbled onto the beach. It was an older gentleman, with an unruly beard and a long raincoat flapping behind him as he walked, and he was carrying a small wooden box. The poor fellow must be baking in this heat, she thought, watching his haphazard progress. She didn't think he'd noticed her so she started treading water, and was suddenly aware of snippets of his voice being carried on the breeze. He walked to the bottom of the cliffs and disappeared out of sight, still talking to himself. Pearl was confused. Where had he gone?

It was several minutes before he reappeared with the box. He crossed back to the steps and then mounted them, returning up the cliffs, presumably to Highcliffe House. Ellery hadn't mentioned any other members of staff, and he was certainly not dressed like a guest, so who was he?

Curious, she swam inshore, striding through the waist-high water as soon as her feet reached the ocean floor, and then she dragged her increasingly heavy legs back through the shallows up the beach. She grabbed her robe, flinging it about her damp shoulders, using the hem to brush the fine shingle from the soles of her feet, before slipping her shoes back on. As she approached the far end of the cove, she realised there was a protruding section of cliff hiding a high narrow entrance to a cave. In fact, the opening stretched upwards twenty yards or so, initially giving her substantial light, and then a run of three high steps carved into the rock led into a more room-shaped space, with visible tool marks across the stone, suggesting this area had been quarried out.

There were two glazed lamps attached to the wall as she stepped inside. Both held thick pillar candles, and on a small shelf to one side was a tin that she correctly surmised would contain matches. Perhaps the bearded man was a regular visitor here. She lit them both and, as her eyes adjusted to the gloom, the sight before her took her breath away.

In the flickering light she could see heavy benches and shelving running around the edge of the cave, with a myriad of bizarre objects upon them: ceramic urns decorated with hiero-glyphics, complicated brass instruments that were covered in lenses and dials, numerous stone tablets with detailed engravings and, on the back table, under a glass dome, was a curious clock face that stood above a circle of seven funnel-shaped receptacles around a Ferris-wheel-like structure. The large brass hand on the dial told her it was approaching two o'clock. As she stepped closer, it was apparent that the funnel on the right-hand side was pivoting due to the weight of its contents, and was dripping something into the funnel directly below it. Pearl squinted. The liquid was silver and thicker than water. Mercury? Behind the wheel was a series of brass gears and cogs linked to an arm that moved the hand around the face. Unlike a traditional clock, the dial had twenty-four markings, suggesting that the hour hand only rotated once each day.

She moved nearer to see the curious object in greater detail, but her wet canvas shoes slipped on the stone floor. Her world slowed down, as it often does in moments of great drama, and she felt her legs slide under the table, her hands flailing about as she went down with an enormous bump. Even though she knew it was futile, she tried to grab at the tabletop but her actions failed to stop the inevitable, and the last thing she remembered before her head hit the solid stone floor and blacked out completely, was the dome jerking from its plinth and the brass structure before her wobbling, as a tiny perfectly spherical globe of mercury slopped over the edge of the funnel, and ran down a groove in the uneven wood.

As she slid to the ground, the silver ball caught the scant light, and she saw it roll over the edge and fall towards her head.

7

It must have only been for a few seconds, but Pearl momentarily lost consciousness, and opened her eyes to find herself staring at the underside of the table. As she focused on the rough wooden edge, she noticed a metallic taste in her mouth and wiped her hands across her lips. Had she swallowed some mercury? Oh well, it wouldn't do her any harm. Calomel had been used for over two hundred years to treat just about every ailment you could think of. Perhaps it would go some way to alleviating the headache she could feel forming as a result of the bump.

She sat upright and touched the back of her head with her hand, checking for blood. Concerned that she'd broken the strange clock before her, she took a closer look, but it appeared undamaged. Immediately, she worried that she would be in trouble for tampering with something that wasn't hers, yet again. All it needed was that outspoken manservant to appear and judge her with his fiery eyes.

What have I become? she asked herself. *A prying busybody, looking for excitement and distraction, just because my life is so predictable and monotonous.* She felt safe with the familiar, and yet there was something deep inside her clearly crying out for more. No doubt Mr Badgerwood would be most displeased to know that his guests were rifling through bureaus and snooping about in caves. The bump to her head served her right for her meddling – her 'just desserts', as her unsympathetic father might point out.

Feeling thoroughly ashamed, she determined to replace the pocket watch, as she adjusted the dome over the mercury clock and extinguished the lamps. She would return to the house and make an effort not to let her father down for the duration of this visit.

* * *

Pearl climbed the steps and walked across the lawn, noticing a quaint octagonal summer house in the distance. It had a slate roof and was freshly painted in a pleasant shade of pale green. High-cliffe House and its grounds had clearly been lovingly cared for over the past two decades. Even the interior of the house was tidy and dust-free – although how much Mrs Dawson and Ellery had seen to the previous day, she wasn't sure. Perhaps everything had been covered in sheets for the past twenty years.

As she passed a high laurel hedge surrounding a private area of garden, raised voices came from within. Céline and her husband were quarrelling in animated Italian, but Pearl had an extremely limited knowledge of the language and understood nothing of what was being said.

There was a final '*immorale!*' before Aldo strode out and crossed the lawns to the west. Not wanting to be thought of as eavesdropping, she ducked behind the hedge and watched him pull open the glazed door of the summer house and stomp inside. Wondering if perhaps Céline had returned to the house, she poked her head around the corner and was surprised to find the elegant French-woman seated on a stone bench, looking quite flushed.

As soon as she spotted Pearl in her bathing robe, she immediately composed herself.

'Darling, how lovely. Have you been to the cove?' She smiled at the young woman. 'It is a picturesque little place, *non*?' She patted the seat next to her, and Pearl, not wishing to appear rude, obediently came to her side.

'Yes, I love the sea,' she said. 'And the pity is we live so very far away from it, right in the middle of the Suffolk countryside.'

'Ah, yes, Raymond mentioned this after the lunch.' Céline looked thoughtful. 'And where is your mother?' she asked. 'She is not accompanying you?'

'I never knew her. She died giving birth to me.'

'So sorry.' Céline patted Pearl's hand. 'So many poor women pay the ultimate price to bring life into this world.' She shook her head in sympathy. 'And your father never remarried?'

'No, I think he loved her very much and has never come to terms with her death.'

'And they met when?'

Pearl didn't want to admit that her father rarely talked about her mother and had been vague on the few occasions he'd discussed his wife, so she stuck to the facts she knew. 'The summer of 1903.'

'And you are how old?'

The woman was overly persistent, Pearl thought, feeling increasingly defensive and ill at ease. Not only did she feel inferior to this glamorous and confident individual, but also unnecessarily scrutinised.

'They met and married within a few months.' She didn't want to contemplate that her creation may have hastened the necessity for a wedding. 'I was born in the May of 1904. I've just turned nineteen.'

Céline leaned closer, her heavy scent quite overwhelming.

'And what do you know of the dinner party this evening? Who is

Mr Badgerwood? Why would you travel halfway across the country for such a gathering?'

The questions were like rapid machine gun fire and Pearl felt they had gone on long enough, so she stood to leave, but Céline grabbed her hand.

'Sorry, you think me rude? But the whole thing, *c'est déconcertant*. I do not like this situation one little bit. Gathering a group of... strangers together like this. For what purpose are we here, I must ask myself? And I just wondered if perhaps we had been told the same thing? Or different things?'

'I'm afraid you must speak to my father. The invitation was sent to him. I didn't even want to come; I find social occasions difficult.' *For just this reason,* she thought – *prying strangers like you, making me feel uncomfortable.*

'Of course. I'm sorry. I am just wary, that is all.'

As Pearl turned to leave, a thought occurred to her. 'Do you know him?' She swung back to the elegant lady.

'Who?'

'My father.'

Céline hesitated a fraction before shaking her silk-turbaned head. 'I have never met Raymond Glenham before this very day,' she replied in her slightly broken English. 'But I look forward to getting to know you and your father better this evening over the dinner. Perhaps then we shall discover more about our elusive host and the purpose of this... *soirée*.'

'Perhaps,' Pearl said, and pulled her robe tighter around her body, before continuing on her way back to Highcliffe House.

* * *

'I say, Paula!' Standfield spotted her as she rejoined the flagstone path. He was still on the terrace, but was now alone at the table, leaning back in his chair, an empty wine glass but a half-full bottle on the table before him, and a cigarette in his hand. Despite Mrs Dawson finally locating an ashtray, he flicked the end with his thumb and allowed a cloud of ash to float to the floor. At least her father was not there to witness the mess.

She toyed with pretending not to have heard, but ultimately could not bring herself to be rude, and so walked over to him.

'Join me?' He rose to his feet as manners dictated. 'I can always call that Dawson woman for another bottle. It will help to take the edge off the dull nature of this gathering. She has at least kept me supplied with plenty of the old fermented grape juice – in this instance, a splendid crisp white, if not sufficiently chilled.'

Did his assessment mean he found the company dull, she wondered. Perhaps she, her father, and the almost silent Aldo, weren't the most stimulating of conversationalists, but the same could not be said for the dazzling Céline. Over lunch she had entertained them with her various exploits and travel adventures, managing to name-drop minor European royalty (and on one occasion major European royalty), silent movie stars, politicians and wealthy socialites – all of whom she had either dined with, been romanced by or knew scandalous gossip about.

'I need to change,' Pearl said, feeling awkward and staring at her feet. Knowing that she only had a damp bathing suit on under the robe made her feel vulnerable, even though it more than adequately covered her arms and legs.

'Been swimming, dear girl? You should have said. I'd have come down to the cove with you.'

'Do you swim?' she asked, remembering his earlier desire to launch himself into the sea.

'Not a bit of it. Can't be doing with all that water. And it's such a hassle getting in and out of one's clothes without my man. Wasn't allowed to bring the fellow. Makes no damn sense but the invitation was quite specific on that point. I'll have to ask that Brown chap for his help later, although between you and me, I don't think he really knows what he's doing. Suspect this might be his first position in service. Bit too vocal for someone who's been trained to know his place, don't you think? Plus, I can't shake the feeling I've seen him somewhere before.' He rubbed at his fleshy chin and shook his head. 'Whole blasted affair smells fishy to me.'

Pearl was in total agreement, but remained silent.

'The Brockhursts would never have stood for such jiggery-pokery.'

'Oh, did you know them well?'

Standfield looked startled. 'What? No, but a fellow in his position was talked about around the county. Brash fellow, flouting his money and connections. You know the sort? Hobnobbing with the well-to-do but not really in their league, if you know what I mean? No heritage, little breeding. I heard he wasn't liked much, and understand he called a spade a spade. The sort to present you with the facts, lay them out before you and wave them in your face, whether they were palatable to contemplate or not. Unlike this Mr Badgerwood, vague about his reasons for inviting us here and a damn no-show to boot.'

'The staff say he's expected later today, so perhaps everything will be made clear on his arrival?'

'Goddam better be – excuse the language. I've been forced to turn down a county ball to attend this. I could be there now, wooing some chit of a thing. Rather fear I'm running out of time to furnish the old estate with an heir. All she needs is sturdy child-bearing hips. Interested?' he asked, staring at her robe and she knew her horror was apparent across her face.

'I... erm, there's this Mr Trowbridge who I... erm, no – but thank you,' she finally managed to finish.

He had also been manipulated into coming to Highcliffe House then, and she wondered how Mr Badgerwood had lured him there. Had Standfield's invite also contained thinly veiled threats?

'Do you know where my father is?' Pearl decided she'd been polite enough, and the damp costume was starting to bother her. She needed to change into something more comfortable, and she wondered what duties her father might have for her next.

'I think he's popped upstairs to catch forty winks. Looked plum exhausted to me. We chatted briefly after lunch and he's not any more pleased about Badgerwood's absence than I am.'

Pearl suspected her father had overindulged somewhat during the luncheon. Mrs Dawson may have professed it to be a simple meal, but the quantity and richness of the foods were more than they were used to. And he was not a man who coped well in the heat. Or in situations where he wasn't in control. All of this was enough to exhaust anyone.

She politely excused herself and, fifteen minutes later, after changing back into her cotton day dress, Pearl Glenham too, was asleep across her large double guest bed, dreaming of clocks – endless rooms packed with shelves and shelves of a thousand different timepieces, all ticking away, and every single one with its hands set to exactly four minutes past ten.

8

Céline swept into the drawing room late, but undoubtedly deliberately so. Pearl knew how these things worked, even if the overt manipulation of others was not her forte. By arriving a good ten minutes after Mrs Dawson had requested they assemble for the pre-dinner drinks, the Frenchwoman ensured all eyes were on her as she entered, and those of the men had barely left her since. Even young Ellery had snapped his mouth closed as she swanned past him and into the room – another exotic cloud of scent Pearl didn't recognise enwreathing the air around her.

Added to this, her evening dress was of gold lamé – and it shimmered and rippled as the evening sunlight caught it. It had a beaded bateau neckline at the front but, rather scandalously, it dropped away to expose most of her bare back. She had on a pair of matching gold T-strap heeled shoes and around her sleek bobbed hair was a rhinestone headband. She periodically threaded her fingers through the string of a long jet necklace and wound the beads around her elegant fingers in an alarmingly seductive manner. Pearl looked down at her simple dress of pink silk and sighed. Part of her thought Céline's dress unbelievably gorgeous, and she coveted it with every fibre of her being, but part of her knew she could not endure such attention. Pale colours that enabled her to blend into the background were best.

Mr Badgerwood had still failed to arrive and, in the end, Mrs Dawson said she couldn't hold the dinner back any longer. Ellery had now changed into something approximating a footman's livery, with a proliferation of shiny buttons running down the front in two neat rows, and he directed them all to the dining room.

They took their allocated seats, but the head of the table remained empty and the assembled company struggled for things to say – returning to awkward small talk. Standfield fiddled nervously with his more traditional white tie, but she noticed Aldo and her father had chosen black.

Pearl was aware that every male in the room was staring at Céline, except for the Frenchwoman's own husband, who seemed far more interested in his food. And, indeed, the meal was sublime. A fresh tomato soup was followed by dainty crab cakes – for how could one be this close to the sea and not indulge in its fruit? The entrée was *filet* of beef, with *pommes noisettes* and grilled asparagus. Mrs Dawson was clearly competent in the kitchen, and was pleased to be complimented as such, especially when she announced that she would be returning with a chocolate mousse – much to Aldo's excitement. The Italian word was evidently similar enough for him to recognise. Pearl did wonder, however, where so slight a man was putting all this delicious food, as she'd had more than sufficient by the second course.

Standfield topped up everyone's glass, whether because he realised how dreadfully busy the two members of staff were, or he was so desperate for a drink that he couldn't wait, she didn't know, but strongly suspected the latter. In fact, for the duration of the meal, he'd dominated the proceedings, on one occasion clicking his fingers at Ellery, determining himself the highest-ranking person present. Her father appeared not to mind, but Céline narrowed her eyes several times at the pompous man.

'This has just arrived, sir,' Ellery said as he entered the room, and everyone turned to the door – Aldo's disappointment that it was not the promised mousse clearly etched across his olive-skinned face. The young man handed a telegraph envelope to Standfield, who took the ornate oriental ivory letter opener from the silver tray, and ran it under the sealed flap, before taking out the single sheet of folded paper within. He cleared his throat.

```
Regret unavoidable delay. Stop. With you by
morning. Stop. Accept my apologies and my
hospitality. Stop. Badgerwood.
```

'What the devil—' Standfield spluttered, as he cast his eyes over the words before him one more time and thumped the table.

'It is no use to get into such a flap,' Céline soothed.

'You can't change the circumstances by losing your temper,' Pearl's father calmly agreed.

'Damn poor show, though,' Standfield said. 'When one is the host, one should do better. So, I say we jolly well have a party at his expense.' He turned to Ellery. 'I say, what sort of state is the wine cellar in?'

The young man stepped forward, hands neatly behind his back, and cleared his throat. 'I understand there are a few nice bottles laid down but it is not my place to sanction their consumption.'

'You heard what the telegram said: *accept my hospitality.* We're stuck on the edge of nowhere, with nothing to do, and I still don't understand what the whole blasted gathering is in aid of, so the least Mr Badgerwood can do is to ensure we are sufficiently fed and watered.'

Pearl was absolutely certain that everyone around the table

considered Standfield to be 'sufficiently watered'. She'd had one small glass of wine with her meal – her father having been over-ruled by the guests – and felt distinctly light-headed as a consequence. Standfield had been drinking since his arrival.

'Very good, sir.' And a couple of bottles of vintage wine, to the delight of Standfield and Aldo, were fetched from the cellar.

* * *

After consuming the highly anticipated chocolate mousse, which also went some way to ease their frustration, the guests retired to the drawing room once more. The evening was pleasant enough for the French doors to remain open and, out of courtesy, Standfield, Aldo and Pearl's father sat on the terrace to smoke their cigarettes. Pearl remained inside with Céline, unable to think of a single thing to say to the slightly intimidating older woman, who had a way of looking down her Gallic nose at her young companion.

As Céline began a highly involved tale about the Shah of Persia, Ellery entered carrying a tray of freshly washed glasses of all descriptions – beautifully etched tumblers, brandy balloons and champagne coupes.

'Please help yourselves to the array of spirits on the sideboard. Mrs Dawson apologises for the old-fashioned glasses but these were all we could find. No Martini or highball glasses here, I'm afraid.'

'An idea most splendid. *Merci*. A *digestif*. Perhaps a brandy. And I shall pour my husband one, as I doubt you have any *amaro*. Pearl?'

Pearl shook her head, considering brandy a drink for men, but wasn't surprised that the thoroughly modern Frenchwoman ignored such conventions.

Like a shark circling the waters, having detected the tiniest drop of blood, Standfield immediately appeared at the French doors.

'Brandy, you say? Be rude not to.'

The men filtered back in and even her father, who was not a big drinker unless someone else was providing the alcohol, decided to partake. Standfield suggested a game of poker and her father, a numbers man through and through, was surprisingly keen to join in, happy to utilise his skills in strategic thinking, self-control and arithmetic. But, much to her father's irritation, the game was undertaken half-heartedly by the others and everyone soon owned to feeling surprisingly sleepy. Perhaps the sea air and good food were taking their toll, and so it was decided that they would retire for the night and prepare themselves for Mr Badgerwood's arrival on the Sunday.

'We need to get to the bottom of this confounded nonsense, Raymond,' Standfield said, now slurring his words slightly and unsteady on his feet as they mounted the stairs. 'When that damn Badgerwood arrives, we must demand answers. Press the fellow and find out what exactly he wants from us.'

'Harlow.' Her father's stern utterance of Standfield's name was a quiet warning. The man was talking too much.

Everyone filtered into their rooms and Pearl was left alone with her father in the corridor, where she decided to push him one last time over his connection to Morton Peverell.

'Why exactly are we here, Father? The failure of Mr Badgerwood to arrive is unsettling, and I'm not convinced that coming to Highcliffe House was a good idea.'

'I told you this was purely a matter of business and that should be an end to it. I do not like being cross-questioned by my own daughter. Goodnight.'

He was lying and that made her uneasy, because she knew that Raymond Glenham was being blackmailed, and blackmailers only had power over those with dark secrets.

* * *

Pearl became vaguely aware that her dream of swimming in the ocean, liberating and peaceful, was taking a more terrifying turn. One moment, she was happily powering through the waves, that glorious feeling of weightlessness and strength; the next, her strong strokes began to falter. She could smell something, and it wasn't the fresh, salty air. A towering ocean liner loomed ahead, with thick, black smoke pouring from its three red funnels.

She awoke from her slumbers with a start. An acrid tang invaded her nostrils, and an accompanying bitter taste filled her mouth. Moonlight from the gap in her curtains illuminated dirty grey clouds billowing and lurching from under her door. She leapt from her bed in sheer panic and raced towards her only exit, coughing and dropping to her knees after a few faltering steps, certain she remembered from somewhere that because smoke rises, the safest place was on the floor. Within seconds her breathing became laboured, each inhalation felt painful and raw, as the heat from the smoke started to burn her lungs.

Her heart was pounding and her brain was racing, desperately trying to work out what was happening and her best course of action. They were all going to be burned alive, because it was obvious to her now that the hallway outside her door was consumed by flames and her escape route was blocked. She could hear the roar of air feeding the beast, alongside the cracking and spitting of splintering wood. Any attempt at escape through the house was useless.

Having initially thought to raise the alarm, and to reach her father, her sensible head realised her only chance of survival was to head for the window, because to open her bedroom door would be suicide. Would she even survive a jump out onto the hard-shingled driveway below?

As she dragged her body over to the window, she began to slow down. Everything felt heavy and she was not getting enough oxygen into her lungs to breathe properly. She became disorientated, as the room was now a fog of smoke, and she felt dizzy, her head spinning and her thoughts a swirling torrent of jumbled snatches of random things. Her hand went to her stomach as she gave a nauseous lurch before vomiting the contents of her stomach over the floor.

It was no longer possible to keep her eyes open. They were stinging badly, so she closed them, a cascade of tears running down her cheeks, as she encountered the edge of the bedside rug with her searching fingers. So nearly there...

Air.

She needed air.

But Pearl knew that all further actions were futile. She was dying. The heat was overwhelming and she was being suffocated. And, as all life was squeezed from her racked body, her last conscious breath was accompanied by her last conscious thought: she'd been right to tell her father that coming to Highcliffe House was a bad idea.

9

A huge, violent gasp of clean, salty fresh air filled her lungs, and made her shoulders momentarily lurch and lift from the cold hard surface beneath her. Pearl opened her eyes to see what she could only assume was the underside of a sturdy wooden table – although the flickering light was poor. A cool breeze danced over her body and she shivered.

If this was heaven it left a lot to be desired – she'd expected bright sunlight, possibly a sweeping hillside meadow dotted with poppies and cornflowers, and her mother running through the grass, arms outstretched to catch her in an everlasting embrace. Although, to be fair, the air tasted unbelievably good. Perhaps heaven was simple things, like breathable air, when you had suffocated to death on thick toxic smoke only moments before.

The back of her head hurt and Pearl reached her hand up to feel a small bump through her hair.

Finally, she realised where she was. This was the cave in Highcliffe Cove that she'd stumbled across that afternoon. And she was lying underneath the table that supported the mercury clock. Sure enough, as she rolled her tongue around her mouth, there was the tangy aftertaste of metal again.

Never having died before, she wasn't sure what the human brain might be capable of doing in those moments immediately after death. Might it replay scenes from her day, as it filed them away in her memory, still plodding on with the mundane tasks biology had assigned it, little realising shortly it would be nicely fried, along with the rest of her body, at temperatures approaching two thousand degrees Fahrenheit?

She pushed herself up into a sitting position from the icy stone floor and tucked her feet beneath her.

No, this scenario was lasting too long to be the final tidy-up of her thoughts; her observations were too detailed; the sensations too real. She pinched her own arm with determined fingers, deliberately digging her nails into the flesh. It hurt. This was no dream or celestial experience.

Frowning, she began to rationalise her situation. When she'd slipped in the cave, she'd blacked out. Perhaps, even though the last few hours had *felt* real, her unconscious brain had been hallucinating, playing out a plausible sequence of events that had culminated in the terrifying nightmare that was her death in the fire. Yes, that must be it. A thankful sigh escaped from her lips.

Clambering to her feet, she extinguished the lamps, before exiting the cave and making her way back up the steep cliff steps. Lifting her face to the early afternoon sun, she revelled in the heat of the day – hot, but thankfully not cook-you-alive hot – and skipped through the wooden gate. The relief flooding through her body was immense. Not usually given to unpleasant dreams, the whole experience had been disconcerting. As she ambled alongside the high laurel hedge, contemplating how extraordinarily vivid her unconscious vision had been, she heard raised voices, immediately recognising Céline and her husband. How curious that she should have imagined this very scenario. The brain truly was a wonderful but mystifying thing, and she thought about the handful of occasions she'd experienced déjà vu in her life – although none had been quite like this.

She was taken aback as Aldo stepped from the enclosed garden and walked to the summer house. Gosh, her unconscious had been alarmingly prophetic.

Like in her dream, she then poked her head around the gap in the hedge and saw Céline on the same stone bench, looking flustered. The older woman hid her discomposure and smiled as soon as she noticed Pearl.

'Darling, how lovely. Have you been to the cove? It is a picturesque little place, *non?*' She patted the seat next to her, and Pearl, an uncomfortable feeling rolling in her stomach, obediently took a seat next to her.

'Um, yes.' She couldn't stop a frown from passing across her face.

'You are a quiet little thing. Rather like your father.' Céline cleared her throat. 'I mean, he appears to be the quiet sort from our brief acquaintance,' she clarified.

'He is generally happier with ledgers and adding machines, than people.'

'And you? You like the numbers too?'

'Not especially. I spend a lot of my time reading – I'm an only child, you see. And swimming. I always find myself drawn to the water.'

'Ah, yes, I also have no brothers and sisters.' Céline looked thoughtful. 'And your mother?' she asked. 'She is not accompanying you?'

Prickles of unease were now running rife across Pearl's skin. This was beyond any déjà vu she'd experienced. The conversation was alarmingly similar to the one she'd dreamed about.

'She died when I was born.'

'So sad.' Pearl snatched her hand from her lap just as Céline reached out to pat it. Aware it might seem rude, she faked an itchy nose to justify her reaction. 'So many poor women pay the ultimate price to bring life into this world. And your father never remarried?'

'No.' She no longer felt inclined to elaborate.

'And they met when?'

'Please excuse me. I feel unwell. Perhaps I swallowed some of the seawater.' She stood up but the older woman was not going to let her off so easily.

'*Bien sûr*, but I must ask why you and your father are here? What did your invitation say of the purpose of the dinner party this evening? Who is Mr Badgerwood? Why—'

But Pearl had already stepped back out to the path, and with her head low, she scurried past Standfield.

'I say, Paula!' he called from the terrace – the same half bottle of wine on the table, the same cigarette in his hand.

Again, she toyed with pretending not to have heard him, but this time it was her curiosity, rather than her manners, that forced her reluctant feet over to the terrace.

'Join me?' He got to his feet. 'I can always call that Dawson woman for another bottle. It will help to take the edge off the dull nature of this gathering. She has at least kept me supplied with plenty of the old fermented grape juice – in this instance, a splendid crisp white, if not sufficiently chilled.'

'Um, perhaps just for a moment,' she said, feeling slightly light-headed. A creeping unease was rippling through her. She pulled out a chair but, as she sat, her bathing robe parted to reveal her bony knees, so she hastily pulled the two sides together.

'Been swimming, dear girl? You should have said. I'd have come down to the cove with you.' He returned to his chair.

'But you're not a swimmer,' she said with conviction. 'Besides, who would help you change?'

'Exactly that,' he replied, slapping his thigh in glee. 'Ridiculous nonsense not being allowed to bring my man. It's proving damn bothersome without him. It will take me an age to dress for dinner... unless you fancy popping by to give a chap a hand?' He gave a lecherous wink but received a horrified look in return. 'Well, no, maybe not. I'll have to ask that Ellery chap, I suppose, although between you and me, I don't think he really knows what he's doing. Think this might be his first position in service. Plus, I can't shake the feeling I've seen him somewhere before.' He rubbed at his fleshy chin and scrunched up his eyes in thought. 'Whole blasted thing smells fishy to me.'

'You can say that again,' she mumbled.

'What? Speak up, girl.' He leaned forward and cupped his hand to his ear. 'Men don't like mousy women, pretending to be all timid and helpless. Can't be doing with it. You'll never bag a husband if you go round whimpering all the time. How old did you say you were?'

'Nineteen,' she said, not having owned to her age before, but reassured that the conversation was taking a completely new turn.

'Hmm... bit young, but not entirely out of the question.'

She didn't dare ask 'young for what?' and instead reached out for the half full bottle of Sauvignon and an abandoned glass that had yet to be cleared away. She filled it almost to the brim, and took a huge gulp. Not used to alcohol, she wondered if a combination of the heat of such a balmy summer day, her exertions in the sea, and that small bump to the head were the real reason for this surreal experience. The wine burned her throat and almost immediately had an alarming, but not altogether unpleasant, effect on her knees. In for a penny... she put the glass to her lips again and downed the remainder, aware her behaviour was totally unacceptable – ladies certainly did not drink like sailors – and instantly regretted her actions.

'I say, steady there, old girl. Don't want your father accusing me of plying you with alcohol for nefarious purposes.'

'Please excuse me, I feel a little... off.'

He stood up when she did, and gave an almost imperceptible nod of the head.

Much like in her bizarre dream, she retired to her room and lay across her bed. Most likely hastened by the sudden intake of so much alcohol, she fell asleep almost immediately, but had absolutely no further peculiar dreams – of slipping in caves, being burned alive, or otherwise.

10

Pearl was awoken by someone tapping on the door to her room.

'Miss Glenham, your father asked me to remind you that drinks are to be served in the drawing room at six-thirty prompt.' The voice was Ellery's. This hadn't happened in her silly dream, but then she hadn't been out for the count for so long. And, of course, this was reality – her thumping headache told her so.

She rolled over to peer at the small clock on the nightstand beside the bed. It was a quarter to six.

'Thank you. I'll be down presently,' she called, sitting up in the airless room. She really shouldn't have drunk that entire glass of wine so quickly, but losing a few hours from such a bizarre day was probably for the best. She could reset herself now and endure the discomfort of a meal with these disagreeable strangers. Hopefully, all this silly repetition nonsense had come to an end.

It didn't take her long to dress for dinner and she met her father on the landing as she made for the stairs.

'There you are,' he said, looking her up and down as if she was an extra pair of socks he was considering purchasing. There were rarely any encouraging words; no 'You look splendid, my dear' or 'Your mother would be so proud'.

'Shall we?' and he put out his arm to escort her down the stairs.

They entered the drawing room and Ellery presented them with a silver tray of sherries. This she had also imagined before, but sherry was a common enough pre-dinner aperitif. Pearl shook her head, noticing that Aldo and Standfield were already present, the former in black tie, the latter in white – as in her dream. The Italian had his nose in his book of poetry, clearly lost in the reverie of Ovid's rapturous words.

Incredulous, but largely mute, she allowed familiar conversations to play out, and felt a bit sick when Céline entered the room precisely ten minutes late. Pearl could have described the woman's outfit to the last bead around the neckline before she even stepped through the door.

It came as no surprise to her that Mr Badgerwood had failed to arrive that afternoon and, as she followed behind the others into the dining room, she reached for the wall in the hallway to steady herself. Ellery pulled her to one side.

'Are you all right, miss? You look rather peaky if you don't mind me saying.'

'Thank you. I'm fine.' She looked into his amber eyes and saw his concern was genuine. 'I'm not really a dinner party person,' she clarified. 'Strange people, new situations and rich foods I'm not used to. And everyone is so much more self-assured than me. I'm sure I shall have little of value to contribute to the evening.'

'Entitled people like Mr Standfield, and flamboyant exhibitionists like Signora Ravello, really get my goat. Don't be intimidated by any of them. You're just as worthy as the next... woman, and by far the prettiest here.' His eyes twinkled and those golden flecks really reflected back the light. He was just saying it to be kind. Céline outshone her, even though the Frenchwoman was twice her age, but his words lifted her spirits nonetheless.

Her father appeared, having returned to the hallway to locate his daughter.

'Pearl, really, flirting with staff?' He tutted and she realised it did not look good for her to be huddled with the manservant in the corridor, heads together, speaking in hushed tones. Her cheeks flushed and she dipped her head.

'My apologies, sir, I thought the young lady looked unwell and I was concerned for her.'

'Hmm...' Her father looked unconvinced. 'I would ask you to bear in mind that she's practically engaged, young man, so I suggest you banish any untoward thoughts. I will not entertain such an association. She is the daughter of a respectable man of business, and you are a manservant.'

'I can assure you, I have no untoward intentions towards your daughter – romantic or otherwise. And, as for your implication that I am somehow beneath the pair of you, this position is temporary. I have ambitions and aspirations far beyond working here.'

Pearl noticed her father's jaw clench – as much emotion as he would allow himself to display. She began to pick at her nails and felt her heart accelerate. Was this to prove confrontational? She dearly hoped not.

'Watch yourself, Brown.' Her father's voice remained calm but his eyes narrowed.

Pearl thought Ellery would lock horns with her father, but as quickly as his temper had threatened to flare up, it died down again.

'I apologise if I spoke out of turn, sir, but my concern for your daughter was genuine. Have you not noticed how pale she is?'

Raymond Glenham frowned at his daughter.

'Really, Father,' Pearl interjected. 'Everyone is hot and fraught, especially as Mr Badgerwood remains absent.'

'If you are feeling off colour, then maybe you should retire?' her father offered, peering at her more closely and perhaps shamed by Ellery's words. 'Better than sitting through the meal with a sullen look on your face.'

'I must admit to not being myself, but the meal will settle my stomach.' She entered the dining room and the gentlemen rose from their seats. 'Perhaps you would allow me to retire early, but I would like to be present for our elusive host's telegram. I shall be intrigued to hear what he has to say over dessert,' she said, and then immediately realised her error.

'Telegram? What telegram? Has there been a communication from Mr Badgerwood?' Standfield asked Ellery, who was then pulling out a chair for Pearl.

'Not that I'm aware of, sir. We've had no explanation as yet for his late arrival. Mrs Dawson suspects car trouble. You know how unreliable these new-fangled motor vehicles can be?'

'My mistake,' Pearl said. 'I was assuming that's how he would contact us, there being no telephone at Highcliffe House, but I'm only speculating.' She dipped her head and slunk into her seat, knowing all eyes were on her, but Céline quickly held court with the tale of her rather humorous encounter with the Shah of Persia – which Pearl could have repeated word for word.

She then worked her way silently through the tomato soup (which was as piquant as that of her dream), the same delicious crab cakes, and an equally pink *filet* of beef. Mrs Dawson cleared the plates and announced she would collect the chocolate mousse. Aldo's face became quite animated as he looked to his wife and enquired, '*Cioccolato?*'

The couple had a brief interchange before Céline's attention returned to her dinner companions.

'I have yet to decide whether there is some chemical in chocolate that makes it such a seductive confection. Or whether it is merely how it melts on the tongue that increases one's ardour. Either way, I suspect my husband will benefit later tonight.' The unspoken implication was verging on scandalous in polite company. Pearl's father gave a reprimanding tut but wisely chose not to address Céline's provocative pronouncement. She noticed the Frenchwoman's slight arch of the eyebrow, however, and the way she had her body tilted towards her father.

'Raymond...' She revelled in rolling her Rs as she briefly reached out for his shoulder. 'Your disapproval is quite amusing. Perhaps it is that you have been too long without the touch of a woman, although you always struck me as quite the puritan.'

Pearl's eyes flashed over to the pair of them, neither appearing to notice that Céline's statement confirmed a prior acquaintance, and then she dropped her eyes to the tablecloth.

Ellery entered the room, casting a quizzical look at Pearl, as he presented Standfield with a silver tray.

'Um, this has just arrived, sir,' and he handed the telegram envelope over, as four sets of surprised eyes swivelled in Pearl's direction. Aldo was absorbed by the fine wine he was swirling around his glass.

```
Regret unavoidable delay. Stop. With you by
morning. Stop. Accept my apologies and my
hospitality. Stop. Badgerwood.
```

'How did you know that our host was not coming?' Céline asked, narrowing her eyes and looking at Pearl.

'I didn't.' She felt sick. It was unpleasant to be under such scrutiny from everyone at the table. She did not court nor enjoy attention like the Frenchwoman. 'But, but... surely it is a natural assumption that he would telegraph us to explain his delay?'

Mrs Dawson arrived with the chocolate mousse, and was filled in on the news, as Céline leaned closer to the young woman.

'But you knew *when* it would arrive,' she pointed out. 'Suspicious, *non*?'

Standfield began to voice his discontent at such an outrageous state of affairs, and angle for access to the wine cellar. Pearl needed to escape, besides she had no room for chocolate mousse, so made her excuses, feigned a headache that she was fairly certain would be returning promptly anyway, and retreated to her bedroom. Let them eat dessert, drink brandy and play their silly card games. She wanted none of it. They were all hiding things – she even suspected the outspoken manservant was not who he claimed to be. All she wanted was for her head to hit that soft feather-filled pillow and this dreadful day to be over.

* * *

It was only a couple of hours later when a bitter smell invaded Pearl's sleep that real panic set in.

How could she have forgotten about the fire?

Clouds of smoke were billowing in through the door, and she leapt from the bed in a state of utter terror. She dropped to the floor immediately, but this time, instead of wasting precious seconds heading to the corridor, she turned for the window. She lumbered towards the faint slit of moonlight cutting through the dark, but her eyes were starting to sting as she reached out, fumbling for the heavy velvet curtains, before yanking them apart. Already, her lungs were hurting and her breathing was laboured and desperate. Clutching the edge of the windowsill, she peered through the glass and saw the silhouette of Standfield's car edged by the moonlight.

She thought for a moment that there was a figure, or an animal, on the driveway but as she began to cough uncontrollably, she felt a familiar lurching sensation, and threw up on the floor.

Window... She must open the window...

Her head started to cloud, as she wrestled with the sash but it wouldn't budge. She checked the locks were open and tried again, but the pane was going nowhere. She was getting weaker with each hard-won breath, and her exertions weren't helping.

Thinking her only option was to smash the glass, she realised she had nothing to hand. She slumped to the floor and began to crawl back into the room, but couldn't remember what she was looking for. Why was she heading towards the fire?

Air.

All she wanted was air...

And then everything went black.

11

To live through the same day twice, was a bizarre phenomenon Pearl had tried to explain away, but when everything started to play out for a third time, she knew this was more than a silly dream or the muddled consequence of her fall.

She opened her eyes to a familiar sight: the underneath of a table that she was certain stood in a gloomy cave, tucked at the bottom of Highcliffe Cove. There was the same metallic taste in her mouth, same sore head, same cooling breeze. And, yes, that life-giving gasp of clean, salty air that jolted her slender body back to life was as welcome as it had been on the previous occasion.

After extinguishing the candles, she walked out to the cove and down to the water's edge.

Utterly bewildered by the situation she found herself in, she didn't feel like climbing the steps and having another awkward interchange with Céline, or being called Paula by Standfield for a third time. It could all wait for her up at the top of the cliffs, because she was frightened now that the whole afternoon might be about to replay yet again over the following few hours. She needed time to herself, and she always thought best when she was connected to the water. It was her lifeblood.

She swept the trailing fabric of the bathing robe under her bottom and sat as close to the waves as she dared. The sides fell away and exposed her white legs, as she wiggled her toes, and kicked off her damp canvas shoes. A frothy wave surged up the shingle a few inches from her feet, paused for a moment, and then receded back down the beach into the swelling of the ocean. It met another advancing wave, which folded in on itself and crept up the shore again, this time closer to her toes, before falling away. The rhythm and repetitiveness was hypnotic.

She lay back on the shingle and stared up at the cerulean sky – two white clouds blobbed onto the plain blue canvas, as though the artist of the universe had merely added them as an afterthought.

What was happening to her? Was she going mad? One of those maladies of the mind that no one could fully understand, where the patient was trapped inside their own head. The important thing was not to panic, for surely that would hasten her decline. She must act rationally, do nothing to alarm her father, and see if things became clearer. Perhaps the nasty bump to the head had knocked something out of alignment and given time all would be well.

She closed her eyes and lay in the sunshine for a long while, allowing the whispers of the sea to comfort her, and those hisses and whooshes did indeed soothe her anxiety. Eventually, she allowed a long sigh to escape from her body as she heaved herself up from the beach.

If this was going to play out a third time, she was determined to be better prepared.

* * *

The time Pearl had spent contemplating her situation allowed the house guests to move on with their day. When she crept past the hedge, there was no animated Italian conversation coming from the other side, and she was relieved to notice Standfield no longer sat on the terrace. Perhaps he had drunk all the wine and gone in search of more. Perhaps he had simply retired for the afternoon, like her father.

This time, Pearl entered the house through the kitchens, not wanting to encounter Standfield in the drawing room, and found Ellery and Mrs Dawson bustling about, busy with their domestic tasks. Two highly polished silver candlesticks stood at the end of the table, and the young man was fixing candles into the sockets, as the cook used a noisette spoon to scoop out tiny balls from the large potato in her hand, before dropping them into the saucepan of cold water that sat on the table in front of her.

'Oh, miss, you startled me. Can I get you anything?' the older lady offered, as Pearl's shadow fell across the table and alerted the cook to her presence. 'Perhaps some lemonade?'

'No, thank you, but I wondered if Ellery might help me with my bedroom window? It is difficult to open, and on a day such as this, I should like to let in some fresh air.'

'Of course,' he said. 'I think there is a toolbox in the boot room. I'll grab it.'

Moments later, they both stood in her room as he rubbed at his chin.

'This has been tampered with,' he said. 'Look, a screw has been driven into each side of the sash, pinning it to the frame. How odd.'

He took a screwdriver from the wooden box. After much fiddling about, he managed to extract them both and open the window – although the air outside was hot and heavy, so it made little difference to the temperature.

'Did you and Mrs Dawson not air the rooms yesterday?' she

asked, curious as to why a window might be screwed shut.

'I arrived shortly before her, but it was apparent to both of us that much of the hard work had been done: bed making, sweeping through and dusting. Someone had clearly been living here recently – there were jars of half-eaten jam in the pantry, the drains were wet, and when I cleaned out the range, the ash was still warm. The cupboards were well stocked with tins and packets, and I merely carried out my list of instructions: collecting milk and cheese from a nearby farm, sorting out the requisite tableware, and, like I say, lighting the range.'

'Are you local?' she asked. 'You talked knowledgeably about the Brockhursts the other day... I mean, this morning.' What felt like two days ago to her was only a matter of hours ago to Ellery.

'I live with my mother this side of Weymouth but it's too far for me to return home each night. Mr Badgerwood has arranged for me to stay at the Fisherman's Arms, the public house between here and the village – bizarre, I know, when there are so many bedrooms at Highcliffe House. Perhaps he worries your virtue is at risk if I remain here.' Her insides somersaulted. 'Or mine is at risk from Céline – I expect there are a multitude of things she could teach me. She is, after all, a woman of the world.'

He chuckled and she didn't know where to look. He sensed her discomfort and painted a more serious expression on his face.

'But in reference to your observation, most people around these parts still gossip about the Brockhursts, even if they'd not known them personally. I believe my mother came across Lenora occasionally in her youth, but I was only four in the spring of 1903.'

'The year before I was born,' Pearl muttered, largely to herself. What was her father doing back then, she wondered. He claimed not to have met her mother until the summer of that year, in Southampton. And yet, every couple of years after her death they had started somewhere new: Basingstoke, Reading, Luton, Bedford.

Now she thought about it, there was a definite trajectory to their movements, until they'd come to rest in Suffolk.

Her thoughts bounced all over the place as she turned back to the window.

'Do you think if someone jumped from here, they would survive?' she whispered, aware her father was in the next room and not sure how soundproof the walls were.

'Is life really that bad, miss? You might be better launching yourself off the cliff, if you're determined. It could be broken bones and a bath chair for you from this height. The cliffs are much higher and a better bet.'

Her horror at his matter-of-fact approach to her abstract query flashed across her face. He gave a weak smile. 'It was a joke but perhaps a poor one. You don't strike me as someone with suicidal intentions.'

'Most certainly not,' she mumbled. 'I was thinking more if there was a fire and I needed to escape.'

He laughed. 'I think the risk of fire in the middle of the summer is quite small. It's not even as though we use candles to light the way to bed any more. Surely, we are all sensible enough to be trusted with the oil lamps?'

It was the first time the source of the fire had occurred to her. How had it started? Was it an accident, she mused, looking at the two screws Ellery had removed from the sash window or, she swallowed hard, were there darker forces at play?

* * *

Pearl was determined the alarmingly familiar events of the afternoon would not play out as they had done on the two previous occasions. Once Ellery had returned downstairs, she changed out of her swimwear, but instead of resting in her room, she took the opportunity to explore the layout of the house and grounds, keen to have more information at her disposal.

There were nine bedrooms upstairs, and she briefly popped her head into them all, with the exception of her father's, as she knew he was resting. At the other end of the corridor was a locked store cupboard – she'd disturbed a fly when she'd tried the handle – and, just beyond that, a smaller set of servants' stairs ran down to the west of the house, coming out next to the kitchens and boot room.

On the ground floor, apart from the drawing room, dining room and library, which she was familiar with, there were two further large reception rooms – one given over to more of the artwork, ancient relics and exotic objects that Virgil Brockhurst had been so taken with. She found Céline in that room, wandering restlessly around as though she were looking for something. Pearl immediately backed out of the doorway before she was spotted. She had her suspicion that any conversation would be along the lines of their previous encounters in the enclosed gardens and she simply couldn't endure the Frenchwoman's nosiness a third time.

Next door was a bright morning room, with a small south-facing conservatory attached. She walked through the former to enter the latter. The white-tiled space was devoid of plants – no one to water them, she supposed – but a small table held articles that would previously have been used to care for the tropical flora – a green metal watering can, pruning scissors, a willow trug and a wooden mounted thermometer. She could see Standfield on the terrace through the windows and didn't want him to spot her, so quickly retreated back into the main body of the house. Besides, the heat on such a day in a room that was largely glass was unbearable.

Finally, she slipped out the front door to assess possible escape routes. All the guest rooms were on the same side of the corridor and faced north, across the driveway, she noticed. The family rooms naturally had the wonderful sea view and southern aspect. A part of her was still searching for rational explanations for the bizarre phenomenon she'd experienced (or that her brain had convinced her she had), and she was determined to be prepared if the fire took hold again. She noticed a cast-iron drainpipe ran down the front of the house, between her window and Standfield's, and thought it might be possible for her to reach it from the wide sill. She was lithe and wiry, and had been quite the tree climber in her childhood – another activity her father knew nothing about. Time was ticking on, she realised; tardiness was unforgivable in her father's eyes, so she returned upstairs to ready herself for dinner.

The afternoon had been satisfyingly different from the previous two: no Ravello quarrel to overhear, no shouts of 'Paula', and an afternoon spent acquainting herself with Highcliffe House and avoiding the other guests. If she didn't interact with anyone, then the same conversations could not take place. But as soon as she entered the drawing room for the pre-dinner drinks, events played out in a stomach-heavingly familiar fashion. Céline was late, the menu was as before, the talk over dinner covered the same topics, and moments before the dessert was served, a telegram arrived. Pearl's overriding emotion continued to be fear. What was happening to her? And how many times was she to experience this? Was the bump to her head responsible? Perhaps she was at this very moment, tucked into the crisp white sheets of a hospital bed, somewhere in Dorset, trapped in a coma, where her mind was caught in this incessant loop, unable to heal itself and allow her to wake up.

Like before, Pearl feigned a headache and retired early. Restless and anxious, she was afraid to sleep and had no intention of being caught unaware by whatever the darkness was going to throw at her, so she seated herself in a low chair by the bed, like a night sentry, wishing she was brave enough to park herself in the corridor and not mind what the others thought. She determined to stay awake and not to be caught out by the fire this time. However, exhausted from all the travel, her energetic swim in the cove, and the oppressive heat of the evening, sleep had claimed her by eleven o'clock.

But this time, when the acrid smoke and suffocating air pulled her from her slumbers, she at least knew which direction to head in. Angry with herself for allowing this to happen again, she dropped to the floor and crawled to the window, certain that her hours of swimming in the lake meant she would be strong enough to climb out to the drainpipe and drop to the ground.

But after unlocking the latches, she had the same difficulties opening the window as before. The smoke started to encircle her and she experienced the familiar shortness of breath and retching. She ran her hands around the wooden frame and her heart sank as she felt the heads of two screws – one each side of the sash. They had been returned to the window, but why?

Then she spotted the figure again in the distance, running up the driveway. She couldn't be certain, partly because her eyes were stinging so badly and her tears made it difficult to see, but it appeared to be a man by his gait. Was he running towards the burning building to help, or circling back to check on his handiwork?

She shouted out and banged on the glass, but it was pointless. Her energy was draining away and her lungs were already filled with the poisonous air.

Sinking to her knees, she curled herself up into a tiny ball, awaiting the inevitable, with one overriding thought: Ellery knew that she'd discovered her tampered window, knew that it had been fixed, and had walked off with both screws in his pocket...

12

_____

Pearl had been incredulous when her afternoon had played out a second time, and extremely frightened by the third. But the fourth time she woke under the table, she was just plain cross – largely because those screws had been replaced, and she was pretty certain she knew who was responsible. Even relatively tolerant people had a breaking point. Dying had definitely brought her hitherto-suppressed temper to the fore.

She stomped up the flagstone path, passing a torrent of rapid and agitated Italian, and ignored Standfield's shouts of 'Paula', not particularly caring if he thought her rude. She might be more polite the next time she stomped past (she was beginning to suspect the strong likelihood of a next time) or she might not. But first she had a young man to confront – quite a heart-thumping prospect, as confrontation was not a strength of hers.

She walked into the kitchens but only Mrs Dawson was present, and then she remembered that the previous afternoon she'd loitered at the beach for nearly an hour. On this occasion, she found the cook washing up the crockery from luncheon, with not a potato noisette in sight.

'What can I do for you, miss?' she asked, looking over her shoulder. 'Are you in need of refreshment? There's lemonade in the pantry.'

'Where is he?' she demanded, her manners left entirely under the table upon which sat a strange mercury clock, in a damp cave at Highcliffe Cove.

'Mr Badgerwood? He is due this afternoon but we've had no word as yet.'

'Ellery,' she clarified.

'He took the candlesticks to the boot room to give them a polish. Is everything all right?' she called out, as Pearl huffed out the kitchens and into the hallway. She swung open the door to the boot room, walked up to the nonchalant manservant and swallowed hard.

'The window,' she said, coming to a halt in front of him.

'I beg your pardon, miss?'

'You screwed it shut. The one in my bedroom. Why?'

She did not need to climb the stairs to assess the validity of her statement. She knew, with absolute certainty, that this would be the case.

'I have absolutely no idea what you're talking about, but I don't much like your attitude, young lady. I may be employed to look after the guests for the duration of this gathering, but I do not expect unfounded accusations to be flung at me, especially when I've done nothing wrong.'

Was it her imagination, or did those amber irises of his flicker more brightly as his ire increased? She had fanned the flames of something – it was possible his own temper was about to match her own.

'The sash window in my bedroom has been screwed shut and if there is a fire in the corridor, how will I escape?' Then she answered her own question. 'I won't, will I? I'll suffocate with the smoke, and everyone along that top corridor will perish with me.'

'I've had nothing to do with the bedrooms since my arrival. Most of the house had been prepared—'

'Yes,' she said, in a steady voice. 'The beds were made, the pantry stocked, and ash still warm in the grate. I know...'

His face crinkled into a perplexed frown, and Pearl, who had hardly ever dared to speak in such a way to anyone in her life before, took a physical and mental step back from the situation. He seemed genuinely bemused and she had to consider whether she'd jumped to conclusions. She'd managed to creep around the house without being seen the previous repeated afternoon, so anyone could have done the same. Wasn't it far more likely that the person who either owned the property now, or who had set everything up for this gathering, was responsible? The problem seemed to be that no one knew exactly who that was.

She bowed her head. 'I apologise.' All at once, she felt overwhelmed by everything, but her father had taught her that any display of emotion was a weakness, so she tried to meet the young man's eye. 'The heat is getting to me.'

Ellery stepped over to a slim wool jacket hanging on the back of the door and took a handkerchief from the pocket. He handed it to her and then pulled a hoop-backed chair out from the table, gesturing for her to sit.

'I'm not surprised. It's an unusually warm summer day and even the coastal breezes are doing little to shift the humid and heavy air. Did the swim not help?' He looked at her attire. 'Not a swimmer myself – somehow I never got around to learning – but I should imagine your dip in the ocean was refreshing.'

'Perhaps I overdid it,' she said. 'Exerting myself in this heat.'

'You certainly look most out of sorts. Wait here a moment and I'll get you a glass of something.'

'Thank you,' she said, surrendering to the care of someone else. 'There's lemonade in the pantry, apparently,' she said to the back of his head, as he disappeared into the corridor and she sunk her own muddled head into her hands.

After a small glass of lemonade and a few minutes in the cool of the boot room, Pearl felt more herself. She went upstairs to change but was too fired up to retire, not used to such extreme emotions, or how to handle them. This whole repeating-day was starting to get to her. Why was God playing such a perplexing game? Was it to punish her for stealing the clocks? Or was He trying to save her from an unpleasant and totally unjust death? She thought about this for a while. Perhaps that was it – He was giving her a chance to survive. If she could prevent her death in the fire, would Sunday come around as it should?

What she needed more than anything, was some thinking time. She found Ellery, thanked him for his kindness and decided to take a walk about the grounds, heading for the wooded area beyond the summer house, and wondering how far the Highcliffe estate stretched.

It was as she stepped under the verdant canopies of the ash, oak and silver-barked birch that she noticed a much older man, perhaps in his sixties or seventies, pacing backwards and forwards in a clearing. With an overgrown beard and tatty raincoat, she was certain this was the man she had seen enter the caves when she'd been in the sea.

Curious, she approached him, but he appeared not to notice her – or perhaps he simply didn't care.

'Good afternoon,' she risked, but he was muttering to himself and tapping one of his hands repeatedly on his leg. Still he paced back and forth, so she tried again.

'I say, hello! I'm Pearl. Do you know where this footpath leads?'

Finally, he looked up, but as soon as he'd made eye contact, his gaze dropped away from hers.

'...Doesn't understand... too precious, too precious...' he muttered.

'It's a glorious day.' She tried again.

'Glorious day,' he repeated and she knew that at least he'd heard her.

'Are you local?' she asked. He stopped pacing and stared directly at her. It was unnerving to be scrutinised so. Was the poor fellow senile? Perhaps the elderly grandfather of a local family who had wandered off without anyone noticing his absence. Or was he something more sinister?

'But *she* isn't dead though, is she?' And his eyes narrowed, as though he genuinely expected Pearl to provide an answer.

'Isn't she?'

He shook his head in reply.

'Well, that's good then,' she said, deciding that a placatory approach was safest.

'Drip, drip, drip, drip,' was his bemusing reply. He broke his stare and began to bite at his bottom lip, before turning towards the trees.

'Wait,' she called, as he began to walk away, but he picked up his pace and disappeared between the trunks and out of sight.

* * *

Pearl had a pleasant meander through the woods, enjoying any activity that wasn't a repeat of previous afternoons. Despite owning more than her fair share of timepieces, she never had one about her person and so it was looking at the position of the sun in the sky, that she decided she should probably head back. She stepped into the kitchens, less intimidated by Mrs Dawson than anyone else at the house, with the exception of Aldo.

'I met a curious man at the edge of the grounds.'

'Oh,' the older woman said, looking up from a bowl of flaked crab and potato, as she formed the mixture into tiny patties. 'Curious in what way?'

'He was an elderly gentleman and didn't seem to know what was going on. I wonder if he's someone's relative and he's gone walkabout. Should we report it in the village perhaps?'

'Scruffy man with a grey beard?'

Pearl nodded.

'I wouldn't pay him too much attention. The lady in the post office told me he's harmless enough. She seems to know everyone around here. Just a bit strange in the head, that's all. Talks a lot of nonsense but he won't harm you. I was advised to steer clear and strongly suggest you do the same.'

But Pearl felt sorry for the poor man. If he was no danger to her, surely engaging in friendly chatter with him would only be a comfort. She didn't want to mention seeing him at the cave, not to Mrs Dawson or anyone else at the house. There was no need to get him in trouble, certainly not until she'd worked out what was going on.

13

Determined not to suffer another slow and painful death, Pearl decided that escaping from the fire was not her best course of action – preventing it was. As she pulled on her provincial pale pink dress and stared at her decidedly unglamorous reflection, she knew that whether it was accidental or not, the fire must start somewhere. Had Mrs Dawson left something on in the kitchens? Would the inebriated Standfield trip over while holding a lamp in the drawing room and let the flame catch the velvet curtains? Or was the strange man from the woods not in control of his actions, and to right some perceived transgression, deliberately put a match to Highcliffe House?

The dinner played out as usual, Pearl now heartily sick of both crab cakes and chocolate mousse, and she excused herself early. Cross with everyone and everything, she had a hard job not letting this show on her face or come across in the tone of her voice. Ellery noticed something was up – in fact, he was the only one present who ever seemed to pay her any real attention. He tried to jolly her up with smiles and the odd comical face when no one else could see, but she was a bubbling saucepan of emotions.

After completing her ablutions and changing into her night-wear, this time she kept her shoes on, as well as her oil lamp alight. She read for a while, a book she'd borrowed from Virgil Brock-hurst's extensive library, and periodically stepped out into the corridor to peer over the banister into the belly of the house. This way, she would spot the fire early and could pinpoint where it started. Maybe she could raise the alarm before the whole thing took hold. The two sets of stairs in Highcliffe House offered alterna-tive escape routes, so hopefully, she could guide the other guests to safety in plenty of time.

At half past ten she heard a noise in the hallway and opened her door a fraction to see Aldo mounting the stairs and clutching his book. He'd stayed up later than the other guests, clearly absorbed in the poet's romantic advice. She'd assumed the guests had all come to bed around the same time, like that first night, but there must be the subtlest of differences on each repeat. And, she recog-nised, it would only take the smallest change for events to play out completely differently. Perhaps, on that first occasion, he had crept back down after they had all bid one another goodnight. Could he be responsible for the deaths – either accidentally, or deliberately? But there was still no sign of any fire when she checked ten minutes later.

It was only when she popped her head out of her room some time after eleven o'clock she saw a thin trail of smoke coming from the right. She had assumed the fire started downstairs, but it seemed that its source was on that very corridor. Without a thought for her safety (there was something about enduring your repeated death that resulted in a flippancy regarding your life), she ran along the hallway, trying to remember who was sleeping where. From her previous exploring, she knew Mrs Dawson had the furthest room, nearest the servants' stairs. She would likely have been the last to bed; locking up the house, rinsing the glasses from Standfield's endless drinking, and perhaps preparing items in readiness for the breakfasts.

But as Pearl headed down the hall, she realised that the smoke actually originated from under the poor woman's door. Did that mean the fire had started in her room? A chilling thought occurred to her. Could Mrs Dawson be responsible for the whole thing? Had she set fire to her room, escaped down the servants' stairs and run off into the night, leaving them all to burn? She admitted to not being local. Could she even be in league with Badgerwood? Yet again, Pearl questioned why anyone would want all the assembled guests dead. What motive could Mrs Dawson possibly have?

She wrapped the hem of her night robe around her hand, wary that the brass knob would be hot, and flung open the door.

But she was too late.

Raising her hand to shield her face from the intense heat, she could only stare at the single bed, which was consumed in flames. Mrs Dawson's slender back was towards her, and there was no movement from the bed. The intense orange glow from the heart of the fire highlighted the small dark lump of her curled body at its centre. Was this all a terrible accident? Had she fallen asleep with the oil lamp burning? Or had someone done this to her? Both options were equally terrible to contemplate, but she didn't have time to stand there staring at the horrific sight. Mrs Dawson was beyond saving but perhaps she could save the others.

She started shouting to raise the alarm.

'Fire! Fire! Wake up, everyone.' She thumped repeatedly on the Ravello's door but there was no answer. In desperation, she tried the handle but the door was locked. Panic flooded her as she ran to Standfield's door. The same thing happened. No answer and no way of gaining access. With tears of hopelessness streaming down her face, she finally burst into her father's room, the last on the corridor, thankful to see him asleep in his bed.

She rushed to his side and tried to wake him but he was extraordinarily drowsy. This was most unlike her restless parent, who tended to suffer from insomnia and often walked around their Suffolk home in the small hours. It made no sense. Surely he hadn't drunk to excess; he simply wasn't the sort. But then if Standfield had been in charge of the spirits, it was not entirely out of the question. Perhaps they had all got carried away over the poker game, which would also explain the lack of response from the other guests. Although, there was also the possibility that one or both of those rooms were currently unoccupied, and the occupant, or occupants, had absconded into the night, having done what they had arrived at Highcliffe House to do: murder everyone else in their beds.

'Father,' she begged. 'Wake up! We need to get outside.' She managed to persuade her mumbling parent to his feet, and they stumbled into the hallway. The fire was now spreading rapidly towards Céline's room, so her priority became getting him to safety. They struggled down the stairs although he now seemed more aware of the sense of urgency, and was more cooperative.

As they made their way towards the front door, past all the display cabinets of curios, she considered how she might raise the alarm. Highcliffe House, like most homes, had no such luxury as a telephone, and Ellery had left the premises a while ago, for his lodgings at the village pub. If she was the only one awake enough to take any decisive action, she would have to make the long journey to the village alone or hope someone would see the flames and raise the alarm.

But her heart was heavy. This was a desperate and impossible situation, and the irony that a vast body of water was only a few hundred yards from the devastating scene was not lost on her. Running to the sea with buckets and back up the steep steps in some vain attempt to put out the fire was as pointless as trying to move a mountain with a teaspoon.

'Pearl!' a voice cut through the dark as she settled her father on the front lawn. Ellery appeared from the shadows of the driveway, running towards her and tugging his hands through his hair. 'My God! What's happened?'

She realised he was the figure she'd seen from the bedroom on the two previous occasions.

'A fire has started upstairs in Mrs Dawson's room.' A rogue emotion caught in her throat. 'I was too late to save her. She's... she's dead and I couldn't raise the others. What are you doing back?'

'I realised I'd forgotten my room key and didn't want to wake the landlord, so returned to collect it, only to see a fierce orange glow in the sky. The whole house will be lost.' He looked genuinely distressed. 'I must try to save the others.' He took his jacket off and wrapped it around his neck to cover his mouth, heading for the open front door but she grabbed his arm.

'No, it's too dangerous.'

'We can't just let them burn, Pearl.'

'I'll climb the drainpipe and smash Standfield's window,' she said, as she prepared to remove her cumbersome robe, not wanting the flapping sides and dangling belt to hinder her ascent, and fully aware that this was not a time to worry about being seen in her nightdress. The devastating licks of tangerine flame were already visible through the glass of the Ravellos' room. If Ellery insisted on standing around discussing the plan for much longer, it would be too late for Standfield as well, so she rushed to the drain and began to scale the pipe, putting her first foot on the bracket that attached a section to the stone wall.

Ten foot up in the air and there was a sudden blast, followed by a deafening roar, as the glass from the Ravellos' window exploded and shattered shards flew outwards. Instinctively, she turned her face away, feeling an intense rush of heat across her back. A surge of dirty grey smoke billowed and swelled outwards, and accompanying flares of amber and gold, now able to feed themselves on the air outside the house, darted into the night.

'Pearl!' Ellery yelled. 'This is pointless. Come back down.'

But she was now at Standfield's window and peering into the darkness of his bedroom. She thought perhaps she could see his sleeping form on the bed, but the light was poor. Pulling down the cuff of her nightgown to protect her hand, she smashed the window, but thick black smoke was already pouring into his room. Tears stung at her eyes, but not from the smoke. This was useless. She wouldn't be able to climb into the room, and even if she did, their only escape route was the window. If he was in there, and proved as drowsy as her father, she wouldn't be able to wrestle him out onto the ledge.

The heat from the Ravellos' window was now overpowering. Her skin was burning and her lungs struggled to deal with the toxic fumes. Everything in her body gave up as a light-headedness came over her and she released her hold on the sill and fell backwards. It seemed she was destined to die regardless. Why not embrace it?

She closed her eyes and felt the chest-heaving sensation of falling, but to her surprise there was no bone-breaking impact of the hard shingle driveway, instead she met with a softer landing. Her watery eyes opened to see the blurry face of Ellery looking down at her.

'You caught me.'

'Of course, although I'm not sure what's going on here.'

'What on earth do you mean?' Her voice was croaky and rough from the smoke damage.

'Did you start the fire?'

'Me?' She was shocked.

There was a further explosion as Standfield's window followed suit. Ellery carried her over to the lawns, where she'd left her father.

'I realise I barely know you, but your behaviour today has been distinctly odd. Arriving at the house so demure and quiet, then accusing me of tampering with your windows, and spending most of the dinner looking decidedly angry with the world.' Perhaps her attempts to conceal her feelings hadn't been as successful as she'd hoped.

He lowered her gently to her feet. Still wobbly and unsteady, she retained hold of his sleeve.

'You'll doubtless think me impertinent, miss, but I wonder if you suffer from some mild neurosis or melancholy. Sometimes hysterical women can do strange things.'

'I most certainly am not hysterical,' she said. 'Besides, I'm trying to save everyone.'

'I'm not necessarily saying this was a deliberate act...'

'Perhaps you're just pointing the finger at me to cover up the fact *you* did this.' Suddenly, she saw everything in a different light and took a step back from the unnerving young man, her pale eyes wide. 'You weren't returning for a forgotten key, you were leaving late after starting the fire, having established an alibi by staying at the public house. Perhaps, you circled back to admire your handiwork, horrified to find my father and I have survived. Of course you have to pretend to help, or it would seem mightily suspicious.'

'All of that could equally apply to you. Saving yourself and your father, and feigning an attempt to rescue Standfield. You were pretty forceful when you told me not to enter the house just now.'

'Oh, for goodness' sake, I nearly fell to my death. Besides, the fire has killed me several times. I'm hardly going to start a fire that takes my own life.'

Ellery's nose scrunched up in confusion. 'What *are* you talking about?'

She realised her comments wouldn't make sense to him and would only reinforce his perception of her as unhinged.

'I mean, it could have killed me, if I hadn't been awake. Do you have any idea how quickly a house fire spreads?'

'No. But you seem pretty knowledgeable. And quizzing me about the windows – as if you knew you might have to escape through them this evening. I had you pegged all wrong. Pretending to be a mouse-like shadow of a girl. They do say it's the quiet ones you have to watch.' His eyes narrowed. 'But your real colours are showing now. Look at you – challenging and outspoken. Very clever. A masterful piece of acting.'

Her father, who was sitting forward with his head in his hands, mumbled something inaudible and she sank to her knees to embrace him. Initially, there was no reaction to her touch – he wasn't a tactile man – but then his hand reached around her body and pulled her close. She let her head fall to his and allowed herself to cry, her tears largely spilling because it took a near-death experience for him to show her any real love.

'Thank you,' he muttered. 'Thank you, Pearl, for saving me, in so many ways.'

She wasn't sure how else she had saved him. Other than physically dragging him from a burning building, she rather felt she'd dragged him down over the years – his duty to bring her up alone costing him money and limiting his career possibilities, as he struggled with their fluctuating finances and the loss of his wife.

'It's too late to save anyone inside.' Ellery interrupted their moment. 'But perhaps some of the valuables from the house could be rescued? I must at least try. It's like a museum in there and I know for a fact that many of those items are irreplaceable. I'll run back to the pub, it's not far, and see if I can get help. Perhaps you're right, it would be madness to try and retrieve them myself. But the fire needs containing, regardless of whether anything can be salvaged.'

They locked eyes and she nodded, before he ran back up the long driveway and into the night.

Pearl leaned back on the grass and stared up at a star-sprinkled sky, finally allowing her eyes to close, letting exhaustion and relief overwhelm her. She'd done it. She'd survived. Surely, that was what this had been about. The universe had given her the opportunity to escape a cruel and unjust death, and face another day. It was heartbreaking that four people had lost their lives, but she had at least saved her father. And now, despite the tragedy that had befallen the other guests at Highcliffe House, she might be allowed to continue her life, however haunted she might be for years to come by this night and her inability to save them.

What a relief it would be to make their way back to Suffolk tomorrow, and leave the horror of all this behind. Possessions could be replaced; people could not... Unless you happened to bump your head in a gloomy cave on the Dorset coast, that is, when – apparently – your life could be replaced on numerous occasions.

14

The gasping breath she took was still welcome but not as desperate, perhaps because her lungs hadn't been filled with bitter, life-sucking smoke only a fraction of a second before, even though it had been circling about her as she lay on the front lawns of a burning house.

Disappointment flooded her body. Her whole day had been reset, yet again, meaning this bizarre phenomenon was not linked to her death, as she'd assumed. If escaping the fire wasn't a way to prevent this inexplicable repeat of time, could she be stuck reliving this Saturday afternoon in July 1923 for eternity?

She was in no hurry to jump to her feet now that she knew saving herself from the fire wasn't enough. There was still no logic as to why time was repeating, or how it was being orchestrated. Was there a higher power who needed her to pass some as yet undefined test? Perhaps she must try to prevent the blaze from starting in the first place – save everyone?

Her eyes focused on a tiny spider, which she hadn't noticed before, dropping down on its silky thread from the underside of the table. Unlike Harriet, who was petrified of these unfairly maligned arachnids, Pearl had always rather admired them. The complicated and time-consuming activity of spinning a web was often undone in a moment as a thoughtless human brushed away their endeavours with a feather duster, or a bolting animal crashed carelessly through the gossamer strands in the night. Undeterred, these stoic creatures would begin the lengthy process from the start, and she sympathised with them, for each time she found herself back in the cave, she had to pick herself up and go through the motions of the afternoon all over again, knowing anything she achieved would be swept away at the end of the day.

Identifying with the plucky spider, she determined that she could do this – be the logical and calm woman her father yearned for. How many times had he stated that they were not the adventurous sort? That a quiet stable life was a happy life? That spontaneity and recklessness led to unhappiness and disaster. Clear thinking and reason were the tools that would navigate you safely through life. All she had to do was look at the facts and put emotions to one side. Allowing her irritation to surface had got her nowhere. Perhaps it was time to present her fellow guests with some unwelcome truths and start ruling scenarios out.

The Ravellos were quarrelling again when she reached the enclosed garden. As Aldo stepped from the hedge, Pearl briefly considered calling out for him. But, as he wouldn't understand her, she instead sought out Céline, whom she didn't much like but envied her confidence and sensuality. She hadn't made up her mind whether the woman was friend or foe, but decided to shake things up a bit. Pussyfooting around had got her nowhere.

'We're all going to die tonight,' Pearl announced, as the older woman looked up at the interloper. 'Unless we do something to prevent it, there will be a house fire, starting at the far end of the upstairs corridor. I think Mrs Dawson falls asleep and her lamp catches the curtains.'

Pearl was still open to the possibility that the fire was accidental. Her innate good nature couldn't possibly contemplate that someone was trying to kill them. After all, she'd never knowingly harmed a soul in her life. Her only crime was the stealing of low-value timepieces, and that surely was no reason for anyone to wish her dead. Members of their party were undoubtedly hiding things, including her own father, but could any of them have secrets dark enough to warrant being murdered?

'*Chére enfant*, what are you talking about?' Céline wriggled uncomfortably. 'How can you possibly predict an accident?'

'I can't explain. Call it second sight, call it whatever you like, but I honestly believe we are about to be caught up in the most terrible fire.'

'Hmm...' The Frenchwoman narrowed her eyes. 'Whilst I find your announcement somewhat overdramatic, there is certainly something funny going on. This Monsieur Badgerwood,' she said with conviction, 'he knows things he has no right to know. That he has assembled us all is most strange, do you not think?'

Pearl thought back to the threatening nature of her father's invite. The time for being guarded was long gone. Besides, she knew that whatever she did or said would be erased from everyone else's memory – save her own. Were she to dance naked around the grounds this very instant, no one but she would remember from the second she involuntarily returned to the cave floor.

'I believe my father was blackmailed into attending, so yes, this whole gathering has been suspect from the start.'

'And yet I must ask myself why you stand here and tell me we shall die? What do you hope to achieve by alarming me? If perhaps your father has asked you to put this idea in my head? Do you not think your words are suspicious?'

The distrustful look that Céline gave her made Pearl squirm. Yet again, she was the suspect, when all she was trying to do was help.

But everyone was on edge, suspicious of one another, because the whole situation was so unnerving.

'I'm not hiding anything,' Pearl said. 'But I think many of you are. Pretending to be strangers when I am certain my father has been to this house before and knows both you and Mr Standfield.'

'Nonsense.' Céline crossed her arms but looked distinctly rattled. 'What did your father say?'

'Nothing. He claims he is here on business and that this is his first visit to Highcliffe House.'

'*Exactement.* I, too, am here for business and the only person that I know in this party is my husband – even though he is the most tedious man here. But perhaps we must keep our eyes, how you say, peeled? Hopefully, Mr Badgerwood can clear much of this up at dinner tonight.'

'Mr Badgerwood will not attend. He will send a telegram during the dinner saying he is detained. But we do need to oversee Mrs Dawson. Perhaps stay up until she has retired for the night – for her own safety, as well as ours, because otherwise we *will* all die – I've seen it in my dreams.'

'Such a bold statement from such a little mouse.' Céline inspected her elegant hands and twirled her wedding band around her finger. 'Clearly everything you say is nonsense, and yet I cannot deny an interest in the supernatural. I had an aunt who had an unnerving gift for divining the future, and it was a fool who did not heed her warnings.'

'Then help me. All I'm asking is that you support my efforts to avoid a disaster this evening.'

The Frenchwoman looked at her, considering her response before speaking, but then made an extremely valid point.

'If you truly believe Mrs Dawson is responsible, then perhaps it is she you should be talking to,' she pointed out.

* * *

'I say, Paula!'

Pearl's nervous stomach was spinning furiously as she scuttled past the annoying older man. She had no time to stop.

'Damnably rude. I only wanted you to join me in a post-luncheon drink...'

But Pearl was already in the kitchen and his words followed in behind. Poor Mrs Dawson looked up at her with expectant eyes, unaware a horrific fate awaited her.

'There's to be a fire tonight,' Pearl began.

'What?' The older woman looked confused.

'I had an... um... premonition that a fire starts in your room after our evening meal and kills us all. It will spread along the top corridor. I suspect your lamp catches the furnishings.'

'I'm always exceptionally careful with oil lamps. This is nonsense. Have you had premonitions before?' She scrunched up her face and looked questioningly at Pearl. It was obvious the older woman was rattled; her hand was trembling slightly and her fore-head was creased in a frown. It must be quite disconcerting to have a stranger predict you are imminently to unintentionally kill the entirety of a small dinner party.

'No, but please trust me. This gathering is unsettling and everyone is hiding secrets.' She reached out for Mrs Dawson's hand with her own, but it was shrugged away.

'Are you some kind of witch?'

'There is no broomstick parked on the front drive,' she joked, but the older woman was perhaps of a generation where these things were taken more seriously. It might have been two hundred years since the last woman was executed in Britain for witchcraft, but the Victorians had been a superstitious lot and it was entirely possible that Mrs Dawson was of such a mind. To be fair, what Pearl was experiencing *was* a form of sorcery. The look the cook threw her across the room certainly made her feel that she should be burned at the stake.

Her courage deserted her and she made her excuses and escaped into the hall. Surrounded by Virgil's curios, she couldn't help but wonder what spirits and supernatural forces the man had inadvertently brought back to Highcliffe House. She looked up at the portrait and decided he was not a man to be trifled with. There was a steely determination about the eyes, which sat with what she knew. If he wanted to do something, he did, probably with little thought to the moralities of his actions. After all, he'd procured the finger of a saint and stolen another man's fiancée.

She pressed her nose to a glass dome and looked at the heart-shaped lead urn within, which a small label told her contained the embalmed heart of some French nobleman from centuries ago, found when his wife's grave was accidentally disturbed. How wonderful to love someone that much and be part of a union so powerful. (And how distasteful of Virgil Brockhurst to put such a thing on display.) It made her realise that the worst thing about this whole situation was that she was totally on her own. What she wouldn't give for Harriet to be nearby. Without a telephone, she couldn't even ring her friend for advice, and any attempt to contact her by another method, such as posting a letter, would prove fruitless in the few short hours left before the whole charade began again.

Having been previously told by Standfield that her father retired after luncheon, she went up to his room and knocked on his door but there was no answer. He'd had a sleepless night at the Weymouth seafront hotel, and had been irritable on the bus to Morton Peverell. Along with his overindulgence at lunch, it appeared his exhaustion had finally caught up with him.

She might not have the closest relationship with her father, but he was the one person here she could trust, so she knocked a few more times and eventually heard a voice from within. She entered and he sat up quite suddenly, embarrassed to be found napping and annoyed at being disturbed.

'I'm so sorry, Father, but I have reason to believe we need to watch Mrs Dawson—' she began.

'What?' He spun his face to meet hers, his eyes narrowed. 'Is she behind the invitation? Do you know something?'

'I dreamed of a house fire last night, one in which we all die, and was alarmed when we arrived at Highcliffe House this morning to realise it was this house.' It was a total fabrication but she could hardly say, *I've lived through this afternoon four times and know with absolute surety that a fire will kill us all in our beds tonight if we don't act together to prevent it.*

'Don't be so ridiculous, Pearl. I've not brought you up to believe in such hocus-pocus. Hard facts and clear deduction are the only truths that matter. Not vague dreams and silly prophecy.'

If only he knew just how much hocus-pocus was at play in her life right now.

'Please, Father, can we at least oversee Mrs Dawson when she secures the house and takes herself to bed?' She reached for his sleeve and gripped it to press home the urgency of her request. 'Ensure all the lamps are properly extinguished? What harm would it do to make certain everyone is safe?' She couldn't face another suffocating death.

He narrowed his eyes and stared down at her hand. 'You are getting overly emotional, Pearl, which is most unlike you. Perhaps you should rest for a while this afternoon. What is my mantra?'

'Emotions override logic and cloud good judgement.'

He nodded his approval. 'I am happy to supervise Mrs Dawson but I do not want any more of this ridiculous hysteria, and certainly am not prepared to discuss the possible merits of some dream you claim to have had.'

It was hardly fair to define her plea in such a way, but she knew of old that any difference of opinion with her father was useless. He had agreed to keep an eye on the cook and that was all she could hope for, although what it might mean if they were able to establish that the unfortunate woman did not start the fire accidentally did not bear thinking about.

15

Pearl often wished she was a bolder person. During her friendship with Harriet Crawley, she'd been continually chided for her submissive behaviour and unexciting life. If only her friend could see her now – the unexciting part had certainly taken a dramatic swerve since her arrival in Dorset.

Harriet was not intimidated by anyone, and it was fascinating to watch how she behaved with her parents. As the youngest of five surviving children, it was almost as though they had given up on parenting by the time she came along. Harriet freely admitted that her older sister had undergone a much tougher upbringing, but as a final unexpected daughter, after an interval of three boisterous sons, Harriet had somehow wrapped her devoted father and exhausted mother completely around her little finger.

Pearl's friend was not one to ask permission, but rather to do a thing and beg for forgiveness afterwards – a strategy Pearl could not quite wrap her head around. Disobedience in the Glenham household had always been met with harsh consequences and prolonged periods of the silent treatment. And when you felt very much alone in life generally, to be excluded even further was the worst punishment of all.

She was trying to be more like Harriet and grasp this difficult situation by the horns but, by the time of the dinner, any attempts to take control had slunk back behind her reserved personality. However, with her father, and possibly Céline, on board with her plans to see Mrs Dawson to bed safely, she had secured a small victory. Would preventing the fire free her from these endless repeated days? Because the sight of the underside of that wooden table was starting to seriously annoy her now.

Ellery entered, as Mrs Dawson retreated to fetch the dessert, clutching the familiar buff-coloured envelope, and uttering a slight variation of his familiar words.

'This telegram has just arrived, sir.'

Céline's head jolted in Pearl's direction.

'Well, well, so your unassuming daughter has supernatural gifts, Raymond,' she announced. 'Either that, or the pair of you are orchestrating a charade most strange. Is it not curious that when she spoke with me this afternoon, she predicted the arrival of this very communication? Perhaps there is something you are not telling us?'

'I can assure you, madam, there most certainly is not.' He turned to his daughter. 'Have you been discussing your overly dramatic night-time visions with the guests, when I distinctly told you not to?'

'What's all this?' Standfield said, as he topped up his wine glass. 'Has someone been having naughty dreams? Suffer from an overactive imagination myself. Rarely get a satisfactory night's sleep,' he lamented.

'It is the conscience of the guilty that keeps the mind from resting,' Céline said, and Standfield threw her a furious look. Perhaps the enigmatic Frenchwoman knew something of his past?

Feeling the need to explain, Pearl relayed her tale of the premonition.

'Let me get this right; you dreamt of people and a house that you had not encountered before?' Standfield was frowning.

'It was more of a feeling. I couldn't see faces clearly, but in my heart, I'm convinced it was this dinner party and the people around this table. You know how vague dreams can be?' she finished, lamely.

'You simply didn't want to come to Morton Peverell,' her father said, embarrassing her further, 'and projected those anxieties into a silly dream.'

'Raymond,' Céline purred, 'these things should be taken seriously. Whether or not you believe in your daughter's second sight, do you not think the subconscious can pick up on the most microscopic of things?' She paused, looking at each of the guests around the table in turn. 'Then I will say what we are all thinking but are not prepared to voice; this soirée is fishier than the water not three hundred metres from this very house. I will freely admit that the circumstances that brought me here were somewhat manipulative and highly suspect. I have not heard of this Mr Badgerwood. And, *oui*, it is that perhaps I have things to hide. So, when this young lady hints things are awry, I am inclined to listen.'

Mrs Dawson returned with the dessert and, Aldo, who probably felt as isolated as Pearl in his own way, reached for his mousse and consoled himself with mouthfuls of fluffy chocolatiness.

'I hope no one is suggesting that the insignificant Mrs D is planning to murder us all in our beds.' Standfield was alarmingly vocal and the poor cook's cheeks immediately flamed the exact shade of red as the dahlias that stood in a blue glass vase on the windowsill.

'Murder?' she gasped, wisely focusing on the dreadful accusation and not the assertion of her insignificance.

'Please calm yourself, dear lady,' her father said. 'My hysterical daughter has got herself worked up about some dream and thinks a fire will rampage through the house tonight.'

'Yes, she did mention it.'

Pearl's father threw her a look that conveyed his incredulity.

'Was there any one you didn't talk to?'

Ellery stepped forward from his place by the side wall.

'If I may speak, sir?' Pearl's father nodded his assent. 'I am staying at the local hostelry but am more than happy to remain at Highcliffe House to set everyone's mind at rest. Mrs Dawson and I can secure the house together and I will make sure that there are no unattended flames or lamps. For added peace of mind, I can sleep in the butler's pantry on the ground floor. There is spare bedding in the attics.'

'Splendid,' Standfield said, and held up his now empty glass to the young manservant. 'Then all this nonsense is sorted. And since we have been abandoned by our gracious host, I feel we should take advantage of his aforementioned hospitality until his arrival tomorrow. I say, young man, what sort of state is the wine cellar in?'

* * *

After the meal, everyone retired to the drawing room. Since her announcement that there would be a fire, along with Céline's conviction that all was not as it seemed and Mr Badgerwood's unavoidable delay, everyone was more on edge than Pearl had witnessed on any of the previous occasions. Aldo had owned to a headache and asked to be excused – at least, that's what Céline had told the assembled company his gabbled Italian meant. But on this occasion, Pearl chose to remain downstairs with everyone, rather than retiring early.

Ellery entered the room with a tray of clean glasses.

'Do you have any cigars?' her father asked, his leg tapping up and down. He didn't smoke cigars at home, and rarely deviated from his set behaviour, so this was a sure sign Raymond Glenham was agitated.

'Of course, sir. Should I serve the after-dinner drinks first?'

In an unusual display of helpfulness, her father relieved Ellery of the tray and placed it on the sideboard.

'I'm sure we can attend to that ourselves. I realise that you are woefully understaffed, but I *would* appreciate that cigar.'

Ellery nodded and retreated, as her father fiddled about with decanters and stoppers, his back to the room, sniffing the contents, perhaps assessing the quality of the liquor within.

'Let me lend you a hand, old bean,' Standfield volunteered, probably frustrated at the length of time it was taking for a drink to be placed in his ample hand. 'Anyone fancy a cocktail? I make a mean sidecar? I say, do we have any orange liqueur?'

'I'll have the first thing that comes to hand – just make it a double,' Céline said, walking over to the sideboard and then picking up one of the decanters and pouring it into a glass, just as Ellery reappeared.

'Take this to my husband,' she said, thrusting a large brandy balloon at him. 'If he must isolate himself, then let him at least be *gai.*'

Ellery passed over a silver cigar box, with its intricate reliefs of dragons curling around the sides, to her father, before leaving the room a second time to take the drink up to the Italian. Standfield continued to pour various liquids into various glasses at the sideboard and hand them round.

'Do you think it was wise for you to admit earlier that you have things to hide, my dear?' Standfield followed Céline outside, but his voice lingered in the room as they passed by.

He was referring to her admission at the dinner table and, although the conversation was private, Pearl leaned forward to better catch what they were saying. She had no guilt over her eavesdropping because all the information she was gathering was intended only to prevent the unpleasant deaths of all those staying at the house.

The Frenchwoman sat in one of the wicker chairs and lit a cigarette. The amber end glowed in the half-light and she studied her portly companion for a while, in no hurry to reply. Finally, she took a drag, and then exhaled with exaggerated thoughtfulness.

'*Everyone* has things they want to remain hidden, Harlow. *Amour non partagé*? The love was not returned.'

Pearl's face remained tilted away from the pair, but in her peripheral vision she saw Céline reach up to his cheek and stroke it gently with her fingertips. She sensed them share a long unbroken look, and couldn't help but wonder if there was, or had been, something romantic there. They were of a similar age, possibly mid-fifties, although Céline had worn considerably better. If nothing else, the familiarity of the Frenchwoman's actions confirmed Pearl's suspicion that these two had known each other for far longer than they were prepared to admit.

'To be here, in this house, for Virgil to invite us, only to demonstrate how indestructible his marriage was. It was hard,' she said.

Pearl could only conclude that Céline had been in love with Virgil Brockhurst but he had not felt the same. For a woman like her, who was used to getting what she wanted, that must have been unbearable, she reasoned. Had this enigmatic woman toyed with the hearts of both Standfield and Virgil? Had she even toyed with her father's heart in the past? No wonder poor Aldo felt the need to consult Ovid about how best to keep her.

Ellery was now furnishing her father with a cigar cutter, and she was interested to overhear the younger man complain that Aldo had been found in the kitchens and had not, in fact, retired to bed. Her attention returned to the conversation on the terrace, but it had moved on.

'Cards?' Standfield suggested, slapping at his thighs and rising to his feet. He poked his head back into the room. 'Can I tempt you with a few hands of poker, Raymond?' His smile dipped and he rubbed at his chest. Perhaps he had heartburn.

'I don't play many games but am not averse to cards,' her father said, walking towards the green-baized card table and flipping it open. 'I was planning on joining you out on the terrace for a smoke. Lords of England. Can't get these any more.' He waved his cigar. 'But I'm not sure I fancy it now. Feeling a bit off colour.'

Pearl's eyes darted in her father's direction. He rarely owned to any such thing.

'Let's make it interesting,' Standfield said, opening his wallet and throwing a crisp white ten-pound note down on the table. Pearl knew that her father's proficiency in all things mathematical, and ability to conceal his emotions, made him a competent poker player. He would doubtless soon be ten pounds richer, if only until she was sucked back to the cove. 'Shall I deal you in, too, signora?' he called out to Céline, who squashed her spent cigarette into the ashtray Mrs Dawson had found earlier, and then took a large gulp of her neat brandy, pulling an unimpressed face and sniffing the glass.

Pearl remained awkwardly in her chair, as three people who were pretending to be strangers gathered around the card table, each of them at various points throwing looks her way, driving home that she was the interloper and that her presence was preventing them from speaking freely. A part of her was done with all this, and another part of her was determined to stay in the room to prevent them chatting about things they clearly did not want to speak of in front of her. Had they already chatted in a previous loop? On the afternoon before, perhaps, when she'd lingered at the cave?

Ellery, spotting her isolation, approached her with two cut-glass decanters, one in each gloved hand.

'Would the young lady like a cocktail? Or perhaps a brandy to aid her digestion after that most excellent meal?' His voice was low and his eyes twinkling. No one else had thought to offer her a drink.

'No, thank you. I don't think ladies drink brandy.' It felt slightly inappropriate to be offered such a drink, and made her wonder, yet again, at Ellery's suitability for the job, until she remembered Céline had drunk it on previous evenings. But then, she was French – they made their own rules.

'Tosh. You don't need a beard to drink the stuff. Perhaps a cigar then?' he offered, cheekily, as Pearl pulled a horrified face. 'I quite agree. Disgusting things. Why someone would choose to set fire to the cured leaves of some plant, and inhale the fumes is beyond me. You might as well hang with the kippers in a smokehouse.'

'Physicians always seem to be promoting the health benefits of smoking.' She shrugged. 'Cigarettes help with coughs, apparently.'

'Depends what you mean by help. When I was a young boy I stole my grandfather's pipe and smoked it in the outside privy where no one was about. I coughed so much I made myself sick.' He paused. 'I don't generally tell complete strangers that, especially attractive young ladies.' He winked, and although it was just his way – she'd seen him wink at the cook and suffer Céline's flirtations with a polite smile – she suddenly didn't want to appear unworldly in front of him.

'Perhaps I shall have a brandy, after all.'

'Very good, miss.'

If he was surprised, he hid it well, and poured her a glass, just as

Mrs Dawson came in to announce that everything was tidied away, and she was keen to head upstairs.

Pearl's father got to his feet.

'I promised my daughter I would escort Mrs Dawson upstairs and secure her lamp.'

'I can do that,' Ellery offered. 'You enjoy your game.' The older man nodded his grateful thanks.

Watching the poker game quickly bored Pearl. It seemed that the players were bluffing in the game as well as in reality; Céline talked of the latest fashions, her previous lovers and riotous exploits as though she were in the first flush of youth, when it was obvious she was far from that; her father boasted of his business acumen, even though the truth was they were often hard up; and Standfield, who was becoming increasingly agitated, was almost shouting about the virtues of the single life, yet he had admitted to her previously that he was keen to settle down and have a son to see the family name continue.

Everyone seemed restless and anxious, including Pearl, who found brandy to be quite disgusting after all. Standfield tugged at his collar, which suggested he was having difficulty breathing.

'Mrs Dawson is feeling desperately unwell,' Ellery announced as he rejoined them all. 'I've left a tin bucket in her room but ensured her lamp was properly extinguished. She is clutching at her stomach and wonders if she has eaten something.'

'Could it be the crab?' her father asked. 'I've the constitution of an ox and must own to feeling rather off colour. Look at Harlow; he's not right.'

Pearl knew jolly well it wasn't food poisoning, as at no time in her previous loops had anyone been ill. She'd noticed her father's leg tapping earlier but his movements were becoming increasingly jerky and his breaths jagged.

Standfield stood from his seat and his body started to spasm as he fell to the floor. His neck arched backwards and his limbs went as stiff as ramrods. The room instantly filled with panic as everyone realised what was happening.

'*Mon Dieu!*' Céline screamed. 'We've been poisoned. Save me! Save me!' She was clutching at an equally panicked Ellery, but he pushed the hysterical Frenchwoman aside and raced over to Pearl.

'Are you all right?' The terror across his face was no act. 'Oh my God, the brandy,' he said. '*Has someone poisoned the brandy?*'

Pearl had been the last to partake and was not yet displaying the same symptoms as the others, although her fingers were starting to feel numb. But if the poison was indeed in the brandy, then it was only a matter of time. Everything played out with horrific and nightmarish inevitability over the next half an hour. They had no idea what the poison was or if there was anything they could do to counteract it, and Standfield's agonising death throes became harder to watch, until he finally found peace and lay perfectly still, with a macabre grin across his face.

Céline became increasingly hysterical until she stumbled screaming from the house and into the night, perhaps to throw herself off the cliff and avoid such a fate – something Pearl was quite tempted to do herself. Poor Ellery was frantic, as he watched Raymond and Standfield die the most unpleasant and wicked deaths before him, unable to ease their suffering. Finally, he pulled Pearl's convulsing body to his, repeating that it would be fine, even though they both knew that it would not.

In her last conscious moments, through the unimaginable pain of every tightening muscle and violent contraction, she closed her eyes, suspecting that when she next opened them, she would see a tiny arachnid descending towards the floor on a silk thread from the underside of a sturdy table. Her final thought was that the fire had not in fact been an accident, and by highlighting its imminence, she had forced the perpetrator's hand.

Someone – probably the mysterious Mr Badgerwood – wanted them all dead, and was prepared to go to any lengths to ensure that this happened.

16

The underside of the table loomed large and Pearl took a moment to appreciate just how furious she was. Not merely cross, like the time before, when she'd suspected Ellery of foul play, but absolutely incandescent with the realisation that their deaths in the fire were deliberate. And the futility of her situation made everything a thousand times worse. What did it matter how she conducted herself over the next few hours? The outcome was inevitable. She would continue to wake every afternoon in a dim cave on the Dorset coast and live through the same few hours in a never-ending loop – destined to die in a suffocating or agonising manner.

Her head fell to the side but no other part of her body moved. She stared at the numerous artefacts stored on the shelves, but wasn't really taking anything in. The building tears, resulting from the pointlessness of her situation, finally spilled from the corners of her eyes, and gravity dragged them down her cheeks, towards the stone floor.

As she lay there, unwilling to engage in a day with such a horrific and inevitable outcome, the whooshing sounds from the sea were amplified as they echoed around the cave. Those waves would never stop rolling towards the shore. You could build the tallest, widest, sturdiest sandcastle but that cruel, relentless tide would inevitably wash it all away and you would have to start again. Children stubbornly built castles of sand, each determined that theirs would be the one to beat the waves, overseen by adults who recognised the futility of their endeavours but allowed them to continue nonetheless. Could she really be bothered to build another sandcastle?

Her head tipped back up to the ceiling. She could take every match from the house, and pour every type of poison she could find down the drain, but she strongly suspected the guests at Highcliffe House would still meet a grisly end. They had been gathered together to be killed – that much was now clear.

Her emotional isolation weighed heavy. Who could she turn to? Even if she confided in someone and they believed her, she would eventually wake up on this stone floor again and would be the only person who remembered any of it.

She had never felt so lonely.

As she lay there with no inclination to move, thoughts of the previous harrowing evening flitted through her mind. Mrs Dawson had suspected food poisoning, but no one had succumbed on previous occasions, and Ellery and the cook were the only two with access to the kitchen. The drinks in the drawing room were a far more likely source, as they could have been tampered with at any point. Mrs Dawson may not have joined them, but the person responsible could easily have snuck her a small glass of something to finish the evening off. Or maybe the older lady had helped herself to a nip of brandy to go in her cocoa before she'd headed to bed?

Then she remembered that Aldo had gone to the kitchens after his feigned headache. Céline was also a victim but it was clearly not a happy marriage, so perhaps he'd taken the opportunity to dispose of her, too. She only had to mention Pearl's fictional premonition and he could have secured a deadly substance from the house at any point in the afternoon. Most homes had arsenic-based rat poison lying about, or preparations that included cyanide or strychnine. She knew nothing of how they worked, or how long before they took effect, but someone obviously did. Whether that glass of brandy had ever reached Aldo, she would never know, but had he doctored the spirits, he would most certainly have declined to drink anything sent up by his wife.

The more she thought about it, the more she realised that with the exception of her father, Mrs Dawson (who she had seen burn in her bed) and Standfield, it could have been anyone – the possibility of an outsider still not ruled out. She couldn't be absolutely certain that Aldo or Céline had died – she was too busy dying herself. If the murderer was clever enough, all they had to do was feign the same symptoms as everyone else and wait for the poison to take effect – or in the Frenchwoman's case – run screaming from the house. The only person who hadn't been displaying any symptoms had been Ellery. Time and time again, he was the one piece of the puzzle that didn't fit.

Eventually, she heaved herself up and returned to Highcliffe House. She knew he would still be in the boot room, so headed straight there.

'Can I help you, miss?'

Her bathing robe had come undone as she'd strode purposefully up the garden path, and she could see his eyes trailing over her swimsuit-clad body, beginning to suspect that he found her attractive, although she'd hitherto been unaware of such things. She pulled the two sides together and tied the belt in a tight knot.

'Are you planning to murder us all tonight?'

'I beg your pardon?'

'Has the elusive Mr Badgerwood hired you to set fire to High cliffe House? Or instructed you to make sure none of us leave Morton Peverell alive by whatever means you deem necessary?'

He put down the half-polished candlestick and his brows knitted together. 'I've not met Mr Badgerwood. I told you that.'

'Enough with the silly games. I can't do this any more. I feel so alone and so wretched. I just want answers and not to die a painful death.'

'I suspect all of us wish for that, when the time comes. Are you feeling quite all right, miss?' He looked concerned and put the candlestick down, before walking towards her. 'Here, take a seat.'

'So you can stab me in the back with a bread knife? You might as well. I'm unlikely to survive the night. And, let's face it, I'll never see tomorrow. Oh, if only Harriet were here – although she'd just be furious at me for not having lived a full life beforehand.' Her head fell into her hands as she sunk into the proffered chair. 'And she'd have a point.'

'Now, miss, I don't know what all this ridiculous nonsense is about, but I suspect you've been out in the sun for too long. Let me fetch your father.'

'He doesn't care. To be perfectly honest, he's never had much time for me. I've long since suspected he holds me responsible for the death of my mother – which inadvertently I was.'

'Talk to me. I'd like to help.' He placed his hand on her shoulder and she felt its warmth.

'Don't you understand?' She was getting agitated now. 'It doesn't matter how long we talk for, how genuine your concern is, or if we make friends and you tell me your deepest secrets – you can even confide in me again about stealing your grandfather's pipe and smoking it in the outside lavatory – because in a few hours I will be facing everything alone again.' She had reached her lowest ebb, and stood to leave. 'There is no point. Life has no point. I know I'm going to die and would rather take matters into my own hands and decide the nature of my exit.'

With that, she swept from the room and headed back out into the gardens, her mind firmly set on a course of action.

She stomped down the steps to the cove and approached the shoreline. The sun was overhead, but already dropping to the west, and the shadows from the cliffs had begun their slow creep across the beach. Her eyes scanned the shingle beneath her feet, sifting through the haphazard rows of flotsam and sea glass left by the tide. Mermaid's tears, as the worn pebbles of glass were sometimes known, cried for the sailors who lost their lives at sea. Harriet's mother, Mrs Crawley, had shared this romantic notion on a day trip to Felixstowe.

Pearl bent down and picked up a small green piece and rubbed her thumb across its smooth surface. Was the ocean crying for all the deaths it had either witnessed or orchestrated in the last thousand years? She let it tumble from her hand as she felt a building pressure in her chest and finally let out a frustrated scream. It felt indescribably good to vocalise all her exasperation, anger and loneliness. Harriet was right; she'd kept her emotions buttoned up for too long. The sound echoed around the cove until it was lost in the whispers of the waves, and she tipped her chin towards the horizon, striding out to meet that thick blue elusive line.

Not even bothering to untie her robe, and without a backward glance, she entered the water. The first wave was bitterly cold across her toes, but she paid no attention to the sensation, dragging her body, and her increasingly heavy legs, forward. So hot and furious by all that was happening to her, the calming of the water was almost immediate. The sea was endless, all-encompassing and so powerful. One minute it could be still and clear, the next dark and ferocious. Essential to life, but also with the powerful ability to end it. Now far enough out to lift her feet from the ocean floor, she began to swim away from the shore, hindered by her clinging robe, but struggling on regardless. Aware she was now approaching the protective arms of the bay, she saw the rocky outcrop to her left – a smattering of half-submerged boulders trailing into the sea like some mythical beast.

She was vaguely aware of noises from behind, possibly the circling gulls along the shoreline, but she ignored them. Carried and twisted by the breeze, they were lost to her. Nothing back on the land mattered any more.

This would be a peaceful death – she had read this to be true. Her head dipped below the water, her brain momentarily shocked by the icy temperature, and she allowed herself to inhale a lungful of water. She refused to fight her inability to breathe, so unlike her painful deaths in the fire.

As the water sealed her ears and amplified everything in her head, a loud silence enveloped her. She began to slip into a dreamless sleep knowing, even if she woke under the wretched table again, she had at least taken control – if only once.

And, as a blackness swept across her mind and everything she knew drifted from her, she was irritated, and rather surprised, to find herself gasping for breath again.

But this time, when she opened her eyes, wet lips were upon her own, and it wasn't the underside of the table that she saw, but the concerned and frightened eyes of Ellery hovering above her face.

17

'I think we've got her back,' Ellery said, as Pearl coughed and spluttered, before tipping her head sideways to heave up a lungful of water.

She returned to her horizontal position and realised her head was across his lap. He was kneeling on the beach, and a dark shadow was cast over them by the figure of someone she couldn't determine, totally in silhouette against the sun.

'What time is it?' she asked, confused.

'Damned if I know because you've just cost me one incredibly sentimental wristwatch, young lady,' he said, with mock severity. 'This gentleman and I rushed into the sea after you, and I didn't give a thought to the salvation of my timepiece, but it's a small price to pay to save a life.'

She scrunched up her face in contemplation. So, this wasn't a reset. They had merely saved her from her self-inflicted fate.

'How did you know what I was planning?'

'Seriously?' His expression was incredulous. 'All that nonsense about the pointlessness of life. You don't need to be a private detective to deduce that any young woman who talks of never seeing tomorrow, might need observing. I can't make you out at all but it's obvious that you're unhappy, are controlled by your father... and possibly unhinged in some way,' he muttered, 'so I decided to follow you. This fellow was loitering at the edge of the woods as I ran across the lawns.' He pointed to the scruffy man she'd encountered in the woods two days before, who was pacing the shingle alongside them, in dripping wet clothes, and mumbling in half sentences.

'Too much death,' the figure said to himself. 'So much to do. Keep everything safe. Keep out of everyone's way. Keep everything working.'

'But you can't swim.'

Ellery frowned, probably wondering how she knew of his limited prowess in the water.

'No, but this fellow can. I waded out as far as I could, but he was able to retrieve you from the seabed. Touch and go there for a moment, but I employed the first aid training my father taught me. Artificial respiration.'

He had placed his lips over hers, she realised, a most intimate act. Her hand went up to her mouth. No one's lips had been on hers before. Ever. He saw her action and they were both momentarily embarrassed.

'Wet, wet, wet...' the old man repeated, wringing his cotton shirt and clearly agitated.

'Please don't let us hold you up any further,' Ellery said. 'Thank you so much for your assistance, Bernard.'

He nodded, swept up his raincoat from the shingle, and scurried away.

'Yes, thank you,' she called after him, even though she wasn't happy at being rescued at all. The one thing she'd thought to control had been taken from her.

'Bernard?'

'So he said. Gather he's local although I couldn't get an awful lot of sense from him, but he's not the one I'm concerned about,' he said, returning to the topic in hand. 'I don't understand why a pretty young thing like you would want to end your life.'

She turned her face away. How could she possibly explain? And she wasn't ending it – not really – merely fighting back.

'Look at me?' he begged, and she tilted her face back up to his. Her stomach gave an unfamiliar lurch. Not only was she not used to being in such close contact with another person, two bodies actually touching so that the heat from one seeped into the other, but also the intimacy of this whole situation was overwhelming. 'What the hell is going on?'

'You'll think I'm mad.'

'Try me.'

In any other set of circumstances, those where her day was not an endless loop of repeating time, she would not have spoken to a relative stranger of this inexplicable phenomenon or magical goings-on, but the very nature of her situation meant that whatever she said to Ellery would be erased in a few short hours, so she had absolutely nothing to lose. Besides, she was curious as to his response.

'I was trying to tell you in the boot room, but probably not making any sense. I've been living the same afternoon over and over again, for the past few days. It doesn't matter what I do, shortly before the stroke of midnight, I find myself transported back to the cave at two o'clock in the afternoon and have to go through this evening's dinner party and subsequent house fire time and time again.'

It made no difference if he was trustworthy or not. He could run up to the house and tell everyone she was a lunatic and they could all have a great laugh at her expense, but when the day reset, none of them would remember the conversation. Besides, she had no one else to talk to and she had a need, deep within her, to share her misery with someone.

'Wait.' He frowned. 'What cave? What fire?'

'There's a cave behind those cliffs.' She shuffled up on her elbows and pointed to the entrance. 'Full of what I can only assume are more of Brockhurst's mystical artefacts. I've disturbed something, or wandered into a crack in time – to be honest, I don't know what I've done – but the universe is getting revenge by refusing to let me move on from today, and after we all die tonight, I return to the moment where I slipped over in the cave.' It sounded ridiculous but she ploughed on. 'Actually, you don't die. You head for the public house and it happens after you leave.'

She studied him for a moment, clumps of wet hair dripping down his forehead and hanging over serious eyes – somehow more lacklustre than she'd seen them on previous occasions. But his expression wasn't dismissive, like that of her father, and he studied her face in a way that told her he was listening.

'Virgil Brockhurst had some very strange things pass through his hands – things that it was rumoured people would do, or pay, almost anything to get their hands on. Signora Ravello certainly believes that some of the objects have supernatural powers,' he said.

'Thank you for not immediately dismissing me as hysterical, even if you are just patronising what you believe is an unhinged near-suicidal woman. It's more than my father did last time, when I told him I had a premonition that there would be a fire.'

Ellery rubbed at his chin and looked thoughtful.

'Perhaps I would have done so earlier, but you couldn't have heard about my grandfather's pipe from anyone else but me, and I know I didn't tell you. I'm not saying I do believe you, but I'm not saying I don't. This whole gathering is odd and I've long been interested in the Brockhursts – remarkable people, by all accounts. All those antiquities from ancient civilisations and their links to mystical religions...'

'Like the Persian bowl,' she said, but it meant nothing to him as he hadn't been present when Mrs Dawson had brought it out to the terrace.

She sat upright and coughed up some more seawater. Ellery rubbed at her back, letting her take her time, and then he stood to help her to her feet.

'The cave has a collection of artefacts that appear to have been separated from those in the house. Let me show you?'

'All right, I'll play along,' he said.

She was relieved that he hadn't mocked her and, even if he was only paying her lip service, it was more than she'd dared hope for.

'We will have to be quick, though, as Mrs Dawson will be wondering why the candlesticks are taking so long. Let's hope Mr Badgerwood hasn't turned up whilst I've been saving a drowning madwoman.' He grinned.

'Oh, he hasn't,' she confirmed. 'Follow me.' She brushed the sand and shingle from her legs and led the way.

'Wow.' They stood in the cave, the flickering candles giving the space an eerie feel. 'I had no idea this was tucked between the cliffs, but then you don't have time to swan about the grounds when you're staff – Dawson and I have been non-stop since we arrived yesterday.' He looked about him in wonder. 'I'd put money on this being an old smugglers' cave. The highly illegal trade of luxury goods was rife along this coastline last century. This is a natural crack in the rocks that's been chiselled out.' His gaze travelled around the dimly lit space, alighting on various objects as he scanned the shelves. 'Look at all these stone tablets. They could be the ten commandments, for all we know.'

Pearl thought it unlikely that the moral laws relayed to Moses three and a half thousand years ago were tucked away in a gloomy cave on the Morton Peverell coast, but then Virgil had certainly got his hands on the most extraordinary of objects, so she didn't comment.

'This is where I keep waking up,' she said, pointing to the table bearing the clock.

'What the heck is that? It looks complicated.'

'It's a sort of mechanical water clock, I think. But it appears to use mercury, not water. I knocked it when I fell.'

He stroked his chin and peered closer.

'That, young lady, is a clepsydra. It comes from the Greek *kleptein* – to steal – and *hydra* meaning water. Pretty sure I read somewhere that Galileo had a mercury clepsydra, but don't quote me on that. However, interference with a clock would make sense if you're playing with time. It looks ancient – perhaps centuries old.'

She hadn't thought much about the nature of the loop before; all she'd been focused on was not dying and preventing the fire. She also hadn't got to the letter C in her undertaking to read the entirety of her father's encyclopaedias.

'What exactly happened?' he asked. 'Did you fiddle with it in some way?'

'I slipped on the wet cave floor, hit my head and knocked the table as I went down. The clock wobbled and a tiny bead of mercury slopped over the edge.'

He lifted the glass dome and dipped his finger into the pool of silver liquid, but it trickled down his skin and back into the funnel – the very nature of the metal making it cling to itself rather than other surfaces. He tried again, this time pushing two fingers in and quickly bending them to catch a tiny droplet, and then he gently rocked his hand. They both watched the pinhead-sized silver ball roll backwards and forwards along the ridge between his fingers.

'Weird stuff,' he said. 'Used in barometers, thermometers and extensively in medicine. Cures all manner of ills.'

'Good, because I swallowed some,' she said.

Ellery lifted his fingers to his lips and let the droplet slide into his mouth.

'What did you do that for?' she gasped.

He shrugged. 'Just recreating what happened to you. Do you think the bang on the head was part of it?' He walked to one of the cave's sloping walls and smacked his head rather forcefully against the side. She winced.

'I have no idea but I do know that I was momentarily unconscious, so a little tap on the cave wall is hardly the same thing.'

He looked around for a rock and picked up a sizeable piece of limestone. 'Then you'll just have to swing this at me and knock me out.'

'Don't be so ridiculous. Are you mad?' she said, horrified by this overly confident man, and not quite sure if he was joking or not.

'Excuse me, young lady. Let's just survey the facts.' A grin was forming at the corners of his mouth. 'You've tried to drown yourself and are trying to persuade me that you are living through some sort of time loop... and *I'm the mad one*?'

He rubbed at his head, perhaps regretting how hard he'd hit the wall, just as she started to shiver. The day was warm but they'd been standing in the shadows of the cave in soaked clothing, and the drop in temperature out of the sun was now hitting her.

'You're cold,' he observed. 'And have been through quite an alarming experience. I need to get you back to the house and dried off... well, you can do the drying off by yourself, but you know what I mean. Besides, poor Mrs Dawson will be frantic. We've got an awful lot to do for the meal tonight, and she's keen to impress Mr Badgerwood *when* he arrives.'

'He's not coming at all, in fact,' Pearl said, as Ellery put his arms about her and guided her out of the cave. He rubbed his hand up and down her damp frame in an attempt to warm her. She didn't really need assistance but rather liked the feel of his touch on her shoulders.

'Not coming?'

'A telegram will be delivered this evening during the meal to say there has been an unavoidable delay and he will join us tomorrow.'

'Right.' He grinned as he looked down at his bedraggled companion, releasing his arm to allow her to mount the beach steps that led to the garden gate. 'Because you've lived through this afternoon a hundred times.'

'About six, actually, but you'll forget this conversation when I live through today again, tomorrow.'

'Fascinating,' he said, following her up to the top step. 'This means all your actions are without consequences. You must have been having the absolute time of your life these past few loops. I bet you've rifled through everyone's luggage, explored every inch of the house, told Standfield exactly where he could stick his inappropriate comments, and, I like to think, finally stood up to your father.'

It was interesting how Ellery's appraisal of the situation had so differed from hers. Her first reaction had been disbelief, then fear, then anger. At no point had she embraced the possibilities, or made any attempt to enjoy the benefits of the bizarre situation she found herself in. Unlike the confident, facetious Ellery, who immediately thought of fun and games, mischief and anarchy.

As they headed for the steps, her mind returned to the sandcastles. Yes, they would never last longer than one turn of the tide, but the joy the children experienced in their construction was worth the ultimate disappointment at their erosion, she finally realised. The one inevitability about life was death, but that was absolutely not a reason to stop living.

18

The pair were greeted by Mrs Dawson as they entered through the kitchen. Pearl was worried about spoiling the carpets or parquet flooring in the main part of the house with their dripping clothing, particularly Ellery's sodden trousers.

'What on earth—' the older woman began.

'Miss Glenham got into trouble down by the shore and I helped her out of the water,' Ellery explained, leaving poor Bernard out of it.

'Oh my goodness. Are you all right? I've had no time to visit the cove but Mrs Lane said it was pretty enough. Fancy owning a house so big that it has its own private beach. Get out of that wet costume and you'll soon warm up. It's really quite glorious on the terrace. As for you—' she looked over to Ellery '—let us be thankful you have another uniform for serving the dinner. You'll have to wear the pants and shirt now, and put those articles through the mangle. They might even dry in a couple of hours, if you're lucky.' She glanced up at the kitchen clock. 'We could have done without this delay, what with Mr Badgerwood due goodness knows when.'

Ellery and Pearl exchanged a knowing look. She didn't think he really believed her fanciful tale, but he was happy to play along and, in a funny way, it was rather sweet of him.

Sitting alone on the terrace, with her pale face to the bright sun, Pearl sipped at her drink. She had on her wide-brimmed green straw hat to shield her eyes and was now back in her cotton day dress. Ellery had made her some brandy cocktail that she'd not heard of, and said it would warm her insides, giving her a cheeky wink as he handed it over. The whole drowning incident, and his lips on hers, had lent a familiarity to their relationship, and she was disappointed this would be lost when she next awoke in the cave. She'd been craving companionship, and now that she'd found it with him, it would be even harder when it was taken away again.

'I say, is it cocktail o'clock?' Standfield was like a bloodhound, able to track the scent of alcohol from fifty paces. 'Everyone buggered off, excuse my French, after luncheon and I couldn't persuade anyone to stay for a tipple, so I nipped upstairs and unpacked the old bags. Bit of a bore without my man but got the old evening attire on a hanger. Need to look presentable for this Badgerwood fellow, after all. In the meantime, I'm certainly up for a bit of social lubrication.'

Whether it was the brandy, or Ellery's words about embracing her situation Pearl wasn't sure, but she decided to be kind to Standfield. Perhaps there were reasons he came across as a washed-up old drunk. You never knew what had gone on in people's lives and there could be any number of reasons for his behaviour. She decided to get to know the man, and enjoy herself as she did so.

No repercussions.

'Do join me. I'm afraid I have no idea what the young man put in this glass, but we can ring for him. Apparently, it's called a sidecar.'

'No need, no need, dear girl. I am quite capable of mixing up a cocktail. They are all the rage in London. I'll make two.'

'This one is sufficient, thank you.'

'Splendid. It'll save me getting to my feet a second time.'

He ambled back inside and returned five minutes later with a tumbler in each hand and a smile lifting his thread-veined cheeks.

'It would rather appear that old Virgil's drinks cabinet hasn't been touched much in the past twenty years. I swear the bottle of Bowmore is the one I gave him back in oh-three, even though this new chap, Badgerwood, has obviously recently restocked. It's an Islay whisky,' he clarified.

Pearl let his words hang there and wondered how long it would take him to notice his slip, but he bumbled on, unaware of his error.

'I may as well try to make the best of being at Highcliffe House,' he grumbled, as he took the seat opposite. 'Had better places to be, mind. No offence,' he added hastily.

'None taken.'

Eventually, she decided she couldn't ignore his previous blunder any longer.

'I thought you didn't know the Brockhursts,' she said, trying to appear uninterested as she lifted the sidecar to her lips. It was a beautiful orange colour, smelled wonderfully citrusy, and tasted delicious.

'Ah, well.' He took a few sips of his own drink, probably stalling for time, although she was certain that adding to his inebriation wasn't his wisest move if he was about to spin her a tale. She may be a quiet girl but that didn't mean she was a stupid one. 'When you move in elevated ranks, you come across other elevated chaps. Brockhurst may have been born to schoolteachers but he quickly amassed enough of the old cheddar through *trade*...' his distaste at the source of the American's fortune was all too apparent '…to buy his way into superior social circles.'

Standfield clearly didn't think Virgil Brockhurst's earned wealth entitled him to mix with the upper classes. He was definitely the sort who only accepted a fellow if he could trace his lineage back to William the Conqueror.

'Came across him a couple of times at shoots and the like. Dorset is quite a close-knit county. Everyone who's anyone knows all the other anyones of importance. Never exactly what you'd call chums, though.' He made a scoffing sound, as though the idea was utterly disdainful.

'And yet you gave him a bottle of whisky.' She couldn't help but point this out. A few short days ago, or yesterday, to be factually accurate, she wouldn't have been bold enough to push a gentleman on such matters, but Ellery was right: she was living without consequences. Her ingrained manners and natural timidity, however, dictated that she did not leap from her seat, grab Standfield by the collar and demand he tell her *exactly* what he was hiding – now that she knew beyond all doubt that nefarious things were afoot.

He coughed and shuffled in his seat.

'One doesn't turn up to a fellow's abode empty-handed. I did come here for a soirée of sorts many years ago but had completely forgotten about it until this instant. They returned to England briefly after the birth of their baby – Joseph, I think his name was. Pleased for the chap – Virgil got the son and heir we all hanker after. But you must understand that I'm naturally invited to a lot of houses, and come across an awful lot of chaps, young lady, and they tend to blur into one.'

Having adequately explained the slip away, in his mind at least, he began to relax, and downed what remained of the first drink, before scooping up the other.

'And talking of soirées, I was invited to a ball at Burbridge

Manor this evening. Old Allington holds one every summer. Always a jolly affair and I'm mightily peeved to be missing out.' He huffed.

Had he been manipulated into attending Highcliffe House, like her father? A county ball sounded much more fun and, although Pearl preferred smaller occasions herself, she could imagine a man like him would be in his element, dressed in his white tie, waltzing some attractive woman half his age around a ballroom. She could bet the alcohol would be flowing far more freely, as well.

'Where is Burbridge?' she asked, not being local.

'Small village outside Dorchester, and the Allingtons are a family of note – have a solid place in history.'

'And the Standfields?'

'We go back enough generations to be respectable,' he said, with obvious pride. 'But the line is in danger of dying out with me. Never got around to marriage, much to the *mater*'s disappointment. Couldn't find the right gal, but always looking. No ring on your finger, I notice.'

'I suspect one is imminent,' she admitted, slightly concerned he was again considering her as a prospect. 'There is a Mr Trowbridge back home who has been showing me particular attention.'

'Pity,' Standfield said. 'You're an attractive little thing and I could have sorted you out quite nicely. You wouldn't have had to do much, and I could have set you up with a sizeable allowance.'

'Tempting,' she said, not meaning it. The age gap was beyond reason, to say nothing of their complete incompatibility.

'...And just a few times a week to sort me out in the old bedroom department – if you get my drift.' He wiggled his eyebrows and Pearl felt the blood drain from her face. He couldn't be serious – she *was* actually young enough to be his daughter.

Her father chose that moment to appear at the French doors. He stepped out on the terrace to join them.

'The heat quite got to me, but I feel sufficiently recovered now.

Perhaps the heat has affected you, too, Pearl, as I noticed that your unpacking was a little slapdash. You have placed socks on the right of the drawer, and undergarments on the left.' He shook his head. 'I shouldn't have to remind you that it's the other way about.' He pulled out his pocket watch. 'Perhaps you could ask the cook to put the kettle on whilst you're rectifying your carelessness. You know I like a cup of tea about now on a Saturday.'

'Of course, Father,' she said, getting to her feet.

'Surely the poor girl can finish her drink first, Glenham? After all, I was practically proposing to the dear thing before you interrupted us.'

'Harlow!' Her father looked quite horrified. 'She's young enough to be—'

'Yes, yes, I know, but plenty of girls marry older men for the money. I'd be under no illusion it was a love match, but think of the bloody great house she'd live in. Pop out an heir or two and everyone is a winner.'

Her father rubbed at his chin in an alarmingly contemplative manner. The money had not perhaps occurred to him. He turned to Pearl. 'Well, you could do worse, I suppose.'

A horrified look swept across her face. Surely she did not have to explain to her father that there would be certain... duties she would be expected to perform. Marrying her off to Simon Trowbridge was one thing – he was at least close in age to her. But Standfield?

'And talking of that great institution, where is Mrs Glenham, Raymond? The mother of this most delectable creature?'

'She passed away giving birth to Pearl.' No emotion.

'Dreadfully sorry, old chap. And you never got hitched a second time? Even if only to give the child a mother and run your household?'

The outdated views of the two men before her were very last

century. The war had surely proved women's worth? Look how they had not only kept the home fires burning, but had also chopped down the trees and heaved the sacks of coal for those very fires proving they had capabilities beyond simply motherhood and domesticity.

'We've managed quite nicely, thank you. Pearl is surprisingly brawny and generally compliant.' She was not amused by her father's description of her attributes, and concerned he might try to persuade Standfield into renewing his interest, but he thankfully steered the conversation in another direction. 'And *you* never married, Harlow?' he asked.

'Well, no, you see, the thing is, got my heart trampled on and never quite recovered.' A brief looked passed between the older men but she caught it. Standfield cleared his throat as he finished his second glass – the first long since empty. 'Turns out she really was the one.' He looked serious for the first time in the conversation, and she felt briefly sorry for the poor man. 'So, it's been a lifetime of liaisons that benefited the body, if not the soul, old chap.'

Her pity promptly evaporated in the heat and, feeling she'd made more than enough effort with Standfield, she excused herself leaving behind two Victorian men to rue the modern age.

* * *

The familiar routine of dressing for dinner, Céline's late but dramatic arrival, and sitting through yet another identical meal was, naturally, interrupted by the arrival of the telegram. Pearl had been expecting it, now familiar enough with how things played out to know the telegraph boy would knock on the door as soon as Mr Dawson went to fetch the dessert.

'This has just arrived, sir,' Ellery said, addressing Standfield as he entered the dining room and trying not to stare at Pearl. He was rattled by her predicting this very interruption, and she knew this offered further proof of her wild story.

The usual disquiet at Mr Badgerwood not attending played out, followed by the shifty looks from the three main players as they acknowledged strange things were afoot and, as always, Standfield took advantage of the situation to gain access to the contents of the wine cellar.

With the loneliness of her predicament hitting harder with every loop, she decided to see what all the fuss over a vintage wine was about. Harriet's voice echoed in her ears – chastising her for not having lived a life. Even Ellery had assumed she'd used her curious circumstances to her advantage, when nothing could be further from the truth. If she was going to die anyway, she might as well do so having tasted a Bordeaux that was beyond her father's pocket. With any luck, if she drank a sufficient amount, she'd sleep through the fire. The smoke could claim her in a drunken stupor and she wouldn't feel a thing. Maybe the humorous perspective that alcohol seemed to imbue in those who had consumed substantial quantities might make living through the whole evening a further time more bearable.

As always, her father insisted that his daughter did not drink when the wine was poured, but Standfield and Céline overruled him. She knew his leg would be furiously tapping away under the table, having been undermined. And, after the assembled company had sunk two bottles of 1870 Château Lafite Rothschild and a dessert wine from Austria (which Pearl thought utterly delicious, and leaned in rather too close to Standfield to tell him so), the assembled company eventually retired to the drawing room.

'*Chérie*,' Céline observed, 'you seemed so quiet this morning, but are a surprisingly chatty little thing this evening. Wine suits you, *non*?'

Her father, alarmed to find his daughter had opinions contrary to his own, particularly regarding suffrage and women in sport (or perhaps he was simply shocked to discover she had opinions), suggested that she had drunk sufficient when the brandy was offered around. It was provocation enough for her to return to the cellar and locate another bottle of the dessert wine – neat brandy not being to her taste. Even though Ellery would not remember witnessing her defiance when the day reset, she wanted to prove to herself that she wasn't the biddable child he clearly thought she was.

She returned to the hallway, clutching the bottle by the neck, and bumping into the aforementioned young man returning to the drawing room with the dragon-embossed silver cigar box. Her behaviour on this occasion had unsettled her father enough for him to ask for the cigars again, she realised.

'What the hell are you playing at?' he muttered, blocking her passage. 'Flirting with old Standfield. If you're not careful, you will get yourself in a situation you won't be able to extricate yourself from.' Those amber eyes of his flashed with the gold flecks of passion.

'Has anyone told you what amazing eyes you have?' she said, ignoring his accusation, and bemused at how the consumption of too much wine allowed your mouth to go right ahead and express your inner thoughts without pausing for censorship. She reached up to his face and draped the bottle-holding arm over his shoulder. 'Like tiny fires.'

'Unless you want to see me erupt in flame and fury, I suggest you hand me this wine, miss, and let me escort you to bed.'

He put the cigar box down and deftly manoeuvred her against the wall, sliding his free hand up her arm to prise the bottle from her fingers.

'Ooo, now there's a tempting proposition. You could deflower me across the floral counterpane, and then in the morning I'd be virginal again. That's got to be a plus of my dreadful situation. Unlimited sexual exploits without any of the consequences.'

He placed the wine on the side table.

'Tempting though that offer is—' his voice was laden with sarcasm '—I am imminently needed in the kitchen. The pots won't wash themselves.'

'You're seriously turning me down for greasy pans and dirty crockery?'

In the most unlike-Pearl manner, she slithered closer to him and pressed her body up against his. She'd been watching Céline over the past few afternoons – all accidental touches and close proximity. But as soon as she felt the heat of his body on hers, he stepped away from her and ran his hand through his hair.

'I don't take advantage of young ladies who are not fully in control of their senses. Your father awaits his cigar and Mrs Dawson will be wondering where I've got to. The pots—'

'Oh, to hell with the pots.' She threw herself at him and pulled his head towards hers to connect her wine-stained lips with his. He hesitated, before his mouth moved against her own, but within a heartbeat, he had dragged himself away and gripped her firmly by the shoulders, preventing her from launching herself at him a further time.

'I really don't know what to make of you, Pearl Glenham. I thought I had you pegged when you arrived – following meekly behind your father and not able to say boo to a kitten, never mind a goose. But there were clearly bigger things swirling beneath the calm blue of the surface. One misguided attempt to drown yourself and the real you has surfaced – a wanton, possibly delusional young lady, who is rather too fond of drink.'

Her face became serious. 'This isn't the real me,' she protested.

'No, I don't believe it is, but after your astounding prediction that a telegram would arrive this evening, the way I see it there are only two options to explain what is going on: either you're behind this whole charade, with you and your father masterminding the whole weekend—'

'Because I'm a woman and couldn't possibly have engineered this by myself?' she asked, with sulky undertones.

'Because you keep insisting you aren't *that* sort of woman,' he clarified. 'Or your outrageous claims are actually true. Assuming the latter, largely because things couldn't get any stranger, what happens now?'

She hung her head like a reprimanded schoolgirl. He wasn't going to kiss her, that much was clear, and she found herself more disappointed than she had anticipated. Why was she drawn to him so? He wasn't similar to her at all – much more outgoing and confrontational. Perhaps that was why. And part of his charm was that he seemed up for anything, including going along with her outrageous claims.

'You go back to the Fisherman's Arms when you've finished clearing up and we all perish in a house fire.'

'Then you have to stop it somehow.'

Her legs were distinctly unsteady and she had to blink several times to focus on his face. She was irritated by him now.

'Do you not think I tried that? We were all poisoned instead. Quite honestly, the fire was a slightly less unpleasant death. But don't worry, I've quite got into the swing of it, and with plenty of alcohol inside me, I doubt I'll feel a thing.'

Her stomach lurched, and she knew she'd had far too much wine. She no longer wanted to return to the drawing room, and was irritated and embarrassed by Ellery's rejection. What had seemed a fun game only moments before, suddenly wasn't so fun any more, but she didn't want him to know how wretched she was feeling.

'Cheers,' she said, collecting the bottle to save face, as she swung away and headed up the stairs to her bed.

* * *

Was it a dream? Or was it really happening? Pearl felt a rush of cool air across her face, contrasting with the warmth of something around her body. Everything was dark and very wobbly, and her head was positively pounding. Her eyes briefly fluttered open and she thought she saw a dark blanket above, dotted with white, as the breeze fluttered around her, but there were so many shapes and coloured lights fighting for space in her inebriated head, that she couldn't discern what was real and what was not.

In the end, she gave up trying to work everything out and surrendered to the apparent weightlessness of her body and her overriding yearning for sleep.

19

In her young life, Pearl Glenham had never experienced the thudding head or bubbling nausea that resulted from imbibing excess alcohol. Harriet, who insisted the benefits of intoxicating liquor far outweighed these rather unpleasant consequences, had frequently tried to persuade her friend to join her as she raided her parents' drinks cabinet, but to no avail.

'Try it, Pearl. Even if you feel wretched the next day, all your worries will drift away and you'll feel free, not troubled by the opinions and judgement of others. It allows the real you to come to the fore, not the version of yourself you present to please your father.'

But now that Pearl had finally embraced the demon drink, it appeared that she was destined never to experience the unappealing side-effects, because when she took her next breath, she felt as fresh as the proverbial daisy – the bang to the back of her head aside. It was one of the benefits of her repeating afternoons – the miraculous restoration of her body to how it had been at two o'clock that initial Saturday, regardless of how she had abused it in the intervening hours.

As she climbed the steps from the cove, she felt relieved that her slate of unacceptable behaviour, specifically her outrageous flirting with Ellery, had been wiped clean by the miracle of the loop. She regretted the drinking, but she did not regret the kiss, nor opening up to the self-assured manservant. He had offered a contrasting point of view from her own – one where she should consider embracing her situation, rather than feeling sorry for herself – and that might be enough to see her through a few more afternoons without crumbling completely. It wasn't that she *wanted* to be rude to people, but she was heartily fed up with acquiescing in every situation, or presenting a quiet and polite façade, when there were so many things burning inside of her that she was desperate to say.

She sighed at Aldo and Céline's quarrel – perhaps one of these repeating days she might find out what it was actually about – and shouted, '*My name is PEARL, you insufferable, self-absorbed drunk!*' in response to Standfield's inevitable exclamation. Unfortunately, this display of bad manners only seemed to pique his interest because his response, heard as she entered the house through the kitchens, was obvious delight at the 'feisty little filly' she was turning out to be.

'What can I do for you, miss?' Mrs Dawson asked, as she stacked up the dirty crockery from lunch. 'Are you in need of refreshment? There's lemonade in the pantry.'

'Only if you have some gin to go with it,' Pearl replied, continuing to say out loud what she was actually thinking, and deciding that there were worse things in the world than to spend the remainder of her ever-repeating life in an alcoholic haze. Last night had been her best death so far. She'd fallen asleep dreaming of kissing the outspoken Ellery, a man whose feisty edge and hypnotic eyes had given her almost the same dizzying sensation as the wine. The dream had segued into the pair of them dancing naked around a bonfire on the beach (which, now she thought about it, was prob-ably the smoke from the inevitable house fire invading her subconscious) only to wake beneath the table, having bypassed the vomiting, raw throat and stinging eyes of her previous unpleasant deaths.

'Miss?' The older lady scrunched up her face, possibly confused that the seemingly timid young daughter of the boring accountant had suddenly become so bold.

'It was an attempt at humour. Please don't be alarmed,' she said, with a dismissive wave of the hand, and thinking of Ellery's flippant nature, and how easy-going he'd been with her the day before, even though she was making extraordinary claims. She was eager to find him and explain everything again, as there was no reason he wouldn't be as understanding about her wild assertions as before. And she'd rather spend the afternoon with him than anyone else in the house. Perhaps she could even engineer another kiss because that had been one experience she absolutely wouldn't mind repeating – day after day after day...

She slipped into the boot room where he was buffing the silverware.

'Hello?' she said, studying him for signs that stepping into the cave may have worked some magic on him too, but he was focused on the candlestick and barely raised his head. How had she not noticed his strong profile and appealing scent before?

'Um, so, any disturbing dreams about living through today more than once?' Had banging his head on the cave wall and touching the clepsydra made any difference? Might he remember anything of their conversation from the afternoon before? And did she really want him to? She'd been somewhat... uninhibited in her attentions last night.

'I have absolutely no idea what you're talking about. I rarely remember my dreams. What a curious question to ask staff.'

Her heart sank. She was in this alone but it had been worth a try.

'Can I get you anything, miss?' He looked up from his task. 'Are you sufficiently hydrated? Too much heat can addle your brain.'

'Actually, I'd like a bloody great sidecar, please. In fact, make me two. Strong ones. With a whisky chaser.'

He grinned. 'Someone's having a bad day, and Mr Badgerwood hasn't even arrived yet. I will see to your drinks presently but there's so much to do for the meal this evening, and a cook and a manservant are barely sufficient.'

'Someone *is* having a bad day... after day... after day, and I wouldn't stress too much about Mr Badgerwood; he may not even turn up.'

'Have you been swimming in the cove?' he asked, taking in her damp attire.

About to politely reply that she had, she paused. 'No, I thought I'd dress for dinner early. Didn't you know? Bathing suits are all the rage in London and are this season's preferred formal evening wear – especially amongst the more avant-garde diners.'

He raised an eyebrow and gave an almost imperceptible nod of respect. 'Well, as long as you aren't contemplating another ill-thought-out suicide attempt. I was rather sore when my wristwatch got submerged yesterday. It was my father's. Seems perfectly restored to its former glory now though.'

Pearl stared at the young man, mouth open, as he screwed the lid on the Silvo and wiped his hands on the cloth.

'Yesterday?'

'*Today*, yesterday,' he clarified, shrugging.

Her hand went to her mouth. 'Oh my goodness... *you remember?*'

'Of course I remember! I was having you on.' He walked over to her, orange-flecked eyes wide and jiggling up and down with excitement. His nonchalant body language changed in an instant. 'Good grief, you weren't lying. One minute I was heaving your unconscious body from the house and collapsing on the front lawns, watching Highcliffe House consumed by twenty-foot-high flames, still not quite believing that you'd predicted this alarming turn of events... And the next, not ten minutes ago, I was staring down at a pair of half-buffed silver candlesticks.' He clicked his fingers in front of her face. 'Bam! Just like that.'

Ah, so this explained her curious dream-like experience of the previous evening. He'd believed her tale enough not to return to the Fisherman's Arms, and then entered a burning building to rescue her – wrestling her semi-conscious body outside.

He caught her expression. 'I didn't want you suffering.' His cheeks momentarily flashed an endearing pink.

Perhaps embarrassed by his noble act, he swept her hands up in his own, pulling her around in a circle as they danced in the tiny room. 'We're going to have *so much* fun.'

'And you remember everything from the afternoon?' she gasped, as he spun her around, and her trotting feet almost lifted from the floor.

'Everything.' He gave her a cheeky wink and finally came to a standstill. 'It was the weirdest thing I've ever experienced. My poor brain might take a while to catch up. I was standing here trying to rationalise everything when you appeared. But I was forewarned. You must have been utterly bewildered.' He shook his head in sympathy and let her hands drop from his, before rallying. 'So, what's the plan?'

'What do you mean?'

'What shall we do? Where shall we go?' He rubbed his hands together.

'But... but you have a dinner to prepare and guests to look after...'

He snorted. 'Tosh to that. The stroke of midnight and everything resets, right?' His head tipped to one side as he tried to establish the rules.

She nodded. 'About a quarter of an hour before, but yes.'

'Then why should I spend the day pandering to an entitled drunkard, a stuck-up and manipulative Frenchwoman, an insignificant little Italian who can't even understand me, and a man who treats his daughter like an unpaid servant and displays all the joy of a dead fish. No offence.'

Was that what people saw when they looked at her and her father? Such a distant relationship? Such a lack of joy?

'...Especially if not one of them will remember my insubordinate behaviour tomorrow morning,' he finished.

'Afternoon,' she corrected. 'I always return to the moment I upset the clepsydra.'

'Oh, yes, and I was mid-candlestick. Right.' He clapped his hands together. 'There's a lovely, cherry-red Austin Twenty sitting in the driveway that has been calling my name ever since Mr Standfield swept imperiously into the drive several hours ago and demanded a stiff drink.'

He untied the dark green butler's apron that had been protecting his clothes and tossed it over the back of a chair. He walked towards the door but hesitated when he realised she wasn't following. 'Are you coming on my little afternoon jaunt or not?'

'Erm, yes, I suppose so. But I need to change. I'm still in my bathing suit.'

'If it's good enough for a London high society dinner, then it's good enough for our afternoon excursion.'

He grinned and she couldn't help but grin, too.

* * *

Pearl and Ellery stood together in her guest bedroom. He'd waited outside for her to slip her dress back on, and was now watching as she gathered a few essential items for the trip – her sun hat and more appropriate shoes.

She walked over to the window that had been the cause of so much distress in the last few days, noting the screws were still in the frame. Stansfield's Austin sat at a jaunty angle, abandoned across the gravel and there for the taking. Was she really about to be complicit in stealing a vehicle and driving through the beautiful Dorset countryside, top down and the wind in her hair, with this relative stranger?

'We can't do this,' she said, turning back to him.

'Because?'

Her words dried in her mouth as she realised that everything she was about to say was negated by their situation. If Mr Badgerwood (or someone in his employ) could murder them all in their beds without ever once having to pay for his crime, then the *borrowing* of Harlow Standfield's car (as technically it would be returned to him within a matter of hours) was an insignificant misdemeanour by comparison.

'See? You're coming around to my way of thinking.' A smug look flashed across his face. 'Besides, I'm determined to use this gift of time wisely. For a start, you can teach me to swim.'

'What?'

'You can swim and I can't.' He shrugged his shoulders. 'I want to learn – in case I come across any more insane women diving towards the bottom of the ocean and forgetting to breathe in the process. I want to get the best from this, not just take advantage of the thrills.' He tapped at his forehead to imply he was a thinking man. 'Learning a new skill would be a productive use of our ever lasting afternoons together.'

Everlasting – he said it flippantly. Did he not worry, as she still did, that this could genuinely go on for eternity?

'And in return, I will help you to become a bolder person, Miss Pearl Glenham,' he continued. 'Without you resorting to alcohol. One good turn surely deserves another.'

She knew he was failing to appreciate the seriousness of their situation, but perhaps she had dwelt on it too much. Between them, they might strike a healthy balance.

He swung the door open to let her pass through first and, as they stepped into the hallway, they met her father leaving his room.

'Ah, there you are, man. I heard voices and they roused me from my slumbers. Could you fetch a jug of warm water and a towel? I need to freshen up.'

'No.'

'I'm sorry?' Her father frowned.

'I'm afraid you'll have to do it yourself. I'm taking your daughter for a spin in Standfield's old jalopy.'

'You'll be part of no such thing, Pearl. Harlow is quite particular about his motor car – told me he hasn't had it long – so I find it hard to believe he's given a servant permission to use it. Besides, you have a job to do, man. I am a guest and I need attending to, and Pearl is my daughter and does nothing without my permission.'

She looked at the man whose every domestic whim she had satisfied for more years than she cared to remember and shrugged. Ellery's eyes were boring into the side of her face and she just knew he was willing her to stand up to her father. She wanted to be assertive, if only for the thrill of finally being in control, but she'd spent too many years of trying not to disappoint him and old habits were hard to break.

All her words died in her throat, and instead the young manservant spoke for her.

'She's coming with me and that's that, I'm afraid. I'm going to introduce the poor girl to the concept of fun. Fear not, I'll have her back before the stroke of midnight – about fifteen minutes before, in fact.' He grabbed her hand, tugging her towards the stairs, and they scampered away to her father's admonishment that people would talk and Simon Trowbridge had better not hear of this outrageous behaviour.

They reached the bottom steps just as Mrs Dawson came from the kitchens, carrying a tray of clean cutlery Pearl assumed was on its way to the dining room.

'Ellery, where on earth have you been? Are the candlesticks done? Would you mind helping prepare the vegetables?'

'Not happening, I'm afraid, Mrs Dawson. I'm off to live a day without consequences. Don't panic. Mr Badgerwood isn't coming. In fact, if I were you, I'd send the lot of them home – it will save them being burned alive in their beds tonight. Farewell, cheerio, adieu.'

As they skipped out of the front door to Mrs Dawson's open mouth and wide eyes, Pearl felt the same thrilling sensations that she did from her stealing. She felt alive.

'I'll assume the old jalopy has fuel, as Standfield obviously plans to return home tomorrow.' Ellery lifted the left-hand seat and tightened what she guessed must be the battery.

'Do you know what you're doing?' she asked.

'Sort of.' He dropped the seat back, gesturing for her to get in, skipping round to the other door.

'Right,' he said, doing something with his foot, waiting for a red light, and then turning the ignition. The engine rattled into life. 'The world is our unopened oyster – amusing because I appear to have the pearl right beside me. Where shall we go?'

20

Dorset was a stunning county. Pearl recognised that there was a beauty to Suffolk too, but the valleys and hills that undulated across this landscape contrasted sharply with the relative flatness of home. Summer was a glorious season to behold, whatever part of Great Britain you were in, but she noticed the subtle differences and revelled in them; from the broad limestone ridges and exposed scarps, to the showy rhododendrons that suited the acidic soil and warmer west country clime. Here, the farmers' hedge-lined fields swept up the hills in a green patchwork of squares, as they whizzed past purple clumps of heath and butter-yellow gorse dotting the roadside. If there were such fascinating differences between these two parts of England, she could only imagine the even more dramatic contrasts and spectacles of landscape on the other side of the globe.

All these things she noticed from her somewhat jerky aspect through the window of the motor car as they headed inland, coming to a halt only when they encountered a T-junction.

'Left or right?' he asked.

She shrugged.

'You decide,' he insisted. 'There isn't a wrong answer. We can go in the opposite direction next time.'

He had a huge grin on his face, possibly because he'd quickly mastered the gears of the motor vehicle. What was it with men and machines? she mused. He was as happy as the proverbial sandboy.

'Let's go left,' she replied, wondering how many days it would take the harsh realities of this situation to hit him. Everything was an adventure at the moment but would he still feel this elated when he found himself staring at a pair of half-buffed candlesticks for the one hundredth time?

'Weymouth it is then.'

* * *

Pearl tumbled out of the car and turned to face the sea.

The seafront here was a much more open space than Highcliffe Cove. No imposing cliffs to intrude on the skyline, and a flat, sandy beach, bustling with people who were enjoying an afternoon of escape from their busy lives. How content they were, she noticed, to sit in their neat rows of wooden deckchairs, facing the sun and breathing in the cool salty air (something she would never take for granted again). Elderly couples watched laughing children scamper across the beach, trailing wooden spades behind them, their metal buckets full of sandy treasures. There was even a young woman dragging a large black perambulator backwards through the sand, determined to be part of the adventure, despite the impracticality of her circumstance.

Ellery rummaged in his pocket and pulled out a handful of coins, squinting at his meagre funds.

'We will have to address our financial situation before our next visit. There must be some money at Highcliffe House. I'll wager old Standfield has some notes tucked away somewhere.'

There was no point objecting to his plan. As with everything they did, there were no consequences, and he had been far quicker than her to embrace this aspect of their situation.

They walked along the Royal Crescent and she stopped to admire the Jubilee clock, whilst Ellery bought her an ice from a cart on the esplanade. He directed her to sit in one of the pretty cast-iron shelters dotted along the front, just behind a crowd gathered around the stripy booth of a Punch and Judy show.

'I didn't believe you, you know?' he said. 'I was playing along because I felt sorry for you.'

'That's all right. I wouldn't have believed me either.'

They exchanged a smile.

'So, I really told you about stealing my grandfather's pipe?'

'Yes, after I'd refused your offer of an after-dinner cigar.'

'Hmm, that does sound like something I'd say. It's fun to shock people, isn't it?'

'I'm not sure fun is the word,' she said, thinking back to her father's horrified face when they announced their planned jaunt. 'But it is empowering.'

'Have to say I'm jolly glad I was born a man. Your lot do have the short straw. Not sure I'd fancy having to submit to a father or husband, whilst keeping house and producing babies.'

'Things are changing. Look at Céline.'

'Oh, she's the sort who would never submit to anyone. But then, she has money, and listening to her boasting over the luncheon, it's obvious she's lived a life where she's done exactly what she wanted, when she wanted. Not many women have that sort of gumption.'

Did she want to be that sort of woman? Pearl asked herself. She hadn't thought so before arriving at Highcliffe House, but there was something germinating inside her that made her wonder. She'd thought familiar was safe, but now that familiar had become identical, there was a growing desire in her to break free.

'Lenora Warren was quite a plucky one, apparently,' Ellery continued. 'Her choice of husband scandalised Dorset high society and the traditionalists didn't like Virgil's new money and modern American ways, but I guess she wanted to escape that kind of judgement. She was quite shocking for her day – accompanying her husband to some pretty desolate and dangerous places. Places respectable women weren't usually to be found.'

'How do you know all this?' Pearl turned to study her surprisingly well-informed companion. 'You have quite a detailed knowledge of the Brockhursts. Are you perhaps related to them in some way?'

'I've just picked up on the county whispers, that's all. People do so love to speculate, and the longer they were absent, the more the rumours spread. There have been various pieces in the local newspapers over the years and, depending on the journalist covering the story, it swings between criticism of their lifestyle and genuine concern at the length of their absence.'

Pearl huffed and crossed her arms. 'Don't talk to me about journalists being genuine. They don't care about the lives of the people they smear with their lies. Some dear friends of mine have been on the receiving end of their evil fabrications. Offscouring of society, as far as I'm concerned.'

Ellery snorted. 'My, my, there is fire in you, after all.' He looked most amused.

'And far too much in you.' Her unusually bold response came out before she could stop herself, but he wasn't at all offended, so she continued. 'I find it hard to believe that you are used to working in service. You're incredibly outspoken for staff.'

He shrugged.

'I saw the advert in the *Weymouth Chronicle* – despite your damning opinion, newspapers have their uses – and thought it was easy money; three days at a large Georgian house by the coast. M presence there is easily explained by the need for employment, but why are you and your father so far from home?'

Although she had initially been wary of confiding too much in this young man, she decided that he'd established his trustworthiness by saving her from the fire and, indeed, the sea. She needed his help to work out who was killing everyone off, what might have happened to the Brockhursts, and how – or rather, if – there was a way to escape this glitch in time. So, she told him about the sinister invitation her father had received, and how it had ended with a thinly veiled threat, fighting her desire to lean forward and wipe a small blob of ice cream from his chin. It would be far too intimate an act.

'Father claims to have no association with Highcliffe House or the people there, but he's not being truthful. He knew about the cove before we arrived, and I'm convinced he has a long-standing association with both Standfield and Céline.'

Ellery rubbed thoughtfully at his chin, found the ice cream and dispensed with it.

'Hmm... she's a funny one, and not only because she's foreign. Do you think her husband really doesn't understand English? Or is he just pretending?'

'I'd thought of that, but I'm inclined to think he's genuine. There's been no slip-up in all the days I've seen him. But perhaps he has a desperate hatred of foreigners – one so great that he wants us all dead.'

'Being married to Céline might do that to you,' Ellery joked. 'And he does read poetry so is bound to be highly emotional.'

'The point is, we don't know who is behind all this, and can't take any of the guests at face value.'

'Standfield's certainly a shifty one. I caught him rifling through Virgil's papers in the study before lunch – not long before you were *admiring* the pocket watch.' He gave her a look that made her squirm. Did he suspect that she'd taken it after all?

'He knew the Brockhursts well enough to visit the house twenty years ago and bring a bottle of whisky as a gift,' she volunteered. 'But they are such a disparate group of people to gather together. My father is hardly in the same social circle as the other two, however much he would like to be.'

'May I speak frankly?'

'Don't you always?' she teased.

'I don't like any of them much – present company excepted. Céline is manipulative, Standfield is too full of himself, and your father is as dull as ditch water. There's simply nothing about the chap.'

'He gets very excited about numbers,' she defended. 'You should see his face light up when he's tapping away on his adding machine. And he's had to bring me up alone. I don't think it's been easy for him.' They may not be close, but she knew her father had made great sacrifices on her behalf.

'Rubbish.' Ellery scoffed in his offhand manner. 'It's you who doesn't have it easy. You run around after him like a lackey, pandering to his every whim. He was telling everyone this when you were down at the cove, but perhaps in not so many words. And yet I'd also wager there is more going on with you than you allow the world to see.'

He leaned closer and memories of the kiss replayed in her mind. It was incredibly disconcerting to have him so near, yet she savoured his proximity, despite the fluttering in her chest.

She bit at her bottom lip. Her mouth felt disturbingly dry and she couldn't stop staring at his lips. Neither of them had mentioned her drunken advances from the night before...

'Quiet as a dormouse when you arrived, and then all over me like a feverish rash last night.' Until now.

The heat that flooded her cheeks was not from the sun. The weakness in her knees was equally unbidden. She tried to defend her actions.

'Is it any surprise that my behaviour has been irrational? I've spent seven days trapped in a repeating existence that I don't understand. I felt so terribly alone and that has made me reckless, confident that my behaviour wouldn't be remembered.'

'Oh, I remember *everything*.' He winked. 'But you're not alone any more. And I do sympathise; Ruby tells me I'm too impulsive for my own good sometimes.'

'I was just using my circumstances to... experiment.' She wondered who Ruby was but wasn't bold enough to ask.

'Experiment? Have you not been kissed before?' he asked, before answering his own question. 'Of course you haven't. Your father wouldn't allow it.'

Starting to feel persecuted, she retaliated. 'Then perhaps I shall use this unexpected gift of time productively. I need to meet some eligible young men and employ the feminine wiles that Céline has so clearly perfected. Live a little.'

He slapped at his thighs and jumped up from the bench.

'Now you're getting it. Tomorrow,' he said, 'the fun really begins.'

21

The evening had ended in an undramatic, quiet fashion, with Pearl overwhelmingly relieved not to have to fight for her life. They'd run out of money early on – Ellery's recklessness was liberating but sobering. By teatime, having spent the last of their pennies in the arcades, they were both hungry but did not even have the proverbial two brass farthings to rub together. It was now heading for half past eleven and they were sitting together on the promenade, looking across at the elegant curve of the pier, festooned in strings of twinkling fairy lights, and under the swinging ropes of equally impressive bulbs that hung between the streetlamps.

He'd told her that the illuminations of this pretty seaside town had been attracting the more discerning tourist for decades and, as she looked about her at the soft rainbow of colours, she could understand why. It was a spellbinding sight to behold and, with the right person, it would be an indescribably romantic setting. As she contemplated this, and repeatedly scrubbed Ellery's face out of this frivolous and imaginary scenario, everything went black and the table once again loomed large. She stared at her spider friend, and was grateful that, unlike this tiny arachnid, she was no longer in this mess alone.

Ellery must have run from the house and down the stone steps without a second of hesitation, because this time she met him on the beach. He bounced over to her like an excitable puppy.

'Rightio, just let me strip down to my undies and then you and I can do this.' He winked at her, bold as you like.

'I beg your pardon?' Her face flushed hot and her mind returned to the scenarios she'd been dreaming of only moments before on the Weymouth seafront – things Harriet talked about from her titillating novelettes. Did he think he could have his wicked way with her, right at that moment, there on the shingle, in broad daylight, just because there were no consequences?

He noticed her hesitate.

'Swimming lessons?' he clarified, and she realised her embarassing error, as he whipped off his shirt and stripped down to his cotton drawers.

Never having been this close to the muscular torso of a young man in the flesh before, only the underdeveloped bodies of children, or the lean frames of older men working in the fields, Ellery's body took her by surprise. His skin was pale, like the marble Greek statues she'd seen in books, not the honey colour of those who work outside. It was dusted with black hairs that ran across his collarbone and down his sternum. The bumps and ridges of his abdomen reminded her of a quilted silk eiderdown, and, goodness, those pronounced deltoids. (Oh, there were pages of particular interest in the encyclopaedia that she had skipped ahead to and studied in great detail – largely those extremely detailed Greek statues...)

She hesitated at removing her robe, which was ridiculous as he'd previously hauled her bathing-costume-clad body from the sea and held her alarmingly close. What on earth was she stalling for? Deciding to adopt her inner Céline, she allowed it to slide down her body and puddle at her feet. She turned her body slightly sideways, pushing a hip forwards, something she'd seen the French woman do, executed a coy drop of her gaze, and gave the smallest flick of her tongue across her lips.

Ellery cleared his throat. 'Last one in's a rotten egg.'

He raced into the sea and, sighing as she followed behind, she acknowledged that her efforts to flirt with him were misguided. He simply didn't find her attractive, and she should probably be thankful; a mutual attraction would cloud the situation.

Out in waist-height water, he proved a fast learner, but was perhaps aided by the buoyancy of the salty sea and Pearl's infinite patience. Her initial efforts were met with his inevitable silliness, as he seemed more determined to lark about than learn.

'Please try to take this seriously,' she chastised, as he pretended he was drowning for the umpteenth time. 'It's a valuable life skill which I find it hard to believe you have not acquired, living so close to the ocean.'

'Never interested me, until now.' He smacked the surface as he jumped up to rise above an incoming wave, and grinned as she wiped the splashed water from her face. 'This reckless woman I met this morning threw herself into the sea, in some futile attempt to escape a glitch in time she was wholly responsible for. Truth is, I've never felt so helpless.' His eyes were serious for a brief moment, as they met her own. 'Good job Bernard was on hand.'

She smiled, not minding the teasing. It was refreshing after a lifetime where all comments she made were taken literally. Her father was often slow to understand jokes and riddles, and so she had largely given up telling them.

'I would come to the sea every day if I lived here. Perhaps I shall select a husband based on geography.' She put a finger to her lips in mock contemplation, enjoying the good-humoured mutual teasing, and finding she had quite the sense of humour when she put her mind to it. 'All my potential suitors must live within two hundred yards of the ocean. It's as good a criterion as any.'

They were facing each other and she took his wet hands in her own, as she encouraged him to lift his feet from the seabed and kick. A shoal of tiny sprats swam by, and they both paused to watch the silvery fish, like a handful of tossed coins, shimmer alongside them and then turn as one, towards the shore, probably hoping to escape the predatory mackerel from deeper waters.

'What an utterly enchanting sight,' she said, turning her face back to his and smiling.

'Indeed.' He held her gaze before swallowing hard.

She finally got him floating and treading water, before he began propelling himself forwards, in the style of a drowning dog, but it was definitely swimming of a sort. It wouldn't take more than a few sessions for him to be competent.

As they began to wade back to the shore, she asked him if he knew anything about the string of rocks that trailed into the sea from the far left of the cove.

'Ah, Sailor's Rest,' he said. 'This whole stretch of coast is fascinating. Look, you can see where the earth has shifted and folded over millennia and the strata now sits at peculiar angles, sharp sections of rock sticking up in the air, like slices of cake that have fallen over on the plate. That particular outcrop is an area that small boats steer clear of, for fear of piercing their hulls, and I would suggest you don't stray that way when you are swimming. I can only suppose that the name indicates sailors have perished there in the past.' Ellery shrugged. 'Locals know to stay away, particularly when there are strong currents or bad weather, but I guess it's what gives Highcliffe Cove its privacy.'

Pearl looked at her prune-like fingers and wondered what the time might be. Too much direct sun was not a good idea, even if her body miraculously healed itself every time she woke in the cave.

'Shall we head back to the house?' she suggested. 'Change into dry clothes and do something reckless for the remainder of the day?'

'Absolutely. I've been thinking about how best to expand your limited horizons, and I've got *so many* ideas. How about visiting the circus for a bit of lion-taming and an afternoon learning the flying trapeze?'

She looked momentarily panicked before she spotted his familiar grin, and flicked water at him in retaliation.

'I've got the hang of the motor car now so we can go wherever you fancy, within reason. Maybe take the right-hand turning this time?' He gave her a cheeky wink, obviously viewing the whole thing as an adventure. 'Just remember that driving anywhere of great distance, like Scotland, would prove futile, as we'd never make it before midnight, and simply end up back here. We are somewhat limited by time.'

'And yet, we aren't,' she replied. 'We have hours and hours and hours. Has it not occurred to you that this could go on for years... that this could go on *forever*.'

Whilst he'd been wondering what mischief they could get up to and what experiences they could embrace, she'd remained concerned that their situation would last for eternity. She also worried that the people at Highcliffe House were choking and suffocating in the darkness, anxious as to what degree they might be experiencing painful deaths.

'You fret about things too much.'

She didn't need to deliver the obvious retort.

'Having spent the morning experiencing the servile life,' he continued, 'I can assuredly say it's not for me. I've a hankering to see how the other half live – find out what it feels like to have people wait on me. Don't you look at women like Céline and envy them their lifestyle?'

She nodded because that's exactly how she felt about the older woman. She wondered what it might be like to walk into a room and have all eyes on her, to click her fingers for a willing member of staff to appear, happy to collect her boots, iron her gowns or fetch her a dish of fancy chocolates.

'I wish I had the courage to say what I thought more often than I do, although I've been so frustrated with this stupid situation that I've been quite sharp with Standfield on previous occasions.'

'I'm all for that. The man is insufferable. And it's about time you told that father of yours where to stick his demands. The people at Highcliffe House all need to be told a few home truths.'

'It won't change anything,' she pointed out.

'No, but by gum it will feel good.'

They climbed the steep steps up to the flagstone path, noticing the Ravellos had long since moved on, but Standfield was still on the terrace. It was sad, really, that he'd come to the dinner party alone and his only friend was to be found at the bottom of a bottle.

'I say, Paula!' They both turned to the terrace. 'Join me.' Standfield tapped at the seat next to him and looked to Ellery. 'You, young man, had better pop to the kitchens and calm that cook woman down. She's been asking after you this last hour. But before you disappear, fetch us another bottle, there's a good chap.'

This time, he'd been sat there long enough for the half-finished bottle to be empty.

'Fetch it yourself. The exercise will do you good. In fact, knock yourself out and head down to the wine cellar. You'll be angling after the good wine soon enough.'

'I say, you can't speak to a fellow like that. Wait until Badger-wood hears of your insolence!'

'No, I'll tell you what's insolent.' Pearl addressed the pompous older man. 'Suggesting to the young daughter of a fellow guest that you accompany her to the bedrooms and test out the firmness of the mattress. You might have found your comments this morning amusing, but I was embarrassed by them. We'd barely been introduced. You are far too old for me and cannot even be bothered to learn my name.'

'What the...?' Standfield blustered, but the pair swept past him and in through the French doors, and Ellery led her up the stairs and into the Ravellos' room.

'Now you can finally find out what it's like to be the alluring Céline. Help yourself.' He waved his arm at the hanging dresses and scattered accessories – of which there were many.

'I feel uncomfortable being in here. This isn't my room. It's not right to look through another person's personal belongings.'

'It also isn't right to murder a houseful of people in their own beds, or poison them after a dinner party, but someone here isn't sticking to the rules. At some point, we'll have to wrestle the knotty problem of who this might be, but I suggest today we play dress-up,' he said. 'You've died half a dozen unpleasant deaths. You deserve a little fun.'

Céline's presence about them was overwhelming, yet there were only traces of her husband. From the moment they stepped across the threshold, expensive perfume wafted around the space. Numerous couture garments were hung from hangers on the cornice of the wardrobe and the picture rails. The woman had brought far too many clothes for a two-day house party. Perhaps she liked to keep her outfit options open, whereas Pearl had travelled with very little. She spied the luxurious gold lamé dress that would invariably arrive in the drawing room ten minutes after everyone else, and the matching gold T-strap heels on the floor beneath.

'This is the dress Céline—'

'Wears tonight,' Ellery finished. 'I was there, remember?'

'Isn't it beautiful?' She fingered the delicate fabric and a small sigh escaped her lips.

'That's the one then. Put it on.'

'I can't wear this. It's an evening gown.'

'Why not? Goodness me, Miss Glenham, you really are hard work. Am I going to have to go through the same reasoning every time I suggest something bold? *There are no consequences.* We are freer than we have ever been in our entire lives. Who cares if you put that gown on and walk into a butcher's shop at three o'clock in the afternoon to order a pound of sausages? Or if you attend the dinner tonight in your bathing suit? And if they do, for how long will they care? Until we approach midnight tonight, by my reckoning.'

'I don't believe the dress will fit me.' She was torn. The dress was exquisite and she had never worn anything so fine in her life. Or anything so sensuous. 'I don't have the bosom to fill it out.'

He coughed. 'I happen to know for a fact that you do.'

'How do you...' Colour flushed in her pale cheeks. 'Oh... when you manhandled me out of the sea yesterday.'

'Yes, your particularly scandalous bathing suit.' He grinned. 'My grandmother, God rest her soul, would have been apoplectic to think women were now walking around exposing their ankles, and prancing about on beaches in articles smaller than their undergarments.'

She pulled the two sides of the robe tighter around her body.

'I say wear it, and to hell with anyone who disagrees – pardon my language. And whilst you ready yourself, I shall nip next door and have a rummage. We need money. Standfield strikes me as the sort to have plenty of cash wherever he goes. Even if I can't turn up any extra funds, I've a hankering to be a gentleman. His clothes will be far too big but I bet he has some accessories that will make this afternoon a damn sight more fun.'

She was still gazing covetously at the dress as a thought occurred to her. 'Aldo is more your build. Check the wardrobe? If I'm to draw attention to myself in evening wear, you can be black tie. Wealth permits eccentricity – look at Horace de Vere Cole and his stupid pranks.' Indeed, his escapades were legendary. The Dreadnought hoax still sat uncomfortably with the Royal Navy thirteen years later. 'We could be Lord and Lady... um, Pembridge?' The name was completely fictitious but sounded convincing. 'Rich as you like and answerable to no one.'

'Now you're getting it. I knew there was a true adventurer underneath that dull, good-girl façade. Embrace the opportunities.' He gave her an unexpectedly charming smile, before swinging the tall mirrored door open. 'Aha! Yes, this should do nicely.'

He unhooked a couple of wooden hangers that held the Italian evening suit.

'Right, Lady Pembridge, shall we convene in the hall in ten minutes?'

Swept up in the giddy excitement of doing something she knew she shouldn't be doing, her stomach whirled and spun – much like it did when she stole clocks. She readied herself. The dress, although loose around the middle, was an adequate fit, and the shoes were manageable, if a little on the large side. She hastily pinned up her hair, using pins from a small glass bowl on the dressing table, liberally dabbing herself with Céline's Guerlain perfume as an afterthought. Catching her reflection in the dressing table mirror, she was surprised at the confident and attractive young lady who looked back at her. How could something as simple as nice clothes have such a dramatic effect?

'My dear Lady Pembridge,' she said to the mirror, 'all you need now is some fine jewellery.' She slid open the slender top drawer delighted to find several velvet boxes within, and selected a simple string of pearls – which she felt was appropriate.

She was about to close the drawer when she noticed the small Persian bowl from earlier. Hadn't Céline warned about its powers to invoke malevolent spirits? She shuddered. Whatever the French-woman planned to do with it, one thing was certain – it wasn't hers to take. As she slid the drawer shut, she felt immeasurably better about her own morally questionable actions at stealing Céline's clothing. If the Frenchwoman embraced the old adage that posses-sion was nine-tenths of the law, so could she.

* * *

Pearl and Ellery met in the hallway a few minutes later and Ellery wolf-whistled as he took in the sight before him.

'You scrub up well, girl... I mean, miss.'

'I think you can safely call me Pearl now, and thank you.'

She wanted to embrace her emerging confidence and respond that he looked equally dashing in Aldo's suit, but couldn't – afraid that he might guess how extraordinarily handsome she found him. Whilst her flippant words to everyone else, like her outburst with Standfield, would have no lasting impact, anything she said to this young man was permanent. She would have to be careful about her honesty and her emotions around him.

'You'll never believe what I found in old Standfield's dressing table?'

She looked up expectantly.

'Serious money. Not just some loose change for a night away but a whole roll of notes. Odd, don't you think? To come to a house party with so much cash? Smacks of potential blackmail to me – like he feels he might have to pay Badgerwood off.'

'Everything about this gathering is odd,' she pointed out, about to head for the stairs when she hesitated. 'One moment,' she said, and turned back to her father's door. She knocked loudly and eventually heard a disgruntled mumble summoning her in.

He was sitting on the bed as she entered, and it took him a moment to appreciate what he was seeing.

'Pearl, *what are you wearing*?'

'Do you like it, Father?' She gave a daring twirl, even though her knees were trembling.

'Where did you get such a thing? It's far too grown up for you,' he muttered. 'Did that flibbertigibbet Harriet lend it to you?'

Pearl took a deep breath and hoped Ellery would be proud of her for what she was about to say.

'I'm not actually here to discuss my wardrobe, Father. I'm here to tell you that sometimes you speak to me with no regard for my feelings, and treat me like a member of staff, rather than a daughter. You make me feel that every request to spend time with you is an unreasonable demand, and you show me little affection.'

The frown across his forehead deepened the more she spoke, and his nostrils flared almost imperceptibly.

'Firstly, Pearl, I do not like being spoken to in such a manner. And secondly, you are fully aware that I am not the sort of man given to frivolous displays of emotion. You know that I love you. Let that be enough.'

'I'm not sure that I do,' she said forlornly. 'If you loved me, you would talk to me of my mother. I have no connection to her, which has left a gaping hole in my life. It is beyond cruel to shut me out like this.'

'I should not have brought you here,' he said, finally getting to his feet, but failing to address her comments. 'Such giddy excitement has clearly led to your current befuddled state. May I suggest you take off that ridiculous frock, retire to your room for the afternoon, and join us all for dinner in a more reasonable frame of mind, and in more suitable attire?'

'You may suggest it, but I will not comply. I am going out for the afternoon with a young man, and I have absolutely no idea where we are headed or what we shall do once we get there. Isn't that an exciting prospect?' she asked. 'Spontaneity, it turns out, is quite exhilarating. You should try it, Father.'

'You, young lady, are going nowhere,' he said with conviction.

'Watch me.' And she walked out of his room, with her head held high, but her knees still betraying her nerves.

* * *

They raced down the stairs and escaped the house before her father had a chance to follow and demand her compliance. Pearl could only imagine the commotion when their disappearance was discovered by the others. Her father, who would still be fuming that his daughter had spoken to him so frankly, would be further annoyed when he realised that there was no one to carry out errands for him. But would he be *worried*? Would he walk to Morton Peverell and contact the police, fearful for her safety, after she'd absconded with a relative stranger? She doubted it.

Standfield wouldn't notice their absence until he wanted a drink and Ellery wasn't there to fetch another bottle, or he struggled with his bow tie. And poor Mrs Dawson would have to battle on, producing and serving a meal for the remaining four guests, alone. Pearl cast her eyes at the confident young man in the motor car beside her. Did he not feel faintly guilty about that?

As they drove down the gravel driveway, she wondered if, without her presence, and with Aldo understanding nothing, her father, Céline and Standfield would be free to talk about the connection they all had, but were so desperate to hide – the Brockhursts.

'Do you feel better for being honest with your father?' Ellery finally asked, as they hared through the beautiful Dorset country lanes.

'I'm not sure. Yes, for getting all those things off my chest, but he didn't address my comments, and it changes nothing.'

Ellery threw her a sideways glance. 'It changes a great deal. It's not healthy to bottle things up.'

'But perhaps equally unwise to be volatile and too quick to react?'

'Maybe there is a compromise?' he offered. 'I have a feeling our friendship may benefit us both.'

'Yes,' she agreed, thinking of a few benefits that Ellery probably hadn't considered, and trying hard not to blush.

22

Heading right at the T-junction took them to Morton Peverell and Ellery slid the car in front of the bustling tea room in the main square. The grocer's van was parked in front of the general stores and Pearl had to remind herself that it was only a few short hours ago Mr Lane had kindly deposited her and her father at Highcliffe House.

They approached the café, which was trying to emulate the Lyons tea rooms of the big towns and cities, but on a more modest scale. Small circular tables, with neatly pressed crisp white tablecloths, were dotted about, and the staff wore black dresses with white Peter Pan collars, and lace-edged aprons.

Heads turned as the young couple entered in formal evening wear. Many of the customers were wearing pretty day dresses and summer hats, but no one else was frivolous enough to wear gold lamé before six o'clock, or indeed in a public space. Several pairs of curious eyes followed their journey across the room, before they seated themselves at a table by the large bay window.

A plump woman approached, her hair pinned up under a starched white cap.

'Afternoon. What do you be wanting, my dears?' she asked in her thick Dorset accent and licking the end of her stubby pencil in readiness.

'A good old cup of tea,' Ellery said, unfazed by the curious glances of the other customers.

'And what do your wife be wanting?'

Whether the waitress was assuming that any couple driving around the coast together on such a splendid summer's afternoon must be married, or whether her old-fashioned sensibilities wouldn't allow her to contemplate that they weren't, Pearl was unsure, so kept her ringless fingers on her lap, under the table. She felt uncomfortable people might think she was an unmarried woman – which she was. But Ellery embraced the pantomime.

'Yes, darling, how remiss of me. What would you like?' he asked reaching out for her remaining hand and holding it briefly in his own.

'Just a cup of tea, please.'

'My wife would also like a cup of tea and, let's be utterly reckless, could you throw in a couple of currant buns?'

The waitress nodded and scuttled off to fulfil their order, as he sat back in his chair, throwing one leg across the other and looking totally at ease. Pearl tugged nervously at her dress and bit at her bottom lip. All eyes were on her and suddenly their play-acting didn't seem such a good idea.

'Such a pretty little village,' he said to no one in particular, and gazing out across the square.

She had to agree, but then the sunshine made everything look pretty, giving extra colour and life to the scene before her. They sat together in quiet contemplation and it wasn't many minutes before they were presented with a pot of tea for two, and a couple of large currant buns, bursting with juicy black fruit.

'Look at the pair of you, all glammed up. I'll wager you're o your way to the summer ball at Burbridge Manor?' the waitress said, depositing linen napkins and a silver-plated knife on the table. Evidently, in her mind, it was the only explanation for such attire.

This must be the event Standfield had mentioned to her when Pearl had sat with him that afternoon on the terrace. Ellery's eyes rose slowly to meet hers across the table and she saw the same daring thoughts flash across his face as her own.

'Yes,' Ellery said to the woman, without breaking Pearl's gaze. 'But I have to admit to being somewhat lost. What would be the quickest way for us to get there?'

The woman gave them directions, which meant more to Ellery than to her.

'You know the Allingtons then?' she enquired.

'Oh, we go way back,' he replied. 'Great friends with my father. Known me since I was knee-high to a very small grasshopper.'

Satisfied, the waitress turned her attention to another customer and Pearl leaned forward, conspiratorially.

'Are we really doing this?' she asked, trying hard to prevent a nervous giggle escaping her lips.

He shrugged. 'I'm up for it, but do *you* have the necessary gumption?' He tipped his head to one side in a questioning manner.

Here she was being underestimated again. Her father knew little of her swimming prowess, and yet she was an extremely competent athlete. Even the village schoolteacher had been surprised when she'd outperformed all her classmates in the newly established Junior Certificate, because she'd never once spoken up in class, but instead had sat at the back, silently absorbing everything.

Ellery looked at her, half-doubt, half-challenge – one she was determined to rise to.

'I'll have you know I have gate-crashed a ball before. On my own.' She didn't explain that she'd slunk in, dressed as a maid, to steal a clock, purely for thrills, because her life was so empty she was desperate to fill it with anything.

He raised his eyebrows and put the delicate china cup to his mouth.

'I find that hard to believe, but then you surprised me by confronting your father, so perhaps still waters do run cavernously deep. Oh, Lady Pembridge, if you can truly let yourself go, then we are in for a thrilling evening.'

After their refreshments, Ellery successfully navigated his way to Burbridge Manor, only taking one wrong turn and quickly being put right by a passing postman. It was now heading for six o'clock and their timing was perfect, as carriages and motor cars were depositing guests at the bottom of a sweeping run of stone steps that led up to the most splendid porticoed entrance Pearl had ever seen. Burbridge Manor was far grander than Highcliffe House, or indeed Boxley Hall.

'Do we brazen it out and walk through the front door, or dart around the back and slip in with the staff? I've a mind to try our luck, tagging on to this group.' He pointed to a small cluster of older couples loitering at the bottom of the steps, as one lady adjusted her cream silk slippers, holding on to the arm of her husband. 'Usually, I find if you have enough confidence, and actively engage in conversation, they don't question you. It's those who look nervous who are challenged.'

She wondered under what circumstances he found it necessary to slip into places he didn't belong.

'Whereas I find blending in and keeping my head down is the best course of action.'

'Ah, yes, I'd forgotten you have form when it comes to gaining illegal entry to balls, but we have nothing to lose, so let's be bold.'

As they approached the group, Ellery must have caught a name on the breeze because he burst into life. 'Wilfred, old chap! Haven't seen you in forever. My father sends his regards, as does old Stand-field – neither of whom can make it tonight, more's the pity.'

His exuberance quite took the party by surprise but, even though the slippered woman began to question their acquaintance, Ellery brushed her polite enquiries to one side, as he showered all the ladies with compliments and helped a gentleman with a walking stick to mount the stairs. Pearl followed meekly behind and the doormen did not question the young couple who looked the part, and clearly knew Sir Wilfred – whoever he was.

Burbridge Manor was sufficiently stately to have its own ball-room, which they were directed to by obliging staff. With high ceilings and a white marble floor, it was a glorious space, full of dancing couples, and with tables and chairs placed around the periphery for those who enjoyed the atmosphere but perhaps did not have the energy or inclination to partake in such a strenuous activity. A musical ensemble was seated on a small stage at the back of the room and the strains of a lively waltz drifted around the lofty space.

'Do you dance, Lady Pembridge?' Ellery asked, bowing as he did so.

'A little.'

'And I was taught by a maiden aunt, so let us show the assembled guests how it is done.' He took her arm and swept her towards the floor, before resting his warm hand across her back as she placed one of hers over his shoulder. Their cheeks were almost touching, and she could hardly believe that she was dancing with such a handsome young man, in such opulent surroundings, wearing such a daring gown. If only Harriet could see her now.

Two dances were enough for her to feel light-headed and hot, and Ellery noticed her discomfort.

'Shall we stop for a drink and then head outside for some air?' he asked, and she nodded her assent.

He deposited her at the edge of the dance floor and went to fetch refreshments. As the top of his head disappeared into the crowd, she stepped backwards only to collide with a rather gangly gentleman, and immediately apologised for her clumsiness.

'Not at all, dear lady. The fault is mine entirely. I am all knees and elbows, with very little control over either.'

He was indeed blessed with extraordinarily long limbs, and had an angular but friendly face. His forehead was large and his eyes somewhat sunken, but his open smile melted her heart.

'No, I'm sure the fault is mine. This is my first time at such a prestigious event and I'm rather at a loss. I'm in a dress I don't feel truly comfortable in and never know what to say to people.'

'I feel exactly the same, dear lady, except I'm not in an uncomfortable dress, obviously, but my suit is rather restrictive. I swear the collar has been so starched that if I turn my head too quickly, I shall decapitate myself.' They exchanged an understanding look. 'Albert Cavendish.' He bowed as he introduced himself. 'But my friends call me Bertie – both of them... That was a joke, by the way. I do have more than two friends. Oh dear, I'm talking too much...' He gave a dramatic bow and managed to bump into the gentleman behind him as he extended his rear. 'Utterly charmed to make your acquaintance.'

She was about to introduce herself, but Ellery chose that exact moment to return with a glass of fruit punch. 'Lord Pembridge, and this is my wife, Lady Pembridge.'

The disappointment in the young man's eyes was apparent to them both, but he returned to his full height.

'I'm afraid I barrelled into your delightful wife. Bit short-sighted but find spectacles such a bore. I either lose them or sit on them. Mother always says I shouldn't be allowed out without a chaperone.' He rolled his eyes. 'I do so wonder why they had me. Daddy is a viscount, so I understand that they needed sons, but they already had the spare. I am, in fact, the youngest of several. Anything after two, is totally superfluous and, in my case, rather a liability.'

Pearl found his self-depreciation endearing. He didn't set her heart racing like Ellery increasingly had the ability to do, but there was something about him that was engaging.

'Lucky fellow, lucky fellow, indeed.' He shook Ellery's hand so vigorously, Pearl wondered if he would pull the arm from its socket.

As they moved to the doors, to partake of some fresh air, she heard Bertie's parting words. 'And it's actually a jolly smashing frock – especially from behind. I say, I hope my observation isn't inappropriate...'

There was a terrace attached to the manor, which was much more impressive than the small, paved area at Highcliffe House. It was surrounded by carved stone balustrades, and there was a further set of wide steps mirroring those at the front of the house, which led down into the formal gardens. Waiting staff were milling about with further silver trays of sparkling drinks, which they offered to the overheated revellers spilling out into the cool night air. Ellery placed her empty punch glass on a tray and grabbed them both a bowl of champagne, before ushering her to a quiet corner. Birds chattered in the nearby tree canopies, and the sweet scent of evening primrose drifted up from the flower borders below.

'Here's to the good times,' he said, raising his glass.

She clinked glasses but said nothing. The good times were more intimidating than she'd anticipated, but perhaps she did deserve them after all; to drink fine champagne, have eligible young men flirt with her (for that's certainly what Bertie had been doing in his own, self-effacing way), and to be in a dress she could never have imagined herself bold enough to wear.

There were certainly worse ways to spend an evening.

23

For nearly a fortnight, Pearl and Ellery lived the high life in a series of repeating afternoons. Each day was slightly different – sometimes they swam before they left Highcliffe House, on other occasions they took a picnic and explored a different section of the coast. It was curious that since he had got caught in the strange loop of time with her, the nights ended earlier; she was disappearing back to the cave at half past eleven now, unlike a quarter to midnight, when she'd first been trapped.

On one memorable occasion, they used Standfield's money to go shopping. Ellery was finally persuading her around to his way of thinking and she acknowledged how exhilarating it was to have the funds to purchase anything that took their fancy, even if their acquisition of the purchases would not last. They drove to Weymouth and Ellery told the staff of various retail establishments that he was shopping on behalf of his wealthy but elderly great-aunt, who was returning to England after decades of living in the jungles of Peru. She was an eccentric, he said, and had given him a quite specific list. He proceeded to order a colourful Ludwig and Ludwig drum kit (to be delivered to a fictional upmarket address), boxing gloves (in size small), and some scandalous nightwear (as his aunt was bringing her young Peruvian lover home with her). She was, he informed the various shopkeepers, a particularly active octogenarian with many hobbies. As he paid in full, they did not question the veracity of his tall tale. Pearl could only stand by in wonder at his boldness and try to contain her giggles.

Most evenings, however, they attended the summer ball in all their finery (or, more accurately, Céline and Aldo's finery), where they could dance the night away, and leave their worries firmly behind the closed doors of Highcliffe House. It was the tonic Pearl needed and the escapism she craved, after having experienced so many traumatic deaths.

It did not take long, however, for the thrills and unaccountability of Ellery's attitude towards their situation, so in contrast to her own, to have its drawbacks. They were being judged by people, and not always in a positive light, which sat uncomfortably with her. It was a hedonism that couldn't continue. The novelty of champagne had worn off and the monotony of the music and conversation was beyond maddening. It had been fun for a while, and given her a newfound confidence, but they wouldn't find the answers to the puzzling questions of Highcliffe House on a dance floor at Burbridge Manor.

After another evening of dancing, they retreated to the terrace as usual, but this time, she walked to the far side, wanting, if nothing else, a different view of the gardens.

An older couple were seated on a wrought-iron bench under the star-shaped blue heads of a clematis climbing the trellis behind them. Pearl rested her bottom on the stone rail of the balustrade, as they introduced themselves to Ellery as the Leightons.

'Do I know you? You look familiar,' the gentleman said.

'Friend of Harlow Standfield,' he replied. It was their only tenuous connection to the ball. He gave the usual assumed name of Pembridge.

'Ah, then I've possibly come across you at his place? He certainly knows how to throw a party. Is he here? Haven't come across the fellow.'

'Another engagement in Morton Peverell, but I know he was disappointed not to be attending tonight.'

'Really? Said he was coming when I saw him at the club last month. Must be something important. So, how do you know him? Tennis? Shooting?'

'Who doesn't know Harlow in these parts?' Ellery said, avoiding a direct answer. 'And he's an easy enough chap to get along with, especially after a drink or two.'

Mr Leighton chuckled. It was a variation of a conversation they'd had on a couple of occasions with other guests.

'Indeed. Doesn't take much to loosen his tongue, and then he either spouts politics, or waxes lyrical about his recent social engagements.' The other gentleman rolled his eyes. 'Morton Peverell, you say? Interesting. Never would be drawn on the Warren affair. And all those months he spent visiting Highcliffe House...'

Pearl's ears pricked up at this. Warren was Lenora's maiden name, and her family had owned the house for generations. She noticed Ellery lean forward to pay better attention.

'Oh, I don't know,' she said joining the conversation and slipping into her role. 'He has opened up to us about it in the past.' She hoped by implying she already had knowledge of the Warren affair – whatever it was – the Leightons could be persuaded to enlighten them further.

'Well, naturally, he would spill the heart-rending beans to someone as enchanting as yourself.' Pearl had never once been referred to as enchanting. She rather liked it, but feared it was more down to the shimmering dress than her sparkling personality.

'Always had an eye for the ladies, has Harlow, but then that was the problem. Once she finished it, there was never anyone who could measure up.'

The pieces immediately fell into place. Pearl had been wrong to assume Céline had been in love with Virgil. It was Standfield who'd loved Lenora. Ellery had mentioned her breaking off an engagement before her marriage. She'd misunderstood the overheard conversation. The Frenchwoman had not been referring to the hardship *she'd* suffered by the strength of the Brockhursts' marriage – but his. Standfield and Lenora probably had a long history – he'd stressed how everyone knew everyone in the county – and she wondered if perhaps they had even grown up together.

'I understand he never quite got over *Lenora*,' she said, testing the water. If she was wrong, she would look foolish, but thankfully only for the next couple of hours.

'He was absolutely smitten,' Mr Leighton agreed. 'And weeks away from the wedding, to boot. Bloody Brockhurst waltzed in and swept her right from under his nose. Never have liked the Americans. No history of their own so they go around the world buying up everyone else's, and then marrying into a bit of our heritage, whilst they're about it.' He crossed his arms and let out a snort.

'It's usually the heiresses coming over here and nabbing our aristocracy, to be fair,' Ellery interjected. 'Jennie Jerome and Lord Churchill being the prime example.'

'Perhaps the Brockhursts have finally returned from their travels,' Leighton's wife whispered. It was the first time she'd spoken.

'Well, well, the mystery deepens.' Mr Leighton looked most pleased with himself, remembering the young man's earlier information as to Standfield's current whereabouts. 'That would certainly explain old Harlow's absence tonight. Damnably odd for Lenora and Virgil to disappear for all those years. I was beginning to suspect they'd died because, let's face it, a few postcards to the vicar's wife saying they planned to be abroad for several years, and then nothing. It smacked of foul play.'

'You're being overly dramatic,' his wife said. 'I told you, no one new has moved into the house. They always did prefer hotter climes, and who can blame them?'

'Exactly. So, if she has returned, it would be enough to make the old dog go sniffing about again. Never could give it up. Made a total fool of himself – writing to her, following her about, that sort of thing. Felt rather sorry for him in the end because he couldn't see when to step away.'

'What were the Brockhursts like?' Pearl asked, trying to make her enquiry sound casual. 'I've heard snippets about them, but I wasn't even born the last time they were seen in this country.'

'I only knew Lenora through Standfield,' the wife replied. 'Astonishing lady. Really embraced life and everything it had to offer. A rebellious child, by all accounts, and an untameable free spirit as a young woman – spoilt by her parents, naturally,' she added, as though this was the ultimate cause of her wild behaviour. 'Only met Virgil Brockhurst once and he struck me as a touch arrogant, if extremely good-looking. But he had money, you see, heaps of it, and I got the impression he used it to buy status and connections – possibly even a wife. They were always off on marvellous adventures, and then she came back from Asia with a tiny baby and my dear old mother was adamant they couldn't gallivant around the world with a child in a knapsack – but they obviously did.'

'He used to take her to the most godforsaken places,' her husband chipped in. 'Rainforests, ice caps and barren deserts. No places for a lady. And certainly not a child.'

'That's why we were all so surprised when they headed off again, but it was simply what they did – defied convention.'

They chatted politely with the couple for a little while longer ut when the Leightons were joined by friends, Pearl and Ellery moved to one side.

'It makes me question more than ever, what happened to that family,' Ellery said. 'Did they meet an unfortunate end abroad, cut off from civilisation, that simply never got reported back? Or have they spent the last two decades living an unconventional life, somewhere where they couldn't be traced, or chose *not* to be traced, and have only now decided to return?'

'Do you think they're behind the fire?' Pearl asked, no longer knowing what to think.

'Heaven knows, but I guess we have all the time in the world to find out.'

24

_____

The twinkling lights from the manor bathed the formal gardens in a charming glow, as Ellery led Pearl down a long, straight path of limestone chippings, lined with topiary box hedges and fragrant flower borders. They'd decided to escape the crowds for a while and she was keen to explore. The confines of the manor after so many evenings now bored her.

Every so often, further paths bisected theirs, and she followed one on a whim into an enclosed memorial garden. Four stone benches sat around a circular bed of low white rose bushes – each bloom resembling a little moon in the black. There was a dark granite obelisk in the middle – the quartz crystals within twinkling in the moonlight. They had learned of the tragic loss of the Allington heir during the war through one of their many conversations at the ball, and Pearl suspected this garden was dedicated to him.

She sat on one of the benches and Ellery joined her, haunting shadows falling at their feet, and the distant hum of revelry muffled by the hedges. The night air was fresh – not seaside fresh – but instead draped in the sweet scents of a summer garden. The rose had surely been selected for their fragrance, as hints of lemons and violets hung about them. Pearl kicked off the oversized shoes and wiggled her toes. She felt her companion's proximity keenly, and shivered, despite the heat.

'We could come here every night until the end of time,' he said. 'Wouldn't that be... well, a ball?' He smiled at his own joke.

'I'm beginning to tire of it. Particularly the people. Aren't you?' It wasn't really her world, but she hadn't minded dipping into it.

'Perhaps, although the thought of eating endless delicious canapés and drinking vast quantities of good wine with no ill effects on my body is somewhat tempting.' He grinned, looking at her face and only dropping his gaze when she dared to raise her eyes to meet his. 'You never did tell me the story behind shy Pearl Glenham creeping into a ball uninvited. Was there no one to escort poor Cinderella?'

'Oh, I wasn't there to dance, or fall in love with a handsome prince. There are things you don't know about me. Things you wouldn't believe.'

He sat up straighter and returned his focus to her face, looking faintly amused.

'Perhaps not there as a guest, then? Don't tell me you play the double bass in a jazz ensemble? Or are you a cabaret entertainer? A burlesque dancer? In that dress, I can quite imagine it.'

She didn't blush quite as openly as she might have done when she'd first met him. Two weeks of evenings strutting around Burbridge Manor, usually slightly tipsy with champagne, and in a revealing gown, had done wonders for her self-confidence.

'I know you delight in teasing me, but I think even you would be surprised to learn I'm an accomplished thief,' she announced.

'Right.' He chuckled. 'The only thing you've stolen is time from the universe, and even that was totally accidental.'

'I'm serious. I steal clocks and pocket watches. Small ones. Cheap ones. From people who will hardly miss them.'

He narrowed his eyes to assess whether she was turning the tables and teasing him. 'You're right – I certainly didn't have you pegged as a kleptomaniac horologist. Is that what you were doing in Mr Brockhurst's bureau?' She nodded. 'Interesting. Why timepieces?'

'You'll think me silly...'

'Does it matter what I think?'

Yes, her inner voice shouted, *it matters more than you know,* but she shared her tale nonetheless.

'My mother died giving birth to me. It broke my father's heart. He doesn't talk about her and has this pocket watch that he keeps set to four minutes past ten. I used to ask him about it but he wouldn't be drawn, and then one day he admitted it was when his life changed forever – the moment I was born and, perhaps in his mind, the moment I sealed her fate.'

It was an extraordinarily sentimental gesture for a man who was anything but, and she tried to explain to Ellery how it had led to her bizarre obsession with this instant in time – how her heart thumped uncontrollably if she happened to look at a clock at this precise minute, or how she set the hands of every stolen pocket watch to commemorate it.

He let out a tiny snort. 'I'm no expert, but I'd say it's unhealthy to have such a focus, little one. Holding on to that moment won't bring her back.' He reached across to ruffle her hair and she felt patronised yet again, but wasn't having it any more. Irritated, she grabbed his wrist to prevent the action, and he froze in surprise as their eyes locked. His arm dropped to the seat but she didn't let go, and he refused to break her gaze.

Her chest heaved and curious sensations fluttered around her body. She was acutely conscious that she was still holding him and, equally, that he was making no attempt to break free. They were locked together and neither seemed prepared to uncouple.

Two weeks of sharing everything, every waking moment – because there was no stretch of time when they were asleep – and she knew him better than she knew almost anyone, save her father. She knew that he had a cheeky sense of humour, and that his own father had died in the war. That he had trouble holding his temper when he was riled by something, even though his outbursts were over in a flash. His enquiring mind and grim determination shone through in everything he did, from play-acting as Lord Pembridge, to the speed with which he'd learned to swim. Their conversations in the Austin as they sped to the manor every evening had taught her about his childhood, and simple likes and dislikes; he adored dogs but was nervous of goats, was good at English but hated mathematics. And, most importantly, she knew every inch of his body, from the scar on his calf from a bicycling accident, to the asymmetry of his ears, and how she felt when he held that lean body of his close to hers. But in all that time, he had not given her any indication that he felt the same.

Until that moment.

The moon cast peculiar shadows across his face, highlighting the contours of his profile, and illuminating his eyes. He seemed to be studying her in almost as much detail as she was studying him and, after a few silent moments, where she retained her grip of his wrist, it was all she could do not to pull him to her.

He swayed in her direction. His eyes dropped to her lips and she thought for a moment he was going to kiss her, but almost as soon as he'd lurched towards her, he pulled back, letting out a long breath and closing his eyes for longer than necessary. When he opened them again, he changed the subject entirely, and she reluctantly released his hand.

'Enough of the hedonism, we must throw ourselves back into the mysteries of Highcliffe House.'

'What?' His brutal change of direction threw her. Where had that electricity evaporated to? What had stopped him closing in on her mouth? Surely she'd given out signals to encourage, not deter. But then she was new to all this. It didn't matter what clothes she wore on the outside, on the inside she was as far from Céline as anyone could possibly be.

'Work out who is starting the fire.'

'Do you regret getting caught up in this infernal loop with me?' she asked.

'Not for one moment.'

'But you could be stuck with me in perpetuity...'

Again, he paused and then changed the subject. Again, she wondered why he was so out of sorts. He always called a spade out for what it was, yet would not address this thing between them.

'Confront your father—'

'I did, that afternoon when we first came here.'

'Not his unacceptable behaviour towards you. I mean confront him about his association with Highcliffe House and the Brockhursts. He will forget any information he divulges, but we won't. Let's start questioning everyone in isolation and find out what they know.'

Pearl had tried that approach on her fourth repeated afternoon but the guests had an unfortunate tendency to share such information with the others. She doubted it would work.

'You must get to the bottom of why he's travelled to Dorset, and what hold Badgerwood has over him. And whilst you're about it find out *why* he won't talk about your mother. It's not normal, Pearl and the not knowing is stopping you from becoming the woman you should be. Already, from our short acquaintance, I can see that you have so much unexplored potential.'

Was this why he was holding back? Did he want her to be a stronger person? Did he view her as a child for letting herself be manipulated by her father? Must she resolve these issues before he pursued anything romantic? If that's what it would take for him to kiss her, then so be it. Perhaps wearing the clothes of a strong woman was not enough – she must have the strength of character to match.

'Only if you actively help me get to the bottom of this glitch in time. I'm serious when I say that I've had enough.'

He let out a long sigh. 'Yes, me too. Endless fun just isn't that much fun, is it? You have a deal.' He stuck out his hand and she shook it. 'But one thing at a time; it's no good us leaving the loop, if you're about to be killed by some lunatic. And the disappearance of the Brockhursts is definitely key. To my knowledge, there was never any sighting of them after the April of 1903. Yes, a handful of post-cards, and yes, someone has clearly been looking after the house and keeping it secure, but their possessions remain untouched, as though waiting for their return. Surely it would have been passed on to a beneficiary had they died?'

Pearl thought back to the letter her father had received back in Suffolk.

'And yet my father's invitation implied that financial matters pertaining to the Brockhursts had now been settled and he was to come into some money. Perhaps their deaths are recent? Or perhaps they have only now been declared dead because so much time has passed since they were last seen? Either way, it must be what Mr Badgerwood is coming to explain, when he eventually shows up.'

'Or perhaps he doesn't exist and Virgil and Lenora are behind Mr Badgerwood's invitation?' he said, rubbing his chin and warming to his theme. 'If they wanted to gather a group of people from their past together, pretending there was an imminent and sizeable inheritance might be a way of luring them here.'

His hand fell to his lap and his fingers tapped out a rhythm on his thigh as he worked through different possible scenarios.

'Brockhurst!' he suddenly exclaimed. 'The name literally mean "badger wood". How did I not make the connection? Perhaps the are behind this, after all.'

She saw it then, too. Brock was a term for a badger, and so hurs must mean a wood or similar.

'We haven't properly considered the possibility that the fire wa started by someone outside the house – someone not sleeping ther tonight,' he said. 'They could easily be alive and returning to see revenge for something. Maybe they were forced into hiding? Black mail? Kidnap? Who knows? But they are returning to delive retribution.'

'So, if Virgil and Lenora are pulling the strings, then we are th puppets,' she concluded, thinking back to the portrait in the hall. dynamic couple – a team – two people not afraid of anything.

'It's certainly a possibility, although,' he said, 'we shouldn discount the guests entirely. Who is to say the Ravellos didn prepare the house, employ Mrs Dawson and myself, and then star the fire? You said their room was locked. We don't know if it wa from the outside or the inside. That woman always gets what sh wants, and strikes me as ruthless enough to dispose of anyone wh gets in her way. You didn't actually see either of them die from th poison; Aldo was out of the room and Céline ran into the night.'

They were disturbed by another young couple stumbling int the garden, possibly looking for a quiet space to be alone, befor noticing the pair of them on the bench, making their apologies, an hastily retreating. Pearl looked again at Ellery's profile, wonderin why everyone else could see what a perfect and secluded spot th was to pursue romantic inclinations, except him. All he wa currently focused on was the conundrum of their situation, and yet, here she was, dressed up to the nines, her whole being inwardly begging for him to kiss her.

'Or perhaps it was Standfield,' he continued. 'Something your father and Céline did to him in the past. Perhaps they were involved in Lenora's decision to jilt him and he can't forgive them. He kills you all and slips out of the house. The man is fairly local, after all. He could have organised the dinner party quite easily.'

'No, he succumbed to the poison,' she confirmed. A judder rippled through her as she thought of his horrific death throes. There was no faking that.

'Your father then?'

'He's a cold man, to be sure, but not a murderer. And I know for a fact that he was drugged and as much a victim of the fire as myself.'

'We can speculate until the cows come home, but what we really need to do is start asking awkward questions. How about we come to the ball for one last night of hedonism, and then focus our attentions on solving this awful muddle? We could return to High-cliffe House early and see what they get up to when we aren't around. Maybe we will even catch the culprit in the act. I do so love a bit of detective work.'

'Agreed,' she said, actually looking forward to confronting the people she had been so intimidated by when she'd first arrived.

25

Within minutes of finding herself in the cave again, she met Ellery in the boot room, as had become their routine, and they climbed the stairs unseen, to change.

Ellery grabbed Aldo's evening suit and left her to her usual preparations, but as she walked towards the gold dress, she hesitated. Cinderella was going to the ball for the last time. And she was going to make her final appearance matter – to Ellery, if no one else.

She selected a different gown from Céline's extensive wardrobe to wear that evening, one in a peacock blue, so adorned with beads and sequins in interlocking swirls, that she wondered if it might feel like sitting on the shingle should she take a seat. She arranged her hair differently, and applied the merest hint of make-up – red lipstick and rouge that she found on the Frenchwoman's dressing table. As she gazed at her unrecognizable and surprisingly sophisticated reflection, she was more certain than ever that she would get her hair cut into a fashionable bob when all this nonsense was over. She had long since felt herself caught somewhere between being a girl and a woman, and knew now which she wanted to be.

As she dressed, she thought of her friend Harriet's ability to play the boys in their village off against each other, remembering her once saying that if she told Freddie she was seeing Gilbert, then Freddie was sure to ask her to step out with him. Did Ellery need a gentle shove? Might he act on the feelings he so obviously had for her if he thought her affections lay elsewhere?

Meeting up in the hallway, as always, she saw the flash of Ellery's eyes as she stepped through the door. Her heart rate accelerated, and she was sure his did also. Were his amber irises burning a little brighter? He ran his hand nervously through his hair, a sure sign that he *did* like her, so what was going on? Certainly not a man to be backwards in coming forwards, his reluctance to make even the smallest overture was bewildering – particularly as he was the one always harping on about no consequences.

'A different dress. I like it. It brings out the blue in your eyes, which often seemed so pale they are almost grey. It suits you. Any reason for the change?' he enquired.

'I thought I might dally with the young man who seemed so keen on me that first evening. You are so right,' she purred. 'I must use this gift of time to experiment. Tonight, Albert Cavendish, the youngest son of a viscount, can take me in his long arms and waltz me around the ballroom. You and I shall drop the pretence of being married, and instead be brother and sister.'

She wasn't used to being so forthright, and it felt quite empowering. Ellery raised a quizzical eyebrow, and she felt his body stiffen as she looped her arm through his. They silently descended the stairs to embark on a drive through the picturesque countryside where her usually chatty friend seemed to have run out of things to say.

* * *

Their visits to Burbridge Manor had been fun, she acknowledged, but neither of them particularly enjoyed the company of stuffy, moneyed people who only wanted to talk about things that were of interest to them: horses and banking investments for the men, and the latest fashions and the management of unruly staff for the women. They sought out Mr and Mrs Leighton for the last time and extracted all the information they could, but the older couple had little more to say, other than add to the speculations they themselves were making. Pearl didn't know Céline's maiden name, so she could only enquire about any connection the Brockhursts had to a glamorous Frenchwoman, and the Leightons did not know of one.

'Shall we arrange to reconvene later, *brother*?' she asked, pulling him to one side. 'I'm now off to accidentally bump into Bertie.'

She gave what she hoped was a smile as enigmatic as that of the Mona Lisa, and ran her fingers along his sleeve. It made him uncomfortable and she revelled in that. Albert Cavendish would be waltzing around the dance floor with an elderly lady. She knew this from their previous loops, and as soon as the music stopped, she would wander inside and contrive to collide into him again.

'If you are determined to employ the *modus operandi* of our esteemed French friend, then that poor chap won't know what's hit him. I have a sneaking suspicion that once you unleash your deeply buried feminine wiles, you will reduce any warm-blooded man to mush.'

He gave the familiar grin that so exemplified their teasing, but the joy didn't reach his eyes.

'Although I see little point in pursuing something that will ultimately lead nowhere,' he added.

'Ah, but I will learn so much, much like you with your swimming lessons, and it will stand me in good stead in the future. Besides, I rather like the young man, and can easily hunt him down when all this ridiculousness is over to pursue any romantic intentions.'

She heard him snort, even though he'd turned his head, and was irritated by his conflicting behaviour: teasing and flirtatious, with body language that suggested he was as drawn to her as she was to him, only to back away when there was the slightest opportunity for him to act on his feelings. It was blatantly obvious he didn't like the idea of her approaching Bertie, but she was frustrated by his dog-in-the-manger attitude about the whole thing.

'I shall use my last evening here more *productively* and see what can find out about the legalities connected to the ownership of Highcliffe House,' he said, his sarcastic swipe not lost on her.

'You've missed your vocation,' Pearl commented, as she placed her punch glass on the tray of a passing waiter. 'You should have been a private detective.'

Either he didn't hear her, or his mind had already raced on, because he gave no answer and instead walked off towards a group of elderly men.

Pearl entered the ballroom, spotted her quarry and engineered a collision, which given Bertie had limbs jutting out at every angle, was not hard.

'I'm so sorry.' She engaged her best coquettish expression and bowed her head. 'How unforgivably clumsy of me.'

'Not at all, dear woman. The fault was probably mine. I'm all elbows and knees.' He gave his familiar grin and introduced himself.

'Pearl Pembridge. I'm here with my brother.'

'May I have the pleasure of the next dance, by way of an apology?' he asked. 'Assuming we have your brother's permission, and that between us we manage not to trip each other up?'

'My brother is not my keeper,' she said, 'and I'd be honoured to dance with you.'

As they moved around the dance floor to a lively two-step, hi arm about her body and her face inches from his warm chest, she was disappointed to feel nothing. The recent encounters that he father had so blatantly engineered with Simon had been equall lacklustre, but she had not known – back then – what it wa possible for a man to do to your insides. Dancing with Ellery had been a sensual experience. If she now understood anything, it wa that any romantic connection with a man had a truly physica element, as important, if not more so, than any meeting of th mind. Your body behaved in unsettling ways that you had n control over – as in most emotional situations. Pounding heart rate deeper breathing, unregulated temperatures, and fizzing sensation coursing – unbidden – through every nerve ending. She didn't wan this youngest son of the viscount, and she certainly didn't wan Simon.

Ellery appeared at the edge of the dance floor. He was engage in conversation with a bearded gentleman but his eyes were fixe on her as surely as a hawk latches on to the scurrying field mous on the ground below.

She leaned into the space between herself and Bertie, an raised herself up on her tiptoes to whisper into his ear. It was banal request to step outside for air, but the action was intimate an calculated. And it was designed purely to invoke jealousy. Her lip lingered for too long by his ear, and she sank back to her heels wit her lips still slightly parted and eyes dipped. This flirting lark wa surprisingly easy.

The pair left the ballroom and sauntered out into the warr summer night. It was now heading towards nine o'clock and th Leightons had retreated inside. The light was falling away quickl the last of the blue sky, darker now, clinging to the periphery of th heavens, as the deep yellow glow from the retreating sun, low an warm on the horizon, sucked the vestiges of light from above. It wa a magnificent spectacle to behold, and proof, should she require it, that the blues of the sea and the oranges of fire were perfectly compatible.

They exchanged a few pleasantries, Bertie apologising after most of his comments, and joking at his own ineptitude.

'I wondered if you could do me a favour?' she ventured.

'Of course. How can I oblige? Would you like some punch? Or perhaps I can secure you a seat?'

Dear man. She hoped that some young woman would come to see his worth. He certainly couldn't see it himself.

'I have lived on this earth for nineteen years and never been kissed – not properly. Not by a young man.' She didn't need to articulate the request itself.

'Gosh. That's rather taken a fellow by surprise. Somewhat of a forward proposal.' He looked slightly shocked.

'Sorry.'

'Don't apologise. I'm not usually the sort of chap that girls get excited about. Doesn't help when you have devilishly handsome older brothers and virtually no chance of inheriting the title.' He gave a wan smile. 'For a fellow surrounded by demure and somewhat sedate women, it's all terribly refreshing.' He scanned for spectators. 'But there are quite a number of people on the terrace. You surely don't mean here?'

She spotted Ellery, loitering in the doorway, not quite in the ballroom and not quite outside.

'Oh, I most certainly do. Time is a curious thing,' she said, explaining further. 'None of us know how long we have in this world. Having so recently come through such an unspeakably horrific conflict as a nation, do you not think we should grab opportunities in life when they present themselves?'

Bertie's eyes fell to the floor, where he studied the laces of his black leather shoes in undue detail.

'Lost one of my brothers in the fighting, you know. Oldest two served, and second eldest never came back from East Africa.'

'I'm so very sorry. So many lives were altered by the war, and the shadows of death still hang heavy, cloaking our attempts to move on, but it's exactly why we must snatch moments like this while we can.' She reached out and stroked his arm to demonstrate her sympathy, as he sucked in a fortifying breath.

'Righty ho,' he said, and clasped her awkwardly by the shoulders.

The kiss, when it came, was rather sweet. He was undoubtedly as inexperienced as her, but his touch was soft and his manner gentle. When she next woke in the cave, her lips would revert to being untouched by his but she would at least know, inside, what it felt like, to be held and made love to by a man.

They broke apart and Pearl heard an older lady tut at their public display of affection.

'I say, that was smashing,' Bertie said, as though someone had just bowled a googly. 'I think you're on to something with this grabbing life philosophy.' Pearl couldn't agree more. 'And yet I know so little about you. It would be spiffing to take you out somewhere, introduce you to the olds, have a pretty girl on my arm... that sort of thing.'

She smiled.

'Absolutely. Highcliffe House, Morton Peverell. Ask in the village and they can direct you.' She could have given any address, even a fictional one, because in less than three hours, none of this would matter and poor old Bertie would be as chaste as ever.

'We need to go, dearest sister of mine,' Ellery said, walking towards them, arm outstretched to stress that it wasn't really a request. Was there a frisson of satisfaction that rippled through her as she noticed his obvious irritation? Not used to manipulating people or their emotions (did her father even have emotions?) she felt incredibly smug, but he was right. They needed to return to the house, and she was curious to find out what had transpired when their absence had been noticed.

The two gentlemen nodded at each other and Bertie shouted a cheery, 'Morton Peverell – I'll be in touch,' to her as she retreated inside.

Safely in Standfield's motor car, she decided to tackle Ellery's obvious jealousy.

'I'm not sure why you're so grumpy. You're the one who told me to embrace new experiences. Ever since you got caught up in this bizarre situation, you've been pushing me to be bolder and braver. Telling me to enjoy our predicament, instead of being consumed by anger and fear, like I was before.'

'I've changed my mind. I preferred the old you. You went too far tonight, Pearl.'

'No consequences,' she reminded him, and he huffed, set his face to the road ahead, and they drove back to Highcliffe House in silence.

* * *

When they finally pulled into the driveway, the house was aflame, earlier than she expected. They'd seen the orange glow on the horizon as they approached the coastline, like a volatile and writhing sunset. It still gnawed at her insides to think innocent people were dying every time, even though she knew preventing their deaths was nigh on impossible. If they were currently drugged, as she suspected, it was at least preferable to the poison.

They parked in front of the house as the fire ruthlessly consumed the top floor, and the familiar but gut-wrenching cracks of splintering glass and roars of flame filled the night air. They sat for a while in the motor car and stared helplessly at the devastation before them.

'I'd hoped we'd be back in time to catch someone playing merry hell with a box of matches, but we're too late. Perhaps everyone retires earlier when we aren't there, or the perpetrator is unsettled by things not going to plan.' He paused. 'I realise there are unspeakable horrors going on within, but you have to admit it's a magnificent sight. Fire is so powerful and all-consuming. It's a life force.'

'I strongly disagree. It's destructive, brutal and out of control.'

'Ah, but you love the ocean. We're total opposites.'

'Water is calming and is the real life-giver. Everything needs it to survive and grow.'

'It's just as brutal as fire,' he pointed out. 'You potter about in a bay, on a charming summer afternoon, and think it's a harmless entity, but had you sailed the seas in a raging tempest, you'd understand it is an equally uncontrollable force.'

'I know which of these elements I'd rather have take my life though,' she said, her focus returning to the devastating sight before them, and her heart aching for the souls being extinguished inside.

Ellery must have noticed how her slender fingers gripped white at the edge of the seat, because he reached out to rest his hand on her beaded peacock-coloured knee.

She threw him a glance, touched that he cared. Underneath his cocksure facade, she realised he was a kind soul.

'It's the smell, more than anything,' she whispered, feeling the need to explain. 'Unless you've died in a fire, you wouldn't understand the physical reaction my body has to the bitter smoke.'

'I'm sorry. I wasn't thinking.'

He opened his car door and stepped out into the night, before coming to her side and helping her from the motor vehicle. She jumped her feet down onto the gravel but he didn't release her hand immediately. Instead, he raised it in the space between them and caressed her skin with his thumb. His eyes were unfocused, almost as though he was looking through everything. Suddenly, he let go and ran his hand through his hair.

'Look, there's something I need to do and it's not connected to the Brockhursts or any of this. Can we each do our own thing for one afternoon?'

She frowned. This sudden tangent had thrown her. She wasn't sure how she felt about his request. It had been the pair of them against the world since he'd got himself tangled in her mess. They were a team and the thought he wanted to abandon her, even for one afternoon, was disconcerting. But then perhaps they had been spending too much time together – goodness, they weren't even apart to sleep, because the night never came. They'd literally been together for days on end.

'You don't need my permission.'

'No,' he conceded, 'but we're a partnership and I don't want you thinking I'm up to anything. I'm certain that between us we can get to the bottom of everything that's going on, but I have to resolve this unconnected matter first, just in case we really are stuck like this forever.'

The pleading in his eyes was apparent.

'But it won't be resolved, will it? Whatever you are setting off to do tomorrow, will be reset like everything else.'

'I can't explain. Just trust me.'

'All right.' She shrugged. She had no choice.

He stretched his arm out to expose his wrist and glanced at the time. She'd not paid much attention to his watch before, but a metal guard protected the glass face and Pearl thought it looked like the petals of a flower, each teardrop shape revealing the glowing numeral beneath. He noticed her interest.

'It was my father's. He wore it on the battlefields – far more

practical than pocket watches in the trenches. It got sent to u
along with all his other personal effects after he...' It wasn't possib
for him to finish the sentence.

'I'm so sorry,' she whispered.

'Take care of yourself tomorrow,' he said, and she had th
strangest feeling he wanted to reach out and touch her face. Sh
saw his hand twitch, but it stayed by his side. 'Spend it at the cov
or steal some food from the pantry and just keep walking. I dor
want to think of you suffering.' His expression was deadly serious.

She nodded.

'I'm chilly. Will you put your arms about me?' she asked. 'Ju
for the time we have left?'

She stepped closer and their sides touched.

'No, you aren't, but yes I will.' He draped his arm about her ar
pulled her close.

And, as they stood together, counting down until the day wou
reset, every cell in her body cried out for him to kiss her, eve
though she knew he wouldn't.

She just didn't know why.

26

The moment Pearl opened her eyes in the cave, she jumped to her feet and raced out onto the beach and up the steps to the house. But, by the time she'd reached the boot room, it was empty and a half-polished candlestick stood abandoned on the table.

She scampered back into the hall and flung open the front door. Standfield's Austin was nowhere to be seen: Ellery was already gone. There was no way to follow him, and no way of knowing where he was. It also occurred to her that without the motor car she couldn't escape the house that afternoon, unless she walked, as he'd suggested.

After so many days of hedonistic pleasure, perhaps it would do her good to stay at Highcliffe House. It wasn't that her body was exhausted – every time she awoke, she felt as fresh as the day she'd first slipped on the cave floor – but more that her mind was so busy and full, that a day doing very little might make a pleasant change. She'd been so focused when she'd been alone in the loop, finding ways to survive and desperate to work out how the fire had started, but Ellery's presence had distracted her, with his strong arms, bold statements and warm eyes.

Despite his suggestion she should stay safe and perhaps have a quiet afternoon at the cove, she decided not to play the role of the helpless female, awaiting his return before anything productive could be achieved. Instead, *she* would confront the guests, and ask those awkward questions they'd talked about. She was a bolder person now than she'd been that morning, so many days ago, and there was no reason she couldn't pursue some aggressive questioning. What was the worst that could happen? Even death itself held no fear for her now.

She returned to the garden and found Standfield on the terrace. Having ignored him moments before when she'd raced through the drawing room to find Ellery, she plastered a false smile across her face and approached the table.

'Ah, Paula, there you are.' He got to his feet as manners dictated and gestured for her to take a seat. His face lit up as she produced an unopened bottle of wine and a corkscrew. She'd taken it from the dining room on her way back from the hallway.

'I say, nicely done! There's still half a bottle here, but this looks a cheeky little number. Let's pop her open and see what she's got. I was going to ring for that lad, or Mrs Dawson, but I see you are a girl after my own heart. Need something to liven things up a bit. It's a dull old affair and no mistake. Been swimming?' His eyes scanned her attire.

'What? Oh, yes. I really should change but it's such a splendid afternoon and I thought sitting on the terrace with a little drink might warm me up.'

'Excellent. Excellent.' Clearly adept at opening bottles, he had the cork out in no time and, reaching for an empty glass, poured her a generous measure. 'Down the hatch!'

Although Pearl had been drinking more in these repeated afternoons than she had in her whole life up until that point, the body she now occupied was as unused to alcohol as the day she'd first arrived – largely because this *was* the day she'd first arrived. She would have to watch herself or she'd give Standfield the wrong idea again.

'Must ask that Ellery chap for his help dressing for dinner later on, although between you and me, I don't think he really knows what he's doing. Think this might be his first position in service. Plus, I can't shake the feeling I've seen him somewhere before.' He frowned and finished up the wine in his glass. 'Whole blasted thing smells fishy to me.' His familiar words echoed around her head.

'Doesn't it just?' she mused. 'But then I suspect everyone is hiding things, including you. I met the Leightons at some social function recently...' she waved her hand in the dismissive manner that she'd seen Céline employ so many times '...and they mentioned in passing how well you knew the Brockhursts or, more accurately, Lenora...'

Her announcement took him by surprise and he choked on his mouthful of wine.

'You're acquainted with the Leightons?' he asked, genuinely surprised. 'I thought you were from Suffolk.'

'You know how it is, darling,' she said, embracing her role. Having worn Céline's dress so many times, and played the part of the fictional Lady Pembridge, she slipped into this more confident personality quite easily now. The wine helped. 'One gets invited to parties and such.'

He put down his glass and peered at her.

'That swim has perked you up no end. It's like a different girl has appeared at the table. You came across as such a shrinking violet this morning, but perhaps you are a rampaging bramble. Do I need to watch out for your vicious thorns?' he joked.

Pearl shrugged. 'Did you keep in touch with Lenora after she broke your heart? Oh, I forget, of course you did – you couldn't leave the poor woman alone.'

Standfield's jovial mood disappeared in an instant. He narrowed his eyes even further and paused before answering. 'Hmmm, so you *are* capable of giving a nasty little prick. I don't know what your father has told you but I won't be blackmailed by a chit of a girl like yourself. Whatever you know, or think you know, I can assure you that antagonising me is not advisable. Once you open up the box, things will tumble out that can't be tossed back in.' His tone was surprisingly menacing, but Pearl was on a roll.

'She promised to marry you, and then met Virgil Brockhurst, and your world collapsed. Was that when the drinking started?'

Standfield's rosy face went even redder, as his nostrils flared alarmingly, and he stood up to walk away. 'I don't have to stay here and listen to all this. Where is your father? We need words.'

'Resting in his room, I believe.' Almost shaking but determined not to be brushed off, she rose to challenge him. 'What happened to her, Mr Standfield? Did you determine that if you couldn't have her no one could?' she said, meeting and holding his eye.

'Tread carefully, young lady, because if you bring me down, you bring your father down too,' he warned, before storming into the house.

He was threatening her, telling her to back off and, for the first time, she was genuinely unnerved by him. What did this odious man have over her father? Because Standfield had just confirmed what Pearl had suspected from the start – her father had done something worthy of blackmail.

* * *

Pearl was determined to confront Céline whilst she still had the courage. As she swung into the enclosed garden, the older lady was standing to leave. Aldo had long since retreated to the summer house, and his wife was now planning to return to the house.

'Darling, how lovely. Have you been to the cove?' She smiled at the young girl. 'It is a picturesque little place, *non*?' This time, Pearl would not be sidetracked by small talk.

'Are the Brockhursts blackmailing you?' She had no interest in lilly-dallying with polite conversation.

'What do you mean, darling?' Céline adjusted her silk turban as part of her stalling tactic.

'The question is simple enough. I don't like the way we've been gathered here, like lambs for slaughter. Everyone has secrets and I believe the person who organised this party knows what they are.'

'We are all concealing things – that I agree with.' Céline slid a cigarette from a slender mother-of-pearl case. 'You included, it would seem. I saw you steal the pocket watch when I was passing down the hallway and you were at the open bureau.' Satisfied she had sufficiently disconcerted the young Miss Glenham, the French-woman flicked a delicate silver lighter and lit her cigarette. 'Pre-tending to be all meek and *innocente* and now you stand before me, revealing your true colours. It was a convincing act and I applaud you.'

Pearl may have been meek and innocent that morning, but she wasn't going to let this arrogant woman make her feel inferior any more.

'And you have a seventeenth-century Persian bowl in your room upstairs, so are hardly in a place to cast stones.'

Céline's eyes briefly flashed wide, before she composed herself and plucked the smallest piece of stray tobacco from her lips. 'A snoop as well as an accomplished actress. Interesting.'

'Are you here for the treasures?' Pearl asked. 'The stone tablets, the Egyptian urns, the clepsydra?'

Now she really had the older woman's attention. Céline's whole body stiffened. 'You have seen these things?' she asked. 'Where are they?' Her eyebrow rose the tiniest fraction of an inch – almost

indiscernibly – but Pearl spotted it. This was an interesting develop
ment. Pearl realised Céline didn't know about the cave. Perhaps the
only person who did was Bernard. Was that what he'd meant when
he said he had to keep everything safe?

'I can cut you in... make it worth your while? It is clear to m
you and your father have little money. Let's talk?'

'I'm not interested.' Pearl's biggest fear was that letting anyon
else near the clepsydra would risk messing with time even more
Two people stuck in the loop was more than sufficient. It wa
imperative no one else was sucked into their predicament.

'Even if money holds no interest, you strike me as a young lad
most *morale* – your thieving tendencies aside. You must understan
that what Virgil was doing was wrong. Many of these artefacts hav
been taken from their rightful owners. They were bought as mer
curiosities, a way for that ignorant American to flaunt his wealt
and feel important, when these objects have powers that you woul
not believe.'

'You'd be surprised what I believe,' Pearl said. 'And I agree wit
you. Perhaps when this nightmare is over, I will try to engineer tha
these items are returned to their rightful owners, but I won't b
charging money to do so.'

Céline lunged for Pearl and grabbed at the collar of her bathin
robe, pulling the young girl's face close to her own.

'Where are these things? Tell me this instant. You don't want t
mess with me, *ma chère*. I always get what I want, and will emplo
any means necessary to ensure that I do.' Her eyes were fierce an
her tone all the more menacing for its softness.

'Actually,' Pearl said, gripping the Frenchwoman's hand, an
removing it from her clothing, even though her insides wer
shaking and her heart was doing nineteen to the dozen, 'you dor
want to mess with me. I do not bow to threats, and even death hol
no fear – not any more. You might like to consider that if I know th

whereabouts of these coveted objects, I am also informed of their powers. You need to be aware that I'm not the only one who knows what's going on here. Bring me down and there are others waiting in the wings who will take my place.'

Much like with Standfield, it was the first time in all these repeating afternoons that Céline had revealed her true colours – and they were ugly and dark. Pearl had pushed them both into a corner and they had turned about and clawed at her. It was also the first time she'd had a serious conversation with Signora Ravello about the historical curiosities and treasures that Virgil had amassed. This was what the unscrupulous Frenchwoman was here for, Pearl realised. And it appeared that she would go to any lengths to get her hands on them.

She locked eyes with Céline, using every ounce of her new-found courage, and attempted to out-stare her companion.

'Very well. I shall play along for the moment, but I have clearly underestimated Raymond, and I am cross at myself for making such an error.'

Pearl sighed inwardly. 'My father knows nothing of this. It's *me* who you have underestimated. He is as bewildered as you by the invitation. Someone has gathered everyone here to enact revenge; placed you together in a remote house on the Dorset coast, where they can dispose of you all as they will. Perhaps they shall use poison, perhaps set fire to the house as you all sleep. But, mark my words, they will see you dead.'

'Then you win,' Céline said, waving her hands in capitulation. 'How much is it that you want? I have money and you clearly don't. Name your sum and you shall be paid.'

Pearl frowned.

'You are behind all this – the invitation, the threats. And Raymond? He was always so calculating.'

There. She had it. Proof that there was a connection between this unpleasant woman and her father. But she also had to consider that either Céline was the most accomplished bluffer to ever exist, or she was not responsible for the gathering.

So, if Céline hadn't started the fire, and it was a big if, who was left?

She'd witnessed her father, Standfield and Mrs Dawson die, Ellery was unlikely to be behind it as he'd tried to save everyone before he'd been caught in the loop, but Aldo, the Brockhursts, and even their son (who would surely be a grown man by now), were still possibilities. But the question remained: what had the guests at Highcliffe House done that was so bad they deserved to die?

27

After bumping into a furious Mrs Dawson in the hallway, who had found a note from Ellery telling her he'd quit with little explanation, Pearl returned to her bedroom to change. No one had noticed the missing motor car yet, but it wouldn't be long. She slipped her dress back on and wondered if she'd been overly blunt with her questioning. As with all things, there was a balance, but she'd alienated Céline and Standfield by being too confrontational. What more could she achieve in this loop? Aldo couldn't speak English, and she doubted there was anything useful she could get from Mrs Dawson, who was always the first to die in the fire and the only person, apart from herself and possibly Aldo, who had no obvious connection to the Brockhursts. Ellery was hiding something but he wasn't a killer, and Standfield had stormed upstairs and was currently in her father's room, doubtless accusing him of all sorts. She could hear the rumble of their voices through the wall.

In the end, she decided to walk into Morton Peverell. Perhaps the locals had more information about Virgil and Lenora. She knew from the Crawleys' experience that gossip spread fast in small communities. Someone might know Bernard's background, why he might have access to Virgil's treasures, or have seen any unusual comings or goings over the previous week. She'd been too busy nibbling currant buns and playing Lady Pembridge to question anyone when they'd stopped at the tea rooms. Besides, a couple swanning about in their evening finery were unlikely to invite confidences. A last-minute thought occurred to her and she slipped into Standfield's room and retrieved the money, which was still on his dressing table. Ellery obviously didn't need funds for whatever he was up to, then.

She crept from his room, pausing outside her father's door to hear low male voices.

'Damn it, man, I've not slept properly for twenty years because of the guilt. Whatever it is you think I've told Pearl, I can assure you that I haven't, and I don't much like the tone of your voice. I will not have unfounded accusations flung at me and would ask that you leave.'

The unpalatable possibility that her father had been involved in the disappearance of some or all of the Brockhursts resurfaced.

She heard footsteps approaching the door and ducked back into her own room. As Standfield stormed down the corridor, she could only focus on the news that her father had done something terrible all those years ago, and tried not to contemplate the possibility it involved the taking of a human life.

Or maybe even three.

* * *

It took nearly half an hour to walk the winding, undulating lane into the village. She knew the route well, having driven it with Ellery on several occasions now. The peaceful nature of such a solitary walk was welcome and not one single breath of the fresh air was taken for granted since her first horrifying night at the house.

There was the rumble of a motor vehicle in the distance and, as it approached, she recognised the distinctive livery of the grocer. Mr Lane slowed down and poked his head out the window.

'Can I give you a lift, love?' he asked. 'Are you heading back into the village?' He must have thought it odd, having only dropped her and her father off at the house a few hours previously.

'That's very kind of you but I'm enjoying the walk.'

'No problem, miss.' He doffed his cap and the van trundled away.

Her mind went back to their encounter with his wife, and a thought occurred to her. Mrs Lane had mistaken her father for someone else – someone from years ago... What if it wasn't a mistake? *What if her father wasn't who he said he was?*

She picked up her pace and regretted turning down the lift.

Arriving in the village, she headed straight for the store – which was just as gloomy inside as it had been that morning. The tiny bell hanging over the door tinkled to announce her arrival and Mr Lane's wife appeared from the back of the shop.

'Hello again, miss. Did you forget something? Gerry said he'd passed you on the coast road not ten minutes ago.'

'Not at all. I've had a splendid lunch at Highcliffe House, and bathed in the sea, but am at my leisure until dinner this evening and I fancied a walk. This really is such a lovely part of the country. I was only popping in to ask you about something you said earlier...'

'Oh?'

'You confused my father with a Mr Hardinger?'

The woman nodded. 'My mistake. It was such a long time ago.'

'I'm not sure it was a mistake. You see, my father's cousin bears an uncanny resemblance to him, and has connections in this part of the world. We lost touch with him for reasons of a personal nature, and it occurred to me that it may be this cousin that you were confusing my father with.'

The last stretch of the walk had been perfect thinking time for Pearl. Recognising that most women enjoyed a bit of gossip, she needed a plausible reason that the older lady might have mistaken her father for Mr Hardinger, without exposing him, *and* explaining away the different surnames. This tale might be a way to get Mrs Lane to open up.

The grocer's wife became quite animated and leaned forward conspiratorially, across the counter. Suspecting useful information was to be delivered, Pearl stepped closer.

'That may well be it,' she concluded. 'Mr Hardinger was in the employ of the Brockhursts, oh, I'm going back maybe thirty years. Some sort of accountant, I believe.' With the similarity in profession, she was now certain Mrs Lane was talking of her father. 'Used to work for old Mr Warren, and then did the estate accounts for Lenora and her husband when she married. Quite a well-off young man. Always smartly turned out and quite fastidious, by all accounts. But not much of a talker, if you know what I mean. No lady friends to speak of.' Apart from having money, Mrs Lane was describing her father to a tee.

'And what happened to him?'

Mrs Lane shrugged. 'We didn't see him very often. He would stay at Highcliffe House when there were financial matters to attend to. I think his company was based in Dorchester, but I don't know more than that. I've certainly not seen him since the Brockhursts left.'

'And was he staying with them on their last visit?'

'Twenty years is a long time,' the older lady apologised. 'I couldn't say with any certainty, but if your father wants to re-establish contact with his cousin, I suggest tracking down the accountancy firm. He may even still be in their employ.'

Pearl gave an earnest nod. 'It is so strange that we should find ourselves staying at Highcliffe House all this time later,' she said.

'Sometimes it's such a small world,' Mrs Lane added, sagely.

'Isn't it just?' she agreed, thinking her world was currently smaller than most. 'Do you know much about the current owner, Mr Badgerwood?'

'Nothing, I'm afraid. All his dealings with us have been via letter, and he's paid ahead every time. Gerry thought there was someone up the big house a couple of weeks ago, but it was probably just Bernard. He lives in the old gamekeeper's cottage in the woods – I say cottage, but it's more of a shack.'

'Bernard lives on the estate?' This was a surprise. She'd thought he was local and wandering around in places he had no right to be.

'Old Bernard was someone Lenora took pity on – she was kind like that. He was a bit simple, difficult to get any sense out of him, and he never could read or write much, but she persuaded her father to take him on, and he doted on her. So much so, I gather it got a bit awkward when she married, but Virgil won him over. Feel a bit rotten really. Think he's been underestimated by the villagers because he talks rubbish, but he's good at following straightforward instructions, apparently, and the Brockhursts always trusted him to care for the place when they were away. He has keys to the house and keeps everything ticking over.'

So, it was Bernard who'd painted the summer house that lovely pale green, kept the lawns and flower borders neat, and stopped the house from falling into disrepair. But why keep those valuable artefacts in the cave? And then she thought of Céline. These objects were the controversial ones, the things Virgil knew he shouldn't have, or that were coveted by others for whatever reason. Bernard was keeping them safe.

'You get less sense out of him as the years go by,' Mrs Lane added, 'but the poor chap always insists she'll return and mutters about keeping it nice for her. He ain't no trouble really, and seems to manage on the money sent by the bank every month, so he's just been left to it. One of the ladies from the church checks on him from time to time, and Constable Carter keeps an eye on the place.'

Pearl remembered Bernard's insistence that 'she' wasn't dead. Eurgh... every time she advanced a few paces with her enquiries, it was promptly followed by a stumble backwards. If he was insisting Lenora was alive, didn't it rather imply that her husband and son were dead? Or was that a massive jump? If their deaths had been at someone else's hand, it would certainly give Lenora a reason to exact revenge. Perhaps she'd even enlisted the help of the loyal Bernard.

'And Harlow Standfield?' she asked. 'I understand he had his heart broken by Lenora?' Was he distraught enough to do something silly?

Mrs Lane, who'd been happy to pass the day with a little gossip, became somewhat wary. 'Look here, why exactly are you asking all these questions? You're just a guest at the house. I can understand wanting to trace a cousin of your father's, but this is all a bit much, to my mind.' She blinked at Pearl, as though sizing her up. 'You don't work for one of those newspapers, do you? We've had that sort sniffing around before. I don't want no trouble, and certainly don't want to drag poor Lenora through the mud. A bit wild, but a kind woman.'

Pearl had overplayed her hand again and roused this lady's suspicions.

'No, I'm not with the papers,' she confirmed, but she'd lost the woman's confidence now with her impertinent questions.

'Do you be wanting something from the shop, or not?' Mrs Lane challenged, folding her arms across her aproned chest.

'Um, yes, a quarter of sherbet lemons, please.'

Pearl paid for her confectionery and decided a little more

subtlety was needed from now on. She paid a visit to the tea rooms and the waitress confirmed that Bernard was the only member of staff Lenora had retained, because their travelling meant they were at Highcliffe House so infrequently. There had been a woman from the village whom the Brockhursts regularly called on to act as cook-cum-housekeeper when they were in England – although she'd long since died. And there were always local girls who would willingly earn pin money undertaking housemaid duties, or serving when they held dinner parties. No one could quite remember who, it was all so long ago, and it briefly crossed Pearl's mind that perhaps Mrs Dawson had been employed on a casual basis back then, and that's why she'd been asked to return for this event. She professed not to be local, but perhaps she meant that she wasn't local now. She'd told Pearl that she didn't know the Brockhursts, but she could be lying. Perhaps she'd seen something that summer, or someone suspected that she had, and that's why she was killed, along with everyone else.

But the most interesting titbit was picked up from two elderly women whom Pearl sat with on a wooden bench at the churchyard. They were both lamenting the loss of grandsons in the war, and often tended the recently erected memorial together of a Saturday, finding solace in their shared grief. It turned out they both also shared a love of sherbet lemons.

They told Pearl that Lenora's former nanny, a Mrs Coombes, had been a neighbour of theirs, and was contacted by the young Mrs Brockhurst back in the February of 1903. Lenora was expecting a baby and confided that she and her husband intended to settle in England for a while, certainly until the child was of school age. She offered the former servant a permanent position nursing the baby – which she'd accepted – but the child came early, and Coombes was out of the county when they arrived back at Highcliffe House. When she finally returned to Morton Peverell, she found to her surprise the Brockhursts had left for foreign adventures again, without so much as a word, and she told anyone who would listen that strange things were afoot.

Neither of the ladies knew where Mrs Coombes might be living now, or even if she was still alive, and Pearl learned very little of use during the remainder of the afternoon.

As the sun began to sink towards the horizon, she decided to head back to Highcliffe House and see if Ellery had returned from his mysterious trip. She'd missed him and felt that had he been with her, she wouldn't have made so many mistakes with her questions. They balanced each other perfectly, she realised.

She walked along the cliff path, choosing this route rather than the road, and focused on the chalky whiteness of the ground beneath her feet, picked out by the half-light. Looking ahead, she noticed a figure approaching from the opposite direction. It was clearly a poacher, as he was wearing an oversized coat that was surplus to requirements on such a balmy July night. She just knew the deep interior pockets would be stuffed with dead rabbits and hares.

'On your own, missy?' he asked, rolling a cigarette as she approached.

Prickles of fear immediately travelled up her arms and around the back of her neck. How foolish she'd been to undertake the walk alone. They were at least a mile from the nearest house and totally isolated. She had made herself vulnerable. The waves crashed into the rocks below and the breeze from the sea tugged at her dress.

He stepped from the shadows and onto the path, blocking her way. She could smell alcohol on his breath and a staleness that came from being unwashed.

'I don't have any money on me, if that's what you're after.' It was a lie. She had Standfield's roll of notes in her pocket but was damned if she was about to hand it over. Compliant Pearl was no more.

'Well, now, I'm a bit down on my luck, see? And I'm fairly disappointed to find you without. So, I be thinking that perhaps you can give me something else... something that wouldn't cost you. Something that might warm us both up a bit.'

Once she realised where this was heading, she was surprised how focused her mind became. She briefly contemplated making a dash for it, but knew that if he caught her, he would easily overpower her.

If Ellery had taught her anything, it was to take control of her own destiny.

A low groan of anticipation came from the man, as he raised his eyebrows suggestively, and the ocean spoke to her in the background.

'I will not be the victim here,' she said, and turned towards the cliffs, running the short distance to the edge and leaping into the darkness, much to the horror and total confusion of the poacher, who stared open-mouthed as she disappeared.

'It was just my little joke,' he said into the night air.

28

Not five minutes later, Pearl climbed the cove steps back up to the house, and saw Ellery coming down the path, gesturing for her to turn back. They passed through the gate together and returned to the beach.

He had only been away for a few hours, but she was relieved and unexpectedly emotional to see him again. Yes, she was a much more independent young lady than when she'd arrived at High cliffe House, but the encounter of the previous night had reminded her that, as a female, she was still incredibly vulnerable in today's male-dominated world. Men would, sadly, always have a physical advantage over women.

'I've so much to tell you,' she said, skipping across the shingle, trying to keep up with his long strides, her bathing robe flapping as she went. He was unusually silent as she filled him in on everything she'd gleaned in Morton Peverell, leaving out the part about the poacher – undoubtedly her quickest and most satisfying death. She reached the cave entrance and turned to face him, only to find he was giving her the most intense look.

'Did you hear what I said?' she asked. 'Céline revealed her true colours and is as scary as the devil himself, but I don't think she was behind the invitations... What?'

Ellery's stare was unnerving her now. He hadn't said a word as she'd merrily chattered on about her day. His eyes pinned hers, his breaths slow and focused. Her stomach began to churn. He was building up to something – she was certain of it. Where had he gone for a whole afternoon without her? What had he been up to?

'Look at how you've changed during our short acquaintance. Confronting scary Frenchwomen and taking yourself off to the village alone. I knew there was a strong woman lurking beneath that meek exterior, Pearl Glenham.'

Woman. That was a noticeable improvement in how he viewed her.

'Have you uncovered something, too? Are the Brockhursts dead? Do you know who started the fire?'

'My afternoon was nothing to do with Highcliffe House. I told you that. It was about something far more important.'

'What is more important than preventing the murder of six people and solving a twenty-year-old mystery?'

Did she imagine a slight upturn of the mouth before he spoke? An extra twinkle flash across his eyes?

'You.'

He cast his eyes about to check that they were alone and then stepped forward and put his hands about her face, before leaning towards her and finally placing his mouth over hers.

Her whole time in Dorset had been a series of unexpected events, brutal deaths and shocking revelations – but nothing had prepared her for this. Too stunned to do anything other than let her hands drop to her sides and engage her own lips with his, she was swept up by what was happening. She'd been dreaming about this for so long that she could hardly believe it was real. The first kiss made her melt, her knees as dizzy as her head, and a wave – not unlike seasickness, but infinitely more pleasant – washed over her. He pulled away a fraction and allowed his bottom lip to drag across her lips, before pushing back into her. Teasing and toying, their mouths found a hundred different ways to connect, and each one was more thrilling than the last.

Fearing her legs would give way under her if these relentless and heady sensations didn't cease, she slid her arms about his waist to anchor herself. Encouraged by her response, he pulled her shoulders towards his body, locking them together in an intensely intimate way.

Eventually the kisses halted, which was somewhat of a relief because her poor body was on the verge of exploding, and she opened her eyes to find him staring down into her face. Oh my goodness – those eyes. The sun behind her reflected back in those amber irises, veritable pools of fire.

'I've wanted to do that for so long,' he finally said, breaking the silence. 'You can't know how much this impossible situation has been eating me up.'

'I wouldn't have stopped you,' she replied, confused. 'That night when we sat together in the memorial garden...'

She was breathless but happy. He had finally made the move she'd been waiting days for. He was the other half to her whole. The mirror to herself. Apart, she was confused and lacking. Together, they made sense. If she was to be stuck in this repeating existence forever, she knew it would be bearable with him by her side.

'I couldn't. It would have been wrong.'

'Why? Because we haven't known each other long enough? Because I'm too young? Unchaperoned? What?'

'Because I'm engaged to be married.'

And Pearl's whole world froze. Ironic, considering time had been a relentless barrage for days now.

29

'We've been together all this time and you never thought to mention this?' Pearl was horrified, and took a step back.

'It was difficult,' he said. 'You tell me when I should have dropped that information into the conversation. Certainly not when you arrived at Highcliffe House. "Hello, Miss Glenham. I'm Ellery Brown – at your service for the duration of your stay. Luncheon will be served on the terrace shortly, dinner is at seven, and I'm engaged to be married".'

But the stronger, bolder Pearl wasn't going to let him off the hook that easily. She was furious and had no desire to hide it. 'Perhaps when you fell into the loop, and the possibility that we might be spending eternity together crossed your mind? Or maybe when we shared that moment in the gardens at Burbridge Manor, and you pulled away, leaving me feeling empty, confused and foolish.'

He ran his hand through his dark hair. 'But I've told you *now*. I realised there was something between us and I've done the right thing, so that this can happen. I can't bear spending all this time with you and not be able to touch you, hold you, kiss you, when it's all I think about from when I find myself staring at a half-buffed candlestick, to the moment everything goes black at the end of the day.'

He moved towards her, perhaps hoping to kiss her again, but she took another step backwards.

'And what? You sought out your fiancée yesterday, broke her heart by calling the engagement off, and now think it's fine to start wooing me, when technically, you are still engaged at this very moment?'

'Yes.'

They stared at each other for a moment before she shook her head, turned towards the house, and stormed across the beach. He made no attempt to follow her as she climbed the steps and, as she strode up the path to the strains of the Ravellos' quarrel, she took a right and decided to join Standfield for a drink.

She felt she needed one, and knew he'd be delighted to have the young Paula join him.

* * *

Pearl and Standfield sunk the remaining wine in record time. Yes, she had been swimming. Yes, the whole blasted affair *did* smell fishy to her. And no, she wasn't looking to settle down, regardless of the size of any allowance that he might be gracious enough to bestow.

Ellery appeared as the last dribbles of the bottle were tipped into Standfield's glass. She could only assume he'd remained on the beach for a while to ponder his folly.

'Aha! Brown. Couldn't fetch us another one of these, could you?' Standfield waved the empty bottle in the air. Ellery nodded and disappeared into the house. He returned moments later, with an open bottle and an extra glass, and pulled out a chair, as Pearl studiously avoided eye contact.

'I say. What do you think you're doing, young man? You're staff. Really! I'm not convinced you're cut out for this line of work. All morning your attitude has been decidedly off. Just wait until Badgerwood arrives – I shall be having words.'

'*He isn't coming*,' they said in unison.

'Badgerwood is an attempt to disguise the name Brockhurst,' Pearl went on to explain in a monotone voice but with no real enthusiasm for her subject. 'I think Virgil and Lenora are back from their travels and out for revenge.'

She picked at a splinter of wood on the edge of the table, focusing on anything but the young man who had just turned her insides to blancmange at the cove, as Standfield spat out an 'utter nonsense' from beside her.

Ellery topped up Pearl's empty glass and then poured himself one – although not, she noticed, Standfield. He held the stem and swirled the contents around, staring at the whirlpool of pale yellow, as though considering what to say next.

'Her name is Ruby. We met a couple of years ago at a dance. Her parents have always been keen to rush us up the aisle, but in my heart, I know we've been drifting along. The very fact neither of us seemed in any hurry to set a date was a sure sign.'

'Get up from the goddamn table, man,' Standfield almost shouted, furious at being ignored, his face red and beads of perspiration now running down his forehead. It was hot and he was rattled. 'It is not appropriate for you to join us, or for you to talk to Miss Glenham in such a familiar fashion. I'm certain she has no interest in your love life. Where is Dawson?'

'So, you told her you wanted to break it off?' She paid no attention to the blusterings beside her, and narrowed her eyes at the young man sitting opposite.

'I told her I'd met someone and fallen in love.'

'Love? Love? What are you wittering on about, boy?'

It was a bold statement and she suspected, by the slightly scared look on his face, a massive admission for him to make, but Pearl was too cross to appreciate the significance of the moment. She felt betrayed by the only person, other than her father, whom she trusted at this house.

'She asked who you were and when we met – the only part of the conversation when I thought she was going to cry, because I told the truth; I'd met you this morning and you were a guest at Highcliffe House.' He shook his head. 'It was a tough one. I could hardly say we'd known each other for over two weeks and been in each other's company practically every hour of the day since then. And she huffed and said she wasn't sure she wanted to be with someone so fickle, and breaking it off was fine by her, but I knew from her face that she was just as relieved as me.'

'You can't be sure of that.' Pearl knew full well that pretending an undesired outcome was welcome was a form of self-defence. Had this Ruby put on a brave face to *save* face?

'I rather feel I'm being ignored,' Standfield grumbled to no one in particular. He stood up and stomped into the house.

'As far as I'm concerned, you're still engaged to be married.'

'Fine,' Ellery said, taking an enormous swig from his glass. 'And if we're stuck in this forever, you can be all righteous and keep your distance until the end of time. I do so hope that your morals keep you company, day after day after day, if you won't let me be there for you. I've tried to do the right thing and make everything good.'

'Nothing about this whole mess is good,' she said, as her father stepped out on to the terrace, followed by Standfield. Frustrated by their peculiar behaviour, Harlow had clearly gone in search of reinforcements.

'What have you done to my daughter? What mess? Have you interfered with her in some way, boy?'

'Damn Lothario, from what I gather,' Standfield said, unhelpfully.

Pearl dropped her head into her hands and willed everyone to go away, as her father took in her attire.

'Dressed like that you are rather inviting unwanted attention,' he pointed out. 'Is that scandalous article your bathing suit? What do you expect, when you fraternise with servants?'

Slowly, Pearl scraped her chair back and rose to her feet, turning so that she was face to face with her father.

'You lied to me.' It took every ounce of self-control to keep her voice level and calm. 'You said that you had never been to Highcliffe House before, and that you didn't know the Brockhursts, and yet I find out that your real name is Mr Hardinger, and you, in fact, worked for Mr Warren *for years*. How could you?' She narrowed her eyes at the same time as her father's expanded, his foot tapping in agitation. 'So, don't you dare presume to tell me what to do or who to associate with. I don't even know you.'

'And I clearly don't know you. How dare you speak to me like that. I'm your father. Everything I have done has been to keep us... you safe.'

'Safe?' She was incredulous. 'This is *the* most dangerous place you have ever taken me to in my entire life. You've dragged me halfway across the country, and I still don't know why. What *exactly* does Mr Badgerwood have over you? Why are we here?' she asked, wanting him to supply a rational explanation and for all her suspicions to be unfounded, but his face returned to the unreadable expression he wore so often. She would get no answer from him.

'I say, we can't have her poking her nose into things that don't concern her, Raymond,' Standfield interjected. 'You said she was a quiet thing, but out of nowhere, she's returned from the cove like a woman possessed. Do keep her in check – there's a good fellow.'

It was the final straw.

'We're going, Ellery,' she said. 'Give me five minutes to change, and then we are out of here.'

Suddenly, her friend was the lesser of two evils. At least he hadn't lied to her face, but rather by omission. And when she'd confronted him, he had explained his reasons. Her father wouldn't even respond to her direct questions.

'You can't go off with him. Be sensible, Pearl. Your virtue is at stake.'

'Oh, I dearly hope so,' she said, and strutted into the house.

'I understand why you're cross with me,' Ellery said, holding open the door to the motor car as she stepped inside. 'But let's put that aside for the moment. I realised something in the cove just now when you were telling me about your day. I've visited that Mrs Coombes you mentioned before, Lenora's former nanny. We need to speak to her again, but it's a fair way so must leave now – at least two hours in the motor car.'

Mrs Coombes apparently lived in Hampshire and as Standfield's Austin Twenty sailed northwards, Ellery filled Pearl in on the details.

'I spoke to her months ago, when I was first interested in Lenora and Virgil, but we have more questions now.'

She looked sideways at him, his profile set to the road, perhaps not realising the significance of what he'd said. His fascination with them was more than a passing interest.

'How old are you?' she asked, wondering if he could possibly be the missing Brockhurst baby. Was he the inside man, whilst his mother orchestrated everything from outside? Was that why he'd lodged at the Fisherman's Arms, to avoid danger when the house was ablaze?

'Twenty-five. Why?'

'No reason. I realised I didn't know, that's all.'

Of course he wasn't, she chided herself, even though his keen interest in Highcliffe House clearly went beyond that of a curious local.

'So, why would you have cause to speak to an elderly lady connected to the Brockhursts? Are you related to them in some way?'

'Not at all, just a young man whose imagination was captured by their strange disappearance. I have a curious mind – you know that. Even as an adolescent, I was forever poring over my father's newspapers at the kitchen table. Particularly loved the juicy murders and society scandals. Do you not wonder at the truth that lies behind every story? I spent months researching the *Titanic* and even have my own theories as to who is responsible for the Whitechapel murders.'

'Then perhaps you should be writing books,' she suggested.

'One day, perhaps I might.' He flashed her a grin before returning his focus to the road, and for the next two hours, he proceeded to tell her his theories on the great unsolved mysteries of the last century.

* * *

Mrs Coombes was surprised to get a visit on a hot July Saturday afternoon but rustled up her guests some tea and cake. They sat in her pretty wildflower garden, although they had to move the table when they realised it was close to the fly-covered corpse of a small rabbit in the brambles, most likely deposited by the tabby cat that sat watching them from the top of the high fence.

The woman really was quite elderly. Her lined face and stooped posture betrayed her years, but she was of lively mind and cheery disposition. Ellery explained they were here to learn more about the Brockhursts and wondered if she would share her tales of the young Miss Warren.

'Lovely girl, she was. And such a mischief as a child.' She chuckled. 'Forever getting into scrapes or disappearing for hours without letting anyone know where she'd gone. "I can't help myself, Nanny," she'd say. "When a thing needs to be explored, I have to be the one to do it." Sometimes that thing was a tall oak, and she'd sit in the boughs until it was time for her tea. Sometimes it was a tumbledown house that she might spend an afternoon pretending was hers. A whimsical young girl but a temperamental adolescent. Her father quite despaired of her at times.'

She nibbled at the slice of fruit cake on the tea plate before her. 'We talked about most of this when you visited before. Is the book not finished?'

So he *was* writing a book. Ellery must have felt the heat of Pearl's gaze boring into him because he turned to face her. She remained cross he hadn't thought to mention the woman until she'd found out about her existence in the village.

'I'll explain later,' he said. This was also the first she'd heard of any literary aspirations. Was that the profession that he'd kept from her? He was an author?

'And Virgil? Did you ever meet him?' she asked the older lady.

'Oh, he was just as restless but a hundred times worse. In many ways they were a perfect match, and in others, I think they fed off each other. She was engaged to be married before they met, you know?' They both nodded. 'Forget the man's name but he was a wealthy landowner from further north in the county. He was besotted. You could see it in his eyes. I remember her introducing him to me once when I came up to the house for high tea. And then she suddenly decided to go abroad with a friend who was undertaking the Grand Tour. Perhaps she thought it was her last chance to travel before she became a wife and mother. The upshot was she met Mr Brockhurst in Florence, and within two days of knowing him, she'd sent a telegram to the other fellow breaking off the engagement. See? Spontaneous.'

'You knew all this?' She turned to Ellery, incredulous.

'I knew she'd been engaged, but I didn't know it was Standfield,' he said.

'Harlow Standfield!' Mrs Coombes exclaimed. 'That's the fellow. Couldn't remember his name.'

She dusted some crumbs from her lap and continued with her tale.

'After the wedding, which they held in the parish church at Morton Peverell and then again somewhere in America for the benefit of his family, they were off again. They returned to Italy for the honeymoon and were home intermittently over the next five years, leading somewhat of a nomadic life – never in one place for long.'

'Did you know Bernard? He also worked for the Warren family, I believe. I don't know his surname, nor much about him really, but I've come across him since I spoke to you,' Ellery said.

'He's still alive?' Her tiny bright eyes signalled her surprise. 'Such a gentle soul, if somewhat an anxious and confused one. Never quite made him out. Clever but stupid, if you know what I mean? Give him a task and he would carry it out precisely. Very focused. But his mind bounced all over the place, and he struggled talking to people. He never could look you in the eye.'

Mrs Coombes' opinion backed up that of Mrs Lane, but that didn't rule out others manipulating him for their own ends.

'He adored Lenora, of course,' she continued, 'like the rest of us, and he got on surprisingly well with Virgil, apparently. Not at first – I think he was jealous of this foreign man who took her from High-cliffe House, but I heard that Virgil cleverly got him involved in looking after all his many curiosities. Bernard liked mechanical things, even if he didn't fully understand them.'

Perhaps that's what he'd been doing when Pearl spotted him in the cove. Had the little wooden box contained something he'd been using to maintain the instruments? Oil for the cogs? Mercury for the clepsydra?

The old lady leaned closer.

'Then I heard from Lenora out of the blue. A letter arrived early in 1903 saying she was expecting, and she wanted to know if I would return to Highcliffe House as a nanny.' And she told the same tale as the two elderly ladies on the bench.

'Mrs Coombes is one of the few people certain that Lenora and Virgil are dead,' Ellery explained, rather matter-of-factly. 'They simply wouldn't have gone off on their adventures again without letting her know.'

Pearl was inclined to agree. But had they met with an unfortunate accident or been murdered? And, if so, who was responsible?

'Could Bernard have been so in love with Lenora that he killed them both because he couldn't have her? A crime of passion?' Pearl asked.

The old lady smiled and reached out to pat her hand. 'That man couldn't hurt a fly. Besides, I don't think it was that kind of love. Now that Mr Standfield, on the other hand, had a bit of a temper; the day she broke off the engagement he rampaged through her gardens and did tremendous damage, I heard. I had a cousin who worked at the house. If anyone was likely to commit a crime of passion, I'd put my money on him. But then it's not just romantic love that drives people to kill, is it? There was that case in the papers recently where a mother sought revenge for the death of her son. Familial love is just as strong.'

Never having experienced strong familial love, Pearl couldn't comment, but the older woman had certainly given her something to think about. After another slice of cake and some polite chatter about the garden, Ellery and Pearl made their excuses. They'd got the information they'd sought and had a long drive ahead of them.

* * *

They drove back in relative silence, Ellery's recent revelation still weighing on her mind. He kept casting her sideways glances as they powered along the dusty lanes.

'I want to kiss those lips of yours more than I've ever wanted anything in my life,' he said. Their mutual attraction hung heavy between them, and all Pearl could think about was their passionate embrace in the cove. He was obviously similarly distracted.

'But you're engaged,' she reminded him. 'Whatever you think you've sorted in a previous loop, Ruby is sitting at home right now, wondering what her fiancé is up to. And she doesn't deserve for him to be wrapped in the arms of another girl.'

'You're being ridiculous.' His tone was sulky. 'Besides, you tried to seduce me on a very limited acquaintance. That's not very moral.'

Pearl huffed and folded her arms across her chest.

'Those were exceptional circumstances. I was alone, confused and frightened.'

'And very tipsy,' he pointed out.

'Don't judge me.'

'I rather think it's you who is judging me. You should be pleased that I've fallen in love with you.'

She swung from frustrated to furious in an instant. How dare he imply she should be grateful for his affections, as though she was someone who wouldn't secure them without his generosity. The fact he'd admitted he loved her a second time got lost in her temper.

'*I should be pleased*?' Her nostrils flared alarmingly. 'Why? Because I'm so unlovable?'

'I didn't mean it like that, but I like this new version of you. You're standing up for yourself. Let's hope that if we get out of this mess, you won't be trampled on any longer. I knew all you needed was a little guidance to slide from that protective shell of yours.'

His grin inflamed her even more.

'How dare you. I'm not some Eliza Doolittle for you to fix.'

There was a pause.

'Is this our first row?' he asked, his eyes twinkling with amusement. They came to a junction and he turned left, putting up his hand to a farmer as they passed.

'You love me?' she whispered, floating back to earth after her soaring temper, and analysing his words more carefully. He'd said this over the table with Standfield too, but she'd heard his words without really listening. This time, however, they cut right through her chest and nestled into her beating heart. Even Harriet had rued the inability of the opposite sex to talk about their true feelings. And here he was, declaring his love twice in the space of a few hours.

He shrugged, as though it was no big deal and pretty much a given.

'How about, instead of squabbling, we concentrate on catching the killer and, when we know your life is no longer in danger, work out how that damn clepsydra is messing with time, so that you can admit you love me too?'

She smiled at his words. They certainly made him rather lovable, but she was not prepared to say as much out loud just yet.

'I do want to move on with my life, so you're right – we should focus,' she said, not admitting her feelings and the wonderful man beside her didn't push for clarification.

He glanced at his wristwatch. 'And, hopefully, this time we will catch someone in the act.'

By the time they pulled into the driveway, she knew the dinner would be coming to an end, assuming poor Mrs Dawson had managed to produce and serve it without Ellery's help. They decided to creep around the side of the house and observe the goings-on within.

The window to the dining room was open, as it had been previously, to allow the cooler outside air to circulate on that hot July evening. Ellery tugged her downwards and out of sight, before they were seen, and they crouched below the sill, catching Céline's Gallic tones as they drifted out into the night air.

'I do not understand, Raymond. You say she is a quiet, compliant child and yet she runs off with someone she met only hours before? *C'est inexplicable.*' The guests were still at the table and, without her and Ellery present, and Mrs Dawson presumably still in the kitchens, they were free to talk unguarded.

'Her mother was impulsive and alarmingly headstrong. I shouldn't be surprised really.' Her father's words were without emotion. 'I'm just amazed this spark has taken so long to surface.'

This was the first Pearl had heard that her mother had any kind of spirit. She'd assumed that the woman had been demure and biddable, like herself. An uncomfortable feeling bubbled in her belly. The way he was speaking about his wife implied he wholly disapproved. Had he really been in love with her? Was there more to their story than she thought, and this was the real reason he'd never spoken about his brief marriage?

'Who, *précisément*, was this mysterious woman you married in such haste?' Céline asked.

'Yes, do tell. Surprised the hell out of me. Always thought women weren't really your thing, old boy.' Standfield's drunken mumble could be heard in the background.

'Someone I met the summer after we were all here.'

Pearl exchanged a glance in the gloom with Ellery. They had long suspected these three knew each other, but he was now placing them at the house together. An uncomfortable feeling swelled in the pit of her stomach.

'Fell in love. Married that autumn. Had Pearl the following year.'

What a way to sum up a romance, she thought, but it was about as much detail as he ever gave.

'And the damn name change, man. What was that all about?'

'We all sought anonymity. Even you took yourself out the spotlight for a few years, Harlow. And Céline was using at least four different pseudonyms back then, as I recall.'

'Steady there, Raymond, old bean. We agreed never to talk of that gathering – remember? I say, are you sure this husband of yours doesn't know what we're talking about?'

There was a pause and Pearl could imagine them all looking to Aldo, who was probably absorbed by his food and head down. Céline said something in Italian and received a curt response.

'He is an ignorant fool, an angry little man who does not have the drive or brains to learn another language, and is not in the least bit interested in our conversation. His wants are simple – feed him good food and he is content. He is with me for the sex, not the conversation.'

'Must we?' Pearl's father implored. Pearl could imagine him flaring his nostrils in distaste. Anything to do with human relations was of little interest to him.

'Oh, you were always such a fuddy-duddy, and yet you cannot have fathered a child without indulging in the pleasures of the

lesh yourself, *non*? We all do it, Raymond, but some of us are
nore open about it than others.' There was real irritation in her
one.

'Let's retire to the drawing room?' Standfield had perhaps
ensed the building tension. 'It's no good expecting that poor cook
o see to us – she's run ragged. We'll just have to help ourselves to
he old after-dinner tipple.'

Pearl and Ellery heard the scrape of chairs and clatter of cutlery.

'It's highly likely the men will come out to the terrace to smoke,'
Pearl whispered to her companion.

'No problem. We can sneak inside through one of the back
oors. I want to have a nosy along the top corridor again.'

They let themselves in and crept along the hallway. Mrs
Dawson was running the tap and stacking crockery but the kitchen
oor was closed. About to climb the servants' stairs, Ellery paused
nd opened the triangular cupboard under the steps and peered
iside.

'Well, this is unexpected. There's a petrol can in here and it's
ill.' He pointed to a bright red Shell Motor Spirit can. 'Don't you
nd that odd, since the Brockhursts didn't own a motor car? This
as been put here recently and I would bet money the contents are
ot intended for a fuel tank.'

'Why would... Oh.'

'It's what we always suspected. Someone comes up these back
airs and starts the fire at the top of the corridor because they can
ake a quick escape. Shall I tip it down the drain?' he suggested.

'So we can all be poisoned again. No, thanks.'

He closed the door and mounted the stairs, with Pearl following
osely behind. Mrs Dawson's room was to their left and the locked
pboard was to their right. He jiggled the handle, disturbing the
y she'd seen on previous occasions.

'And this door won't open.'

'It's a storage cupboard that was probably locked in the past t
keep household supplies safe.'

'But why lock it now?'

'This house hasn't been occupied for twenty years. Maybe th
key has been misplaced over time?'

'Hmm...' Ellery rubbed at his chin. 'The naturally inquisitiv
side of me is always suspicious of things others don't want you t
see.'

They entered Mrs Dawson's room and he quickly looke
through her case, but she had even fewer personal possessions tha
the others – not needing evening wear, jewellery, or changes o
shoes. They walked the length of the corridor, pushing at doors an
peering inside, but they had been into all the guests' rooms at on
point or another, and there was little new to see.

The rooms on the right were more unsettling, with person.
possessions dotted about. Even though the Brockhursts hadn't bee
at Highcliffe House all that often after their marriage, it still felt lik
a home, with generations of accumulated clutter. The spaces we
tidy, but bedspreads and rugs were faded in patches from years o
streaming sunlight, and everything felt shabby and neglected. Pea
found the master bedroom particularly poignant – a tiny woode
rocking crib by the bed, that had surely been Lenora's before it ha
been the baby's – Joseph, Standfield said his name was.

Apart from the petrol can, there were no obvious signs of imm
nent fire-making, so Ellery led the way down the main staircas
They tried not to make any noise, but the drawing room door w
flung open by a striding Standfield, possibly on a return visit to t
wine cellar. He looked up and spotted them as they turned t
quarter landing.

'What the blazes? Here they are,' he called over his should
'I've caught the blighters.'

30

'Fancy stealing a chap's motor car and disappearing off into the blue. There'd better not be so much as a scratch on her. She cost me several hundred pounds.'

It didn't take many moments for everyone to tumble out into the hallway and investigate the commotion. Even Mrs Dawson stepped from the kitchens further down, wiping her hands on a tea towel.

'Pearl.' Her father sounded vaguely irritable. 'Where have you been? Running off with a manservant like that. People will talk, and if it gets back to Simon, you can wave goodbye to any chance of a ring on your finger. He won't want someone who is spoiled.' There was no indication he'd been worried for her safety, just her marriage prospects.

She assessed the sea of cross faces and noticed that Céline was the only one who appeared faintly amused by the situation.

'Well, well, who's been a naughty girl?' she said, putting a cigarette to her lips and flicking her lighter. 'Has Daddy kept you on such a tight rein that you absconded at the first opportunity? I hope the young man has at least shown you a good time this evening. He looks the sort who knows how to make a young lady happy.' She raised an alarmingly suggestive eyebrow and no one knew quite what to say or where to look.

'You still haven't answered me, Pearl.' Her father remained calm but persistent.

'Ellery is my friend,' she said, employing her newfound confidence. Ellery looked disappointed but she couldn't forgive what she felt was a betrayal. Not yet, at least.

'Nonsense. Really, Pearl, you can't go around attaching yourself to random men – and a servant, for goodness' sake. You only met the fellow a few hours ago.'

'On the contrary, Mr Glenham, I have spent several evenings with your daughter and we are quite well acquainted.' Ellery spoke for the first time.

Her father spluttered at this piece of information.

'What? Have you been seeing her behind my back? I don't understand. You said you were from Weymouth and my daughter lives in Suffolk.'

Not addressing her father's comments – how could he without everyone thinking him mad? – he chose instead, to defend her.

'She's a remarkable woman, who I rather feel you have a tendency to overlook.'

'It's not your place to tell me how I view my own daughter.'

'Come on, Raymond, you still think of her as a child and I can assure you she is far from that.' His eyes came alive, and her father frowned as the young man used his Christian name. 'A proficient swimmer, a quick mind and a surprising wit. She displays such determination when the odds are stacked against her and, goodness, how she rises to a challenge. Scaling drainpipes to save the life of another, and if you've never seen her stride into a ballroom full of people when all eyes turn in her direction, then you've never seen her at all. Do you even know any of these things about her?'

'Drainpipes, indeed. And Pearl is not the sort to go to balls.' And with that, he dismissed everything the young man had said. In his mind, the manservant was clearly talking nonsense.

'Ellery,' Mrs Dawson reprimanded, stepping forward, but her voice was hesitant. 'How could you leave me to manage this alone? Mr Badgerwood will have to be told. Don't expect to get paid.'

'There is no Mr Badgerwood,' he said, totally exasperated. 'Have you not worked out that it's a pseudonym for Brockhurst yet?'

Pearl was initially frustrated that he was revealing their hand, until she remembered it didn't matter what they said or how much they disclosed, it would be a blank slate for these people in approximately three hours.

'Someone has gathered you all together for one reason alone – murder,' Ellery continued. 'There's a petrol can concealed at the bottom of the servants' stairs and if you think today has been a scorcher, that will be nothing to the toastiness you'll experience tonight when you're all burned alive in your beds. What *exactly* are you all hiding?' He looked at each face in turn before shaking his head. 'I don't understand... Why does someone want you all dead?'

'Look here, young man,' Standfield blustered, visibly upset by his revelation. 'You can't just go around making bold statements about secrets and murderous intentions with no proof. I rather think you are deflecting from the real matter at hand – what have the pair of you been up to?' But he looked distinctly unsettled by the suggestion nefarious things were afoot.

'Do you really want to know, Harlow, old chap?' His familiarity unsettled the older man, but Ellery didn't give him the chance to comment. 'Pearl and I are frankly rather miffed that you've been spinning us a web of lies. We've been talking to the Leightons and now that Lenora Brockhurst broke your heart, and it was a love you never got over.' He looked at her father. 'Mrs Lane told us that your real name is Raymond Hardinger and you used to work for the Brockhursts.' He spun to Céline. 'Although you, signora, are more of an enigma. We know you're a thief, and have likely made a career of stealing valuable antiquities and being paid handsomely to return them to their country of origin.'

The three accused looked between themselves, like guilty schoolchildren caught cribbing each other's work, until Céline elected herself the speaker on behalf of them all.

'None of these revelations are proof of anything.' She shrugged. 'Raymond chose not to tell you about his previous employment, perhaps he has his reasons. And Harlow might choose to keep his broken heart to himself. It is no business of yours. Equally, all my dealings with Virgil were – how you say? – above board.'

Pearl's father backed the Frenchwoman up. 'Everyone has their secrets – even my daughter, it would seem.' He narrowed his eyes.

'Hear, hear.' Standfield crossed his arms over his chest. 'Are you actually accusing us of something? Or just highlighting a few things you uncovered by poking your noses in business that most certainly isn't yours to poke about in?'

Aldo put his hand out to his wife and uttered a stream of rapid Italian – presumably enquiring as to what was going on.

'Oh, do be quiet, you stupid man. I don't have time to explain.' Aldo, suitably dismissed by his wife, shrugged and turned toward the stairs.

'Oh no you don't, mister.' Ellery stopped him with an outstretched hand so there was no ambiguity. 'We need to keep together. I suggest we all retire to the drawing room.'

He guided everyone through the door and Standfield made a beeline for the chinoiserie sideboard, probably thinking a drink would help pass the time.

'Perhaps it's best you don't touch the spirits,' Pearl warned. 'There is someone either watching this house, or within it, who will stop at nothing to kill us all this evening and we suspect we are imminently to be drugged so that we sleep through the fire tonight

The murderer may resort to poison if they believe their scheme has been uncovered, and the decanters on the sideboard, which we've all had access to throughout the day, are where my money is.'

'A fire? Where are you getting all this nonsense from?' her father asked. It was a perfectly rational question but her answer was far from rational.

'Because Virgil had an ancient mercury clepsydra and I stumbled across it. It's been resetting the day for the pair of us, so we have spent that gift of time investigating you all.' She had absolutely nothing to lose by uttering the truth. This bolder Pearl wouldn't give a fig what these duplicitous people thought about her. Let them think she was crazy – maybe it would lower their defences.

Céline was the only one not to laugh. Instead, her face belied her surprise.

'Virgil acquired the Abydos clock? It went missing at the turn of the century but I did not know he had obtained it. Where is it?' she demanded. 'It doesn't control time, of course – ridiculous notion. But its... loss was felt quite keenly and I know for a fact those who guarded it are most anxious for its return. Most anxious.'

Mrs Dawson's eyes expanded to the size of saucers. 'Insane – the lot of you,' she declared. 'I'm leaving. It's not worth the wages. I'll walk into Morton Peverell in the dark if I have to.'

'That might not be a bad idea,' Pearl said. 'We know the fire likely starts in your room, and believe petrol is used as an accelerant.'

A lifetime with a man who displayed little emotion had left Pearl unused to reading people, but she was certain that the terror she saw in Mrs Dawson's eyes was real, and the poor woman started to shake, rocking backwards and forwards, and tugging at her sleeves. The others might be dismissive of their ridiculous-sounding prophecies, but the cook believed them. Pearl thought

back to when she'd announced previously that there would be
fire, and decided she was indeed a superstitious individual. On thi
occasion, it would serve her well. Tonight, Mrs Dawson would nc
be cremated in her own bed.

'No. We stay here, where we can all keep an eye on each othe
Who is to say she's not behind all this?' Ellery reasoned.

Although Pearl did not agree – Mrs Dawson, her father, Eller
and Standfield were all in the clear as far as she was concerned
she acquiesced.

'Perhaps he has a point. You don't want to be stabbed on th
driveway.' Mrs Dawson, who still looked somewhat stunned by a
the revelations, merely nodded and collapsed into a nearby chair.

'This is nonsense,' her father said. 'So, we sit here staring a
each other throughout the night and then what?'

'I strongly suggest that in the morning you all go home,' Elle
said. 'I've told you Badgerwood doesn't exist, and it's possible one
the Brockhursts has engineered this dinner party – even though
believe something happened to that poor family, or at least some
them. But someone wishes you all ill. The sooner you escape th
place, the better.'

'I've had enough of this. I don't like feeling cornered, and tha
exactly how I feel. Like a rabbit with one leg in the damn steel tra
I'm not waiting for the poacher to return – I'm heading home th
instant,' Standfield announced, heaving himself to his feet. 'I ho
you have left sufficient fuel in the old jalopy.'

'*Non.*' Céline put up an elegant hand. 'The young man is rig
No one leaves. You could return and set the house alight in t
early hours. We all stay.'

'Then I'm going to need a stiff drink to see me through. I *was*
my way to the wine cellar earlier.'

It seemed he needed alcohol to function, in the same way th
his motor car needed petrol to drive. Pearl reminded him that t

spirits may have already been drugged, but Standfield argued that decades-old bottles of unopened wine were probably safe.

They jointly decided that if anyone needed to leave the room, they must go in pairs, and those pairs would be based on the unlikelihood of the two people being in collusion. When Céline said she needed to powder her nose, Pearl went along. When Mrs Dawson offered to make everyone tea, her father oversaw its production. And when Standfield visited the cellar, Aldo, who had his instructions relayed in Italian by his wife, accompanied him.

Pearl looked at the mantel clock. They only had minutes until she would be staring at her tiny eight-legged friend again and nursing a sore head. It appeared no one was to be murdered that night.

'*Saluti!*' Aldo and Standfield sat together in the corner. They had an appreciation of fine clarets in common, if not a language.

She stood by the French doors, looking into the moonlit-dusted garden, as something caught her eye. Were they mistaken in their belief that one of the guests was behind this? Time and time again, the possibility that Lenora was alive crossed her mind – that she had returned to right an unforgivable wrong from the past.

Because moments before everything went black, Pearl saw someone outside, lurking in the shadowed bushes by the buddleia, and all of the guests were in the room with her.

31

'We have to focus on the Brockhursts and the people who cared about them,' Pearl said to Ellery, as he strode down the path to meet her, like they'd done so many times on that same sunny July afternoon. 'There was someone outside last night. I saw them in the bushes.'

Pearl had recognised the figure – or thought she had. It was the silhouette of a flapping coat that had been the giveaway. A man who had worshipped the mistress of the house, and would, by all accounts, do anything for her.

'We questioned people at the ball and locals from the village but have overlooked the one person who knew Lenora from a child and has been at the house all this time...'

'Ah, Bernard,' Ellery said.

'I met him in the copse before you got dragged into all this. He insisted *she* wasn't dead – Lenora, I assume. I didn't think much of it at the time, because the poor man isn't quite the ticket, but what if he is the key to all this? It's easy to dismiss the wild ramblings of someone who is unwell or confused, but the things he's saying must come from somewhere...'

'Do you really think she's orchestrated this whole charade?' His forehead wrinkled.

She shrugged. 'Let's ask him.'

They made their way to the small cluster of trees where she'd bumped into the older man before. She couldn't remember the time of their encounter, so tracking him down might prove difficult, but after a few minutes, Ellery spotted him in the distance. He was tugging at his straggly beard and talking to a squirrel.

'Hello.' Pearl gave her kindest smile as they approached. 'We are friends of the Brockhursts. Do you know where they are?'

Bernard looked momentarily alarmed and mumbled something incoherent, as the squirrel scampered up the gnarly trunk of a big oak. Ellery stuck out his hand but the old man just stared at it.

'I understand you worked for Lenora?' she ventured.

'...Must keep out the way... Don't talk to anyone. Can't lose my job. I love my job.'

'We won't tell anyone that we've seen you.'

She smiled again, but the old man dipped his head and began to turn away. It sounded suspiciously like someone had threatened him, if he was worried about the security of his employment. And if that person didn't want him conversing with the guests, that probably meant he had information of value.

'...Mow the lawn, paint the summer house. It's how she liked it...'

'And the summer house is such a delightful colour,' Pearl said, scurrying to keep up with him as he began to walk away. Her eyes briefly met Ellery's, knowing she'd lost the old man's interest. He was becoming increasingly agitated, and kept glancing over his shoulder at them, as his pace increased.

'Bernard, I have a gift for you. A very special wristwatch.'

Suddenly, Ellery had Bernard's attention. He stopped walking and turned back to look at the item being held out in front of him, his eyes flashing up to the young man's as if to ascertain the offer was genuine.

'It was my father's. The numerals light up in the dark,' Ellery explained. 'Radium paint makes them glow when the light is poor so the officers could see the time in the trenches.'

Bernard kept blinking, moving slightly closer to him and fascinated by the timepiece.

'Like hers... a bracelet that tells the time. Tick tock. Tick tock.'

'Men wear them now. They're all the rage. Do keep it, old chap.'

The watch was of enormous sentimental value to Ellery but Pearl knew he wasn't giving it to Bernard – not really.

'Where is Lenora?' she asked gently, not even sure if Bernard had any concept of the passing of time.

'They aren't coming back, are they?'

'The Brockhursts?'

'The chickens were everywhere...'

The answer was nonsense, and his face scrunched up in distress. His breathing became faster and he started to rock backwards and forwards, his head nodding as he moved, and she was reluctant to push this vulnerable man further.

'She's all right, though, not like the others. She didn't die.'

And with those final words, he closed up completely, clutching the wristwatch to his chest and hobbling away. Pearl's eyes met and held Ellery's, both fully aware that, by implication, someone certainly had.

*   *   *

'Mrs Coombes is right – something unpleasant happened to the Brockhursts,' Ellery said as they made their way back to Highcliff House. They had discreetly followed Bernard to a small cottage on the edge of the grounds, and watched him enter, clutching the wristwatch as though it was made of gold. At least they knew where to find him now, if they needed him at some point in a future afternoon.

'Not Lenora, though, if Bernard is to be believed,' Pearl ventured.

'But if she's behind all this, where is she? She can't be Céline – Lenora wasn't French. I guess Mrs Dawson is a similar age, but the other guests would have recognised her. She must be the elusive Badgerwood and she's kept out of sight all this time.'

'But Badgerwood is surely a man,' Pearl reasoned.

'Why? Because he's signed himself as Mr? If Mary Ann Evans could call herself George Eliot, Lenora could certainly become a Mr Badgerwood.'

He had a point.

'I think we need to talk to the guests individually,' he said. 'When we confronted them last night, they clammed up and presented a united front. Let's see what we can get from Céline as she's the one we know the least about, but I suggest we are better prepared this time.'

As they came out of the woods, he darted over to a small shed on the edge of the gardens, nipped inside and reappeared a few moments later.

'As I suspected there's some nasty stuff in there: arsenic-based rat poison and an old bottle of strychnine sulphate from a Weymouth chemist – probably procured for moles. It's the most likely candidate for the poisoning from the way you described the deaths. There was a case in the newspapers only last year of a woman murdering her lover with the stuff.'

Pearl shuddered, not wanting to be reminded of what was undoubtedly the worst death of her many lives, but the poison being so easily accessible, and only a stone's throw from the house, meant everyone had the opportunity to commit the crime.

The Frenchwoman wasn't in the enclosed garden, as a good h.
an hour had passed since their day had reset but they eventua.
found the enigmatic Céline in the large reception room filled wi
Virgil's artefacts, clearly sniffing around. Her face briefly flashed
deep shade of guilty as soon as they entered, and they could bo
see she was concealing something behind her back.

'I'm going to cut to the chase.' Pearl had no intention of bot
ering with polite chit-chat. 'You were blackmailed into coming he
as my father was, but why?'

Céline looked at Pearl's attire. 'You have been swimming?' It w
obvious that she was giving herself time to think – women li
Céline didn't like to be caught on the back foot.

'Answer the question,' Ellery said.

'Ah, an interesting development. The two of are you are in coll
sion. How charming – the thief and the hired hand. You both stru
me as not worthy of my attention earlier. How wrong I was.'

Pearl took her time to respond, mimicking the cool demeano
of Céline, not wanting to be underestimated any longer.

'I keep forgetting that *you* are unaware of all the things I kno
that you've stolen the Persian bowl, how threatening you can
when provoked, all about Standfield's broken heart and that r
father is really Mr Hardinger. So let me lay down the facts, and th
you can fill us in on the rest.' One of the Frenchwoman's eyebro
rose a fraction of an inch. 'Quite frankly, I don't have the energy
hear your tiresome observation that I've changed from the lit
mouse I appeared to be this morning, or your surprise at the inf
mation I'm about to present to you. You're a dangerous woman w
turns ugly when backed into a corner, so let's not pretend any mo
and instead talk plainly.

'As far as I'm concerned you can take what you like from t
house – the bowl and whatever it is you have behind your bac
but we need information from you to prevent several horrific deat

in this house tonight. Something happened here twenty years ago, and someone is out for revenge, so I'd appreciate your cooperation. Do you think you can manage that?'

Her heart was thumping but she'd never felt so powerful in her whole life. She knew what a dangerous adversary Céline was, but she'd hopefully presented herself as an equal.

Céline narrowed her eyes but dipped her head in acknowledgement.

'Good. Why were you blackmailed into coming to Highcliffe House? And is it enough for someone to want you dead?'

Céline paused for a moment before answering, but she had turned pale.

'That is personal and you will not extract that from me – a small error of judgement that I regret.' She waved her hand in the air to demonstrate it was something that could simply be batted away. 'It was not the threat, however, but the bait that made me attend. Monsieur Badgerwood implied that he was open to discussing the... repatriation of various artefacts.'

She had come for the treasures. Pearl had suspected as much.

'Lenora Brockhurst, the woman who broke Standfield's heart, what do you know of her whereabouts?'

'What exactly has Raymond told you?'

'My father has told me nothing. You've known him for twenty years, so you'll appreciate that he's a closed man.'

'And yet, you know all these surprising things and I must wonder at the source of your information. What is your reason for making these enquiries? Because what happened here before, and what is happening now, it is nothing to do with you. I understand you were not even born when the Brockhursts were last seen in this country.'

'But I'm caught up in it now, and my... friend and I have reason to believe that some rather unpleasant revenge is about to be administered by persons unknown, at which point we *will* be caught up in it, and that's not fair.'

'Unpleasant, *comment*?'

Finally, Ellery took the reins. 'I can assure you Mr Badgerwood has no intention of delivering on his promise because he doesn't exist. What you have failed to realise is the invitation was a trap, luring you here to be killed.'

Céline snorted. 'Ridiculous.' But her eyes didn't mirror the conviction of her words. She was unsettled. Pearl was certain of it.

Ellery patiently explained about Badgerwood again, trying not to show his frustration that he was repeating information he had given out previously. Having been warned about Céline's dangerous side by Pearl, he'd suggested an insurance policy as they'd walked back from the woods. If it wasn't Lenora behind the fire, that left Céline and her husband as the only two within the house that no one had ever seen perish. What he was about to say was a complete fabrication, but the Frenchwoman wouldn't know that.

'I left a sealed letter with my mother before I took up this position. She has been instructed to forward it to the county police should anything happen to either one of us – for example, should we disappear, or appear to befall an accident. Inside the letter amongst other things, I have suggested you are investigated, and al the information I've gathered about your dealings over the years is contained within. I do so hope it will prove unnecessary. All we are asking for is the truth about the Brockhursts. And that, along with the information we have recently gleaned from Bernard—'

'*Qui?*'

'The old man who worked for the Brockhursts.'

'He's still alive?' Céline looked incredulous.

'Alive and still living here on the grounds of Highcliffe House.'

Céline paled, and finally sunk into the leather button-back chair beside her. 'He absolutely adored Lenora, but then everyon did.' There was no attempt to hide the bitter edge to her voice. 'She was so full of life, bubbly – like the champagne, and so kind... the sort who is beautiful without necessarily being beautiful, if that makes sense?' She sighed. 'I did not know her well. We met out in Egypt, just after the turn of the last century, the year your queen died, where Virgil was stripping that country, too, of its treasures. I was keeping an eye on him for various governments, and I levered myself into his social circle. I will say this for the man – he may have lacked breeding but he always threw a party most *magnifique*.' She smiled at the memory.

'Bernard rather gave us the impression Mr Brockhurst is dead but that his wife is alive.' Ellery tested the waters.

'The man is – how you say? – simple. I'm not convinced you can trust what he says.'

'Is it possible that Lenora is behind all this?' Pearl asked. 'And Bernard is in on it? Perhaps she's been secretly visiting Highcliffe House over the years—'

'Yes, that must be it,' Céline said, a little too quickly. 'Although what she wants with me, I cannot imagine. Virgil knew nothing of my motives for our friendship and the last time I saw them, we all had the most pleasant evening.'

'And those motives were what, exactly?' Ellery asked.

'Virgil had *acquired*, from a private collector, an illustrated manuscript that was part of the haul taken by the British army in 1868, after it defeated the Ethiopian emperor. Such a scandal – the British raided his treasury after he killed himself. I became part of the Brockhursts' circle in order to negotiate the return of the manuscript, which was of supreme religious significance to its people.'

'And if you failed to negotiate, I presume you would simply have stolen it?' Pearl surmised.

'It is not stealing if the item was stolen in the first place.' Céline's voice was sharp. 'But Virgil had a price and I paid it, so there is nothing more to tell. *C'est ça.* Will you assure me your letter will be destroyed now that I have cooperated?'

'If we both survive until tomorrow, then yes.'

'And I may take certain... items away with me without being challenged?'

'We won't stop you. I can't speak for anyone else.' Ellery shrugged and she nodded.

'Then I will heed your warnings and watch my back, but if you still believe I am in any way tied up in this, you are – as the English say – barking up the wrong tree.'

But then, Pearl reflected, as Céline swept from the room clutching something in her hand, she would say that, wouldn't she?

32

Pearl spent part of the afternoon helping Mrs Dawson in the kitchen. Her father forbade it; she ignored him. Standing up to him was getting easier. She was polite, but firm. It was as good a way as any to while away the afternoon, and she was competent in the kitchen. Besides, she wanted to spend her time with Ellery, even though she remained cross with him. In her heart, she knew what he'd said made sense. His relationship with Ruby was over, and it was hardly his fault that he couldn't do anything about it. Pearl was drawn to him like a mesmerised moth to those eyes of flame. He made her happy, he made her laugh and he set in motion the most curious sensations to ripple through her body.

Céline had confirmed their suspicions that she was mixed up with stolen antiquities. Interesting how easy it was to get people to confess things when they thought you already knew the truth, so Pearl found an opportunity to speak to her father alone, after he'd rested in his room, hoping to trap him similarly, but got no further. Although he did not deny his real identity, nor that he had previously been in the Brockhursts' employ, he was too calm and measured to be drawn into admissions, unlike the more volatile Céline.

'But why would a former employee be invited to the house for dinner party all these years later? I don't understand, Father. And why was your employment terminated? You'd worked for Mr Warren for years.'

'There is no great mystery, Pearl. I was offered a better-paid position elsewhere, yet I remained friends with the Brockhursts and even had a postcard from them both that autumn.'

'A postcard?' This was new information.

'Yes, they were travelling through South America, I recall, and by that stage were in Peru.'

'And you didn't think it strange that they never returned to England?'

'To be honest, I did not think of them much at all. I had lost my wife. I was bringing up a small child alone. I had other concerns.'

She felt guilty then. Perhaps he didn't openly demonstrate his love for her, but he'd had no wife to share the burden of parenting, only employed housekeepers. There had been occasions he'd sat with her through the night when she was poorly as a child, and he'd always been interested in her academic achievements, if not her sporting ones. He was hiding something, undoubtedly, but perhaps that was tied up with the mystery of her mother and was not to do with the Brockhursts at all. That his marriage had been unhappy, or perhaps even scandalous, had not occurred to her before.

Ellery suggested they let the day play out as it had done originally, and confront the guests again after the meal, when their stomachs were full and the wine had loosened their tongues. Having helped prepare the dinner, Pearl readily agreed, determined to eat it. Besides, she liked watching Aldo's contented little face as he worked his way through the courses. He was the one constant oblivious to it all and happy so long as he had a plate of moderately good food and a glass of excellent wine in front of him, drifting about the house unfazed by all the goings-on – the fiery spats with his wife aside.

When Céline finally made her glamorous entrance, Ellery leaned towards Pearl and flashed his eyes in the Frenchwoman's direction. 'You wear that dress so much better,' he whispered. A thrill of exhilaration rushed through her at his words.

Céline ensured her arrival on this occasion was even more dramatic by announcing that Bernard still lived on the grounds. Standfield choked on his drink and her father, whose expression rarely betrayed much, lost the colour from his face. Pearl exchanged a glance with Ellery, acknowledging that their three main suspects were therefore unlikely to be in collusion with the old man. If not one of them knew that he still worked at Highcliffe House, then the person behind all this was looking more and more likely to be an outsider. Bernard had been warned to stay away from the guests, and had even had his job threatened. Someone wanted him kept quiet.

The conversation over dinner was stilted. The atmosphere was one of suspicion, made worse by Badgerwood's telegram. After the meal, everyone retired to the drawing room and the pair decided to continue their established method of keeping everyone safe by gathering them together from that moment. This included insisting a bemused Mrs Dawson joined them. She clearly felt uncomfortable at the request, claiming her place was in the kitchen, but they wanted to keep the poor woman from harm. Anyone could be lurking outside, a bottle of strychnine in their pocket and murder in their heart.

'May I top you up, sir?' Ellery asked, swooping in on Standfield and replenishing his glass without waiting for an answer – not that anyone in the room doubted what his response would be. He nodded but was clearly ruffled by the way Ellery and Pearl had taken charge.

'Look here, I don't know why you young upstarts think you have the authority to boss us all about, but it's simply not on,' Standfield said, hitching up his trousers and settling into a large wingback chair. 'Herding us in here like cattle.'

'And yet, you *will* listen to us, and you *will* do as we ask, because we have power over every one of you. And the source of that power is knowledge,' Pearl said, deciding now was the time to reveal her hand.

She relayed the established facts to everyone in the room for what felt like the umpteenth time, ignoring the uncomfortable looks as the secrets spilled across the heavily patterned carpet. And then she presented them with the biggest surprise of all.

'Bernard told us that Virgil Brockhurst is dead.' She was stretching the truth somewhat, but the reaction was interesting.

'He saw something?' Standfield immediately jumped to his feet and was shot a murderous look by Céline. He returned to his chair looking sheepish. 'Although, I can't think what that could possibly be...'

'We plan to contact the police in the morning and ask them to investigate his death, and I wonder who they will discover has the biggest motive. Signora Ravello clamouring for treasures he wouldn't relinquish, or Standfield because Virgil stole his fiancée away?'

Standfield spluttered into his drink and Céline's nostrils flared alarmingly.

'Then you lied to me,' she said. 'You extracted information from me on the promise I would not be investigated.' She looked as though she was about to say more but Pearl's father stared at the agitated Frenchwoman, as Ellery surreptitiously topped up her glass.

'Exactly what information did you reveal?' her father asked Céline, looking slightly more wary.

'Nothing about you, Raymond, although now you have rather proven that you have something to hide.' She made a good point.

'Quite honestly, old chap, if all our secrets are out, I don't see why your daughter should go on believing everything was tickety-boo with you and old Brockhurst, when that's simply not the case,' Standfield chipped in.

Her father's eyes narrowed briefly as he looked across at the portly man, but he refused to be goaded and remained quiet. Standfield shuffled his bulky frame towards the edge of his seat, clearly preparing to say more.

'Harlow...' Céline warned, but Standfield was now too lubricated to care.

'Funny old business with the accounts. Virgil accused him of swindling him somehow. Don't know the details, don't even know if it's true, but we were all invited to Highcliffe House in oh-three and rather think Virgil wanted to put his affairs in order.'

'His suspicions were unfounded,' her father asserted. 'I do not need to defend untruths, and you need to consider that perhaps silence is golden.'

'Look, these youngsters clearly know things between us and the Brockhursts weren't exactly peachy, so it's no use pretending otherwise. Doesn't mean any of us wished them harm. I'm just saying, they came back to register the child, and Virgil organised a small get-together, but after most of the guests had gone home, he took the opportunity to get a few things off his chest – ranting at Raymond for sloppy bookkeeping, challenging Céline over missing artefacts and warning me off his wife. So, yes, things were... uncomfortable with the Brockhursts when we arrived, but by the time they left for foreign shores, we'd all had it out, and parted as friends.'

'*Exactement.* You are seeing dark things when there are not dark

things to see. I told you, our business matters were concluded satis-
factorily.'

Standfield raised his glass into the air and waved it about, the
contents slopping dangerously close to the edge.

'He even said to me later how wrong he'd been to vent. Don'
think they were getting much sleep with the little fella. Surprised
they hadn't employed a nursemaid, to be honest. Poor Lenora wa
doing it all.'

Interesting, thought Pearl, that they did not seem to know o
Mrs Coombes' imminent employment back then.

'*Oui*, and I heard you drinking brandy on the terrace by the en
of the evening, and remember thinking how *magnifique* it was to se
two former love rivals overcome their differences and behave lik
gentlemen.'

'Yes, yes.' Standfield was becoming increasingly animated and
in Pearl's opinion, now overplaying his hand. 'And Raymond, ol
bean, do you remember joining us for a cigar, and how we talke
about their next adventure?'

Her father raised his left eyebrow the tiniest fraction of an inch

'Off to the Orient, as I recall? Starting in Constantinople.'

Her father coughed. 'I fear you are mistaken, Harlow. It wa
South America.'

'What? Oh, right. Whatever you say.'

Not only could these three people not get their story straight,
was also terribly convenient that the last time they had all seen th
Brockhursts, it had been such a friendly and forgiving occasion. If ev
there was a time the air at Highcliffe House smelled fishy, it was now.

Céline slid from her seat, the gold lamé catching the light, an
walked to the French doors, absent-mindedly looking out into th
night.

'There were suitcases everywhere,' she said. 'They had bare

ınpacked from their last trip, and Lenora was already making ɔreparations to leave – talking of how the baby would struggle in he heat abroad. What was the name again?'

'Joe,' her father said, as Céline's inability to remember, or even are about, the sex demonstrated her total lack of interest in chil- dren. It was no wonder that she'd never had any of her own.

The Frenchwoman took a drag from her cigarette. 'They wanted ɪ registered in this country but had restless feet and had no inten- on of staying in England for long. She did not have family ɔmaining and Virgil wanted to take the child to America at some oint. And then it cried in the middle of the hors d'oeuvres and enora had to leave the table to soothe it.'

But this was not what Mrs Coombes had told them. The former anny was convinced the Brockhursts were settling at Highcliffe louse for a few years at least. Céline was lying.

'Forgot that,' Standfield chimed in. 'Feel bad really. None of us ɪowed any interest in the little fellow. To be honest, I couldn't ɪmember his name either, but he must be a man now. About your ɜe,' he said, looking at Ellery.

All eyes swivelled in Ellery's direction, and Pearl felt her heart ɪte increase. Over their afternoons together, it had become quite ɔparent that there was more to his interest in the whole affair than ɪet the eye. Could he really be Joseph Brockhurst? After all, he was ɪe one continually telling her to question things because people ɪd. He *said* he was twenty-five, but she only had his word for that. ɪe wanted to trust him with all her heart, but could she? He'd let ɪr down before.

'The brutal truth is, someone wants to burn this house down, ɪth you all inside...' Ellery said. As always, the easily spooked Mrs ɪawson gasped, and Pearl noticed the three guests looking at each ɪher. Aldo remained head down, absorbing the wise words of

Ovid. 'And Bernard's assertion makes us wonder if revenge fo
Virgil's death might be the reason.'

'Please don't tell me you are foolish enough to listen to th
ramblings of an imbecile?' Her father looked most disappointed, a
she was in his unkind assessment of Bernard. 'Honestly, Pearl, I'v
taught you better than that. Three upstanding citizens are sittin
here telling you what happened on the last occasion they saw Virg
and Lenora, and some simple fellow has imparted fragments an
half-truths. And you suddenly suspect us of heinous crimes?'

'How can you all be of a mind that the Brockhursts went sailir
off into the sunset, when no one has heard of them for twen
years?' Ellery said. 'Something happened to them back in th
spring of 1903, why can't someone admit it?'

'You English are so overdramatic.' Céline rolled her eyes, as sl
took a cigarette from a silver case. 'They sent postcards.'

'Which could have been sent by anyone,' he pointed out.

'Then what are you suggesting? Someone here murdered tl
whole family? I had no reason to want Lenora or her son dead.' Th
implication hung in the air, however, that Virgil was not
favoured.

Pearl was getting better at reading people, and it was obvious
her that they were clustered together like hunted animals, faci
outwards to see off the predator and acting as one. But who we
they defending? She'd already seen Céline's ruthless side, and ha
little doubt the woman could kill if driven to it. Standfield had lc
the woman he loved and remained bitter. Perhaps there we
desperate circumstances where he might remove Virgil from t
equation, but she could never believe he could kill Lenora, or
innocent child.

And then there was her father. Such a scandal, unfounded
otherwise, attached to his profession would have undoubtec
ruined him, whatever he claimed. He wasn't capable of a crime

passion – there was little passion within him. But a calculated crime that would make the ledger of his life balance nicely? Maybe.

The evening played out with no further drama. They could prove nothing but they did have more information. Ellery pacified everyone by saying they would be free to leave in the morning, but that remaining together was for everyone's safety. Anyone who needed to leave the room did so with someone accompanying them, as before. Standfield instigated a game of cards but no one's heart was in it and, as Pearl stood looking out over the gardens, her thoughts returned to Bernard, if only because she was running out of other options. Could he be seeking revenge for whatever he may or may not have seen? Just because the poor man was a bit simple didn't mean he wasn't capable of murder... did it?

But she dismissed this thought almost immediately. Mrs Lane said he could barely write, and this whole gathering had been cleverly orchestrated; detailed correspondence and instructions to staff, to mention nothing of the detective work involved to track everyone down. Her father and Céline had gone to great lengths to conceal their previous identities. No, this was not something Bernard could have executed – certainly not on his own.

She sidled over to Ellery, who was observing the poker game from a distance.

'I need to speak to Bernard again. Alone. He's outside in the bushes.'

'But we're insisting everyone sticks together. They'll kick up a fuss if you go outside. Or follow you.'

She glanced at the mantel clock. 'We have about ten minutes before me being outside is moot, because I'll be flat on my back, staring at the underside of a table in the cave. Can I borrow your father's wristwatch again? And can you create a distraction?' He nodded, undid the strap, and handed it to her. She slipped it behind her back as he wandered over to the sideboard and pretended to stumble on the edge of the rug. There was an almighty crash as he pulled the tray of glasses to the floor. And in the noise and general chaos, she slipped through the French doors and out into the night.

* * *

Bernard was watching the house from beneath the buddleia, but as soon as he realised Pearl was heading his way, he began to retreat towards the summer house and the woods beyond.

'Please wait,' she called. 'I know you don't know me, but I'm a friend of Lenora's. I need to know what happened to the Brockhursts. I just want to talk.'

Lies sat uneasily with her, especially those that were so blatantly untrue. She hadn't even been born when they'd disappeared, but she suspected Bernard's grip on the passing of time was tenuous.

He slowed down but was still walking away. She sped up and came to a halt in front of him.

'This is for you.' She held out the watch, which was at its best in poor light. The bold numerals glowed an eerie green and she could see Bernard was intrigued. He looked at her, down to the watch and then back to her.

'Take it. Honestly. I've been told that you are very good with mechanical things, and Lenora would want you to have this for all the hard work over the years. The gardens look lovely and I know she was right to trust you to keep all their treasures safe.'

He nodded. 'He said people would come. Keep them safe. Keep them working. I was good at that. "You're very good, Bernard," he said. "You keep them working."'

'You must miss Lenora very much.'

'She was nice. Not everyone is nice to Bernard.'

Pearl reached out and gave his arm a squeeze.

'You're nice. You gave me a watch.'

'What happened to them? Do you know?'

But she was losing him again. He started to rock from foot to foot, and his head began to bob up and down.

'...All that shouting... Should be buried properly, not with the sailors. Bundled up.'

And in that moment, Pearl realised Bernard *had* seen things that night, and knew with absolute certainty where the Brockhursts, or certainly Virgil, had been for the last twenty years.

33

Picking herself up from the cave floor, a few moments later, Pea[r]
studied the clepsydra in more detail, removing the glass dom[e]
completely to get a closer look. She could see that the pressure fro[m]
the weight of the mercury was forcing the overspill up a tube an[d]
back into a higher funnel, which then dropped when it was full an[d]
made the wheel turn. Following the complicated arrangement [of]
cogs and gears that turned the brass hands on the clock face, sh[e]
noted again that with twenty-four markings, the hour hand woul[d]
only rotate once each day. It was unlike anything she'd ever see[n.]
Where had it come from? And had Virgil known of its powers?

Part of her resented it for making her relive the same afternoo[n]
over and over, but part of her knew without it, she would be lor[g]
dead, and her relationship with Ellery would never have had t[he]
chance to blossom – although she was still torn as to whether th[is]
was a good thing or not. As much as he had given her the streng[th]
to be the person she really was, and awoken her most intima[te]
emotions, she still suspected him of keeping things from her; h[is]
unusually keen interest in the Brockhursts remained puzzling.

She lifted the dome to replace it over the timepiece, assumi[ng] hat it was to protect the dripping mercury within. Perhaps it evapoated, like water – although as a more viscous substance, it would urely be a slower process. Part of Bernard's care over the years night have even involved keeping the levels topped up.

As she lowered it over the workings, she caught the delicate heel of funnels with the glass and yet more mercury spilled out, hich rolled to the edge of the sloping table, moving as one silver lob.

'Bother.' She crouched down and saw the liquid metal nestled a a dip on the cave floor, catching the scant light and looking for all he world like a shiny silver coin. She tried to pick it up, but her ngers couldn't collect the slippery substance.

'What's keeping you? You're usually scampering up the path by ow.' She turned to see a familiar silhouette in the entrance of the ave.

'Stupid clepsydra. I've knocked it again and some of the ercury has run under the table.'

'I wouldn't worry. The joy of our situation is that everything will e back as it was before by the end of the day,' he said, and she cepted he had a point.

They walked out into the blinding sunshine and, instead of turning to the stone steps, she approached the water's edge. He uld see she looked pensive and followed. Gulls were circling ove a patch of water in the distance, doubtless following a shoal fish, and a rogue wave rushed towards them, forcing them both take a step back.

'Did you get anything from Bernard?' he asked, correctly rmising that this was the reason for her detour.

She let out a long exhalation of breath. She knew what she had do but it was not going to be a pleasant undertaking.

'Sailor's Rest,' she said. He followed her gaze to where the left-nd side of the bay curled round on itself and the jagged outcrop

of rocks spilled out to sea. 'I don't think it's just sailors resting ou
there.'

Neither of them said anything for a moment. Her words wer
self-explanatory.

She stepped out of her shoes and took a deep breath.

'So, you're going to swim over to investigate? Even if you're righ
there won't be anything left. Creatures will have disturbed the
and the sea will have washed everything away.'

'"Bundled up," Bernard said. But regardless, I have to check.'

'Then I'm coming with you. I can't wait on the shore, doir
nothing.'

'I'm not sure you're proficient enough in the water. Even thoug
it looks calm, we don't know what riptides might pull you into tl
rocks. You'll just have to be patient.'

'Not in my nature. Besides, it's one of the advantages of o
present predicament,' he said, ever cheerful. 'If it all goes wrong, I
meet you back here shortly and we can try again.' He looked in
her eyes, forcing her to pay attention. 'I'm not asking permissio
Pearl. I don't want you doing this alone.'

It was in that moment, those fiery glints of gold reflecting t
passions he often couldn't control, that she realised how strong h
feelings were for him. She loved him. Her life had been a lonely o
until she'd met Ellery. Her father had fulfilled his duty of care, b
not much beyond that. Harriet was a good friend, but an indepe
dent spirit. This was possibly the first relationship where she w
considered part of a 'we'.

She turned away, not wanting him to see her face. With h
back to him, she sensed him move closer as she slid the ro
from her shoulders, letting it fall to the shingle at her feet. I
reached forward and his hand rested on the pale skin of her ar
It was as if he knew the significance of the moment – as if
could feel her finally accepting that her feelings towards h

could no longer be brushed aside. She shuddered. His touch was electric. He leaned forward and let his lips brush across her shoulder. She didn't stop him, neither did she react. Her feelings were swirling, as were the currents beneath the waters stretching out before her.

As his tiny kisses travelled up to the nape of her neck, she reached her arm back to stroke his hair, half turning her head so that their cheeks met. There was a moment of stillness, where in any other circumstances she might have swung back to face him and planted her lips on his. She loved him, but still wasn't certain that she could completely trust him. And what was love without trust?

Her gaze returned to the sea and she watched the waves roll towards her; relentless and never-ending. Ellery slid his arm around her waist and pulled her close.

'When this is all over—' he began.

'For me, things have only just started. None of this will end well. I think we are about to sail straight into the raging tempest you warned me about.'

'Just remember,' he reiterated, 'we're in this together.'

He let her slip from his embrace and she strode confidently into the water, the iciness of it biting into her skin. Ellery began scrabbling around behind her, removing his clothes. She turned to see him in his white vest and long underpants, hopping on one foot to remove his trousers.

It wasn't long before he'd caught her up, more hesitant than her to submerge his body beneath the gentle waves, but they were soon both swimming out to the edge of the cove. It was not the place to talk, as waves splashed into their faces, and she could see him focused on his stroke. It would have been faster and safer had she swum out alone, without babysitting him, but she recognised he wanted to be seen as her protector and whilst she was physically more capable of dealing with this situation, he was mentally stronger.

As she kicked out, her foot scraped across something rough beneath the surface.

'Careful,' she called back. 'We're over the rocks now.' She ducked beneath the water and opened her eyes, trying to gauge the hazards below, but everything was blurry. There was a flattish area of rock to her right and she made for it, resting her feet and surveying the outcrop.

'Over here,' she called.

He joined her and was able to stand, but the current made keeping still difficult, and their bodies swayed in the water, bumping together. She reached out to hold him and steady herself. Their eyes locked and they stood for a few moments clinging to each other.

'Stay here whilst I scout around.'

He nodded, but she knew he didn't feel safe.

Diving underwater again she navigated her way between the jagged boulders. A brown crab scuttled along the surface of a submerged rock, and more of the small silvery whitebait zigzagged ahead of her, hoping they were safe from the bigger fish if they were closer to the shore.

She surfaced, surprised to find how far she'd drifted from Ellery, gave him the thumbs up and then dipped down again, but her eyes stung from opening them in the salty sea. It might be bright sunshine above, and relatively calm waters, but she was looking for a long abandoned needle in a rocky haystack.

And then she saw it: a dark mound, wrapped in seaweed covered ropes. She resurfaced, needing air to breathe and a moment to think. Looking down, through the water, she could see it was wedged between two submerged boulders, and a loose edge of tarpaulin flapped gently with the push and pull of the tide. She gave Ellery a thumbs up and then down she went, propelling herself towards the ominous bundle. She tugged at the canvas but knew what she was about to find. It was obvious from Bernard's words. She couldn't hold her breath for much longer, and her stomach was spinning faster than the paddles of a butter churn, but she had to see.

And, as she peeled back a slimy corner of the waterproof cloth, she saw the twisted threads of chicken wire, and through that, the smooth yellowing sphere of a human skull.

In her heart, she knew she'd found Virgil Brockhurst.

34

Time was of the essence, and they returned unseen to the house. Pearl quickly changed out of her bathing suit, before they borrowed Standfield's motor car and headed into Morton Peverell to raise the alarm.

They discussed the plan of action as they drove through the winding country lanes. Obviously, anything the police discovered that day would be lost again by nightfall, but Pearl needed to know exactly who was down there, and she wasn't prepared to investigate herself. Even though it would likely just be bones, she couldn't bear to carry such an image, knowing it had once been living, breathing flesh and blood. Her actions might be reset by the clepsydra but her memories wouldn't, and they would haunt her always.

Whilst Ellery had been very much redundant when she discovered the body, it was now her turn to take a step back and allow him to take the lead. He took her straight to a stone cottage with 'County Police' above the front door, and she didn't think question how he knew the location of the police station in a relatively small Dorset village, so many miles from his home.

A middle-aged woman answered their knock, and informed

hem that her husband, Constable Carter, was off-duty and out the
ack, digging up new potatoes. As Ellery dashed round the side of
he police house, Pearl stood awkwardly on the doorstep, knowing
e would have more authority than her purely because he was a
nan. She would be dismissed as hysterical or overemotional. It
vasn't fair, but it was how it was.

It wasn't long before the constable came to the front door and
nformed his wife he was off on his bicycle to see about launching a
oat out to Sailor's Rest. Pearl thanked Mrs Carter for her time, and
ney returned to the motor car.

'He wanted to leave any investigations until Monday, but I
npressed upon him that now that the body had been disturbed, it
as compromised.' Ellery opened the door for her and she slipped
ito her seat.

'I hardly touched it,' she replied.

'We know that, but we also need any investigation to happen
day, or we won't learn anything useful before the day resets. Let's
ead back. It will be some time until they can raise a boat, but I said
e'd meet them at the cove, to point out the location of our grim
scovery.'

was a further two hours before anything was brought to the
rface. Pearl and Ellery had directed the constable as best they
uld, having remembered which of the protruding rocks were
osest to the bundle, and then they sat together at the top of the
ff, watching the tiny fishing boat and three men scour the
tcrop. She was sure the constable didn't like their presence, but
ey were on private land and far enough away not to be a nuisance.

Pearl knew that, yet again, everyone at Highcliffe House would
rrently be furious that the manservant, Raymond's daughter, and

Standfield's car had disappeared. No one there had been alerted t
the search as, from Constable Carter's point of view, this was merel
the investigation of a suspicious bundle spotted in the water. Unt
there was something to report, he saw no point raising the alarm.

When the tarpaulin was located and heaved aboard the sma
vessel, Pearl suddenly didn't want to watch any more. It had bee
found and that was enough for her. A strange feeling pulse
through her body and she turned her face away. How desperate
sad for someone, or several someones, to be missing for near
twenty years and for no one to have investigated their absen
until now.

She told Ellery that she would take herself to the summer hou
for a while, not wanting to return to the house and face the gues
He decided to intercept the boat when it returned to the shore ar
find out what he could. Although she doubted he would get ar
information from the constable, she'd noticed that he had a gift f
wheedling information out of people, and someone else on t
boat might be more forthcoming.

Tired from all the exertions of the day, she sat in a wicker cha
and watched through the summer house windows as du
descended. Soon the glorious sunset they had witnessed on
many occasions would give a repeat performance. Those fier
colours of fire and heat that had been a precursor to the real thi
on so many occasions would grace the skies to the west. Would th
be any closer to ending this repeating nightmare by the time t
sun set? she wondered.

'Two adult bodies,' Ellery said, half an hour later, opening t
summer house door and making her jump. 'The boat owner le
few things slip.'

'No baby?'

He shook his head. 'Two of them, wrapped in chicken wire, a
then a boat tarpaulin tied around the outside. Well thought o

really. Boats and swimmers steer clear of Sailor's Rest, and it's on the edge of private property that, as it's turned out, no one has lived in for twenty years. They were wedged between two rocks and weighted down with stones and an old anchor. He reckons the wire was to stop bits of them becoming detached and washing up on the shore—'

'Don't.' Pearl paled. She didn't need that level of detail.

'Sorry,' he said, and reached for her arm, 'but whoever did this didn't want to prompt a missing persons inquiry. The Brockhursts would have been the first people they'd have tried to contact, as their land edges Sailor's Rest.'

'So, is it definitely Virgil and Lenora?' she asked.

He shrugged. 'The chap said we can't even be certain of the sex at this stage, but unofficially, going by some jewellery on one of the bodies, yeah, the constable seems to think so.'

Suddenly, the reality of what she'd found hit her with all the force of a tornado, and she had to catch her breath. A small sob escaped her lips and tears sprang to her eyes. Ellery noticed her distress and pulled her close, placing his arm about her shoulders – which, of course, made everything worse.

'I don't know why I'm so upset. I never knew them.'

She thought of the portrait. A handsome young couple in love, prepared to take on the world, and at the start of their biggest adventure of all – parenthood.

'They were real people who we've learned quite a bit about over the past few days. To be honest, even I feel a bit choked up.'

She felt his lips brush the top of her head and the warmth of his arm, holding her body to his. It was safe harbour, nestling into him. This was what she'd been missing for so much of her life, she realised, floating around, untethered, in a vast ocean of loneliness. Yes, her father had been there for her when she'd scraped her knee or had a bad dream, but he'd not held her close, whispered

soothing words into her hair, or kissed her cheek. Touch. She'd
been missing touch. And, as she let her head fall onto Ellery's broad
chest, she wanted nothing more than this particular moment to be
on an endless loop.

'What on earth are you doing with my daughter?' Her father's
voice cut through the gloom, and they turned to see him peering
through the window. 'We came out to the terrace to partake of an
after-dinner cigar and Harlow heard voices.'

He wrestled with the door and stepped inside the summer
house.

'She is an innocent and practically engaged to be married. I was
right to be suspicious of you. Are you behind this whole charade?
Inviting us all to Highcliffe House for reasons that are still not
apparent, in order to seduce my daughter? You have spectacularly
failed to do the job you were employed to do and left poor Mrs
Dawson quite beside herself. Badgerwood isn't coming until tomorrow, and I find myself wondering if you know more than you are
admitting.'

She did not respond that Badgerwood was Brockhurst. That in
all likelihood, Lenora and Virgil had been lying together at Sailor's
Rest for twenty years, missed by no one. They were fast running out
of suspects for the fire now, and she looked up to Ellery's face
wondering one final time if he'd played her all along – even though
her heart couldn't bear the thought that he had.

'I'm not Joseph, Pearl,' he said, reading her mind. 'I promise. I'm
exactly who I say I am.'

She felt his grip tighten slightly as if to reinforce the truth of his
words.

'The pair of you need to come back to the house and explain
yourselves,' her father continued. 'I'm most disappointed, Pearl.' He
shook his head. 'Most disappointed.'

They followed him across the lawns to the terrace, where Stanc field sat with a brandy balloon in his hands, swirling it around and occasionally inhaling the aroma.

'Up to no good in the woodshed?' He guffawed at his own joke, and Céline sauntered out, also clutching a brandy balloon, to meet the returning runaways.

'Not at all, dear fellow,' Ellery replied. 'We've actually been investigating the murder of the Brockhursts. Their bodies have been found this very evening in amongst the rocks of Sailor's Rest.'

There was a smash as Céline's glass slipped from her fingers and shattered on the flagstones beneath her feet. All eyes turned to her and she quickly composed herself.

'Not Lenora? She was such a darling. Oh, how *affreux*.'

Pearl couldn't make up her mind whether the older woman's reaction was borne of guilt, or shock. She very much doubted Céline had genuinely been fond of Lenora, just jealous of her.

'If I were to ask any of you about the last time you saw the Brockhursts, I have no doubt that you would all claim that they were alive and well,' Ellery said, 'planning their next big adventure, but this discovery rather throws all that into question.'

'Confound it, man.' Standfield rose to his feet. 'What are you implying?'

'You tell me? We know you were at the party they held just before they disappeared, and now you have all been invited to Highcliffe House under mysterious circumstances. Pearl and I have reason to believe someone wants you dead. If I were a gambling man, I'd say revenge for their murder would be a pretty good bet.'

Her father, as logical as ever, took the reins of the conversation.

'The discovery of bodies, which at this stage I presume are unidentified, proves nothing. Even should they be confirmed as Virgil and Lenora, I doubt even the most experienced coroner could determine when they had entered the water. They sailed round the world, leaving when they wanted, to go where they wanted, and were accountable to no one. For all we know, they could have returned from their travels and sailed out to Sailor's Res together. They used to have a rowing boat somewhere about here.'

'And then rolled themselves in chicken wire, wrapped a tarpaulin around the whole thing, and anchored themselve down?' Ellery's words hung in the air.

Aldo, who was curious as to the nature of the fuss outside, cam to the doors clutching his book and asked his wife something in Italian. Pearl heard the word *assassinio* somewhere in her response and the small, dark man shrugged and returned to Ovid. Food an poetry seemed to be the only things that moved him. The deaths c two strangers certainly hadn't.

Pearl took it upon herself to go through the monotonous task c filling the astonished guests in on their discoveries. It was startin to get wearing, having to repeat herself every afternoon, but sh couldn't deny the satisfaction she felt watching their astonishe faces – not only at the presentation of information they ha thought unknown to others, but also at the complete personali change in the timid young girl she'd been that morning.

Ellery was right – it was better to let things out than bottle the up. She'd been tempering her emotions for far too long. She als liked being important. And there was no doubt everyone on th terrace was hanging on her every word – possibly worried abou what she might say next. Power was addictive.

'Frankly, I've had enough of all your lies, given that we know th Brockhursts were murdered.' She had absolutely no proof of thi but Ellery was the only person on the terrace who knew that. 'Ar everything we've discovered points to it being one of you. Yc certainly all had reason to want Virgil out of the way, although wh poor Lenora did to deserve such an end, I can't imagine. So, who going to own up to the crime?'

Mrs Dawson chose that moment to step out through the Fren

oors. She'd forgotten about the cook and her confused arrival
ather took away from Pearl's dramatic moment.

Standfield got to his feet, claiming he needed another drink,
nd stepped inside. Céline and her father remained tight-lipped. It
as only when they realised Standfield had taken a long time
pping up his glass that Ellery went in search of him.

'Where the devil is he?' His voice floated out into the warm
ight air. He must surely be asking Aldo, but they all knew there
ould be no useful response. The three of them looked at each
ther and returned inside. Ellery had disappeared and they heard
e thunder of feet up and, barely a minute later, down the stair-
se. He burst back into the room, red-faced. Pearl walked over to
im and he spoke quietly into her ear.

'His room is empty and the Austin is no longer on the driveway.'

'Perhaps he's already been drugged by the brandy, and he won't
t far.'

'And, in approximately an hour he'll be back at the terrace,
lling you Paula, and demanding I fetch another bottle of wine.
teresting, though.'

'Yes,' she agreed, because nothing smacked more of guilt than
nning away.

But it was, in fact, less than twenty minutes later, just after
even o'clock, when she found herself flat on her back in the cave.

35

Before Pearl had found herself trapped in an endless loop of tim
her life had been a dull trudge towards an inevitable and undesir
marriage, interspersed with the snatched moments of peace and j
she got from being near water, and the occasional heart-thumpi
thrill of stealing. But now, here she was, having died multiple tim
in multiple ways, and trying to solve multiple murders. She thoug
back to her life before arriving at Highcliffe House and sighed
herself. The old adage 'be careful what you wish for' could not
more apt. Aesop had warned of this centuries ago, and now s
appreciated the truth of his words.

As she heaved herself up from the ground, a puddle of silv
caught her eye. There was the mercury that she'd knocked over
the previous loop, nestling in a small hollow of the uneven ca
floor. Everything else had returned to how it was the very mom
she'd first collided with the clepsydra; she was in her bathing su
damp from swimming in the sea; the candles were still casting th
flickering light across the cave; and Ellery would be in the be
room staring at a half-buffed candlestick... but the mercury had

returned to the funnel. The mercury was key. It was the very thing driving this circle of time.

She wanted out of this impossible situation, and so allowed her mind to re-examine what they knew – from her father's strong aversion to the sea, to Céline's temper, and Harlow's dramatic flight. She considered who might be seeking revenge, who might be *capable* of murder, and even considered the fly-covered corpse of the dead rabbit at Mrs Coombes' house.

These were the almost invisible wisps of a spider's silken threads floating in the air before her, and she had to anchor them down. She had theories, but she needed evidence and, for the first time, wondered if the Brockhursts had inadvertently left any clues behind. After all, the house had barely changed in the twenty years since they had last occupied it.

She met Ellery on the path as usual and asked him to cover for her whilst she searched the property for anything that might shed light on their disappearance.

'I'm hopeful there will be something we've overlooked. After all, the person behind the invitations is expecting everyone to be dead by midnight. They won't be worried about letters or links to the past.'

'Must I really polish that second candlestick *again*, aid in the production of a meal I am heartily sick of, and bow and scrape to people who do not deserve such attentions?'

'Don't be such a whinger. Unless you've also died from smoke inhalation *several times*, and suffered a violent poisoning, you don't get to complain,' she teased.

He put his hand out to her elbow and looked serious for a moment. 'Fair point.'

After changing out of her damp costume, she searched through those bedrooms that had not been given over to the guests, starting in the master bedroom.

It was a light, airy room, with unfashionable busy wallpaper covered in huge purple flowers, and curtains of a similar shade hanging under pelmeted windows. The small wooden crib in the corner remained as poignant as before. She started to the right of the door, and searched through the furniture and cupboards until she came full circle.

Ten minutes later and she'd discovered nothing of significance, but that was almost the most significant thing about it – there were a few personal possessions, but the items she would expect to find, like a dressing table set, a jewellery box, or perhaps some perfume, were missing. It was almost as if they *had* left for foreign travel. Undergarments were absent from the drawers, and several empty hangers were in the wardrobes. There was no luggage either – although it was possible this was stored elsewhere.

The other bedrooms threw up nothing, so she retreated down stairs and, after assessing the coast was clear, slipped into the library. She returned to the bureau and began to look through Virgil's personal papers, her heart racing the whole time. It was a similar sensation to when she stole the clocks and watches and even though it wouldn't really matter should she be discovered, she would rather not have to explain herself.

In amongst the papers, she found proof that a Raymond Hardinger had worked for the Brockhursts, as well as details of provisions for Bernard during his lifetime, but it was a slender album of photographs that proved the most useful. It belonged to Virgil and contained a few images from his childhood – photography not being as accessible as it was now, and probably very expensive back then.

One Brockhurst family grouping caught her eye in particular; was taken on the steps of a wooden colonial-style porch, between two white entrance pillars. About a dozen people of various age dressed in formal Victorian clothing, stood in rigid poses with stern faces. She flipped it over to see the names of the assembled group neatly written in a swirling hand, carefully labelled from left to right. Why had none of these people missed him? Or made an effort to track him down in the last twenty years? But she did find what she was looking for, startled to recognise a young face in the group, and tucked the album back where she'd taken it from. Everything was starting to make sense.

There was a small mahogany writing slope in the morning room. She opened it up and stroked the green leather, imagining Lenora sitting before it to deal with her daily correspondence. In the compartment beneath the slope itself, she found some loose letters addressed to Mrs Lenora Brockhurst – the use of her married name indicating these were sent after her marriage. They were all in the same hand, and all relatively brief, written by Standfield, expressing his adoration and begging her to be his. On one occasion including the slightly threatening sentiment that if she could not consider returning to him, she did not deserve to be with anyone. Had these been what he'd been looking for that morning when Ellery had caught him snooping?

Finally, she scouted around the boot room, not because she thought there would be anything relating to the Brockhursts' disappearance in there, but because she remained suspicious of Ellery and knew he hung his coat on an iron hook behind the door. She searched the pockets of his jacket, but they only contained his handkerchief. To her surprise she found a metal lipstick case had rolled under the corner cupboard – an item not invented when Lenora had lived at Highcliffe House – and certainly not something worn by respectable ladies back then. It was a deep plum colour and she pocketed it to show to Ellery, wondering whether to tease him and ask if it was his. Her sense of humour had definitely crept from the woodwork since arriving in Dorset.

Just as she was leaving, she noticed a key, which she assumed was to Ellery's room at the pub, and next to it was the corner of an envelope poking out from under his box of polishing materials. It was the letter from Badgerwood setting out the terms of his employment, and he would have been referring to it since his arrival. She scanned the words, not even sure what she was looking for...

Dear Mr Brown,

I am writing to inform you that you have been successful in your application for the temporary position of manservant, from Friday 6th July, until Sunday 8th July. As discussed, you should arrive at Highcliffe House no later than one o'clock and are free to leave on the Sunday evening when the guests have departed and all the duties listed below have been completed.

I have also secured a cook-cum-housekeeper for the duration. Mrs Dawson will arrive the same afternoon, and the necessary delivery of food and other supplies will come from the local grocers on that day. I have arranged for you to stay at the Morton Peverell Fisherman's Arms both nights. It is within walking distance, and you may retire there when Mrs Dawson dismisses you, returning each morning at seven prompt.

There will be five guests: Mr Harlow Standfield, Signor and Signora Ravello, and Mr Raymond Glenham and his daughter, Pearl. Most of these guests will have traveled quite some distance, but all of them are expected to arrive around 11 a.m. on the Saturday morning. You will take their luggage to the appropriate rooms, assist in personal matters for the gentlemen, and be of service in any other capacity deemed necessary. You will also have duties in the kitchen, helping Mrs Dawson to prepare and serve the meals...

There followed three pages of detailed instructions, concerning ho was sleeping in each room, and a list of tasks he needed to omplete before the guests arrived, and during their stay. Mrs awson, it said, had more comprehensive instructions, being the enior member of staff, and he should take further directions om her.

And suddenly Pearl knew, or thought she did, who had killed e Brockhursts, what was in the locked cupboard at the top of the rvants' stairs, and who had gathered everyone at Highcliffe ouse, with the intention of murdering them all in their beds.

36

Pearl's search had taken longer than anticipated and there was n[c] barely an hour until the meal. Because she needed to work throu[g] a few possibilities in her head, she retired to her room to change f[] dinner, having first told Ellery to continue with his habit of plyi[] everyone with drink – it usually loosened tongues, and she felt[] was their best bet for spilling any beans still lurking in the jar.

The last thing she did, before descending the stairs, was[] approach the locked store cupboard, brushing that same fly aw[] from her face as she turned with some trepidation to face the do[] Using a poker she'd taken from the fireplace in her bedroom, s[] managed to prise it open. The lock was not substantial and she h[] surprisingly strong arms for a young woman her age, thanks to t[] swimming.

The door swung towards her and the scant light fell up[] shelves of folded laundry, an assortment of buckets and brus[] and, as she had suspected, a small figure across the narrow fl[] space, wrapped in a stained sheet. Her eyes caught the purp[] tinged curled fingers of one waxy exposed hand, and two more fl[] crawling black dots against the whiteness of the linen. A poman[]

had been hung from the ceiling to hide the smell, but it underlaid the air and she heaved.

She pulled the door back to close it. She didn't need to investigate any further. The person was not known to her and, out of respect, she would leave them undisturbed.

'Gotcha,' she muttered under her breath, and turned to join the assembled guests for pre-dinner drinks.

* * *

Pearl was precisely fifteen minutes late, ensuring all eyes were on her. Ellery muttered that he'd been so frustrated by how long her investigations had taken, he'd resorted to talking to Aldo in the drawing room as they waited for everyone to come down for dinner – a somewhat one-sided conversation, but he was trying to be a more patient person, as she'd requested.

'Well?' he asked, desperate to know what she'd uncovered.

'Do you trust me?'

He locked eyes with hers. 'Always.'

'Then follow my lead… '

Pearl began with the shock announcement that the Brockhursts' bodies had been discovered in the cove and that someone in the room was responsible. Bernard had seen things. Every time one of them tried to speak, she spoke over them. She had no time to listen to repeated pleas of innocence, when she knew they were all far from that.

'Enough with the lies and excuses. I don't think there is anyone here who isn't hiding something – with the possible exception of Signor Ravello. And that includes myself and Ellery.'

'Me?' Her friend looked wrong-footed, and frowned at her, lowering his voice. 'I told you; Ruby will be sorted as soon as—'

'Not that. But it's not relevant at the moment.' Pearl had never interrupted so many people in her life, and yet again relished being in control.

'I'm sure I have no secrets,' Céline purred. 'Certainly nothing relating to this affair, only things I have kept from my husband – but doesn't every married couple?'

So, Pearl told her that they knew she'd been stealing antiquities for decades, but the Frenchwoman, as ever, gave little away.

'Silly little girl with your nonsense theories. Pure speculation.'

'We could all go up to your room and investigate why you have a valuable Persian bowl hidden in your drawers, if you like?' she offered

Céline's eyes became the usual suspicious slits, and Pearl could tell she was furious to be exposed by such a surprisingly bossy young woman as herself.

'And the stolen watch that *you* have, Miss Glenham. What of that?'

'Yes, I've been stealing clocks and watches for the past couple of years. And that's exactly what I meant when I said we are all hiding things. I'm not proud of it, and I'm certainly not making excuses but I have long held an obsession with a particular moment in time Four minutes past ten was when my mother passed away, and I suspect my father's inability to connect in any meaningful way with me, has led to that becoming an unhealthy focus.' She did not dare look in his direction, but felt his eyes on her. He said nothing in response to her comments. She hadn't expected him to.

'But I digress, signora. You were invited here in the spring of 1903, where Virgil either confronted you, or caught you stealing things and threatened to expose you,' she continued. 'I suspect lengthy prison spell beckoned. And that would not have suited someone such as yourself.'

Her eyes turned to Standfield, who wriggled in his seat and hastily downed his drink.

'And you had been harassing Lenora, writing letters and refusing to accept that she'd chosen Virgil over you. He'd had enough. I feel certain he loved her just as much as you did, and she was besotted with him, by all accounts. You struggled to accept this painful truth.'

'Absolute tosh. You have no proof.'

'I have the letters, actually. She kept them.' Even Ellery looked surprised at that. 'And you...' she looked to her father '...had been swindling the Brockhursts for several years. Don't even bother to deny it. I have proof of that too.' She didn't, only Standfield's words from before, claiming Virgil had confronted his accountant and made such accusations.

Her father cleared his throat. 'He was mistaken. I even got a letter from Virgil a few months later from Norway, as they travelled through Scandinavia. It was an apology, in point of fact, clearing me of any wrongdoing—'

'Goodness, they covered practically every continent that autumn.' Pearl rolled her eyes and caught Ellery's raised eyebrow, both noting that it was a letter this time, not a postcard, and from an entirely different destination.

'I had one, too,' Standfield chipped in. 'The fellow must have been in a forgiving mood. Said no hard feelings and all that. Asked me to be godfather to the little boy. You don't ask a chap that if there still bad blood.' He sat back in his chair and crossed his arms in a most self-satisfied manner.

Everyone focused on Céline, who was lighting up a cigarette.

'So typical of men – pulling up the drawbridge to save themselves. And yet you *are* hiding things, Raymond. Do explain to the assembled ladies and gentlemen why you felt the need to siphon funds from your most generous employer.' Raymond's lies had nearly angered her. 'To fund your dirty little habit...' She turned to

Pearl. 'You surely must be aware that your father cannot resist the lure of a wager?'

Pearl felt her temper rising. *Her father was a gambler?* Was this why she had endured such a frugal childhood? He was in a respectable profession with a moderate income, and yet they were often short of money, and he was always asking her to make economies. Of course, it would be related to probability and numbers – poker, she suspected. It all made sense now. Clearly the man had been frittering it away for years.

'And you wanted to marry me off to a wholly unsuitable man to claw your way out of a hole of your own making.' She was indignant. 'Did Simon owe you money? Or did you lose me in a wager? Actually, don't answer that; I don't want to know. You are such a disappointment.' Oh, how it thrilled her to say that.

'Where have you got all this information from, Pearl?' he asked, still frustratingly calm, despite the unpalatable truths spilling out.

'Oh, father of mine,' she said in her sweetest voice. 'You wouldn't believe me if I told you.'

Ellery topped up everyone's drinks, and Mrs Dawson entered announcing dinner was now ready.

'Ah, Mrs Dawson, just the lady,' Pearl said. 'Do pull up a chair and join us. We are having quite a jolly time here, and I think you need to be aware of the calibre of people you've been slaving away all afternoon in a hot kitchen for.'

'No, that wouldn't be proper, and the meal will spoil if we don't start serving promptly. Ellery?' She looked for him to back her up, but he shook his head.

'This is Miss Glenham's moment,' he said. 'We must all listen to what she has to say,' and he pulled out a chair for the cook, as Pearl ran through the accusations she'd levelled at each guest for the benefit of the bemused cook.

Aldo's nose was still buried in his *Ars Amatoria*. She smiled erself; here they were exposing the darkest of secrets and he was ignorant of it all, absorbed in a book detailing how to hold on to his wife. Would he be so keen to study such things if he knew the truth about her?

'I will not be painted as a common criminal.' Céline stood up to court the attention she so revelled in. 'What Virgil, and other arrogant collectors, were doing was wrong. It is a disease that has spread, ever since all these jumped-up little countries decided to sail around the globe, invading everyone. Stripping nations of their treasures to display them in their private residences because they were wealthy and could pick and choose from the spoils. Do you honestly believe *all* the items from the Boy King's tomb Mr Carter discovered last year will go to the museum in Cairo? I have already been advised to keep my ear to the ground by those I work for. Things are missing and the spirits of the ancients know it. Do not dismiss the curse – or think Lord Carnarvon's recent death is coincidental. These are the real thefts – sacred items, magical items, taken from cultures and religions that depend on them. How dare the wealthy acquire such relics with no regard for their sanctity?'

'So you steal these items back and return them to their original owners purely from the goodness of your heart?' her father said wryly, still smarting from her outing of his secret.

'I have expenses.' The Frenchwoman was indignant.

'Enough of the bickering. Why will not one of you own to the murders, when we know the truth? Bernard saw *everything*,' Ellery said, supporting Pearl. 'He has already directed the police to the bodies, wrapped in tarpaulin and hidden in Sailor's Rest.'

An icy chill swept the room. Regardless of who had committed the crime, the matter-of-fact nature of his announcement was beyond shocking; even Céline reached for the mantelpiece to steady herself. 'He is currently speaking to the officer in Morton Verell about the events he witnessed leading up to the murders.

We have agreed to keep an eye on you all here until Constable Carter can send reinforcements.'

'Stupid man, always lurking in the bushes. What he saw, or thought he saw, will not be taken seriously.' Céline was quite self assured, but Standfield was rattled.

'Well, I'm not having that.' He rose to his decidedly unsteady feet and banged his empty glass down on the small table next to his chair. 'I'll not go down for something that was an accident. I don't care what that simple fellow has told the police, but the only person who should be swinging from the neck in this room is you, Céline. You are the cold-blooded murderer.'

And all eyes swivelled towards the accused, as she slid a small pistol from her beaded bag, manoeuvring herself so that she had her back to the fireplace, and waving it at everyone in the room.

37

Céline tipped her head to one side and assessed her stunned audience.

It was only at this point that Pearl realised how ill prepared they were. They should, in fact, have approached Constable Carter, rather than just pretending that they had. That would have been the sensible thing to do. Have him lurking nearby, out of sight, only to appear if and when they elicited a dramatic confession from the true perpetrator – who, it would suddenly appear, was Céline. But Pearl was confused, her theory had been more complicated, and was thankful the universe would give her a hundred further opportunities to get this right.

Aldo sprung into action as soon as his wife produced the weapon. He looked genuinely horrified. Whether that was because he didn't know about the pistol, or was unsure whether she would use it, she wasn't certain. Pearl knew little about guns but knew the Frenchwoman would have no qualms in shooting anyone who challenged her.

Aldo began shouting at his wife and she replied in calm Italian. Was he to be the first casualty? But at no point did she wave it in his direction, and he moved to stand by her side, as their animated conversation continued.

'You silly people – it's as if you think Virgil was the first time I have taken a life. When people get in my way, I remove them. When people serve my purposes—'

'You marry them?' Pearl finished for her.

'*Exactement.*' She shrugged. 'Such a shame Aldo has scruples – he has already chastised me this very morning when he discovered I was here to take certain items from the house. I had not realised until recently that all these treasures still lay untouched within, and assumed the house had been sold. But it was worth the trip, after all, and my husband will stick with me. He may be stupid but he knows I am the best thing to happen to him and his ridiculous olive groves. Do excuse him as he gathers our things, but we must be off now. We will be borrowing your delightful little motor, Harlow. hope you don't mind.'

Standfield muttered something inaudible as Céline nodded at her husband, and he left the room.

'I'm somewhat worried, you see, the imbecile Bernard will not be able to adequately explain to the constable that it was all very heat of the moment,' she continued. 'And I wouldn't want anyone to think I'd planned to dispense with the American, but he was being so unreasonable. The party had come to an end, the two young girls they'd hired for the evening had returned to the village, but he asked Harlow, Raymond and me to remain.'

Mrs Dawson had risen almost silently from her seat and was making her way slowly to the doorway, but Céline spotted her.

'Please return to your seat, dear lady. I really can't have anyone scampering off and telling tales. And now that the cat has escaped the bag, I feel I should justify my actions that night. Everything got a little out of control, did it not, my friends?' She looked between Standfield and Pearl's father. 'The wine was flowing and the heads were hot. Lenora was exhausted. She had been a lot more fun back in Cairo but she'd just had the child and it was keeping her awake. Frankly, she looked awful – pale and drawn, and exactly why I did not choose the path of motherhood for myself.' She pulled a disgusted face.

'I highly suggest you don't incriminate yourself any further,' Pearl's father warned. 'We won't try to stop you leaving. I'm in no mood to be a hero and would suggest no one else in the room gets any funny ideas about tackling Signora Ravello. She is not a woman to be trifled with.'

'And wouldn't that suit you?' Céline purred. 'If I leave now, halfway through my tale, I can be blamed for the entirety of that night when we all know it was more complicated than that. I care not what people think. Let the facts be spoken aloud in this room, or I can disappear. I've done it before. The simple truth is Virgil refused to hand over certain artefacts, and instead threatened to expose me – so I shot him.'

Neither Pearl nor Mrs Dawson could prevent the gasps that came from their mouths.

'And this is exactly what Bernard is now telling Constable Carter.' Ellery continued the bluff. 'Killing us serves no purpose. He was in the gardens that night and saw everything through the window.'

'Then he also saw Harlow kill the woman he professed to love?' Céline asked, moving her gun and shifting the focus.

With her heart doing a million miles an hour, Pearl tried to remain calm and sift through these revelations. Although she hadn't known exactly who had killed the Brockhursts, she'd been sure that Céline, Standfield and her father had all been party to the murders, mainly because she was convinced the fire was revenge. There was only one reason to kill everyone in the house – they all bore some responsibility for the deaths. Spouses and daughters were collateral damage.

'Absolutely. He saw *you* shoot Virgil, and *Harlow*... kill Lenora. Pearl couldn't specify the manner of the poor woman's death because she didn't know it. She doubted Bernard did either. Perhaps all he'd seen was the bodies being taken out to sea, but that was enough. And then he'd muttered something about it to the wrong person and set in motion this dreadful chain of events.

'Then I hope he witnessed the stupid man fawn all over Lenora the second her husband lay dead on the floor? Telling her he would take care of her and had always loved her. And how Lenora, in her grief, told him a few home truths.'

Standfield was angry now, muttering and getting to his feet, as tears started to tumble down his red cheeks. 'She told me that she never loved me. That I'd become an embarrassment, and that she would never be mine. *Never*. I couldn't bear it. I worshipped her. would have done anything for her...'

'This has to stop,' Raymond said calmly. 'It's foolhardy to talk of these things. The police have no proof, bar the ramblings of a simple man.'

'I need to speak of it. It haunts every day of my life; only the drink can take the edge off my pain, and even that hardly works any more. She would never be mine, you see.' He turned to Pearl. 'But there was a chance she would go on to find someone else... I was so angry, so drunk, so desperately in love with her... I didn't mean to. The older man collapsed, sobbing, to his knees.

'The emotional fool slapped her across the face. Damn hard. Céline filled everyone in on the next part. 'And she hit her head on the hearth when she went down. Raymond dealt with the blood and the bodies. I simply couldn't bear it and he was so much better at controlling his emotions.'

'So, you were all involved?' Ellery finally realised. 'Céline kill

'irgil, Standfield pushed Lenora, and Raymond helped to
lear up?'

Standfield nodded. 'Made a pact to part ways and never meet or
ilk of it again. As guilty as each other. So, shoot us, Céline, and let
iy twenty years of torment finally be over. I damned well deserve
'

'But you didn't kill anyone, Father. These two may hang, and
ou will doubtless serve time, but you aren't a murderer.' Pearl
ung to that, at least.

'Oh, but he is darling.' How Céline enjoyed her moment. She
aved the gun around, rather too recklessly for Pearl's liking, and
ausing just long enough to get everyone's attention. 'We all took a
ie that night. Do let me tell the entirety of the tale. After all that
ama, and with two bodies at our feet, we knew if we did nothing,
ir crimes would be discovered, so Raymond and I, more clear-
inking than Harlow, who was weeping like a child on the hearth
ig and clutching at a lifeless corpse, decided to make it appear as
ough they'd left on their adventures again. They were always
ivelling. I offered to pack the cases. Giving such a task to a man
ould be foolhardy, as they would not think to include the neces-
ry things. Harlow agreed to return with his carriage the following
y and take the luggage away. And Raymond – who we all know
is a disturbingly clinical mind – suggested dumping the bodies
it at sea. And all was going well until *l'enfant* upstairs started
ving.'

'Forgotten about the little mite,' Standfield said. 'We all had. Not
e of us had paid the slightest interest in him all night.'

Pearl's blood ran cold as she realised where this was leading.
r father had killed the baby. He was as guilty as the rest of them –
ire so. The child was an innocent. That's why they'd all been
ackmailed into coming to Highcliffe House. They were all
irderers.

She felt slightly sick and reached for the back of the neare[st] chair.

'I was *persuaded* that if I didn't help deal with the mess these tw[o] had created, I would be dragged down with them regardless,' h[er] father said, looking at Standfield and Céline with narrowed eyes.

'Which means you'll also hang, Hardinger,' Standfield sai[d] calling her father by his real name for the first time, but the unner[v] ingly calm accountant merely smiled.

'No, I won't, because despite the fact everyone here thinks me [a] cold and calculating man, I simply could not bring myself to har[m] the baby. I may fail to understand the extreme reactions of others [in] many situations, but I'm not inhuman. Jo Brockhurst is in this ve[ry] room. Jo Brockhurst never died.'

Three pairs of eyes swivelled in Ellery's direction. As the on[ly] male approximately the right age to be the son of Lenora and Vir[gil] Brockhurst, it was the natural conclusion to draw.

Ellery rolled his eyes and chuckled. 'I'm five years older th[an] this missing baby, and I'm the very spit of my mother.' He waved [a] hand across his face. 'These colourful irises are a family trait. [As] much as I'd love to step in and claim the Brockhurst inheritan[ce,] I'm certain that you've got your facts wrong, Mr Hardinger.'

Her father looked at Céline and Harlow in turn, his face s[till] unreadable.

'Both of you are so innately selfish, so uninterested in the li[ves] of others, that neither of you even took the time to establish the s[ex] of the baby...'

Pearl's stomach began a slow swirling – a torrent of underc[ur] rents and eddies, pulling everything that she thought she was do[ing] in a spiralling whirlpool of emotion.

'Jo,' her father said with steel in his eyes, 'was short [for] Josephine.'

38

The eyes that had hitherto scrutinised Ellery now turned to Pearl. She noticed that Céline had let the gun drop to her side, such was her shock.

'But I was born after this all happened. I wasn't alive that summer.'

Even as she said the words, the truth came flooding towards her, saturating her in a chilling wave of comprehension. Ellery had said it so many times – just because a thing is proclaimed as true, doesn't mean it is. Her academically advanced behaviour as a young child now made sense. She was a year older, perhaps more, than her father... than this man before her... claimed she was. No wonder they had moved about so much when she was small, and an infant remembers nothing much before the age of four. She would not know how many birthdays she'd had, and their itinerant lifestyle in those early years, ensured no one else did either. How easy it must have been for Raymond Hardinger to arrive somewhere new, call himself Glenham, and create some tragic tale of a young wife dying in childbirth. No wonder he had never talked of her mother – she didn't exist...

Except she did...

'*Lenora and Virgil Brockhurst were my parents?*' Mrs Dawson let out a shriek and slithered from her chair to the floor, and Ellery took advantage of the general chaos to do exactly what Raymond Hardinger had warned them not to do only moments earlier; he snatched the gun from Céline and twisted her right arm behind her back, forcing her in front of him. Standfield, meanwhile, helped the cook back to her feet.

'Lock the French doors, Pearl,' Ellery instructed, 'and pocket the key. Let's keep everyone together, shall we?'

Pearl gave Céline a look she could only wish had the power to kill. This ruthless woman had murdered her father. Shot him in cold blood because he threatened to expose her for something that deserved to be exposed. There was a part of Pearl that wanted to run at her and claw her stupid French eyes out with her fingernails, inflict pain that would endure for twenty years, like the pain she couldn't even begin to process. Her parents had been taken away from her, but she hadn't even known they were hers to grieve over. It would take time for her to sort this all out in her muddled head.

She was clenching her fists so tightly that her nails were digging into her flesh, and so she took a deep breath and rationalised her thoughts. Anything she did to Céline would be undone in a matter of hours; besides, it would make her no better than the serpent standing before her.

Standfield caught her eye and, unlike Céline, he had the grace to look ashamed. A crime of passion was still a crime, and she hated him with equal fervour.

'It was an accident,' he said. 'I'm truly sorry for it. I loved her.'

'You *will* pay for what you did,' Pearl muttered under her breath.

'Then I shall be thankful to have had such a good run. As the Good Book says, "Be sure your sin will find you out".'

Pearl felt her nostrils flare and never wanted to hit someone so much. It was as if he'd stolen cookies from the pantry, not taken the life of a beloved wife and mother. Ellery must have noticed her distress because he stepped closer and leaned slightly into her, his warmth reassuring and calming.

'You never were married then, Raymond?' Céline wriggled uncomfortably as Ellery held her tighter. 'Must admit I was rather surprised to hear that you had. You never showed any inclinations either way, as I remember.'

'Simply not the romantic sort,' Raymond said. Finally, he could avoid Pearl's horrified glare no longer.

'Why did you call me Pearl?' she asked, desperate for answers.

He let out an impatient sigh, as though he was explaining a simple maths problem to an idiot.

'Because when I made the decision to save you, I was rowing out to Sailor's Rest. Harlow had helped me get the bodies down the steps to the shore, but wanted nothing to do with killing the baby. I told him to leave. That I'd take it from there. It was approaching ten o'clock but it was pitch dark. The moonlight illuminated the floor of the boat and all I could see was that shock of white-blonde hair sticking out from the dark blanket Céline had wrapped you in. It made me think of pearls in the sea.' He swallowed. 'I'm aware I am different to other people, but I'm not a killer. And the truth is, I was lonely.'

Raymond's shoulders slumped slightly, but the moment that Céline scoffed, he regained his composure.

'I decided to forge a new identity, to give you a home. After depositing the bodies, I just kept rowing, coming ashore further down the coast, where some locals helped me through that first night with you.' He turned to face Pearl properly. 'Perhaps I did an inadequate job but I did try, every day suspecting the police would come looking for us. I was waiting for the bodies to be discovered or for someone to demand an investigation into the disappearance of the Brockhursts – but neither of those thing happened.'

'Until now,' Ellery pointed out.

'I had no particular desire for a wife, but wondered if a child might make an undemanding companion, and perhaps nursemaid for me in my dotage. You must admit you have proved exceedingl useful about the house, and from a remarkably young age, too?'

Pearl was incredulous. Her mouth was slightly agape as he justi fied his decision to save her from the raging waters, and there was moment when she considered that all three had deserved to die i the fire.

'So, keeping me was not born of compassion, but instead calculated assessment of the pluses and minuses of having daughter to care for you?'

'I am fond of you,' Raymond finally said. 'In my way.'

'All these years, I held on to the exact minute this mythica woman died, fundamental to who I was and what I'd lost, but meant nothing.'

'It meant a great deal. I'm not sentimental, as you know, b technically, four minutes past ten was the time *my* daughter wa born – the moment I climbed into the water to better position the bundle, and my pocket watch stopped working.'

'No.' She was adamant. 'I'm not the daughter of a calculatin emotionally barren man, who considers eating fish on a Tuesd the height of daring.' She shook her head. 'I'm Josephine Broc hurst – daughter to an extraordinary couple, born of love a destined for adventure.'

As she said the words, she allowed herself to consider how tr they were. She'd spent a lifetime believing her quiet nature and clos horizons were hereditary when the truth was she came from unt lievably intrepid stock. Ellery had seen it in her, and shown her ov

ιe repeating days that they'd spent together, that she was capable of
ɔ much more than she thought, even before the truth of her
ɑrentage had come out. And for that she would be eternally grateful.

'I say, where's that funny little Italian chap of yours got to,
éline? Isn't it about time he burst back in and whisked you away?'
ɪandfield muttered, not remotely interested in the family drama
ɪaying out before him.

It occurred to them all then that Aldo had indeed been gone an
ɪtraordinarily long time. Pearl exchanged a glance with Ellery,
ho still had Céline's arm bent behind her back, to prevent her
ɔm escaping.

'I'll check,' Pearl volunteered.

'No, I'll not have you confront a possibly dangerous man alone,'
ɪ replied. 'We all go. Out into the hall,' he directed, and everyone
ɔved as one, Ellery pushing Céline through the door first, and
ɪarl bringing up the rear. Mrs Dawson had recovered sufficiently
join the group, but her face was pale and her posture stooped.
ιe threw repeated glances in Pearl's direction as though she also
uldn't believe the transformation in the quiet young woman of
ɑt morning.

'Signor Ravello?' Ellery called up the stairs, just as Standfield
ɑde a foolhardy dash for the front door, weaving between the
ɪplay cabinets, and flinging it wide, only to stare out at the drive-
ɪy, open-mouthed.

'The bastard's taken my motor car!'

'What?' Céline screeched, wriggling against her captor to ascer-
ɪn the truth of this statement. '*Trahison* of the worst kind. He has
ɪtrayed me.'

Aldo's decision to make a run for it confused Pearl. Only guilty
ɪn ran, as Standfield was proving for the second time, and she
ɪs not sure what crime the Italian had committed. She'd assumed

he was not involved in any of Céline's past escapades. Had she g
this all wrong?

'Planning to go somewhere, Standfield?' Ellery asked. 'Yc
wouldn't have got far.'

'You wouldn't have shot me.' The older man was defiant.

'Not to kill – just to incapacitate. I'd go for a kneecap, old cha
and I should warn you all, I'm a crack shot.'

The threat was enough to make Céline wince and possib
reassess any escape plan she'd been formulating. Even Raymor
blinked twice in rapid succession.

'But if you'd run, you wouldn't have found out the truth of th
gathering,' Pearl said, scrabbling to get everything back on tra
and preparing to reveal the biggest secret of all. 'Do you not want
know who orchestrated this elaborate charade? Who doubtl
spent months, if not years, tracking you all down, in order to k
you all in this house – the house where you committed yo
heinous deeds – and make the three of you pay for your crimes?'

'Do you know who is behind all this?' Ellery was incredulo
His face fell. 'You didn't say.'

'And you've always been totally honest with me?' s
challenged.

He did not reply.

'*Who*? Who is behind this?' Céline was verging on hysteri
now. Any hopes of her husband rescuing her had driven out i
the Dorset countryside. 'We've all known from the start tha
wasn't the Brockhursts inviting us to Highcliffe House. They w
several feet under the sea, for Christ's sake. But I was promi
treasures…'

Pearl ushered everyone back into the enclosed dining roc
ignoring Ellery's searching looks.

'Who owns the house?' Ellery eventually asked Raymond. 'W
inherited after they died?' He released Céline and remained in

doorway, facing the assembled company as they retook their seats, and blocking the only exit. If they swarmed at him, Pearl had no doubt he would go for the knees, as he'd threatened. These people deserved no kindness, and now that he knew she was Josephine, his anger at what they'd done would be all the greater.

'To the world at large, they are still alive,' Raymond pointed out. 'I know for a fact certain trusts were set up, because they travelled so much. Bernard, for example, had been granted use of the game-keeper's cottage and a small income for his lifetime.'

'But someone other than Bernard has been inside the house recently. It was given a thorough spring clean before Mrs Dawson and I arrived. Surely the Brockhursts had a will?'

'They did, but I was not privy to its contents – although it was suggested to me in Badgerwood's invitation that I had been left a bequest,' Raymond said.

Pearl took a deep breath. 'The truth is, Virgil had a relative and, although they can't have been close, after a while they naturally began to wonder what had happened to him and started to investigate.'

The photograph had been key. A familiar face staring back at her as she'd browsed the album in the library. The accent had thrown her at first but the evidence was indisputable.

'I don't know how many years it took, or exactly what was uncovered, but they eventually visited Highcliffe House, and I can only think that Bernard gave them cause to believe the Brockhursts were dead. He did see something that night – if only the bodies being taken out to sea.' Of course the chickens were everywhere; the wire from their run had been removed, and he'd seen Raymond with the baby. '*She didn't die*,' he'd insisted. Little Josephine was safe, and not bundled up with the others.

'Honestly, I have no idea how the three of you were implicated or how you were tracked down, but you had to pay for your deeds.'

She paused for effect, as she had seen Céline do on so many occasions. 'You were gathered here by Virgil's sister, Myrta, and this very evening she planned to kill us all in our beds by starting a fire that would rampage through the house.'

'Nonsense,' Standfield said. 'Virgil never mentioned a sister.'

'Well, I can assure you he had one, and she's in this very room. Aren't you, Mrs Dawson?'

And five sets of eyes turned to the silent cook.

39

Mrs Dawson?' Standfield spluttered, falling into an upholstered chair. 'This dowdy old thing is Virgil's sister?'

'Oh, I don't think she's that dowdy, are you?' Pearl turned to the insignificant woman, still reluctant to accept that she was related by blood to the architect of this horrific house party. Myrta narrowed her eyes.

'I found a rather daring lipstick in the boot room,' Pearl explained, 'which I assumed was Céline's at first, until I remembered that she only wears red, so concluded it must belong to someone else who'd been at the house recently. It's certainly not Bernard's – plum doesn't suit his colouring.'

Her attempt at a joke was lost entirely on her father, but Ellery smiled.

'And there is a family photograph that includes her as a young woman, in Virgil's bureau. She really was quite the elegant lady.' He turned to the cook. 'But then I imagine if you don't want to be recognised, you become the opposite of the thing people know you . And, of course, the joy of this whole gathering, was that not one of these people had ever met you before.'

Pearl could see Myrta was assessing what to do next. To deny her identity was futile – it would come out eventually. There would be a birth certificate, people who could identify her, records in America that they could track down – all when they had longer than an afternoon to investigate. But Pearl had accused her of dreadful things – crimes she still had yet to commit – but dreadful things nonetheless.

'Nonsense. She doesn't sound like an American,' Standfield pointed out.

Mrs Dawson, or rather Myrta, decided the jig was up.

'Very clever, honey,' she said, a hint of her American accent creeping back in. 'Thirty years being married to an Englishman sweetheart. One I met in Calcutta, on a trip with my brother. A man my brother forbade me to marry, but I did so regardless and we didn't speak from the moment the ring was on my finger. And living under the Raj, surrounded by the extreme Britishness your nation always inflicted on the conquered world, was enough for me to perfect your accent.'

But there had been clues. Mrs Dawson had referred to Ellery's trousers as pants on the afternoon that he'd rescued Pearl from the sea, and Mr Badgerwood's written instructions to Ellery had talked of the guests 'traveling' a long way – the spelling favoured over the Atlantic.

'That's the problem with estrangement,' she continued. 'You just aren't kept up to date with family news. So, you can imagine my surprise when my husband passed away three years ago and I decided to contact my brother again, that no one had heard from Virgil in over fifteen years.'

'Myrta *Brockhurst* – badger wood. I see it now,' her father said.

'Oh, Ellery worked that out ages ago,' Pearl said, dismissively.

'Plain old Myrta Smith now, honey. Part of the problem; Virgil always said I deserved better. Perhaps that's why he left me the

ouse, but I have no need of it or his stupid treasures. However, it
urns out if no one has seen you for seven years, and reasonable
fforts have been made to track you down, your estate can be
ettled. I guess I wanted to see where he'd made his life, more than
nything. He was always so good to me when I was... unwell as a
id.'

'So, was Pearl correct?' Ellery asked. 'Was it Bernard who told
ou that they'd been killed?'

Myrta shrugged. 'I wanted to know about my brother, find out if
e'd been happy since our quarrel. Initially, I assumed something
rrible had happened to them abroad until the old man started
uttering about bodies in a boat and people scurrying about in the
arkness. He mentioned a man who came to the house to talk
imbers, some young woman from abroad, and Standfield – who
· knew quite well through Lenora. For the sake of a few after-
oons drinking your unpleasant English tea in his hovel of a home,
managed to extract enough information to establish the truth.
kes one wandering mind to recognise and understand another, I
ess. Eventually, I paid someone to track you down, and the very
ct you all came confirmed your guilt.'

'I say, cooking us all in our beds is rather extreme. Exactly
w unhinged are you?' Standfield banged on the arms of his
air, furious that this woman had planned his demise, momen-
ily forgetting he was responsible for extinguishing a life
mself.

Perhaps it was his careless use of the word 'unhinged', or
rhaps Myrta was finally at breaking point after years of planning,
earching and almost executing the ultimate revenge. She leapt
m her seat and launched herself onto the bumptious older man
h all the rage and fury of a rabid cat, clawing at his neck and
tting in his face.

'How dare you,' she screeched.

'Well, there is our answer,' Céline pointed out, in response
Standfield's question. 'Exceedingly unstable, by the looks of things

'I will not have those unfounded accusations launched at m
again,' Myrta screamed, as Pearl rushed to pull her from Standfiel
not because he didn't deserve it, but because with a loaded gun
the room and tensions running unbearably high, she wanted
restore a modicum of calm.

Myrta Smith, Pearl suspected, was not quite of sound mind. B
then was her mental instability any more alarming than the co
calculated way Céline went about disposing of people?

'Virgil was the only one who understood,' Myrta wept, mo
placid now that the younger woman had a grip on her arms. 'Savi
me from the sanatorium when I was younger and begging o
parents to let him take me abroad – away from all the mean-spirit
people who picked at me, pulling on the loose threads of my ex
tence until I unravelled completely. He was the best of brothe
even though it took me too many years to realise it. And you all to
away any chance I had of reconciliation. You deserve to die for wh
you did.'

Céline flared her nostrils, Standfield's face went beetroot r
and even Raymond swallowed hard. But they said nothing. Wh
could they say? Their guilt had been established.

'You will be held accountable for your murderous plan, rega
less or not of whether you had the opportunity to enact it,' Ell
said to the cook, as Pearl guided her into a chair.

'But I think you'll find that all I've done is invite a group
people I've not met before to my own house for a dinner pa
However odd that may seem, I have committed no crime.'

'Maybe not, but procuring a corpse will undoubtedly lead
criminal charges being brought against both you and whiche
local morgue or undertaker you dealt with.' Pearl felt little satis
tion from this victory. The woman had committed murder time a

time again, but the fact all her victims were currently alive and well would make a prosecution somewhat tricky.

'What the devil?' Standfield blustered. That a further body was somehow involved in this mess was news to everyone else in the room.

'Oh.' Ellery finally caught on. 'The locked cupboard?' She nodded. 'And when you saw Mrs Dawson burning in her bed...'

'Exactly. Myrta has been here for several days, and Highcliffe House is sufficiently off the beaten track so no one would particularly notice whether or not it was occupied. Besides, the villagers know Bernard lives on the estate, so odd comings and goings, or a light on at night, would not raise suspicion. She cleaned the place up in readiness, ordered in food from the village, and sent out invites to the guests and instructions by letter. Somehow – although the exact details don't bear thinking about, she secured a corpse and concealed it before Ellery arrived, turning up later than him to avoid suspicion.'

Pearl could only wonder at the despicable depths of human nature. Myrta, as the sole beneficiary of her brother's fortune, now had the wealth to buy anything she needed to enact her twisted revenge – enough to hire a private investigator, put on a lavish dinner party, even procure a corpse.

Myrta stared at her hands like a reprimanded child choosing to ignore the admonishing parent.

'Tonight, you planned to slip a sleeping draught into our drinks—'

'I bet it was in the glasses,' interrupted Ellery. 'The ones I carried through into the drawing room, because she couldn't guarantee everyone would drink brandy. Unfortunately for you, Pearl, there were occasions you had no after-dinner drink at all.'

Several confused faces listened to their muddled tenses as they exchanged theories.

'And you planned to set fire to the upstairs corridor when we were all asleep,' Pearl continued. 'A house fire was the perfect way to kill several people in one go without raising suspicion. Badgerwood was only ever a means to lure your victims here and either you organised a telegram in advance, or paid someone to send it for you, ensuring everyone remained overnight, all desperate to meet the man claiming to have something that would benefit each of them, and too intimidated by his threats not to attend.'

'What telegram?' Céline asked.

'Oh, it doesn't arrive for another half an hour,' Ellery said dismissively.

'I still don't understand – what do you need a body for?' Standfield was agitated and began pacing in front of the fireplace.

'Because an investigation into the tragic fire that raged through Highcliffe House would ensue if Mrs Dawson was missing – don't forget Ellery knew who was here,' Pearl said. 'But if all persons were accounted for, then the case could be closed. Myrta Smith could access her brother's money, or perhaps even sell the land, even if she had cremated the house in her fury.' The logic was muddled, but then so was Myrta. 'Only you and I will ever know what you planned for us all tonight.' She met the cook's eyes and held them for as long as she dared, fancying that she could see her guilt deep within the pale irises, even without her knowledge of the fire from living, and dying, through it so many times.

Myrta, she now realised, had been clever, adapting as best she could every time they had poked an unexpected stick into the spokes of her carefully constructed plan. The day Ellery had removed the screws from her window, there had been ample opportunity for her to pop upstairs and replace them. And, as soon as Pearl had announced her suspicions about the fire, although doubtless startled as to how Raymond's daughter could possibly have known of her intentions, yet again she'd adapted by poisoning everyone, claiming to be sick herself.

When Pearl revealed they were all to be burned alive, Mrs Dawson had been genuinely shocked at how the young woman knew of her murderous scheme. It was not her superstitious nature, as Pearl had wrongly assumed at the time. And on the days they had foiled her completely, she was doubtless regrouping. Heaven knows what she would have come up with, but Pearl was certain that she would have got them all in the end, by some means or another.

She turned to the cook. 'Kind of you to spare Ellery – arranging for him to stay nearby. But Aldo and I have nothing to do with this.'

'I thought the baby had been murdered too,' she whispered. 'Bernard was so frustratingly jumbled. I had no idea you were my niece.' She put her hand out to Pearl in a gesture of friendship, but Pearl just stared at it, and made no effort to move.

They were startled by a loud knock at the front door and all heads swivelled towards the hallway.

'This must be the police you summoned,' Céline surmised, now resigned to her fate. 'It is truly over and I am not sorry.'

Pearl and Ellery exchanged a glance, knowing that it wasn't. They had failed to organise any such thing, but Pearl went to investigate regardless, and was astonished to see Constable Carter and another young policeman she recognised from the time the fishing boat had been launched, standing the other side of the door.

Aldo was behind them, raising his eyes in acknowledgement at Pearl, as the constable started to speak.

'We were informed that there was a madwoman here, brandishing a gun.'

40

The two policemen were taken to the drawing room and all th
nasty little secrets that had been uncovered were relayed to ther
The younger officer took notes, and Constable Carter formal
arrested Standfield, Céline, Raymond and Myrta. The intricacies
their crimes and the charges that would be brought against the
could be sorted another time, but his main priority was to get the
all safely behind bars and ensure they were not a danger to ther
selves or others.

Ellery explained that they would need a boat to recover t
Brockhursts.

'And I'm afraid there is an unknown corpse in a cupboard at t
top of the stairs,' Pearl added.

'So, let me get this right: three bodies and four perpetrator
Constable Carter said, looking bewildered. 'That's quite a cri
wave for Morton Peverell.'

'There would have been eight bodies if this evil witch had g
her way.' Standfield pointed at Myrta. 'And I'd be one of them.'
shivered.

'I think I would rather have perished in a fire than face wha

come,' said Céline, forlornly. 'I will not suit prison.' Of the four of
them, she was the only one certain to hang.

'Well, now, I don't have four pairs of handcuffs so we'll have to
improvise. Henry, see if you can find some rope – there's a good lad.'
The younger man nodded and went off in search of a suitable
restraint. 'I'm not sure how I'm going to get them all to the station.
I'll have to organise a military truck from the nearby base. Should
do the trick. And after that, I would ask that the three of you remain
in the house, and someone will be over to take statements in the
morning.' He shook his head. 'These things always happen on my
days off. Still, it gives me a valid reason to skip Reverend Tidyman's
sermon tomorrow, so it's not all bad.'

It was only as the truck pulled away two hours later, that Pearl
allowed herself to contemplate the enormity of all that had
happened in the last few hours. She had finally solved the mystery
of the Brockhursts' disappearance and worked out who had started
the fire that had killed her so many times. The biggest shock of all –
that her whole life had been a lie – would take many months to
come to terms with.

Ellery glanced at his watch.

'Not long now and I'll be staring at a half-buffed candlestick
and you'll be nursing a sore head in the cave. Perhaps we should
use the rest of today to decide how we're going to let this all play
out tomorrow. I'd really rather not be in charge of a loaded
weapon this time, and there's no need to investigate the cupboard
again.'

'No, it ends tonight,' she said. 'This evening has been unbearable and I can't repeat it. To do so might lead to *me* committing
murder. I don't want to see any of their evil faces again.'

'Not even Raymond? He saved you?'

'He saved me to save himself. I feel sorry for him – perhaps he
loved me in his way – but what he did was wrong. I've grown up

with very little tenderness shown towards me. And what is li[fe]
without it?'

She locked eyes with him and gave a small smile, accepting sh[e]
was now over her childish sulk about Ruby, and acknowledging
herself that a huge part of her anger had been jealousy. Ellery ha[d]
won her heart and changed her outlook. No longer was she th[e]
compliant and ordinary girl who had arrived at Highcliffe Hou[se]
that morning, but instead a strong woman with a voice and a desi[re]
to live a more extraordinary life.

'Shall we head down to the cave and finally wake up to Sund[ay]
morning?'

'You know how to stop this interminable loop?' He was wid[e]
eyed. 'You really are full of surprises this afternoon.'

'I have a good idea, but only time – quite literally – will tell. [We]
need a lamp, the wood-mounted thermometer from the conserv[a]
tory, a paintbrush and a wide spoon.'

'Yes, sir,' he said, saluting her.

* * *

They stood in front of the clepsydra, Ellery holding the oil la[mp]
aloft as she lifted the glass dome and set it on the table.

'The mercury is the key,' she said, getting down on her kne[es]
and bending under the table. 'The weight of it makes the fun[nel]
beneath drop and the wheel turns, moving the brass hand arou[nd]
the clock face. And if some of the mercury is missing, the lar[ge]
hand never reaches midnight—'

'So, time can't move on without the correct weight of mercu[ry?]'
He realised what she was saying.

'Exactly, and that's the theory I'm about to test. I think Célin[e's]
right; some of these artefacts have powers we will never und[er]
stand. I think even Virgil... my father... knew that. He wante[d]

own these things because he was an acquirer of curiosities, but he also employed Bernard to maintain them *and* protect them. He instilled in him over the years that they must be kept safe. He'd already had a saintly finger returned to the Catholic church, and encountered Céline in Egypt, sniffing around, and he knew there would be others.

'So, when Bernard saw the Brockhursts taken out to sea and realised they were dead, he made sure no one could come for Virgil's precious curios, and continued to care for them for the last twenty years, simply because that is what he'd been told to do. Poor man,' she said. 'He told me on more than one occasion that *she didn't die*. He must have seen Raymond take the baby, but neither of us knew the baby was standing right in front of him as he said it.'

'Will you tell him?'

'Of course. Perhaps tomorrow – if we ever see it. I will also make sure he's taken care of.' She sighed. 'There's so much to sort. I don't know where I stand legally, or even what will happen to Myrta. Where do I even belong now? But one step at a time. Let's make sure there is a tomorrow first.'

She took the flat spoon and used the paintbrush to sweep the slippery beads of silver liquid into it – an adaptation of a dustpan and brush. It was fiddly and they kept rolling away, but eventually she'd retrieved the mercury from the floor and tipped the silver puddle into the funnel that was slowly draining.

'We must get every last drop,' she said. 'Hand me the lamp.' She crawled around and found a tiny bead of mercury she'd missed, no bigger than the head of a pin, reflected in the light. 'It's how I worked this out,' she explained. 'When I was first caught in the loop, the time reset fifteen minutes before midnight. When you joined me, the day finished half an hour earlier.'

'Of course. The mercury we both swallowed.'

'I have to assume that's what pulled us both back. And when I knocked the clepsydra the other day and more rolled out—'

'The day finished even earlier.' He grinned. 'You're one hell of a girl, Pearl,' he said. 'Or should I call you Josephine?'

'Pearl for now, I think. Pass me the thermometer.'

She prised the glass tube from the wooden mount and used a piece of rock from the floor to break the end. 'Two drops should do it.' And she carefully allowed two beads to fall into the funnel.

'Will we still be pulled back?' he asked. 'The mercury is still inside us. We're never around long enough for it to pass through our systems.'

She shrugged and reached for his wrist, glancing at his father's wristwatch.

'I'm afraid I can't tell you with any certainty unless we are still here in another... fifty minutes. Let's hope today we *finally* see the stroke of midnight.' And they both smiled.

* * *

They tidied up as best as they could and took the lamp out to the cove. The evening was warm, as it always was. They paused by the shoreline as Pearl's eyes were inevitably drawn to the jutting boulders that marked Sailor's Rest.

'It's awful to think they are still out there,' she said.

'At least they are together and have been so for the last twenty years. We can bring them back to shore and make certain they are buried properly. They will be treated with the respect they deserve.'

He lifted up his arm and placed it about her shoulders, pulling her a little closer to his body.

'Thank you,' she whispered.

Tears were building in her eyes, exacerbated by the cool breeze blowing in from the sea. His touch was electric, and being so close to the thing she wanted more than anything in the world, but convincing herself she couldn't have it until everything with Ruby was properly resolved, was starting to break her.

He twisted his body towards hers and bowed his head until their foreheads were touching. Every part of her was pulled in his direction, and all she could think about was that kiss by the cave. She tipped her chin upwards slightly, allowing her lips to make the briefest contact with his mouth.

He pulled back and studied her face.

'What was that?'

'It was an accident. I brushed your lips as I looked up. I told you I don't dally with men who are engaged to other women.'

'Really?' His eyes twinkled and he lurched forward, and pressed his lips firmly and resolutely on hers. 'I do apologise. I tripped. Understand that I take my engagement seriously and wouldn't trifle with the feelings of someone when I was betrothed to another.'

They stared at each other in the challenging way that was becoming so familiar, seeing who would be the first to break the gaze. But the more she looked into those eyes, the heavier her breaths became. Her heart began to thud and her stomach rolled. Finally, she could bear it no longer and reached her arms up, sliding her hands about his neck, pulling his mouth to hers, as her morals slipped to the shingle by her feet and were washed away by the endless lapping tide.

* * *

Having spent most of her life without kisses, it was surprising how addictive they were. To be connected with another person in such a way was incredible, and the fact that this person was Ellery felt right.

'I'm starving. Let's see what we can rescue of the meal,' he said, as they broke apart, and she reluctantly nodded.

He picked up the lamp and they climbed the steps to Highcliff House.

They stumbled across Aldo in the kitchen as they went in search of food, sitting at the pine table, tucking into his third dish of chocolate mousse, with his open poetry book on the table beside him. He looked up as they entered and smiled, giving them both the tiniest nod of the head, then scraped his chair back and stood for Pearl. From the looks of the abandoned plates and dishes, the drama of the evening had done nothing to diminish his appetite.

'What I don't understand is how Aldo managed to make himself understood by the police,' she mused, as they both nodded back at him. He dabbed the linen napkin to his lips and gathered up his leather poetry book.

'Perhaps Constable Carter speaks fluent Italian,' Ellery joked. 'Or he was creative with his sign language. Who cares? He turned out to be the only honourable one amongst the lot of them.'

Aldo walked towards the door, but paused and turned to face them. 'I only ever wanted a quiet life. I was always happiest in my olive groves.' He shrugged. 'My mistake was to marry someone such as Céline. But I have the last laugh – no? You learn so much when others think you do not comprehend their words.'

Pearl's mouth dropped open. 'But, but—'

'She frightened and bewitched me in equal measure. It was easier this way. And once you start a lie, it is so very hard to stop, *vero*?'

She thought about all the lies that had been carried for the last twenty years. Those despicable people had spent two decades looking over their shoulders, wondering if their heinous actions would ever be discovered. It was no way to live. And she rather revelled in that. The lie that Aldo had carried was insignificant

omparison. He knew exactly what sort of woman he was married
o and, luckily for them, was principled enough to see she was
unished for her sins.

'I am to bed. The day has been long and... surprising. But now
ou must tell the truth to the young lady or you will lose her, *signor*?
he good truth you did tell to me, and the not so good.'

'The truth about what?' She turned to Ellery, confused.

Aldo excused himself and Ellery gulped as he took her hand
. his.

'Please try to understand...' he began. 'All this started before I
new you.'

41

Turns out that you really shouldn't rant to a foreigner who y
don't *think* understands a word you say, as a way of venting yc
frustrations over your romantic situation... particularly when tl
foreigner secretly understands every word.

That afternoon, as Pearl had scoured the house for evidence
her suspicions, Ellery had been ensuring she wasn't discovered
he went about his duties. This involved steering Céline away fr
the library on one occasion, and keeping an eye on the poet
reading Aldo, who dressed for dinner early and chose to re
quietly in the drawing room whilst his wife prepared herself for I
grand entrance.

Under the mistaken belief that the quiet Italian did not und
stand English, Ellery was both frustrated and unbelievably prc
that Pearl had decided to solve this thing alone, and had sha
these sentiments out loud.

'Ah, reading the poetry of love, again?' he'd said, as he m;
sure all was ready for the pre-dinner drinks. Aldo had looked
from his book and stared at him blankly. 'Don't mind me, old ch

Just killing time whilst the girl I love gets to the bottom of a twenty-year-old mystery. There's evil in this house and she's determined to root it out.'

Aldo had nodded politely but Ovid had demanded his undivided attention.

'But what would she say, I wonder, if she knew the truth? That I work for the *Dorset Herald* and secured this job purely to further investigate the Brockhursts and print a story I've been working on for some time. Turns out she's not terribly keen on newspapers and it's how I make my living. I've been a fool, Signor Ravello, a damn fool. Kept something from her once, and that didn't turn out too rosy...'

Ellery began to relay this one-sided conversation with Aldo from earlier.

'*You're a journalist?*' Pearl stepped back from Ellery, nostrils flaring and hands shaking.

It had been obvious from the start that he was not trained in domestic service, but his prior knowledge about the Brockhursts, his visit to Mrs Coombes, and his willingness to help her all now made sense. Was that also why Harlow had recognised him? Perhaps Ellery had covered some society event and his face had stuck in the recesses of his mind.

'I wanted to tell you sooner but you had this tainted view of our profession, and I didn't want you to think badly of me. I'm sorry that your friend's family were embroiled in a scandal not of their making, but my job is important. There are some stories that must be told.'

'Well, congratulations. Now you have one – and what a story it is.' She couldn't stop a bitter tone creeping into her voice. 'It has everything: murder, secrets, passion, untold treasures, hidden identities, drama and heartbreak.'

'And a happy ever after?' he asked, a trace of pain sweeping over his features.

'Not for us, I'm afraid. Not in the way you mean. This is such a betrayal. It's not just your distasteful occupation, but your dishonesty.' She shrugged. 'But you will have the scoop of your career, and I have found myself, at last.' She shook her head. 'I'd been looking for such a long time...'

'But—'

'I'm not sure what you want me to say? You're about to splash scandal and personal information across the front pages of a newspaper, and it affects my parents... and me.'

'I didn't know they were your *parents*. Hell, *you* didn't know they were your parents.' Ellery ran his hand through his hair.

'You lied to me twice, Ellery.'

'No.' His voice was suddenly firm. 'I failed to pass on information to you twice, which, with hindsight, you had a right to know. But this whole situation has been somewhat... unusual.'

'You can be as pedantic as you like, but we both know that you've used me to get your big story,' she said. 'This could be the making of your career. You'd better grab a notebook and start writing it up. And do keep your eyes peeled for news of Josephine Brockhurst in the future. She may have had an unremarkable childhood, but she will become a remarkable woman.'

'Yes,' Ellery said, all fire absent from his amber eyes. 'I'm certain that she will.'

* * *

As she lay across her bed a little while later, clutching the stolen silver pocket watch, having cried herself out, she took little satisfaction when the hands jerked forward in unison to announce it was midnight.

As she finally waved goodbye to Saturday, she decided to also wave goodbye to the broken-hearted Pearl Glenham. Josephine Brockhurst would do this alone. She would be stronger, braver and a real force to be reckoned with.

Josephine Brockhurst could be anyone she wanted to be.

42

THREE WEEKS LATER

'Isn't this thrilling?' Harriet said, standing on the dock and lookin across at her friend, as the enormous black hulk of the ocean lin cast them in shadow. 'To think we will be in New York within week, Pearl.'

She couldn't get used to her friend's real name, but the voyag had been booked for Josephine Brockhurst – guest of Mr, Mrs ar Miss Crawley. News of her true identity was slowly leaking out ar the Crawleys had offered to help her escape the media attention f a while. After all, avoiding the public eye was the very reason th had planned their trip in the first place.

Josephine had stayed at Highcliffe House for nearly a week, n certain where her home was any more. The police had taken statement from her and she would be needed as a witness for t forthcoming trials. And then she had returned to the house she shared with the man she'd thought was her father, mainly to colle her possessions and consider what she should do with her li Harriet had asked about her time in Dorset, but what could s possibly say? In the end, she relayed the bare facts, knowing eve ing would come out soon enough, but any mention of clepsydras nd handsome, lying menservants were omitted from her narrative.

Harriet couldn't believe what a difference three short days away ad made to her unadventurous friend. She put it down to the 10ck of discovering her true parentage, and the whole ghastly 1siness of their murders, but Josephine knew the change had been .ore gradual, and largely due to Ellery challenging her perspective 1 life. But for now, she was to sail across the Atlantic, and perhaps 1e day even beyond, no longer afraid of the unknown. Just as well, :cause she had no idea what the future held. The grieving process as proving complicated, and the legalities of everything had yet to : sorted, but her small world had opened up and she was going to nbrace it.

Her romantic disappointments would ease in time. Besides, she 1s pretty certain that the youngest son of a viscount would ppily court her, should she decide a husband was absolutely cessary.

'There is a man waving at you.' Harriet scrunched up her face d leaned forward, squinting into the distance.

Josephine turned and realised it was Ellery, the man she'd just en thinking of and had hoped to avoid until the trials.

He pushed through the crowds and came to a halt directly in nt of her, as her friend discreetly stepped away.

'How did you track me down?' She couldn't bring herself to ke polite conversation, but his unexpected appearance made her mach flutter. She so badly wanted to be cross with him, but the mory of their kisses kept slipping into her thoughts.

'Oh, I remember now,' she continued, determined not to revert he compliant woman he'd first met at Highcliffe House. 'You're a rnalist, looking to ruin decent people's lives with that one big eer-making scoop. I keep forgetting, because you failed to reveal

that small detail to me in all the days we spent together. That, an
the fact you had a fiancée.'

'Pearl. Josephine. You need to let me—'

'I've been waiting for the sensational story to break. An insi
account of the Brockhursts' murder. A world exclusive by Elle
Brown – "My time with the daughter assumed dead for twen
years".'

'Josephine—'

But she was on a roll and there were still things she needed
get off her wildly thumping chest.

'When I turned up at Highcliffe House I felt so inferior. I sat
the terrace that lunchtime and I was intimidated by everyone the
Now I realise that you are not people to look up to, or to be in a
of – not one of you. You were all only concerned with your ov
selfish wants and needs. As long as you came away with a sca
dalous feature about the Brockhursts – you didn't care who y
hurt in the process.'

'JOSEPHINE!' Ellery's voice was sharper, and he reached out
grip her shoulders, ensuring he had her full attention. The fire
those amber eyes of his flared alarmingly. She swallowed a
decided to let him speak.

'The whole point is, I do care who I might hurt in the process. A
the moment I realised it was going to affect the woman I love
stopped and walked away. Yes, I could have easily written a sen
tional newspaper article about everything that happened to us dur
that gathering and my career would be set for life – the murder of
Brockhursts, my intimate friendship with their daughter, and
scheming of Virgil's estranged and mentally unstable sister. But
happy to bury that all in a box, twenty feet under the soil, even tho
my editor has sacked me for stepping away from the story. There
be other scoops, but there will never be another woman like you.'

He reached for her right hand and lifted it up with his own, bringing it to his lips.

'I love you. That was never a lie.'

He'd given up the story for her? It took her a moment to process his words. Three times now he had declared his love. Perhaps he was telling the truth. She realised how easy it would be to fall into his arms and let him make everything all right. But things were more complicated. He was talking to Josephine Brockhurst, not Pearl Glenham – although Pearl was still very much a part of who she was. Maybe that was the problem; she hadn't forged her true identity yet. She needed more time.

'I'm afraid I still don't really know who I am. And before I declare any foolish feelings of love, I have to work that out. This trip to America is a huge step for me, and a chance to investigate my heritage, so I'm going to embrace it. Who knows where it might lead? I could be gone for months.'

He digested the news and slowly nodded his head.

'I understand and I'll wait,' he said, caressing her face with his fingers. 'I can be very patient when I put my mind to it. Besides, there's plenty to keep me busy whilst you sail the seven seas. Thought I'd give novel writing a try. Got this splendid idea for a science fiction novel. H. G. Wells seems to do well enough out of them. It starts with the main character wandering into a cave and knocking over an ancient clepsydra...'

He grinned and she fell in love with him a little bit more. Because it was love, she accepted that now, and hoped that they would be together in the end, whenever that might prove to be. Fighting that inevitability was almost as pointless as trying to stop the tide coming in.

'I want to make it a romance,' he continued. 'There will be a powerful love running through the story. You know the sort of thir

– two people who appear total opposites but the universe knows that they complement each other perfectly?'

'Fire and water?'

'Exactly,' he agreed. 'Everyone says they don't mix, but what do they know? I shall do my utmost to ensure it has an uplifting ending. What do you think? Is it unrealistic for two people so very different to fall in love and live happily ever after?'

He looked nervously at her face, so much hanging on her reply.

'Not at all,' she said, smiling now. 'In fact, I rather think it's how all the best romance novels end...'

ACKNOWLEDGEMENTS

A huge and heartfelt thank you to everyone who helped me with the book. I was very nervous about this one but my enthusiastic editor, Isobel Akenhead, and ever-supportive agent, Hannah Schofield, were with me every step of the way. I am still so thrilled to be part of the amazing Boldwood team and their passion and professionalism continue to blow me away.

For research help, the charming Barry 'The Legend' Strickland-Hodge, from the University of Leeds, went above and beyond with his knowledge of poisons, and his attention to detail was wonderful. I only wish I could have squeezed in more of the fascinating information he imparted. What a guy.

Leila Anni had the genius idea of a water clock as my McGuffin, which I ultimately tweaked to become a mercury clepsydra, but without her inspired suggestion, this book wouldn't have been quite the same.

To my son, Peter, who is so patient when I need to brainstorm, even if he is doing it upside down on the sofa, with his feet in the air. He's always been restless and, even as an adult, nothing much has changed.

To Kate Smith and Clare Marchant who both beta-read an early draft and assured me the book had legs. Thank you, girls, you are the bestest.

To the author pals that I chat with EVERY week (you know who you are). We started video calling in the pandemic for the sake of our sanity, but now we just do it for the gossip and the LOLS.

And finally, to my amazing family, my many friends, and my gorgeous readers. I wouldn't be doing this without you all.

Jenni x

ABOUT THE AUTHOR

nni Keer is the well-reviewed author of historical romances, often ith a mystery at their heart. Most recently published by Headline 1d shortlisted for the 2023 RNA Historical Romantic Novel of the ar.

gn up to Jenni Keer's mailing list for news, competitions and odates on future books.

sit Jenni's website: www.jennikeer.co.uk

llow Jenni on social media here:

facebook.com/jennikeerwriter

x.com/JenniKeer

instagram.com/jennikeer

bookbub.com/authors/jenni-keer

Boldwood

Boldwood Books is an award-winning fiction publishing company seeking out the best stories from around the world.

Find out more at www.boldwoodbooks.com

Join our reader community for brilliant books, competitions and offers!

Follow us
@BoldwoodBooks
@TheBoldBookClub

Sign up to our weekly deals newsletter

https://bit.ly/BoldwoodBNewsletter

Printed in Great Britain
by Amazon

48256526R00188